COUNT MY LIES

COUNT MY LIES

A NOVEL

SOPHIE STAVA

SCOUT PRESS

New York Amsterdam/Antwerp London Toronto Sydney New Delhi

SCOUT PRESS

An Imprint of Simon & Schuster, LLC
1230 Avenue of the Americas
New York, NY 10020

First Scout Press hardcover edition March 2025

SCOUT PRESS and colophon are registered trademarks of Simon & Schuster, LLC

Manufactured in the United States of America

ISBN 978-1-6680-7934-8

To my mom and dad

"If you tell the truth, you don't have to remember anything."
MARK TWAIN

"I always thought it would be better to be a fake somebody
than a real nobody."
TOM RIPLEY, *THE TALENTED MR. RIPLEY*

1

'm a nurse." The words fall out of my mouth before I can stop myself from saying them, loud and clanging like a pair of tin cans tied
to a back bumper. If I could reach out, catch them by the tail, and
reel them back in, I would, but it's too late. They've been heard; two
heads turn.

I should walk away. Or laugh, say I was just kidding. But when
the dad and little girl look up at me from the park bench, his eyes
shining with hope, her eyes shining with tears, I feel such a rush that
I don't do either. Instead, I kneel beside the girl and smile broadly,
first at her, then at him.

"You need to ice it," I say to the man, my voice clear and steady, the
slightest air of authority that I assume someone in the medical field
would naturally possess.

The thing is, I'm not a nurse. I never have been. What I am is a liar.

I had heard the little girl's wails from across the playground, long
drawn-out sobs that drew me toward her. I've always been nosy, leaning in to hear strangers' conversations, taking a step closer to read over
someone's shoulder, glancing at the person next to me on the subway,

straining to see the text messages on their phone. It's another bad habit of mine. Add it to the list, okay?

"Let me see," the dad was saying to the little girl as I walked up, holding her bare foot in his hand. "Where'd it sting you? Here? Or here?"

I'd wanted to help; he'd seemed so flustered, so unnerved by it, that, almost without thinking, I'd opened my mouth and the lie had dropped out. Clunk, onto the sidewalk, startling them both. I meant well, really, I did. I know, the road to hell, right?

Now, I glance around at their belongings. Just a paper sack lunch beside them, contents strewn over the bench. A half-eaten sandwich. Apple slices, already browning, carrot sticks. Two drinks: a can of grapefruit-flavored sparkling water, a juice box.

I grab the can. It's cool, not cold, but it might help. "Here," I say, holding it toward the man. He takes it. Our fingers brush, just slightly, his surprisingly soft. "Is the stinger out?"

The dad frowns at his daughter's foot. She's still whimpering, but the intensity has lessened. She's looking up at me, eyes wide. Her face is tear-streaked. Snot leaks from her nose. She's doll-faced with bangs and long lashes, a real cutie. So is he, to put it mildly. I can still feel his fingers against mine.

"I think so," he says. "Would you mind taking a look?"

A flick of pride. He trusts me. Of course he does. I'm a good liar— and, well, there's the convenient fact that I'm wearing scrubs.

"Sure," I say, smiling. Still kneeling, I reach out and lift up her little pink sole smudged with dirt. She's four or five, her foot tiny in my too-big hands. They've always been large for a woman, even when I was a kid. Mitts, my aunt would always tease, holding her palm up to mine. I'm still self-conscious about them, keeping handshakes brief, tucking them into my pockets, under my thighs when sitting.

I squint at the bottom of her foot. There's a small red welt and, in its center, a black dot. The stinger. I suck in air between my two front teeth, shaking my head. "It's still in there."

He frowns and peers down at it. "Should I—?"

"You need to scrape it out. With a credit card or something with a flat edge. Don't squeeze it; it could make it worse."

I'm pleased by how competent I seem, how knowledgeable, like I actually know what I'm talking about. I do, I guess; I also happened to step on a bee in this very park, late last summer. I'd spread out a blanket and kicked off my shoes before I lay down to read. When I got up, my sneakers still in the grass, I felt a sharp jab on the bottom of my foot. I sat back down to examine the injury, cursing under my breath, and saw the crushed bee, the stinger still stuck in my skin. I squeezed carefully, forcing the stinger to the surface. It was only later, when I googled it in a blind panic, that I realized my mistake.

By the end of the day, my foot had almost doubled in size, turned bright pink, swollen as a little sausage. It took three days for the itching to stop and another four before the swelling went away entirely. I limped on it dramatically for the whole week, recounting the saga to anyone who so much as raised an eyebrow in my direction. Although, truth be told, I might have claimed it was a swarm, not a single bee. The point is, I do have *some* experience in this area.

The dad reaches into his back pocket, returning with his wallet. "Thanks," he says gratefully. "If you weren't here, I'd probably have called 911." He smiles to show me he's joking. His teeth are bright white, straight and even. He's handsome in an obvious, teenage-heartthrob sort of way, probably early thirties, my age.

He slides a credit card from one of the wallet's slots. "Let me see your foot, sweetheart," he says.

As he drags the card across her sole, I see the name on the card. Jay Lockhart. *Jay Lockhart.* I like the sound of it, like it would roll off my tongue if I said it out loud. Jay as in Gatsby, love-crazed millionaire, charming, hot-blooded. I look back at the man—Jay—and decide it fits him, with his boyish smile, playboy face.

"Got it!" Jay announces, triumphant, holding up an infinitesimal black speck—the stinger, presumably—between his thumb and forefinger. "See?" He shows it first to the little girl, then to me.

"Good work!" I say, smiling at him. He looks so proud, like he's just placed in an Olympic event. Maybe not gold, but bronze, still very respectable.

When he smiles back, I feel a slight blush color my cheeks. It feels like we're sharing the victory together, like he might reach out and hug me, his winning teammate.

"Feel better?" he asks the little girl. She nods, stops sniffling. He reaches out and wipes her wet cheeks with his thumb, smooths her silky bangs. I notice he isn't wearing a wedding band.

"You should ice it when you get home," I say, standing back up, "to keep the swelling at bay. And you might want to give her some Benadryl, just a half dose, maybe. It'll help with any itchiness."

"Seriously, thank you. Can you say 'thank you,' Harper?" Jay turns to the little girl. "Say, thank you, Miss . . . ?" He trails off and looks back at me, for my name.

"Caitlin," I say. Another lie. I don't even know where it comes from. Have I ever even met a Caitlin? Once, maybe. When I was younger, I think I did ballet with a girl named Caitlin. Or was it Carly? We were in the same class at a local community center, but that's where our similarities ended. She had long, waist-length hair she wore in a beautifully woven braid down the center of her back, sparkly barrettes clipped into the sides, and brand-new ballet slippers, their pink satin gleaming. I danced in old socks. She was the best, whatever her name was, the lead in the recital. I was Sugar Plum number six. The young girl with the bee sting, Harper—her name bougie, but cute, exactly what you'd expect in this neighborhood—also has a single, glossy braid, her bangs neatly combed. Maybe it's why I thought of the name: she reminds me of her.

"Thank you, Miss Caitlin," Harper dutifully recites.

"My pleasure, Harper," I say. "I hope your foot feels better soon."

She offers me a tentative smile, staring up at me with her big brown eyes. Then she looks back at her dad. "Can I finish building my castle?"

Jay nods, smiling, and she slides off the bench to a scattering of sand toys on the ground.

He looks back to me. "I'm Jay, by the way," he says, standing up and extending his hand to me. He's taller than I expected, well over six feet.

"Nice to meet you, Jay," I say. When we shake, there's a current. At least, I feel one. He didn't have to introduce himself, but he did. That's something.

There's a pause, then he says, "Everyone's a liar, right?"

My heart stops beating, lodges itself in my throat. "What?" I manage. *How could he—?*

Jay smiles, then gestures toward my hand, dangling by my side. I'm still holding my book, the one I was reading when I first heard Harper wailing, my fingers tucked between the pages where I left off. It's a well-worn paperback copy of *Murder on the Orient Express*, the edges of the cover curled up, soft with wear. "Sorry." He grimaces apologetically. "Did I spoil it? It looks like you've read it before. I just assumed—"

"Oh." I let out a little laugh, exhaling in relief. "No, it's probably my tenth time. You've read it, too?"

Jay nods. "I loved the detective, Hercule Poirot. My parents gave me a box set of the series for my twelfth birthday. I always tried to solve the case before he did. But I never could." He shakes his head ruefully.

I laugh. "My favorite Agatha Christie is *And Then There Were None*. The ending was—" I make an explosion noise. "Whoa. I never saw it coming."

"I haven't read that one. It's that good?"

"I could bring you my copy," I offer. "Do you come here a lot? I'm usually here a few times a week." I hold my breath and feel my heartbeat accelerate. I'm probably overstepping. I often do.

But here's the truth. I know this isn't their first time at this park. I've seen them here before. Twice, actually, earlier this week. I'd been hoping for another sighting today, pleased when I saw them approaching. Harper's crying really did catch my attention, but I'd also been keeping an eye on them as I leafed through my book, glancing up every few pages or so, watching her on the monkey bars, the swing.

That first day, Tuesday, I noticed Jay before I noticed Harper. I'm pretty sure all the women at the park did. Not only because he was one of the few men here, but because he looks like he belongs on a movie set in LA, not on a playground in the heart of Brooklyn.

Like I told him, I'm here most days, ducking out of work for an afternoon breather, so I'm familiar with the regulars. I often see the same kids with the same nannies, the same groups of moms sitting next to each other, chatting on the benches as their offspring bound through the playground, shrieking. I like this park, how happy everyone seems, the sunlit patches of grass, the smell of the honeysuckle bushes that line the perimeter. It's busy even in the colder months, the kids bundled up, their cheeks rosy.

"That'd be great," Jay says, responding to my offer, "but my wife is usually the one who brings Harper here. I had the week off, so I've been the one on park duty. It's back to the grind on Monday."

When he says "my wife," my heart sinks, which makes me feel even stupider than I already do. What, did I think this was the start of a romantic comedy, that I'm Liv Tyler in *Jersey Girl*? I know it's an outdated reference, but what woman doesn't fantasize about a widowed Ben Affleck finding comfort in their arms, grief-stricken and vulnerable? A motherless little girl gazing up at them adoringly? Yes, it's a little morbid, but I can't be the only one. Oh god, am I?

"I'll tell her to look for you next time she's here," Jay says. "Apparently, this is Harper's new favorite park."

I force a broad smile as if the thought of meeting his undoubtedly beautiful wife fills me with unbridled joy. "Great," I say, hoping to sound chipper. "I'm usually here around this time. Maybe I could bring the book to her."

Here's how I know I'm not pretty. No married man would tell his wife about the gorgeous, single woman he befriended at the park. Not unless his IQ was below functioning, or he was hoping to be smothered in his sleep later that very night. And Jay doesn't appear to be stupid, or to have a death wish.

But I'm not surprised. I know I'm not the sort of woman who is a threat to other women. My nose is slightly too large, jaw angular. On good days, I tell myself that I'm handsome, like one of those black-and-white movie actresses, strong-featured. Greta Garbo, maybe, if the lights are low. And I don't do myself any favors. I know I could spend more time on my appearance; I don't have to look quite as schlubby as I do.

I could dress better, for one, but instead I wear what's comfortable, clothes I've had for years that should have been donated—or tossed—ages ago: high-waisted jeans with holes in the knees, button-up flannels, oversized, stretched-out sweaters. Thanks to the ebb and flow of fashion, it might actually be cool if it was intentional—or if it wasn't paired with half-brushed buns and cheap, plastic-framed glasses, scuffed sneakers. I do have contacts (and a hairbrush), but most mornings I'm running late, scrambling out the door partially dressed, just-burnt toast crammed in my mouth; the contacts (and hair brushing) usually fall to the wayside.

It's not that I don't have nicer clothes—I do—I just haven't had a good reason to wear them recently. Because instead of cardigans and slacks, I wear scrubs to work. Mauve-colored, to be specific. My boss, Lena, handed them to me on my first day with a proud smile. She picked the shade herself.

I'm not a nurse, but a nail technician at a small, boutique day spa that offers seventy-five-dollar manicures and pedicures, sugar waxing, and a three-page menu of signature facials. Nurse, nail tech, what's the difference, really? Oh, right, everything. The chasm between fixing a broken arm and a broken acrylic is wide and deep.

Currently, along with the scrubs, I'm wearing the aforementioned plastic glasses, a pair of gold studs, and a chain-link choker I grabbed on my way out.

I touch my hand to the necklace. I found it at a little shop I passed on my way home from work a few weeks ago. I'd stopped in to kill time, not intending to buy anything, but as I walked by the check-out counter, I noticed it through the glass case, the gold glinting. The salesgirl offered to put it around my neck so I could see how it looked. It fit perfectly. The chain was delicate, tiny links woven together, with, right at the base of my neck, one tiny iridescent pearl. I paid for it and wore it out. When Natasha, my coworker, commented on it the next day, I told her it was a family heirloom, passed down from my grandmother.

But—prepare to be shocked—even with the earrings and choker, I'm no ten. Jay's wife probably looks more like Liv Tyler than I ever will. The Daisy to his Gatsby. Lithe, with high cheekbones. Full lips, curls spilling down her back. No frizz in sight.

"Five more minutes, Harp." Jay stoops to touch the top of the little girl's head. She nods absent-mindedly. She seems to have forgotten about her bee sting and is now playing happily by our feet, pouring sand from a shovel into a bucket, then tipping the bucket upside down.

I shift my weight from one foot to the other. I should go—I'm due back at work in less than ten minutes—but Jay is far more interesting than what waits for me there. And he said he only has five more minutes. If I walk quickly, I'll be able to make it back on time. So instead of leaving, I say, "You said you had the week off?"

He nods. "Harper's preschool is closed for spring break, so I took the week off, too, to spend some time with her."

"What do you do?" It's another bad habit of mine, talking too much, asking too many questions. It's probably the same reason I lie: to fill the silence, keep people from walking away.

Look, I'm painfully aware of how pathetic that sounds. It's just that my job is so boring. My life is so boring. Bland and dreary. I'd do almost anything for a sneak peek into someone else's. And his seems especially interesting. Technicolor, so bright you have to squint. I'd bet everything that I'm right.

"I started my own company last year, in online game development.

Which basically means I'm a big nerd," Jay jokes, smiling, eyes flashing. I notice he has a dimple in his right cheek.

He's not a nerd. Far from it. He never has been. You can tell just by looking at him. Like I said, he's tall, really tall, at least six-three or six-four, with dark hair that he keeps raking his hand through, brushing it from his eyes. His jaw is strong, clean-shaven, skin tanned and smooth.

"Sounds exciting," I say. "Starting your own company."

"It can be." He shrugs. "Not as altruistic as a career in nursing, but it pays the bills."

Right, I'm a nurse. I smile modestly as if I deserve his compliment. I wish that I did.

Jay glances at his phone. "Shit, we have to head out. I promised I'd have Harper home by three."

"Is it that late already?" I say, feigning surprise. "Shoot, I have to run, too." Of course, it's back to my real job, nary a patient in sight. "It was nice to meet you."

"You too, Caitlin." His smile makes me feel like he means it, my stomach flip-flopping. "Like I said, I'll tell my wife to keep an eye out for you."

I grin back, showing my teeth. "I'd *love* that." I'm a liar, remember?

I watch as he and Harper leave the park, hand in hand, their arms swinging. When they reach the gate, Jay turns, gives me one last wave. I wave back but wait until they disappear from sight before I turn and leave, too.

It occurs to me, though, on the walk back, that the reason I'd thought he might be single is that he wasn't wearing a wedding ring. I can't help but wonder why not.

2

"M om?" I call out when I get home from work, easing the front door shut behind me and setting my keys on the little table in the entryway. "I'm home!"

"Sloanie? Is that you?" That's my real name, Sloane. Sloanie, Sloanie, full of baloney. And yes, I live at home with my mother. I know, I know, another notch on my belt of accomplishments. I'm working on it. Really, that's the truth. Hand to heart.

"Yeah, it's me, Mom," I answer loudly. I kick off my shoes, drop my purse next to them, and walk down the short hallway into the living room. She's in her recliner with the TV on, wearing a light blue tracksuit and thick wool socks like a character from a seventies sitcom. I cross the room and bend over to drop a kiss on her cheek, glancing at the screen. *Murder, She Wrote*, her favorite old show. She's likely seen this episode at least three times before.

"How was work?" she asks, lowering the volume from blasting to blaring. She squints up at me, looking far older than her age, her short, wiry hair almost all gray, the lines across her forehead, around her eyes and mouth, deep.

"Fine," I say, shrugging. "I'm going to get dinner started. You hungry?"

She nods and points the remote back at the TV, the sound returning to an assaulting level. I'm surprised the neighbors don't complain.

Both my mother's eyesight and hearing are declining. Years of working on her feet as a house cleaner have ruined her back, leaving her hunched and aching, her joints stiff. She's had rheumatoid arthritis since her thirties, managed by medication, but it's taken its toll, finally rendering her unable to move most days, let alone work.

She spends her days in a well-worn corduroy armchair in the corner of the living room, a heating pad on her backside, legs stretched out before her, peering through smudged glasses at the TV as reruns of *Unsolved Mysteries* and *Forensic Files* degrade the screen. She drinks cup after cup of oversweetened, lukewarm coffee, followed by one whiskey at five, then another cup of coffee before bed, this time, decaf. It wasn't my plan to be living with my mother in my thirties, but at least I can keep an eye on her. By now, taking care of her is second nature, something I've done for as long as I can remember.

I head into the kitchen and open the fridge. There's some leftover roast chicken from the dinner I made last night that I warm up and shred into a bowl, along with a handful of chopped-up cucumbers and carrots, some romaine lettuce. A modest attempt to counterbalance the Chinese takeout my mother frequently has delivered for lunch. I divvy the salad between my plate and my mom's, then head back into the living room.

"Thanks, Sloanie," my mom says, taking the plate from me. Then she mutes her show. She likes to hear about my day when we eat.

"I did Dolly's nails today," I say, biting into a carrot.

I've been working at the day spa—Rose & Honey—for almost a year now. I wandered in one afternoon when I saw the *Help Wanted* sign posted in the window. I'd walked by the black-and-white awninged storefront at least a hundred times, but had never gone in. By that point, I'd been out of work for months. I couldn't get hired anywhere, at least not doing what I was qualified for. I'd get through a few rounds of interviews, but no job offers materialized. I knew why, of course, so it didn't come as a surprise, but that didn't make it any easier. Doing nails sounded like a reasonable alternative, something I could be good at if I tried.

The woman at the front desk looked pleased when I asked for an application. She pumped my hand vigorously, introducing herself as Lena, the owner of the spa. She was a heavyset, Eastern European woman with impeccable makeup, kohl-rimmed eyes framed by long lash extensions, porcelain skin, pouty red lips. She'd opened the shop a few years ago, she told me in thickly accented English, and she was adding another manicurist to her team, someone reliable, someone she could count on. Why not, I thought, how hard could it be?

When Lena asked if I had a cosmetology license, I said that I did, that I'd recently passed the exam. I figured I could find a certificate to doctor, if and when she offered me a job. I was invited back for a practical interview, which, she explained, meant I'd be demonstrating my skills and giving her a manicure. I spent the next week on YouTube, pausing the videos at each step to practice on my mother, filing and refiling, painting and repainting. I memorized the steps, which were easy enough—clean, clip, file, buff, cuticle care, exfoliate, moisturize, base coat, paint, top coat—and showed up with my own set of manicure tools that I'd bought at a local beauty supply store with a twenty-five-percent-off coupon. When I was done, Lena examined her nails, smiled, and offered me the job.

"You have good hands," she'd said, nodding appreciatively at them. I looked down. Next to Lena's, they seemed even bigger than usual. Who'd have thought my big hands would turn out to be an asset? The pay was twenty-one dollars an hour, she continued, plus at least an extra thousand a month in gratuities, sometimes more; her clients were generous, Lena told me, alluding to the deep pockets in Cobble Hill. It was slightly less than I made in my last position, even with the tip money, but as they say, beggars can't be choosers.

I accepted the job on the spot, handing over a forged cosmetology license that I'd Venmoed some guy online fifty bucks for. Lena glanced at it, distracted by a ringing phone, then told me I could start the following day.

It's a good job, mindless, easy, and most of the clients leave at least twenty percent, sometimes thirty, at the end of their service. Between that and the social security checks my mom collects, we have enough for our rent, our bills, but it's not nearly enough to keep me from wishing for something better—something *more*—or from dreading the sound of my alarm clock each morning, its blaring chimes grating.

"And how is she?" my mother asks, referring to Dolly—as in Parton. An homage to the Queen of Country herself. I make up names for my regulars, the ones I see week after week, women I've come to know through their too-loud phone conversations or idle chitchat. Dolly Parton is really Laura Hoffman, but they share the same big blonde hair and oversized chest. Laura even has a slight Southern twang, although she grew up in Texas, not Tennessee like Dolly. She's a Dallas transplant, having moved to New York after she met her husband while he was on an oil expedition—or whatever tycoons do when they travel for business.

"Her stepdaughter wants the Lamborghini," I say. Laura's

husband—very old and very wealthy—died two years ago. She's been in litigation with his children since, fighting over every last cent the old coot had to his name. Which was quite a bit. Laura updates me on the developments when she comes in every week. She lives in a penthouse in Manhattan—on the Upper East Side, where else—but she has a son from a previous marriage in Brooklyn Heights, a few streets over from Rose & Honey, so she drops in on the days she meets him for lunch. Heads turn sharply when she walks in, a blinding contrast to our typical bougie Brooklynite clientele.

"But," I continue, "Laura says she'd rather sell the car for parts than see that spoiled twat riding in it. Her words, not mine."

"Where do you park a Lamborghini in Manhattan?" my mother asks. She sounds genuinely curious.

I shrug. "She said something about a private garage? Neither one of them even *drives*. Laura says Cassie doesn't have a license. Instead of a car on her sixteenth birthday, she got a driver."

My mother snorts, rolling her eyes. Her tolerance for wealthy women is lower than mine. I like Laura, though, how she opens the window to her soap-opera life, offering me a glimpse inside. She also treats me like a human being rather than an inanimate object who happens to know how to file nails, which is more than I can say about most of my clients.

"But she found out her son's expecting his second baby, so she was in a good mood. She tipped double." Laura usually hands me a fifty on the way out—one of my only cash tippers—but today it was a Benjamin, crisp, green, newly printed. I started to protest, but she waved me off with an exaggerated wink.

This isn't the whole truth, though. She likely gave me the extra money because at the start of her manicure, I had mentioned that I'd spilled coffee all over my MacBook, frying the hard drive and subsequently erasing the last fifty pages of the novel I told her I've been working on. Her hand, nails still wet, flew to her mouth. *Oh no, Sloane!*

Obviously, there is no MacBook, no novel. But the lie was as much for me as it was for Laura. I wish there was a half-written manuscript on a laptop, that I spent evenings hunched over a keyboard instead of days hunched over women's feet. Christ, anyone would. I had no idea she'd double her tip. If I had, I wouldn't have said it. I swear.

It's just that the truth is so uninteresting. Amending it, changing the details, adding in color, is something I started when I was a kid, a bad habit—like biting your nails or picking at scabs—that I never grew out of. In fact, I grew into it, the lies rolling off my tongue more and more naturally, almost reflexively, until it became instinctive, part of who I am. It almost doesn't occur to me to tell the truth anymore. Why would I? When you tell the truth—at least, if the truth is boring, which it almost always is—people begin to fidget, their eyes glazing as their attention wanes. Eventually, they realize, snapping to with a sheepish *Oh, I'm sorry, what were you saying?*, trying to feign interest.

I hate that look. The fake, vacant way they smile at you. I always have. It makes me feel unimportant, like a crumpled piece of paper, tossed on the floor instead of in the wastebasket. I used to get it all the time when I was younger. My mom and I moved around a lot, hopping from town to town, apartment to apartment, school to school, as she changed jobs, one after the next. I was always new, always standing at the front of a classroom, palms sweaty, as the teacher instructed me to introduce myself. I'd start haltingly, staring at my shoes, saying that I was born in Florida, that I'd moved from whatever Podunk town we'd just come from, and I'd look up to see that no one was even paying attention. The girls were passing notes and whispering, the boys kicking each other across the aisle. The teacher would shush the class, but even she was distracted, writing on the chalkboard or handing out worksheets. I stared longingly at the girls, wishing I was the one being whispered to. But my pants were too short, sneakers too scuffed, shirt too faded to catch the eye of anyone. It was a shitty feeling, the invisibility. Every time, I wished we didn't have to move, but I understood why.

My mother was hardworking, scrupulous to a fault, but when her arthritis flared up, she was housebound, unable to work, spending the day with her hands and feet submerged in water as hot as she could stand. When I got home from school, I'd climb into bed with her and rub her joints with castor oil and Tiger Balm, turn on one of her favorite movies to distract her from the pain. Eventually, her employer would begin to complain about her absences, giving her a warning, then another, until she came home with a final paycheck.

We'd move when the landlord started banging on the door, shoving late notices through our mail slot. We would find a new town, twenty miles in whatever direction, another shabby apartment that didn't run background checks, and I'd start a new school. Rinse and repeat. I got used to it, though, expected it every few months.

It was just the two of us, making our way in the world. I never met my father, didn't even know who he was other than a brief fling in my mom's early twenties. Her parents—my grandparents—had died a few years after I was born, and her sister was older, living hours away. We were fine on our own. We had to be.

In fifth grade, when my mother and I moved to Whispering Pines, Georgia, a tiny suburb on the outskirts of Macon, I told myself things would be different this time. On the first day, when the recess bell rang midmorning, I followed the class out to the blacktop where a group of pigtailed girls circled around me. "Where are you from?" one of them asked. You could tell she was cool by the number of neon-colored rubber bracelets looped around her wrist, hot pink and lime green, bouncing when she walked. She had bangs, and when I got home that night, I gave myself bangs, too, standing on a chair in front of the bathroom mirror, kitchen shears in hand.

"California," I said. I didn't know where it came from. We hadn't moved from California; we'd only driven an hour north, not even crossing state lines, just one county to the next. By the grace of god, the teacher hadn't asked me to the front of the class that morning, hadn't mentioned me at all. I was a blank canvas, a tabula rasa.

As I watched the girls' faces light up, something inside of me swelled. I knew I'd said the right thing. The girl with the bracelets beamed at me. "Are you famous?" she asked excitedly.

I shook my head no, but when I saw her disappointment, I quickly added, "But my dad is. He's in the movies."

Their gasps were audible. And just like that, I was special. It was so easy.

That day, so unlike all my previous first days, everyone fought to sit next to me at lunch. I told them about the beach and the palm trees, describing in detail what it was like to wade into the breaking waves, the colors of the seashells I found on the shore. One summer, I'd won a sandcastle-building contest, I said. Of course, I'd never seen the Pacific. I'd been to Daytona a few times, which aided in my descriptions, along with scenes from my favorite Disney movie, *Lilo and Stitch*, and my second-favorite movie, *Flipper*. After lunch we played handball, and the girl with the bracelets—her name was Bianca—asked me to be on her team. I was elated.

When they asked to meet my dad, I told them he was on set, filming a new movie. It *could* be true, I reasoned with myself. It's why the lies never seemed so bad. I had no idea where he was or what he did. How did I know he *wasn't* an actor?

I knew I should stop, but I couldn't help it. I wanted so desperately for people to like me, and it was the only way I could think of. It was no more complicated than that: I wished I was more interesting, so I pretended to be. Sloanie, Sloanie, the big fat phony.

But the irony is that the more elaborate my lies became, the further I had to keep people away. I could never invite anyone over. They'd want to know where my puppy was, the one I said we'd adopted over the summer. His name was Pickles, I told my classmates, and he was the runt of the litter, black with white spots. They'd want to see the princess bed I'd described, the one with the sparkly canopy and unicorn sheets. They'd want to meet my dad, the movie star, and swim in our backyard pool with the waterslide. Of course they did. It was why we were friends. And it was also why we could never be friends. Not real ones, at least.

Then, another lie occurred to me, one that would solve all my problems. I came to class one Monday with a long face and whispered into Bianca's ear that there'd been a fire at our house over the weekend. Everything had been lapped up in the flames, our home with the backyard pool burned to the ground. My canopy bed was gone. So was our dog.

I told her we had to move into an apartment across town, but that it was only temporary, until they rebuilt our house. Maybe she wanted to come over after school one day? The apartment wasn't as nice as our house, I said, but there was a park across the street we could go to, and I'd saved some of my Barbies before I ran out. Bianca nodded, wide-eyed.

By recess, everyone had heard. My teacher, Miss Newberry, pulled me aside at lunch and asked me what happened. I repeated the story I told Bianca, about how my mom had left the stove on, the fire alarm sounding in the middle of the night. She touched my arm, her eyes soft and sympathetic, and told me if there was anything I needed to let her know. And that I didn't have to turn in any homework assignments that week. I was pleased as punch.

The next day, Miss Newberry announced to the class that the school would be hosting a fundraiser for me and my family, to help us during this difficult time. It would be a bake sale, and she would be sending a sign-up sheet home for everyone's parents. I smiled shyly, overjoyed by the special attention. But, unsurprisingly, the fundraising never happened. One of my classmates' moms called mine that night, asking for our new address to organize a meal train for us. I was coloring on the floor of our living room when I heard my mom say, "What fire?" into the receiver, and I knew I was toast.

That Thursday, I sat with my mother in front of the principal, my legs dangling over the chair as he droned on, lecturing me about the consequences of the lie. My mother was mortified, to say the very least.

I was embarrassed, too. Mostly because I'd gotten caught. If I had the chance to go back, I would have done it again. It was worth it for the way everyone looked at me those two days.

I was too young for detention, so the principal made me write an apology letter to my classmates and Miss Newberry. My mother took away my television privileges for a month. But neither punishment taught me not to lie. It taught me to be a better liar. I didn't make the same mistakes at my next school.

We moved again at the end of the year. In sixth grade, I told one of my classmates that I rode horses on the weekends, after I finished reading *Black Beauty*. She did, too, she exclaimed happily, then invited me to her riding club the following weekend. I made up excuse after excuse about why I could never go. Trips to my fictional aunt and uncle's house in the mountains, dance classes, sleepovers with friends from my old school. All of which meant I had to stay home, alone in the apartment, while my mother worked, instead of with the friends I'd made because of the stories I'd told. I'd stop by the library on Friday afternoons to stock up on the books I spent the weekends reading. Books that kept the loneliness at bay, whose details wove themselves into the web of lies I spun.

I lied through middle school and high school, then through community college and beyond. Small lies, usually, but lies, nonetheless. I should have stopped by now—I'm an adult, for god's sake—but I haven't. I can't. I just want so badly to say the right thing, be the right kind of person, that when I open my mouth, out comes what I think someone wants to hear, whether it's true or not.

It's not that there haven't been any consequences—aside from visits to the principal's office. I've lost friends here and there, job opportunities when my references were checked a little too thoroughly. I'm a good liar, but I'll have slip ups, or someone else will refute my story, and I'll be exposed.

Sometimes, there are stretches of time that I lie less. Usually after I've been caught. I try to change, try to be honest, but after a few weeks, I hear myself saying something that isn't true, something I hadn't even planned on lying about, and I slip right back into my old ways like I would into my favorite shirt. It fits, just right. Snug, comfortable, well-worn. Other times, when things are going well, like when I had the job before this one, I don't feel the need as often. I still do it, unable to help myself, but the urge isn't as strong.

But here's the part that makes me an even bigger freak. Sometimes I believe my own lies. They feel real. I get swept up in the fantasy, the telling of it, the retelling, lying in bed at night adding to the story, drifting off and dreaming about it. I think it's because I've always felt like there had to be more to my life than what it was. I couldn't just be this poor kid with no dad. He had to be out there. He had to be *special*, which meant I had to be special, too. Doesn't everyone want to feel special?

"So, a good day," my mom says. Both a question and a statement. Right, the hundred-dollar tip.

"Mm-hm," I answer. It was a good day. A very good day. I consider telling her about Jay and Harper, but I don't. I'm not quite sure why. She's the one person I don't lie to, the only person who thinks I'm interesting, just as I am.

Even so, I want to keep them to myself, for now. And leaving something out isn't the same as lying, not quite. It's what I tell myself, anyway.

My mom hands me the remote. "You pick the movie," she says. "I picked the last one."

I give it back. "No, you choose. I'll get dessert. We still have that pint of Rocky Road."

"I'll take two scoops." My mom settles back into her armchair as she starts scrolling through the list of trending titles on Netflix. We watched a thriller last night, one about a woman whose husband isn't as perfect as he seems. Few husbands are, at least in Hollywood, apparently.

In the kitchen, I load our dishes into the dishwasher and dole out what's left of the carton into two bowls, tossing the empty container into the almost-full recycle bin. I make a mental note to take it out before the collectors come on Monday. I dim the lights on my way back to the couch, handing my mom her bowl before taking a seat. The title sequence of a movie—another thriller—begins to play, cheesy music rising, and I take a bite of my ice cream, turning the cold spoon over in my mouth.

Almost immediately, I tune out, the screen blurring, sounds fading. All I can think about is Jay and Harper. But mostly Jay. His smile. I wonder if I'll see him again.

Before I go to bed, I take my paperback copy of *And Then There Were None* off my bookshelf and put it in my bag. Just in case.

3

I get to work late on Monday morning. I snoozed my alarm three too many times, then ran out the door as I struggled with the zipper on my hoodie. Luckily, no one cares what time I show up at the spa, as long as I'm there by my first appointment, which, today, happens to be at ten thirty.

Mondays are typically our quietest days, and this Monday is no different. The spa is practically empty. Chloe, one of our three rotating receptionists, is behind the desk. Out of the group, I like her the most. She's a nineteen-year-old sophomore at Brooklyn College, cooler than I'll ever be. Her jet-black hair is bleached platinum—her Korean parents almost disowned her when they saw it, she told me gleefully—cut into a sleek bob, short bangs. She wears oversized plastic tortoiseshell glasses, wide-legged jeans, and crop tops. If it's slow, I'll do her nails, usually a neon color, bright yellow or orange, like a highlighter.

Behind Chloe, a lone woman is getting a pedicure in one of the four spa chairs that line the left wall. Only one of the six small treatment rooms is occupied, its door shut, sign flipped to *In Session*. It will pick up a bit in the afternoon, but not by much. Lena takes Monday mornings off, so a lot of the girls stroll in closer to ten than nine, when the shift officially starts, with the exception of the opener, who arrives at eight in case of a walk-in.

A thick bloom of eucalyptus and lemongrass wafts over me as I walk through the spa. Under it, the acidic smell of polish and acetone. It used to bother me when I first started, the heady fumes making my eyes water, but I've acclimated. I hardly notice it anymore, except for the days I work a double, when it seeps into my clothes, clings to the fibers of my scrubs, my hair, my skin, the chemicals following me home, into my bed, into my dreams.

I deposit my purse and coat into the break room in the back and make myself a cup of coffee before my first client arrives. Last year, Lena purchased a Keurig for employee use as a Christmas present. She keeps the cupboard stocked with espresso pods and French vanilla–flavored creamer. She beams when she sees someone using it, still impressed by the ingenuity of her own gift-giving.

I take a sip of coffee and peek my head out into the nail bay. It's empty, the woman in the pedicure chair now at reception, handing Chloe her credit card. Even though the tips are less on these slow Mondays, I prefer this pace to the end-of-week rush, the manic, caffeine-fueled women staring impatiently at the clock as we churn through client after client. It gives me a chance to catch up with the other nail techs, gossip between appointments.

As if on cue, Natasha, my co–nail tech, walks into the break room. She smiles when she sees me.

Natasha is a few years younger than me, a half-Vietnamese Jersey girl—her mom from Ho Chi Minh City, her dad a second-generation Sicilian from East Hanover—with pink-streaked black hair that she pulls into a high ponytail at the crown of her head. She wears her scrubs skintight over a push-up bra, always a pair of gold hoop earrings the size of a bangle bracelet. It's a pain-in-the-ass commute from Jersey City, but she makes three times the money here as she would across the river; the Hoboken housewives are a tad less generous with their wallets.

"Morning, Slo," she says, popping a coffee pod into the machine. Her acrylics clack against the plastic buttons. "Have a good weekend?"

I nod. "It was great." I offer her a creamer from the glass canister. "I met someone," I say, smiling, thinking about Jay. "At the park on Friday. And he took me to dinner last night."

In reality, I spent the afternoon making Alton Brown's root vegetable panzanella for my mom, and we both fell asleep in front of the TV watching *Seinfeld*. Jay, I'm sure, was with his wife and Harper, the three of them cuddled together in Harper's bed, Harper in the middle, reading bedtime stories. Later that night, when I moved from the couch to my bed, I googled him in the dark, under my covers, his LinkedIn profile the first hit. I studied his list of jobs, then searched for his socials, disappointed to find they were all set to private.

"Oh yeah?" Natasha says. Her microbladed brows shoot up with interest. Then, "Tell me *everything*."

I grin. "Well, for starters, he's super handsome. And great in bed. Like, really, really great," I add for emphasis.

Natasha hangs on to my every word, tickled by my fabricated tryst. She wants to hear more, I can tell. Like me, she's single, scouring dating apps between clients, agreeing to dates with men who show her the least bit of interest. Most Monday shifts are spent commiserating about our shared lack of success, comparing the worst messages we received over the weekend, the lurid pickup lines, the grainy photos that linger in your mind long after you've deleted them.

"Where'd he take you for dinner?" she asks.

"La Vara," I say, not missing a beat. It's where Laura mentioned her son had taken her last week, said they served the best sangria she'd had in years. "The cocktails were amazing."

"And you went home with him? You bad girl, you!"

I nod. "You would have, too, if you saw how good-looking he was. But he was a total gentleman. He made me breakfast this morning before I left." I smile modestly. Natasha looks green with jealousy. "Buttermilk pancakes," I add. I can't help it.

"Are you going to see him again?" she asks.

Before I can answer, the front door rattles, and I hear Chloe offer a sunny greeting. I peek out, see two women at the front of the spa. Quickly, Natasha and I down the rest of our coffees and wheel our nail carts to our stations, where we settle onto stools, turn on the faucets.

In front of me sits a college-aged girl in an Aviator Nation sweatshirt and oversized Celine sunglasses pushed up like a headband, her pant legs pulled up to midcalf, feet in the tub as it fills. The color she's picked out is sitting on the armrest next to her—an electric blue. She has earbuds in both ears, sighing every so often, as if the person on the other end of the line is giving her a headache. She doesn't seem to notice my existence, or if she does, doesn't acknowledge it.

Her attitude is commonplace. Most of the women whose nails we do rarely look at us as we work, our bodies hunched over their feet and hands. There are a few regulars who remember our names, engage in real conversations, but the majority of clients only speak to us when barking instructions—*not too short, now,* or *no, not like that, more rounded!,* an *ouch!* and a glare every once in a while if we yank a cuticle too hard—but we're otherwise invisible to them.

Next to me, in Natasha's chair, is a nondescript middle-aged woman. She's flipping idly through a magazine, her Hermès bangles jangling with every page turn.

"Too hot?" I ask my client, motioning to the water in the basin. She looks at me blankly, then gestures to her ear and mouths, *I'm on the phone.* She means to say, *Don't talk to me, peasant.* I nod as a confirmation. Fine by me. If she doesn't care about whether the water scalds her, then neither do I. I turn the water slightly to the left, a few degrees warmer.

"Mine's too hot," the woman in front of Natasha announces loudly, overhearing my question. "Too hot," she repeats slowly and deliberately, staring intently at Natasha. Then she looks to me. "Can you let her know it's too hot, please?"

I smile tightly as Natasha adjusts the faucet. An embarrassing number of women assume an Asian girl in a nail spa has little to no grasp of the English language, never mind that Natasha was born less than twenty miles from here, both of her parents college professors. We've long stopped wasting our breath correcting them, but it still rankles me, makes me want to crank the water as hot as it will go, turn their white skin red, watch it blister.

"So," Natasha says, once the pedicures are underway, turning slightly toward me. She keeps her voice low and neutral. "I'm dying over here—are you going to see this guy again or what?"

I nod, grinning. "Definitely. He has a business trip later this week, but said he wants to see me as soon as he gets back. He said he'd take me to see *Funny Girl* if I wanted, with Lea Michele." I'd heard several of my clients talking about the show, how hard it was to get tickets.

I wonder if Jay takes his wife to the theater and decide that he probably does. He's probably taken her to La Vara, too. I picture them at a table for two, flutes of champagne sparkling, faces aglow in candlelight, their cheeks flushed, smiles wide, fingers interlaced across the table. I feel a surprising, hot flash of jealousy.

The smile I stretch across my face is as stiff as plastic. "This one?" I ask my client, reaching for the blue nail polish on the tray next to her. She stares at me a moment, eyes blinking slowly, before pursing her lips and nodding. *You're bothering me again,* she's telling me. *And it's not even worth my breath to say it out loud.*

Briefly, I imagine uncapping the bottle and ruining her two-hundred-dollar sweatshirt. If I didn't have bills to pay, if I didn't desperately need this job, I might. I let my smile grow even wider, part my lips to show her my teeth, then bend forward over her feet. I imagine hell isn't much different than this.

Natasha leans toward me. "Ask your new boyfriend if he has a friend. The last place a guy offered to take me was Subway. Which wouldn't have been terrible, except he followed it up with asking if I wanted to see his foot-long." She looks disgusted.

I nod. "I'll ask him," I say to Natasha. "Maybe we can double-date."

We turn back to our clients, both smiling. This time, my smile is real. *Your boyfriend,* she called him. I like how it sounds. *This is Jay,* I imagine myself saying, *my boyfriend.* If Natasha asks about double-dating again, I'll tell her that most of his friends are already married. I'm sure that part's true, at least.

4

At one thirty, I take my afternoon break and start toward Quail-wood Park. It's only two blocks away, just over a five-minute walk. I feel anticipation mounting as I near, even though Jay said he was going back to work this week. I can't help but hope that he's taken an extra day of vacation or gotten off early, picked up Harper on his way home because he'd enjoyed our conversation as much as I had. What's more likely, though, is that he spent the weekend with his beautiful wife and darling child, never giving me a second thought. But a girl can dream, right?

It's a bright, warm day, perfect late spring weather. The little park is swarming, filled with kids and their moms and nannies, screeching and laughing, arms and legs bare. I take two slow laps around the play structure. No Jay. No Harper. I let out a sigh. I stop, then scan the park a third time. Still no sign of either of them. It's unsurprising, but that doesn't keep me from being disappointed, which is stupid, I know.

When I'm sure, really sure, they're not here, I spread my flannel shirt on a little grassy patch under a full-branched tree and sit down cross-legged, take a book out of my bag. It's a dog-eared copy of *Rebecca* that I've read a hundred times. I open it to a bookmarked page, but I can't concentrate. I stare at the same paragraph for several minutes before I give up. All I can think about is Jay. The dimple in his right cheek. The electricity I'd felt when his fingers grazed mine. I wonder what he's doing right now. In a meeting? Sitting in front of his computer, chin resting on his hand? I groan and close the book, returning it to my bag, then pull out my earbuds and tap the Spotify icon on my phone.

I scroll, finding the song I'm looking for, the one I've had on repeat lately. The noise of laughing children fades. I mouth along as Taylor Swift sings about how everyone agrees: it's her that's the problem. Same girl, same. Sighing, I close my eyes. Every few minutes, I open them, glancing up at the playground. Just in case. After ten minutes, just when I'm about to pack up and head back to the spa, I catch sight of a familiar face. I freeze. It's Harper. And she's looking my way. My heart skips a beat like a tiny hiccup in my chest. I'd think my eyes were playing tricks on me, but I'm sure it's her because she's wearing the same purple shirt she had on last week, the one with a white sequined unicorn on the front.

She has her arm outstretched, and I realize she's pointing—at me. At least, I think she is. Eagerly, I look for Jay, but instead I see a woman next to her.

She looks like she's in her late twenties or early thirties, dark hair, sunglasses, a wide-brimmed hat tilted back on her head, also looking in my direction. She turns to Harper, then takes off her sunglasses and looks back toward me, squinting. She says something I can't make out, and Harper nods.

Then a smile spreads across the woman's face. She begins to wave. *Oh shit.* I look behind me, just to make sure, but there's no one there.

I'm sure now; she's waving at me. Tentatively, I raise my hand and wave back.

The woman takes Harper by the hand and the two start toward me, crossing the rubber playground mats onto the grass. Slowly, I un-cross my legs and stand awkwardly as they approach, then take out my earbuds, one by one, slipping them into my pocket. My phone drops to my side.

"Hi," the woman calls out as she nears. Her voice is loud and clear, like a bell. She's smiling, her teeth an iridescent white. "I'm Violet." She stops in front of me, extending her right hand. "Jay and Harper told me all about how you helped them with her bee sting. You're Caitlin, right? The nurse?" She glances at my scrubs.

I nod slowly. Right. Caitlin, the nurse. I slip my hand into hers. Her palm is soft, cool, fingers slender, but her handshake is firm. I no-tice her nails are well manicured, recently painted. I wonder where she gets them done, if she's ever been into Rose & Honey. I decide that she hasn't; I'd remember her.

"You're Harper's mom," I say. "Jay's wife." Of course she is. She's gorgeous, just as I knew she would be, but in a more interesting way than I'd imagined. Her nose is strong, brows thick under glossy bangs. She reminds me of a marble statue, handsomely angled features, smooth, hand-polished skin. *Venus de Milo* at the Louvre, a throng of people crowded in front of her, staring. How I imagine I look when I'm daydreaming, the lights dim.

Violet nods, still smiling. "I was hoping we'd see you here," she says warmly. "So I could say thanks for the other day."

I give her a small, modest shrug, looking down bashfully. It was nothing, my shoulders say. Really, though, it was *nothing*.

"Can you tell Caitlin 'thank you,' Harper?"

"Thank you," Harper parrots. She's wrapped herself around Violet's legs, peering at me from behind her waist.

"You're welcome," I say. "I was happy to help."

There's a pause, then Violet asks, "What were you listening to?"

"Oh." I glance down at my phone, caught off guard. "Taylor Swift," I say, hesitating, just slightly. I considered making something up—a podcast might have made me sound more interesting—but the album cover fills my screen; she probably already saw it. "*Midnights*."

I silently hope that she's not one of those people who finds pop music cliché—listening instead to underground indie bands or one-named folk artists who record songs in cliff-side studios on the rain-drenched coasts of Ireland—but luckily, her eyes light up.

"So good," she says appreciatively. "It's one of my favorites."

I grin and nod. "Mine, too."

We stand there, smiling at each other, sort of shyly, a comfortable silence between us. I do a quick appraisal, glancing her over. She's the same height as I am, but thinner, legs long. Her eyes, like Harper's, like mine, are a dark brown, wide and long-lashed.

She wears a sleeveless white button-up and a pair of beige linen shorts, cinched with a linen belt around her waist, a pair of nude wedges. The top button of her shirt is undone, and when she bends over to talk to Harper, I can see the lace of her bra, her full breasts. The hat she wears is a camel-colored wool fedora, the brim tipped up. It makes her look cool, like one of the girls I always longed to sit with at lunch in high school.

Under the hat, her hair is a mahogany brown, almost reddish, and I wonder if it's natural. It brushes the top of her shoulders in loose, shiny waves. Just then, she takes off her hat and rakes a hand through her hair, then smooths her bangs, brushing them from her eyes. They're just a millimeter too long, dusting her lashes. It suits her, though, the way they frame her face, and I find myself imagining how I'd look with the same cut. I haven't had bangs since fifth grade, when I took scissors to them myself.

As if she reads my mind, her hand goes to her forehead. Her left hand. There's a perfectly round, pebble-sized diamond on her ring finger. It glints in the sun, as do the matching studs in her ears. "I know, they're too long," she says. "I need a trim. It's at the top of my to-do list, but, well, you know." She motions to her daughter, then waves her hand in a sweeping motion, like *and everything else*, laughing. "That must sound incredibly sad—that trimming my bangs is at the top of my to-do list."

"If you think *that's* sad, you should see my to-do list," I say. "'Sad' doesn't even *begin* to describe it. We're talking tragic. *Sophie's Choice* tragic. Bambi-losing-his-mom tragic. *Titanic*, 'I'll never let go, Jack' tragic."

Violet laughs, an open-mouthed, throaty chuckle. "You're funny," she says, when she stops, smile still on her lips. "What's on your to-do list that makes it so tragic? Now I'm curious."

"Well, nothing, actually. I don't even *have* a to-do list. That's what makes it so sad." It's not totally true—there's a stack of unpaid bills on our kitchen table, the bag of recycling on our back stoop that I have to take out, and a dentist appointment I need to make—but I don't want to bore her. No one wants to hear about someone else's oral hygiene needs.

She laughs again. "Not having a to-do list sounds like the opposite of tragic. It sounds glorious. Kate-Winslet-ascending-the-stairs-at-the-end-of-*Titanic* glorious, if we're keeping with the theme."

This makes me smile. She's funny, too.

She puts her hand on Harper's shoulder, gives it a gentle squeeze. "Well, we won't keep you. I just wanted to say how much I appreciate—"

"Will you push me?" Harper interrupts, looking up at me with her chocolate eyes. Her dark brown hair is in the same neat braid today, secured with a pink ribbon.

"Push you?" I frown.

"On the swings." She points toward the playground with her tiny finger.

I look toward Violet, who smiles apologetically at me. "Only if you want to," she says, shrugging. "I completely understand if you have better things to do."

"No, it's fine," I say hurriedly. "I'd be happy to. No to-do list, re-member? Let's go!" I'll be late getting back to the spa, but I decide it's worth it. My next appointment isn't until three; as long as I leave by a quarter to, I'll be fine.

Harper puts her hand in mine and pulls me toward the swing set. I lurch forward, surprised by her strength, then regain my footing and fall into step behind her.

We wade through the little bodies darting across the play-ground, the three of us in a trailing line. When we reach the struc-ture, Harper happily climbs onto the swing, wiggling her legs in anticipation. I put my hands on the small of her back and push. She's light as a feather. Once she gains momentum, I take a step back, toward Violet.

"She's sweet," I tell her. "And she was really brave when she got stung."

Violet smiles at me. "She's a good kid. Eager to please. But I'm warning you, she could swing for hours. I'm not sure if you know what you've gotten yourself into."

I smile back. I like Violet already. And I especially like that she seems to like me. I give Harper another push.

"Do you live around here?" Violet asks.

"Not too far," I say. "Near Second and Bond."

"That's right near us!" she exclaims delightedly, as if I've shared some extraordinary news. I beam, happy that I've said the right thing. "Well, a few blocks away. We're in Cobble Hill, off Clinton and Kane. Have you lived here long?"

I nod. "Since high school."

We live in Carroll Gardens—the neighborhood just south of Cobble Hill—a small pocket in Brooklyn filled with young families and swanky boutiques, close enough to the water that when the wind blows, there's just the slightest tinge of salt in the air. My mom and I moved here before it was wildly trendy, when the rents were still reasonable, before the restaurants and bars earned Michelin stars, before it cost north of one-point-five million for a two-bedroom, one-bath.

We moved to take care of my aunt, my mom's older, and only, sister. Her health was, as my aunt put it, in the shitter—kidneys failing and liver not far behind—and she needed someone to take her to her weekly dialysis appointments. It was only a matter of time before she kicked the bucket, she'd say, sighing.

We moved into her spare bedroom, sharing a queen bed and tiny closet between the two of us. My aunt was right: she died less than eighteen months later. We emptied her room a week after the funeral, packing up her clothes, dismantling her hospital-style bed. My mom waited another week, then ordered a bed set from Macy's and moved into my aunt's old room, leaving me in the guest room.

Before my aunt died, she added us to the lease as co-tenants, so we pay the same rent each month as she did when she moved in in the late nineties—just under a thousand dollars. The neighbors above us pay four and a half times that much. If we were looking for a place to live today, we'd be lucky if we could get into a studio in Queens.

Cobble Hill, where Violet lives, is an even nicer neighborhood than ours, filled with new money, couples with trust funds, seven-figure salaries. The brownstones are all renovated, façades refurbished, restored to their historical glory. If she and Jay can afford a home there, they're even wealthier than I thought.

Just then, Harper leaps off the swing, joining Violet and me. She slips her hand into Violet's. "I'm hungry, Mom. Can I have my M&M'S now?"

Violet nods, glancing at the Apple Watch on her wrist. The band is gold-linked—real gold, no doubt. "Sure, baby. I didn't realize what time it was. Let's get going." She reaches into her pocket and holds out three M&M'S. "Can you say goodbye to Caitlin?"

"It was nice to meet you," I offer. I try to keep the disappointment from seeping into my voice. I wish they weren't leaving. I feel like I should hate Violet—poisoned with jealousy of her beautiful face, her rich, handsome husband, her cute-as-a-button daughter—but I don't. Quite the opposite. She's as interesting as Jay is. The Daisy to his Gatsby, just as I'd imagined. I shouldn't be surprised. He isn't the type of man to be married to a boring woman.

"You, too." Violet smiles. "I'm so glad we ran into you today."

She looks like she's about to turn to leave. "Actually," I say quickly, hopefully, "I was planning on grabbing some frozen yogurt—do you guys wanna come?" Lena might kill me, but I can't just let them walk away.

Violet scrunches up her nose. "We'd love to, but I have to run to the market—our fridge is practically empty."

I nod as if it's no big deal, a smile on my face, pretending to be unaffected by her answer. Then Violet cocks her head, as if considering something. "But . . ." She hesitates briefly, then continues, "Would you want to come over for dinner tonight instead? As a proper thank-you for helping Harper the other day."

My disappointment blooms into excitement, its leaves unfurling. She wants me to come over. I don't know what to say, suddenly speechless.

She smiles. "It'll be totally casual," she says. "I'll make something easy. I mean, if you're free?"

I nod, delighted. "I'd love to," I say, finding my voice. "Can I bring anything?"

Violet shakes her head. "No, please, just yourself." She glances again at her wrist. "It's two thirty now—how does six sound? Jay gets home from work around then, and that gives me enough time to stop by the market."

At the mention of Jay, the tiny butterflies in my stomach extend their wings, their flapping intensifying. I think of the copy of *And Then There Were None* in my bag; I could give it to him in person. "Six is great," I say, smiling broadly. I usually don't leave the spa until closer to six thirty, but I'll make up an excuse to duck out early. I worry if I ask to come later, she'll rescind the invitation. Kids are early eaters. *Another time*, she might say, and I can't risk that.

"Perfect." Violet grins back. "What's your number? I'll text you our address."

I leave the park as happy as I did when I met Jay.

5

race back to the spa, giddy, arrive out of breath. I'm late; I've been gone for an hour, well over my allotted thirty-minute break. Lena won't be pleased. She despises tardiness.

I pause at the front door, wiping sweat from my brow. Through the glass, I can see Chloe at the reception desk, sipping a to-go coffee. When she notices me, she motions for me to come in. I inhale deeply, trying to slow my breathing, then step inside.

I'm distracted, scanning the spa for Lena, when Chloe stops me. "You have a deluxe pedicure waiting," she says. "She was booked with Natasha, but Natasha had to squeeze in a walk-in, and she's not done yet." I catch the annoyance in her voice. I should have been here to cover the walk-in, she means; I am the wrench in the schedule.

"Sure, no problem." A quick glance toward my station tells me the client is already seated, feet soaking. "Let me just grab my cart."

I duck my head as I beeline toward the back of the spa, trying to keep a low profile. If I hadn't been in such a hurry, maybe I would have taken a closer look at the woman in my chair. I should have.

I relax when I reach the break room and see that Lena's office door is shut. She's not here. She doesn't close it when she is, leaving it open even if she's on a personal call, her baritone voice audible throughout the spa. I deposit my purse in my cubby and take a minute to compose myself.

I redo my bun, smoothing my flyaways, then grab my tiered roller, push it over to my station. The waiting woman is reading, her head hidden behind an open hardcover book. A thin bracelet is looped around her right wrist, one delicate green gemstone dangling. I see it, but fail to place it.

"Do you have a color picked out?" I ask, smiling up at her. What happens next feels like it's in slow motion.

As the woman lowers her book, the first thing I notice is her hair. A surprising flash of red, her ponytail draped over one shoulder, bright auburn. Goosebumps prickle the back of my neck. I know the color, that shade. It's then, my stomach clenching, that I finally look at her face. High cheekbones; a heart-shaped mouth; a thin, sloped nose. It's her. She looks exactly the same, even though over a year has passed. The blood drains from my cheeks. I feel like I might faint. If I wasn't already seated, my knees would have buckled beneath me. *What is Allison doing here?*

She recognizes me at the same time I recognize her. My surprise is mirrored in her face, her mouth dropping open, her blue eyes wide, almost bulging.

She has the same thought as I do. She doesn't have to say it for me to know; I can see it plain as day. *What is she doing here?*

I open my mouth—to say something, anything—but she springs into action before I have the chance to speak. She jerks her bare feet out of the basin, water sloshing over the sides. The surprise on her face has turned into something else, a mélange of anger and fear, a chocolate-and-vanilla swirl.

"I told you to stay away from me!" she says, high-pitched and shrieky. She's scrambling for her purse, struggling to hook the strap over her shoulder.

I glance around desperately. Natasha is staring at me, other patrons craning their necks. It's noisy in the spa—Chloe on the phone, the other line ringing, women chatting—but Allison's voice rises above the din, hinging on hysteria.

I turn back toward her. "Please," I hiss, holding my hands up in defense, hoping to somehow defuse the situation, dampen her anger. "Please, I didn't know you were coming in, I swear, this isn't what you—"

But she's not listening. "You're supposed to leave me alone!" she yells. She's managed to put her shoes back on, a pair of strappy sandals, block heels, and has edged by me, started backing toward the entrance, strands of hair loose around her face, a phoenix rising in the sun.

Allison gets to the front door, then raises a finger, points it at me. It shakes, just slightly. The gemstone on her bracelet—the Bulgari I recognized but couldn't place—dances. A pink flush stains her cream-colored cheeks. Her lips are sealed together tightly. She wants to scream, but her mouth won't open. She stands there, finger outstretched, trembling, staring at me, and I can feel my heart pulse in my throat.

Then she's gone. The door slams behind her, little bells on the handle jingling merrily. The room is silent. At least, it is to me, chatter and clatter no longer audible, as if someone pressed a mute button.

"What the—?" Natasha starts to say, but I'm already on my feet, headed toward the back, to the break room. I can feel everyone's eyes on me, boring into the back of my head. My face is burning. There's a steady rush of white noise in my ears, loud, deafening. Blindly, tears stinging my eyes, I grab my purse, turn, and rush back through the spa.

"I need some air," I mumble to Chloe on my way out. I think I hear Natasha call out after me, but I don't turn around. I have to get out of here. I wonder if I'll ever come back. Maybe, if I'm lucky, a black hole will swallow me whole and I'll disappear, poof, just like that. Vaporized into a million tiny atoms.

I fumble with the doorknob, my palms slick with sweat, then push out onto the busy sidewalk, gulping as if I'm coming up for air, lungs full of salt water.

I don't stop walking until I'm three blocks away at the mouth of a narrow alley, flanked by two apartment buildings. It's there my feet stop moving, refusing to take another step. I lean against the brick wall, cool from the shadows, then sink to the ground, staring blankly at the pavement in front of me—dirty asphalt, black splotches of gum. Eventually, my breathing returns to normal, my heartbeat slows.

Of all the gin joints in all the towns in all the world, she walks into mine. She does look a little like Ingrid Bergman in *Casablanca* with her clear blue eyes, sharp cheekbones. Of course, though, it's not such a coincidence. She lives only a few neighborhoods from here, in one of those newer buildings, fifty-seven stories tall, her apartment high enough to see across the water to Manhattan. I loved that view, loved leaning against the floor-to-ceiling glass wall in her living room, watching the sun set and the lights brighten throughout the cityscape until everything glittered like an endless sea of stars. If the windows were on the other side of the room, you'd have been able to see the roof of our apartment. Only a sixteen-minute walk from my front door to hers. Twenty, maybe, if you counted the steps across the marbled lobby, the time it took the elevator to carry you to the thirty-sixth floor.

So it wouldn't have been strange if our paths had crossed earlier, if today wasn't the first time I'd seen her since late last fall. Almost eighteen months have gone by. Has it really been that long? Some days it feels longer; others, like it was yesterday.

I used to look for her. I scanned the faces on the sidewalk, searching for hers, wondering if she'd appear, if I'd catch a glimpse. But I never did. It was like she vanished. Eventually, I stopped looking. Stopped wondering. Instead, I pushed her out of my mind. I packed her up tightly in a cardboard box and shoved her into the corner of a cobwebbed attic.

Until today. Until there she was, right in front of me. I'd almost touched her, taken her foot in my hand.

There's a dull ache in my chest. I wish I had a chance to explain. If she'd just been willing to listen, maybe things would have been different. I think maybe I should have followed her out, run down the sidewalk after her, but it probably would have only made things worse. If that's possible.

The chime of my phone startles me, its chirping shrill in the noiseless alley. My eyes flutter closed, and I brace myself, sure it's Lena calling to fire me. Who would have been the one to tell her? Chloe? Natasha? One of the other manicurists that I'm friendly—but not friends—with? I reach into my purse, my stomach heavy. But it isn't a call from Lena. It's a text from Violet. Immediately, the weight lifts. I smile. A ray of sunshine peeking through the clouds.

I wipe my face with my sleeve, sniff. The message lights up my screen. *Here's our address! See you at six!*

I click on the link. Google Maps drops a pin in the heart of Cobble

Hill, and I touch my finger to the thumbnail image of the street view. It's a beautiful brownstone, two stories instead of the traditional three, but wider than most, a steep set of stairs leading to a black front door.

I copy the address, then plug it into Redfin. The same image of the brownstone pops up with a small tag in the upper left corner that reads OFF MARKET. I thumb down the page and see that it sold last April for three-point-two-five million. Three-point-two-five *million*. My smile broadens. Tonight, I'm going to a three-point-two-five-million-dollar home for dinner. *Me.*

I close out of Redfin, look up from my phone. The alleyway is filthy, littered with flattened cardboard boxes, a dumpster against the opposite building. It smells dank, of wet, rotting leaves. I stand up, straighten my shoulders. I need to get out of here.

When I step onto the sidewalk, out of the shadows back into the light, I turn left. Away from the spa, toward home. I'm not going back to work. It's a risk—if Lena isn't pissed about the commotion, she will be about me skipping out—but I can't face my coworkers, their uneasiness, how they'll look at me, but not really, their eyes flicking around nervously before catching each other's. No, I can't go back. And, I realize, looking at the time, I need to get ready, out of these scrubs and into something nicer.

I won't let Allison ruin my evening. She's taken enough from me as it is.

I pack up what happened and put it back in its box. I unhinge the attic door and hoist it up, slide it back into the shadowy darkness, out of sight, out of reach. Everything is fine. Everything is *fine*, I repeat to myself, over and over until it is true. By the time I reach my apartment building, I'm no longer thinking about Allison. I'm thinking about Violet. And about Jay.

At home, I make a quick veggie scramble for my mom and bring it to her with a tall glass of iced tea with a mint garnish, cubes of ice clinking against the cup.

"You're not eating?" she asks, glancing up at me.

"I'm going out for dinner."

She raises an eyebrow. "Oh?"

I nod. "I met someone. A friend, maybe. At the park. She invited me over tonight, to their house."

"That's nice," my mom says. She looks like she might say more, her lips slightly parted as if she's waiting for the right words to form. But she just smiles and turns her attention back to her show. An old *Dateline* episode about a home invasion gone wrong. I watch for a moment—one of the victims is recounting the night—then leave the room to get ready.

In the bathroom, I trade my glasses for contacts, blinking rapidly as they go in. I rarely wear them. When I do, they dry out my eyes, leaving them red-rimmed and itchy by the end of the day. I'd get used to it if I wore them more, but I'm usually running late or out of contact solution. I look better without my glasses, though; some people look great in them, but the lenses make my eyes small and beady—so I'll grin and bear the dry eyes, at least for tonight. Carefully, I apply some mascara, then run a brush through my hair, pulling it into a high ponytail, wet my hands to smooth down the frizz.

I try on three different shirts, finally settling on a high-necked black tank, then tie my flannel around my waist. Even though the days are getting warmer, the nights are still cool. I take my scrub pants off and pull on a pair of jeans, ones without holes, then zip on some black boots.

"Don't wait up," I say to my mom as I leave, dropping a kiss on her forehead. She snorts, then smirks. We both know she'll be asleep in her chair by eight thirty. I'll come home and the living room will be dark, the TV flickering, volume still cranked high.

"Have fun," she says.

I smile. I will. I know I will. I've never been so sure of anything.

6

The Lockharts' house is only fifteen minutes from ours. I walk quickly, taking small, brisk steps. My heart is beating in double time, my nerves wired, but in a good way, like at the end of a date you never want to end, smiling nervously at each other, the air charged, night brimming with possibilities, or on Christmas morning, right before you walk into the living room. I keep reaching into my bag to make sure that the book for Jay is still inside. It is, of course, but I can't help myself.

I arrive at the address two minutes after six. From the sidewalk, I stare up at the house, the same brownstone from the Google Maps image. It's even more impressive in person, bigger, the wrought-iron railings shinier, its recently restored façade pristine. Worth every penny of the three-point-two they paid for it. I'd whistle under my breath if I knew how.

I climb the stoop and pause on the top step, shifting my weight uneasily from one foot to the other. Briefly, I see Allison's face, her whip of red hair. Suddenly, I consider turning around. It feels like I'm here under false pretenses. And I am, I guess. If I walk away now, no one will be the wiser. But then I catch sight of Violet through their front bay window. She's bending over Harper's shoulder as she colors at a small table in their living room. Violet is pointing to the drawing and nodding, smiling, cheeks slightly flushed. I blink Allison away. I know I'm not leaving.

I straighten, tighten the flannel around my waist. My name is Caitlin. I am a nurse. One, two. I tick off the lies that I've told, repeat them until they feel real. Then I knock.

A moment later, the door swings wide. Violet stands in the doorway, a little breathless, eyes shining. She's wearing the same outfit she had on earlier—the linen shorts, white shirt—covered by a frilly, paisley-print apron. She's also put on a cardigan, the sleeves pushed up.

"Caitlin, hi! Come in!"

I step from the porch into their entryway. In front of me is an oak staircase, leading to a second floor, and to the right, a large living room with the window I saw from the street. On the other side of the living room, a kitchen. There's music playing in a low murmur, a woman's voice, a guitar. The house is warm and smells like freshly baked bread.

"Follow me," Violet says, motioning with her hand. "I'm just finishing up dinner. Jay should be home any minute. Harper, say hi."

I follow her through their living room into the kitchen. Harper glances up from her miniature table as we walk by, smiles and waves, then continues drawing, humming under her breath. "Let It Go," from *Frozen*, I think.

The kitchen is bigger than most in Brooklyn—certainly bigger than our shoebox with a stove—with bright white cabinets, shiny gold accents, a six-burner oven, and a French-door refrigerator. To the right, there's a dining nook with a table set for four, but large enough for at least six, a large rattan lamp shade hanging above it.

"Sit, sit." Violet points to a bar stool on one side of the marble-topped kitchen island. There's a fragrant bowl of gardenias in the center of the counter that smell like a garden after it's just rained. "Everything's almost ready. The pasta's boiling; the sauce is simmering. I just need to take the bread from the oven."

I hang my purse over the back of the stool and slide onto the chair. Looking around, I want to pinch myself. If you'd told me this morning that this is where I'd be for dinner, I'd have laughed, said you were as big of a liar as I am.

"You want some wine?" Violet asks, pulling a half-empty bottle of white out of the fridge, glass fogged with condensation.

I shake my head. "No, thanks. I don't drink." I surprise myself, telling her this. It's true, but something I rarely admit. I wait for her to raise her eyebrows, cock her head at me in surprise, like I've revealed I have a third nipple. *You don't* drink? Most people act as if I've told them I skin puppies for sport. My god, the horror!

Instead, Violet breaks into a big, warm smile. "Me neither!" She returns the bottle, then reaches into the back of the fridge. "I'll pour us something else. Do you like ginger?"

I nod, elated. Another three-nippled freak, just like me. I love that we have something in common already. "Sure," I say.

"Perfect." She pulls out a can, shuts the fridge, and grabs two champagne glasses from the cabinet behind her. The can snaps loudly when she opens it, a sharp, crisp crack. Carefully, she fills the glasses, foam rising.

"My favorite ginger ale," she says. "No one would ever know it's not champagne."

She smiles and hands me a glass. "Cheers."

I touch my glass to hers, then bring the rim to my lips. It's sugar sweet, a little spicy. "Delicious," I say.

"Right?" Violet says. "It's my signature move, actually: ordering ginger ale at a bar, asking for it in a champagne glass." She scrunches up her nose. "I *hate* telling people I don't drink. Saying no is never good enough, is it? They always want to know *why* you're not drinking, like if you turn down a drink there's something seriously wrong with you."

I nod emphatically. "Totally." I rarely go out with friends, but she's right, on the occasions I do, I make something up—I'm on antibiotics or I went at it a little too hard the night before. The truth—that it gives me hives, giant red puffy splotches the color of overripe cherries—is far less appealing.

"The worst is when they give me a little coy, knowing smile, glancing at my stomach, like they're in on some stupid secret. Like the only reason on the planet a woman wouldn't drink is if she's pregnant." Violet rolls her eyes.

"So would you hate me if I asked why?" I say, leaning forward on the counter. I can't help myself. Remember, I told you I was nosy. "I can go first—I'm *highly* allergic. It actually might be worth a glass or two if I didn't look like a smallpox patient. It turns out people don't *love* being in close quarters with Typhoid Mary." This, unfortunately, is also true. I'd learned this my first weekend in college, when I'd taken a sip of warm beer at a house party and almost instantaneously turned into a tomato; the rate at which people distanced themselves was alarming.

Violet laughs. "Assholes, all of them." Then, "Oh, fuck!" she cries. She runs to the stove. The water is foaming, bubbling up and out of the pot, spilling down the sides. "I'm a terrible cook," she says, smiling over her shoulder at me helplessly. "But it'll be edible, I swear."

I study her as I sip my ginger ale, watching as she glides around the kitchen, her glossy, dark brown hair gleaming, soft waves bouncing. There's something effortlessly cool about her, even as she flounders.

She turns back toward me and opens her mouth to say something, but before she does, there's the sound of a door opening and closing. We both look toward the living room.

From where I'm sitting, I can see Jay in the foyer, his hand still on the doorknob. Then he turns, facing the living room. I can see him, but he doesn't yet see me. There's that flutter in my chest again. He's even more handsome than I remember, in a collared shirt and loosened tie, pressed navy khakis, but he wears a clouded expression, his face drawn, not easy and relaxed like it was at the park.

"I'm home," he calls out.

He shrugs off a brown leather bag and slings it over the stairway banister, walks into the living room. He pauses at Harper's little table, bends over to give her a kiss, smooths her bangs, then comes into the kitchen.

Violet smiles at him brightly. "Jay, you remember Caitlin, right?"

At this, his face changes, softening around the mouth and eyes. He looks at me and smiles, that same smile from the park—wide, dimpled, full teeth. For a moment, I forget how to breathe. "Of course," he says. "How could I forget our savior? Guardian angel. Patron saint of the park. Good to see you again, Caitlin."

I blush. "It was just a bee sting," I say.

"Well, your expertise was highly appreciated," Violet says. "You were the hot topic at dinner that night. They both couldn't stop talking about you."

Jay's smile seems to freeze. He hesitates, then says, "She's right. If you hadn't come over when you did, Harper wouldn't have been the only one in tears."

I give a little laugh. "You're welcome, then. I'm glad I was able to help."

He surveys the kitchen, his eyes settling on the champagne flutes in our hands. "I see you've already gotten started," he says, deadpan.

Violet rolls her eyes at him good-naturedly. It's a silly joke, one that he's clearly made before. It reminds me of being a kid, ordering a Shirley Temple at dinner, the waiter winking at me conspiratorially—*hitting the sauce pretty hard, I see!* It's more charming coming from Jay. "Can I get you a beer?" she asks him.

"I'll get it," he answers, crossing the kitchen. I like how he doesn't fall into that 1950s stereotype, the one that gets off work and plonks into his armchair, accepting—expecting—a cold drink prepared lovingly by his perfectly coiffed, apron-clad wife, though Violet happens to be both.

As he moves toward the fridge, their bodies brush. His back against hers. They both turn, catching each other's eyes, holding a beat. I look away, feeling both embarrassed and jealous by the intimacy, a brief sharp twinge in my stomach.

Jay pops open his beer and takes a swig, leaning against the countertop next to the stove. Then, he raises the bottle in my direction. I smile and do the same. We both drink.

"Need help?" he asks Violet, and she nods at him gratefully. "The Parmesan, can you grate it? Oh, and grab the serving bowl from the top cabinet, would you? The pasta is ready to toss."

He complies, setting his beer down and retrieving a large bowl from an upper cabinet in the corner of the kitchen. He sets it down next to her and picks up the cheese and begins to grate it. As he works, Violet drains the pasta into a colander in the sink, then transfers the noodles into the bowl, ladles in the simmering sauce.

"Okay," Violet says, surveying the kitchen, hands on her hips. "I think we're ready to eat! Harper, come wash your hands!"

A few minutes later, we're all seated, Jay and Violet on either end, me across from Harper. Violet dishes out the pasta while Jay passes around a basket of warm, crispy bread. I take a slice, then offer the basket to Harper, who takes two.

When everyone's been served, Violet holds up her glass. "Cheers. Thanks for joining us tonight, Caitlin."

"Cheers!" Harper shouts, holding up a plastic cup of milk. I smile at her and touch my glass to hers, then to Violet's, then, lastly, to Jay's. Our eyes meet and we both smile.

"Thanks for having me," I say, after I've taken a sip of my ginger ale. I look again at Jay, then back at Violet. "So, where'd you guys meet?"

I expect warm smiles, eyes glazing as they remember the night, but neither of them looks at me. Instead, they look at each other, their gaze holding steady. I can't read the expression on either one's face. Violet breaks first, glancing toward me and waving a hand dismissively.

"College," she says. "I wish it were a more interesting story, but it would probably bore you to tears."

It wouldn't, I want to assure her, but there's something about her tone that stops me, slightly clipped, but somehow, almost too cheerful. I look to Jay, hoping he'll say more, but he doesn't. He's staring at his plate, a strange tight-lipped smile on his face that looks ironed on.

I shift in my chair, wracking my brain for something else to say, but before I have the chance, Harper yells, "Look at this! A worm!"

She's holding up a noodle, wiggling it dramatically. We all laugh. Quickly, Harper becomes the center of the conversation, loudly chattering on about her day, happy as a clam when I ask her about her favorite book, announcing that it's *Winnie-the-Pooh*. She smiles when I tell her it's one of my favorites, too.

"Nina read me all of *The House at Pooh Corner*. It's a *chapter* book," she says proudly.

"Who's Nina?" I ask.

"Our nanny," Violet jumps in. "Well, former. She stopped working for us a few months ago. A shame, really. Harper loved her. We all did. Didn't we, honey?" She turns to Jay. "She was the best, huh?"

Jay stops chewing, blinks, then nods, once.

Violet sighs, turning back to me. "I've had the hardest time finding a replacement." She launches into a story about the series of interviews she's had over the last couple of weeks, how one candidate showed up two hours late in stage makeup, apologizing about an audition that ran long, only to go on to say that she didn't have any practical experience with kids, but she had played a mom in a commercial once. "Apparently," Violet says, "if you want a good nanny in New York, you need to find one when your child is in utero."

I smile; she's right. "Actually, I used to be a nanny," I say. "Before I got into nursing." This—believe it or not—is true. I started in college when one of my professors said she was looking for someone to pick up her daughter after school. She recommended me to another colleague, and before I knew it, I was booked almost every weekend. I liked it so much I switched degrees—from English to early childhood education—and began nannying full-time when I graduated. Eventu-

COUNT MY LIES

ally, I began working at a local preschool, one not too far from here. It's the job I lost before I started working for Lena. But I don't share that, of course.

Violet smiles back. "Well, no wonder you're so good with Harper!"

I feel an unexpected pang. I had been good at my job. It's funny: all my lying, which is generally considered a social faux pas at best, an egregious moral failing at worst, is partly what made me so well-liked by my students. I was a master storyteller, a spinner of tales, the queen of make-believe. The kids loved my outrageous stories, enthralled by the exaggerated accounts of my weekends, an adoring audience. Never once did they ask if it was true. They didn't care.

I was devastated when I had to leave. If I close my eyes, I can remember the last day like it was yesterday. There was no warning, the rug ripped out from under me so fast I'd lost my footing. I wanted to argue, wanted to scream that it wasn't fair, that it was all just a misunderstanding, but I knew it would be a waste of breath. No one would believe me over her.

Tears stung my eyes when I told the kids I was leaving. Leaving and not coming back. They asked why, but of course I couldn't say. My throat was tight, and no words came, so I just knelt and held out my arms. They filed in one by one and pressed their little bodies against mine. The principal was standing in the doorway, leaning against the frame with her arms crossed, waiting to walk me out. I still miss them: their sticky fingers, their shrieking, their gleeful laughter.

I force myself to smile back at Violet. "I really liked it," I say. "Loved it, actually."

Before I can say anything else, Harper knocks over her cup of milk, reaching for another slice of bread. Both she and Violet yelp in surprise. Instinctually, I leap up, grab the roll of paper towels next to

55

the sink, and race back to sop up the puddle, just before it drips onto the floor.

"Thanks," Violet says, smiling gratefully at me.

"Once a nanny, always a nanny," I say good-naturedly. Theirs is exactly the kind of family I would have loved to work for when I first started out. In fact, they still are. I picture myself in their kitchen, making a snack for Harper, cutting peanut butter and jelly sandwiches into heart shapes; in their living room, folding her tiny unicorn shirts as she colors happily by my side. It takes all my willpower not to offer to step in, to tell Violet she doesn't need to interview any more candidates, that I will gladly take the role. God knows, after today, I'll need a new job, and badly. I swallow the bitter memory of this afternoon, biting down on the inside of my cheek.

Dinner continues with small talk, Harper interjecting with anecdotes about her day. Violet listens attentively, encouraging her to elaborate on her stories. Twice I sneak glances at Jay, only to see him staring at Violet, watching her. I can understand why. She's glowing, wisps of hair framing her face, cheeks pink as she laughs. If she notices Jay's eyes on her, she hides it, her attention focused on Harper, on me, making sure my plate is full, that I'm enjoying the food. Once, she catches me looking at her and smiles. I smile back, enchanted. I wonder what it would be like to be as beautiful as her, to have that magnetic pull. Like magic, I imagine.

Just after seven, when our plates are scraped clean, glasses empty, Violet clears her throat and looks at Jay, then cocks her head toward Harper. He nods.

"You ready for a bath?" Jay asks Harper. Immediately, she begins to pout, about to protest, but Violet interjects, "Two M&M'S if you make it upstairs in thirty seconds or less!"

Harper lights up. "Red ones?"

Violet nods. Harper squeals and leaps from her chair. She races from the kitchen to the living room, her little feet thumping across the hardwood, then to the stairs, scrambling up them on all fours. "I did it!" Her little voice is faint, somewhere above our heads, and we all laugh.

Still smiling, Jay asks, "How many has she had today?"

"A handful?" Violet shrugs. Then, to me, "I'm not above bribes." She winks. "In fact, it's the only way to parent, in my opinion."

Jay looks like he might say something else, but instead, he scoots his chair back, stands. "I'll let you know when she's ready for you," he says to Violet. Then to me, "If I'm not back down before you leave, great to see you again, Saint Cait."

We both smile up at him. His tie is gone, shirt open at the collar, sleeves rolled up. I like how he says my name. My fake name. He even has a nickname for me. It makes me feel warm, gleeful. "You too," I say. Violet and I watch as he leaves the kitchen, disappears up the stairs.

"He's really sweet with Harper," I say. It's cute that he's worried about her sugar intake, that he's the one who fills her tub, who wraps her in a fluffy towel when she's done.

"She adores him. Everyone does," Violet says, letting out a little laugh. "He's like that; he makes people feel really . . ." She searches for the right word. "Special."

I know what she means. I felt it at the park the other day. He has this way about him, a charisma that pulls you into his orbit. Even if he wasn't married, I'd never stand a chance with him—he's leagues out of my own—but there was something about how he smiled at me that made it feel like maybe, in some alternate reality, we were fated.

I insist on helping Violet clean up, an excuse to stay more than anything else, clearing the table, rinsing dishes, loading the dirty plates and silverware into the dishwasher. We work in a comfortable silence, laughing when one of us bumps into the other, pots and pans clanging in the background.

When the kitchen is clean, counters wiped down, Violet takes off her apron and hangs it on a hook near the fridge.

It should be my cue to leave, but I linger. I'm not ready to go. I'm afraid if I walk out now, I'll never see the inside of this house again. Violet and Jay and Harper will fade until I'll wonder if I made them up.

Violet looks at me and smiles. I brace myself, waiting to hear that it's getting late, how she should head upstairs to help put Harper to bed. Maybe, before she does, I'll offer to run out, grab some pastries from a nearby bakery for dessert. I kick myself for not picking any up on the way. But as I open my mouth, she asks, "Want some tea? Coffee?" She sounds hopeful, like she's afraid I might say no.

I nod, biting down on my lip to keep from grinning like a buffoon, silently cheering in my head. "I'd love a tea." She's not ready for me to leave, either.

"Great, I'll heat some water," she says, smiling. "Go sit down." She motions to the living room. "I'll be right in."

I leave the kitchen, head toward the oversized couch against the wall. Gingerly, I sit down. I sink into the cream-colored cushions, pillows soft against my back.

From the couch, I look around the room. Across from me is a big bay window, gauzy white curtains pushed wide. It's dark outside, and the light from the lamp in the corner creates a reflection on the panes so I can't see out. Under the window, two armchairs are angled toward each other, a small side table between them, a stack of books on top. I can't make out the titles, but they look like novels, thick and worn. And in the corner, to the left of the armchairs, is a small kid-sized table for Harper, the one she was coloring at earlier this evening, topped with canisters of crayons and colored pencils. Next to it, a bookshelf and a few woven baskets piled with toys, stuffed animals, baby dolls.

It's one of those homes that feels cozy and warm, but fastidiously neat. Everything is in its place; no piles of junk mail or kicked-off shoes, no discarded jackets, no unhomed tchotchkes. Then I notice something strange.

Other than one framed picture of Harper on the bookshelf, grinning at the top of a slide, her hair in pigtails, there are no photographs. Everything on the walls is art; watercolors and oils of seascapes, waterlilies, one painting of a faded white-and-red umbrella on an empty beach. Oddly, no pictures of Violet or Jay. No wedding photos, no images of her, hair pinned back, elegant in a white gown, walking down the aisle, or him in a tuxedo, gazing at her adoringly. No vacation pictures, no family portraits. Only the one lone picture of Harper. Which seems weird. If I looked like Violet, if my husband looked like Jay, the walls would be plastered with our faces.

I get up and walk toward the entryway. Allison had photos everywhere. Blown-up, gallery-framed prints of her children, of herself, her husband. It was how I knew about their annual summer trip to the Catskills, that she wore a marigold flower crown at her baby shower. For her fortieth birthday, I surprised her with a bouquet, bright yellow. "My favorite," she'd said, burying her nose in their petals. "How'd you know?"

There were other pictures in Allison's house, too, not on the wall, ones she hadn't wanted me to see. An image of them, dozens strewn across her carpet, pops into my head. I force it out. Maybe Violet hung their family photos upstairs, or—

"Here you go."

I turn, startled. Violet is standing by the coffee table, two mugs in her hand. I hadn't heard her come into the room.

I walk toward her and take the tea, smiling in thanks. The cup is steaming, the porcelain warm to the touch. I sit back down and inhale deeply. It smells like orange rinds and spicy cloves, nutmeg. The bags are the expensive kind, delicate meshing instead of the flimsy paper ones filled with overdried, ground-down leaves.

"So," Violet says, settling next to me on the couch, smiling warmly. She curls her legs under her. "Tell me about yourself. You used to be a nanny and now you're a nurse?"

I don't let my smile falter. I knew it would come up; I'd thought about what I'd say when it did on the way over. But now, I have another idea. A better one—for me, and for Violet.

"I *was*," I wheedle, slowly reeling back the lie, one turn of the spool at a time. I take a sip of my tea. "Well, nursing school. My second year. But I just put in a leave of absence, today actually, to take care of my mother."

It was another thing I'd learned. If pressed about the lie, you backpedal. Answer noncommittally, add some new details, so that later, when they think back on it, they're not sure exactly what they were told. Then change the subject, but just slightly, a natural segue. In this case, introducing my mother into the conversation.

Violet takes the bait. "Oh, I'm so sorry, is she sick?"

I nod. "She has lupus." It's lie number three. I'm Caitlin, I am a nurse, and my mother has lupus. One, two, three. "It's been rough, but her doctor started her on a new medication that seems to be helping. I just want to be available to her while she adjusts."

"That's good to hear!" Violet says. She smiles as if she really does care.

It's Natasha's mother who has lupus. She's described it to me in detail, from her initial symptoms to the diagnosis. They had no idea what was wrong with her for almost a year. They thought it was Lyme disease at first, or fibromyalgia. The whole thing fascinated me. Only recently had she found a course of treatment that gave her some relief. Arthritis, in comparison, doesn't quite hold the same weight.

"I gave up my apartment and moved in with her, to keep an eye on her," I continue. "It was cheaper than hiring a live-in nurse. It's temporary, of course, until we figure something else out, or she gets better."

Violet nods understandingly. A woman living with her mother in her thirties is pathetic—unless said woman is a caretaker and said mother is ailing; then it is selfless, noble, really.

Then, before Violet has a chance to probe any deeper, I plant the seed that's just occurred to me. "You know, since I'm taking some time off, I could babysit Harper if you ever need an extra set of hands. I mean, if that's helpful." I hold my breath.

I need her to say yes just once, to give me the chance to show her how good I am at the job. Because once could turn into twice, especially if Harper asks for me to come back, then into a third time, then a weekly occurrence, a set schedule. Most of the families in this neighborhood have live-ins, and I'm sure the Lockharts have an extra room in this big house; maybe, just maybe, one day Violet might realize how helpful having me around is. It won't matter if Lena fires me. Or, if she doesn't, I could quit. I'd finally be able to tell my mom I'm moving out. The thought is exhilarating.

Violet beams at me, and I feel a rush of pleasure. "Thank you! I really appreciate that. Like I said, it's been so hard to find good child care. By the time I get back from dropping Harper off at school, I feel like I have to turn right back around and get her. I can't remember the last time I even vacuumed." She looks around the living room, seemingly embarrassed.

"Well, I'd be happy to," I say, pleased with myself, with my plan. "Not that you can tell your house needs vacuuming. It looks beautiful. Have you lived here long?"

"Not really. We moved here about a year ago, for Jay's work." Violet shakes her head. "I can't believe it's been that long already. I still haven't met very many people yet. Which is why I'm so glad you agreed to come over for dinner tonight." She smiles at me, and I smile back.

"Where'd you move from?" I ask. I already know from Jay's LinkedIn profile, but I want to hear it from her.

"San Francisco. We moved there after graduation so I could go to law school. My family lives in the Bay Area and my dad offered me a job at his firm when I passed the bar. We were there for almost ten years. It was hard to leave. We had a really good community out there. If it wasn't such a promising opportunity for Jay, I don't think we would have moved. Not that it isn't nice here," she adds. "It's just different. Have you been?"

"Once," I say, nodding. I haven't, but I looked it up as I got ready for tonight, taking a Google Maps tour through the city, then looking up the top places to visit, the top attractions and best restaurants. "I stayed in Nob Hill off Polk Street."

Violet lights up. "I love that area! We lived right around there when we first moved to the city." She smiles wistfully, remembering. "What about you? Have you lived in this neighborhood long?"

"Since forever. My mom and I moved here when I was in high school. To take care of her sister. She died not long after we moved, but we ended up staying. And we've been here ever since." I shrug.

"And your dad?"

I hesitate, surprised at the question. No one has asked about him for a long time. Usually if I don't bring him up, people take that as a cue, though I don't mind that Violet hasn't. I consider making something up about him, but I decide against it. There's something about the way she's leaning in, her body angled toward mine, that makes me want to tell the truth, like she's interested in me for me.

"I've never met him," I say, honestly. "He bailed right after my mom told him she was pregnant with me. It was a summer romance. My mom was waitressing in Daytona Beach, and he was there for a few weeks visiting a friend from college."

Violet's eyebrows rise. "And they never spoke again?"

"Not as far as I know. She said it was for the best, though. She knew she was going to have me, and she didn't need him trying to talk her out of it. She said once, after I was born, she called the number he'd given her, but it was out of service." I tell it to Violet the way my mom told it to me, like it would have made no difference at all whether he had picked up or not. "I didn't care," she always told me, squeezing my hand. "I knew I could do it on my own." But I've never stopped wondering what would have happened if he had.

"Wow," says Violet, sitting back against the pillows.

"The only thing I know about him is he was from Philly. Well, a suburb, just outside. She told me she doesn't even remember his last name."

"Philly?" she repeats. There's a funny look on her face.

"Yeah." I smile. "She still has a Phillies jersey of his. He gave it to her the first night they met, on the beach, when the sun went down. Have you been?" I ask.

She starts to nod, then—"Vi?" Jay's voice floats down from upstairs. "Harper's ready for her kiss," he yells.

The strange expression disappears so quickly that I wonder if I imagined it. "Be right up!" she calls back. "Sorry," she says to me. "That's the deal. If Jay does bath and stories, I do the good-night kiss and the tuck-in."

I glance at my phone. It's almost eight thirty. "It's okay. I should get going anyway," I say. I don't want to leave, not yet, but I don't want to overstay my welcome, either. I have to play my cards right tonight.

"You don't have to," Violet says. "It'll only take a minute."

"No," I shake my head, setting my empty teacup on the coffee table. "Really, I probably need to check on my mom."

"Okay, *fine*." She smiles and we both stand up. "Thanks so much for coming over tonight," she says. "And for your babysitting offer. Really, I appreciate it."

"Anytime," I say, following her to the foyer. *Just once*, I think, *that's all I need*.

She walks me out onto the stoop. Then she gives me a small wave and gently eases the door shut, disappearing back inside. Through the glass, I can see her walking up the stairs. I watch until I can't see her anymore.

I turn, feeling giddy, like I'm floating. I pause when I reach the sidewalk, looking back up at the brownstone. The windows are lit, the house softly glowing behind the drawn curtains. It's hard to believe that I'd just been inside, part of their evening, that maybe soon, I'll be part of their lives.

When I get home, my mom is asleep in her armchair, as I knew she would be, lightly snoring. I take the remote from her lap and turn down the volume on the TV, then pull the knit blanket on her legs up to her chest and switch off the light on the side table next to her chair.

Quietly, I make my way to the bathroom my mom and I share, easing the door shut behind me. After I've taken out my contacts, brushed my teeth, and put on some old sweats, I climb into bed and close my eyes. But I can't sleep. I lie there, replaying the evening, thinking about Violet and Jay and Harper. Their beautiful home, its warmness, the smell of it. The way I'd felt at the kitchen table, like I'd belonged. The way Violet laughed at my jokes, how she leaned closer when she asked me a question. There was something about her—about them, all of them—that felt electric, special. It made me feel special, too.

I turn over under the tangle of my sheets, too hot, the darkness like a thick blanket. My dresser casts a looming shadow on the opposite wall. I wonder what they're doing right now, in their bedroom, under their covers. What does Jay wear to bed? What does Violet? Do they sleep with their limbs entwined, pressed against each other, or sprawled, fingers and toes brushing throughout the night? Had he pulled her to him when she got in, his mouth on hers, hungry, urgent?

Then I imagine it was me getting in that bed, not Violet. Falling asleep next Jay, his body warm and heavy, his breathing deep, arm slung across my chest. The idea of it, of him, of his skin against mine, makes me feel hot all over, fever flushed. I throw the covers off of me, flip my pillow to the cool side. *No, Sloane.*

I turn my thoughts back to Violet. "Let's do this again sometime," she said. Had she meant it? Or was it just something she'd said to be polite, a thoughtless offering, tossed out without a second thought?

No, she liked me. She wouldn't have asked me to stay after dinner if she hadn't. She wouldn't have asked all those personal questions. Through the darkness, I smile. She wants to be friends with me as much as I want to be friends with her. I'm not wrong. Not this time.

7

I brace myself when I walk into work the next morning, silently rehearsing what I'm going to say about yesterday. About Allison. I don't know *who* she was, I've decided to claim, donning a perplexed look, my face a well of confusion. It *was* disturbing, I'll agree, which is why I left. It's a reach, but disgruntled clients aren't entirely unheard-of; every so often there will be an outburst, a dispute over the bill, dissatisfaction with a service, a perceived slight, and voices will rise, hostile and accusatory. Then the scene fades. It's over and the spa readjusts, settles back into its normal din. This doesn't have to be any different from any of those other times. Who says it isn't?

Chloe looks up from the computer when I enter the spa, a customer-ready sunshine smile on her face. When she sees it's me, there's a shift. Her smile falters. She seems nervous, eyeing me cautiously, like a deer in the middle of the road, staring into bright white high beams.

"Lena—?" I start, and Chloe shakes her head. "She's not here. I don't think she's coming in today. She mentioned something about her sister being in town this week."

I nod, relieved. I'd forgotten about her sister's visit. Lena had been talking about it for weeks. It would be the first time they'd seen each other in almost two years. Something about an issue with her visa.

I offer Chloe an apologetic smile. "Sorry," I say. "About yesterday. I think that woman must have thought I was someone else. It really freaked me out."

"That was *crazy*," Chloe says. She seems to relax, her nervousness dissipating.

"I *know*." I lower my voice and take a step closer to the reception desk. "That's New York for you. Chock-full of lunatics."

Chloe nods, agreeing. "She made a last-minute appointment. Said she'd been referred. If I had known—"

"You couldn't have," I say, interrupting her. "Let's just forget about it." I thumb toward my station. "I'm going to get set up."

I smile at Chloe, pleased she believed my retelling of the afternoon, then go to grab my kit.

Already, the spa is loud and noisy. We're booked with back-to-back appointments all morning, women wanting their fingers and toes to be just the right shade of pastel pink, fire-engine red. I should be focused. But I'm not. I'm distracted, reaching into my purse to check my phone, waiting for a message to appear, putting it into my pocket, taking it out again. I stare at the screen as if I can manifest her name if I try hard enough. I'm a broken record, my mind snagged on last night's dinner, the evening playing and replaying, over and over.

By eleven, my stomach is in knots. I've had to redo two of the nails of the woman in front of me after I smudged her polish as I fidgeted, jiggling my leg as I worked. *Why hasn't she texted yet?*

And then it vibrates, my phone buzzing against my thigh in my front pocket. I reach for it and grin when I see the alert. It's a message from her. From Violet. A rush of elation floods through me. I quickly unlock my phone and open the text, scanning quickly.

Hi! it reads. *So much fun last night, thanks for coming! I think you left your jacket here—a red flannel? Want me to drop it by your place?*

I smile, my stomach fluttering. I wasn't sure how long it would take Violet to find the shirt. I was starting to wonder if she'd even know it was mine. Before I left their house, I untied it from my waist, just as she turned to walk me out, her back to me, leaving it balled in the corner of the sofa, half tucked under a knitted throw pillow. It wasn't obvious, a flash of red—the sleeve—barely visible.

Okay, I know how it sounds, I do, but I needed a reason for her to text me. Sure, she said she'd love it if I babysat for her, but I'm not the only person who lies. And people get busy—work, kids, errands that pop up unexpectedly—before you know it, it's been a week, then two, a month, then six. She planned to call, but instead, I'd dissolve into her memory until I was blurry, out of focus, and then, even if she squinted, I'd be hard to make out. *Who?* she'd ask if Jay mentioned me, then—*oh, right, the nurse. What was her name?*

I couldn't let that happen. She was too interesting, too nice. I didn't want her to slip through my fingers. So I found a way she wouldn't.

"Excuse me," I say to the woman in the chair, then turn off the nail lamp and hurry into the back. I need some space to figure out how to reply.

In the break room, I study my phone, biting a fingernail as I compose my response. I type and delete, type and delete. I want to get it just right.

Finally, I press send. My message says: *Oh, sorry about that! Can I pick it up tomorrow morning? Maybe we could grab coffee?*

I don't have to be at work until eleven, so we'd have several hours to pick up where we left off. I hold my breath, waiting for her response. My lungs begin to burn. Then a message. I release the air, a smile spreading across my face.

When I read it, my face falls. *Actually, tomorrow morning Harper has a doctor's appointment.*

Then my phone lights up again. *Meet in the afternoon instead? Does 1ish work? Same park?*

I do a silent cheer. *Yes!* I write back. *I'd love to. See you tomorrow!* One p.m. is smack in the middle of my shift, but I can't say no. Not now, not at the beginning of the friendship, when it's so fragile it could disappear with the slightest breath, like a dandelion, naked in the wind. No, "no" wasn't an option. I'll figure something out. Beg Natasha to cover for me or fake a phone call midmorning. *It's my mom,* I could say, pale-faced, *she needs me.*

I return my phone to the front pocket of my scrubs and hurry back to the woman I'd left waiting. She gives me an irritated sigh when I sit down, her eyes flicking to the clock on the wall, but I don't care. I smile broadly at her, apologize for the delay. In fact, I can't stop smiling. Not even when I get a ten-percent tip instead of my usual twenty. It was worth it.

"You're in a good mood," Natasha says when we have a break, a rare moment when both our chairs are empty.

I nod, grinning. "That guy just texted, the one that I went out with last week. He said he wants to take me out again tomorrow night."

She raises an eyebrow. "I thought you said he was away on business."

"He is," I say quickly. Right, I *had* said that. "But he's coming home early. One of his meetings was canceled, so the trip was cut short."

She stares at me for a long beat before giving me a wistful smile. "Where's he taking you this time?"

I shrug. "I don't know yet. He said he'd pick me up at seven."

"You're so lucky. The last time I was picked up for a date was"— she taps an acrylic nail against her front teeth—"right, it was never."

She's right. I am lucky. Lucky that I've met someone as nice as Violet. "I know," I say, nodding. "I keep wanting to pinch myself."

On my way home, I pass by the small shop where I bought that necklace, the one I told Natasha was a family heirloom. I slow, something catching my eye. In the window is a mannequin, dressed in a bohemian floral-print dress, puffy sleeves and a high neckline, a leather bag hanging from the crook of her stiff arm. But I'm not interested in the dress or the purse. I'm staring at the wide-brimmed felt hat on her head. Almost the exact same hat that Violet was wearing at the park yesterday. It even has the same thin leather tie around the head, looped in a small bow at the back.

After a minute, I walk into the store. There's a mechanical bell sound as the door opens. *Ding-dong!* The woman behind the desk looks up, smiling at me as a greeting.

I smile back. I start to wander, then turn back to the salesgirl. "That hat, in the window—" I say.

"The fedora? It's so cute, right?" she says. "We have it in a few other colors, too. Here, follow me." She hops off her stool and motions me toward the back of the store to a table with a variety of hats in different shades: tans, beiges, grays, and blacks.

"I'm going on vacation next week," I say, walking behind her. "To Europe. I've been looking for a hat to bring."

"How fun!" she exclaims. "I've never been." She clucks regretfully, then sighs and picks up a caramel-colored one, the same as in the window—the same as Violet's—and hands it to me.

I take it and offer her a sympathetic smile as if I can relate to her longing—which of course I can. I've never been to Europe, either.

"Try it on," she says encouragingly. "It'll be perfect for your trip."

I unwind my hair from the messy bun on top of my head and smooth it down. It's long, almost midway down my back; I haven't been to a hairdresser in eons. Then, gingerly, I place the hat on my head, tilt the brim up like Violet had worn hers. The salesgirl points behind me, to a mirror on the wall. "Check it out." Then, "I'll be up front if there's anything else I can help you with," she says, starting back to the counter. Then she smiles. "It looks great on you, by the way."

I turn toward the mirror. To my surprise, it does look good. The hat hides my frizz and frames my face flatteringly. I look more put together, more chic. I smile at my reflection. It's nice to see myself like this.

I haven't always been such a schlub. Not that I've ever been as gorgeous as Violet, but there was a time when I made more of an effort. Before I lost my job, my hair was usually trimmed (and combed), my clothes unwrinkled, blouses instead of T-shirts, slacks instead of baggy jeans. Venus de Milo I was not, but it was better than how I look now. Maybe I could look like that again. Maybe I could look better than before. More like Violet. And this hat could help.

I take it off and turn it over, examining it. The price tag reads eighty-five dollars. Christ.

I should put it back. I shouldn't be spending my money on things like this. Last night I told Violet the truth about one thing: I am planning to get my own place. I have been for ages. In fact, I almost signed a lease. About eighteen months ago, now. It was a newly renovated studio in Brooklyn Heights on the third floor of a seven-story building, flooded with light. I had first and last months' rent, the broker's fee, but my application fell through. The management company wanted to call my employer. Had it been a month earlier, it wouldn't have been a problem, but as luck would have it, I'd lost my job the Friday before my broker called to let me know they'd started my background check. I asked if I could just show my last two pay stubs, hoping it would be enough, but the answer was no. And even if it hadn't been, without a job, there was no way I'd have been able to afford the rent. So poof, just like that, there it went.

I thought getting hired at Lena's spa would put me back on track, but because so much of my income is in tips—an unreliable stream of revenue, according to my broker—I'm not the desirable applicant I once was. So I'm waiting, waiting and hoping, the deposit still in my savings. It's why the idea of being a live-in nanny is so appealing: no background checks, no proof of income, just an invitation and an open door.

I run my thumb over the soft brim of the hat. I shouldn't. But a moment later, I start toward the counter, the hat in my hand. I leave wearing it.

8

At a quarter to one the next afternoon, I tell Natasha that I need to run a quick errand and ask her to keep an eye on my station. Luckily, I finished my twelve o'clock appointment early, and my next one isn't until two. Begrudgingly, Natasha agrees to get my two o'clock started if I'm not back, and I promise to make it up to her. I'll bring her a coffee and her favorite Danish in the morning, an apricot strudel from a bakery around the corner. She'll forgive me—I know she will.

Before I go, I put a loose sweater on over my scrub top, swap my scrub pants for a pair of leggings. I walk toward the park, a spring in my step. I'm wearing the hat I bought yesterday, too. Today, I feel slightly self-conscious about it, like I'm an imposter, playing dress-up. I'm not sure if it suits me, but I decide to leave it on, tipping up the brim like Violet had done.

Harper is already on the swings when I get to the park, Violet behind her, pushing. They both smile when they see me. Violet says something I can't hear, and Harper leaps off the swing and sprints toward me. Violet follows, giving me a wave. She's in a dress today, high-collared with tiny white polka dots, long-sleeved, that hits mid-calf, and the same wedges she wore the first time we met.

Harper slows when she reaches me, smiling shyly at me. Violet joins us a moment later, placing her hand on Harper's shoulder. "Hi," Violet says. "Cute hat."

"Thanks," I say casually, but my chest swells with pride, thrilled I decided to wear it. Then I squat down to Harper's level.

"Hi, Harper," I say. "I love your shirt. Red, just like the shirt Winnie-the-Pooh wears!" Harper's face lights up. "Do you like honey as much as he does?" I ask.

She nods. "My mom puts it on my strawberries. Sometimes," she says, leaning closer to me, "I lick it off a spoon. If I'm really good, Mom buys me a honey stick from the market. But that's our secret."

I laugh. "Yum! That sounds delicious."

"It is," she says. "Do you know how old I am?"

I shake my head. "Can I guess?"

"Okay," Harper agrees. She looks delighted by my request.

"Are you twenty-five?" I ask. When she shakes her head, giggling, I pretend to be shocked. "What? Older? Twenty-eight? Thirty?!"

She giggles. "No! I'm almost five. My birthday is in August. August twenty-second. I'm going to have chocolate cupcakes with pink sprinkles. And I asked for a kitten, but Mom said no." Then, to Violet, "Can I go play over there?" She points to a sand pit in the corner of the park. Violet nods, and Harper bounds off, limbs loose like a puppy. She beelines for an abandoned plastic bucket, faded from the sun, and begins to scoop sand into it.

"Want to sit?" Violet motions to a park bench a few feet away.

I take a seat beside her. She smells like the bloom of gardenias on her kitchen counter. "Oh!" she says, remembering. "Here." She reaches into her bag and pulls out my red flannel shirt. "Before I forget."

"Thanks," I say breezily. I take it from her and put it into my purse. I'm pleased with myself, by how well the plan worked. "Sorry about that."

"It's no problem," she says. Then she leans toward me. "I love your necklace," she says, squinting to get a better look. I put a hand to my neck. The pearl is cool and smooth. "Where'd you get it?"

"It was my grandmother's," I say, repeating the lie I told Natasha.

She looks disappointed. "Shoot. I was hoping you'd tell me where I could buy it. I've been looking for one just like it."

I want to kick myself. Now I wish I had told the truth. I like the idea of us wearing the same necklace. "Well, she bought it not long before she passed, actually. I can find out where, if you want?" I offer. "I think it's probably somewhere local. My mom will know."

Violet brightens. "I'd love that, thanks." She smiles and looks back toward Harper. She's now forming sand patties with another little girl, shaping them carefully with her small hands then pretending to eat them in one bite.

"Are you home with her full-time?" I ask.

Violet nods. "I left my job when we moved out of San Francisco. I hired some help—Nina—after we got here, so I could start studying for the New York bar, but that didn't work out, so . . ." She trails off, shrugging. "We'll see. It's funny, though: this job, the stay-at-home-mom gig, is a hundred times harder than my job as an attorney. But it's more fun." She smiles. "I never got to spend Wednesday afternoons at the park before I was a mom."

"Do you want more kids?" I ask. Immediately, I wish I could take it back. It's too personal a question, too premature, given that we just met. I hope she doesn't take offense.

The smile on Violet's face doesn't falter, but it changes. Her eyes flick to her lap, then back up at me. "I did. I thought we'd have a big family. At least three kids. But—" She stops abruptly, clears her throat. "Harper has some medical issues. It's been hard for us. All of the doctor visits, appointments with specialists."

A lump forms in my throat. "What's . . . what's wrong with her?" I ask.

"It's her heart." Violet looks down at her hands again. She fiddles with her diamond. "It's weak. She had an infection as a baby, and it damaged the tissue. Blood doesn't always pump correctly. She has these fainting spells. Not often—the last one was over a year ago—and usually they're just a few seconds, but once she needed a defibrillator."

We both look over at Harper, who is still playing happily in the sand. My heart aches for her. And for Violet. And Jay.

"It's probably why Jay was so flustered about the bee sting the other day. We're always holding our breath, hoping she's okay. Jay won't even talk about it. Pretends like everything is fine. I don't think he wants to admit that we could lose her, you know?" Then Violet smiles. "But she's tough. We don't treat her any differently—we don't want her to feel like she can't do anything any other kid can. But it's one of the reasons I'm having such a hard time finding another nanny. I really want someone with a medical background, you know, just in case."

Then Violet bites down on her lip, looks at me sheepishly. "Which brings me to the real reason I wanted to meet up today. Aside from returning your jacket, of course."

I stare back at her, waiting for her to explain, hoping, hoping—

"I know you offered to babysit every once in a while, but I couldn't help but think, I don't know, would you be interested in more than that? Maybe nannying a few shifts a week? Just until you go back to nursing school?"

"You want me to be your nanny?" I repeat.

Violet nods. "It would just be a few hours a week. I was thinking Tuesday and Thursday afternoons when Harper gets out of school, a Friday here and there? Then I could dedicate a few hours a week to studying again. Maybe take the bar next February. Please tell me if I'm overstepping, but I had to ask. Like I said, we have a hard time trusting people with Harper, and with your background, it just seems so . . . *right*."

My heart feels like it's beating in triple time. It's exactly what I wanted, what I hoped for when I made the offer, but—and this is a big "but"—that was before I knew Harper was sick. She needs a real nurse, not a make-believe nursing student. I should say no. I should tell Violet the truth. I know I should. I want to do the right thing, but I also want her to like me. I want so badly for her to like me. And when you want someone to like you, you tell them what they want to hear.

"I—" I start, unsure how to finish. "I'm—"

"I'd pay you, of course," Violet says. "Thirty-five an hour? Is that fair?"

Thirty-five an hour is more than I make at the spa. More than I made as a teacher. A couple of nannying shifts a week would be another thousand dollars a month, at least. And if—when—I do a good job, maybe those few shifts will turn into more. Maybe a live-in position, like I hoped. It would mean I could move out. I'm happy to take care of my mom, I always have been, but in the last few years, the walls have been closing in, the apartment becoming smaller, making my life smaller, me smaller. I want to start living for myself, for once, finally stand on my own two feet. This offer could make that happen.

Violet stares at me hopefully, eyebrows raised in anticipation. She wants me to say yes. I want to say yes.

A smile breaks out across my face. "I'd love to," I say. I can't help myself. It feels like kismet. Every moment from Harper's bee sting until now, everything falling into place, just so. The last eighteen months have been so hard, but this—a chance to start over—is what I've been waiting for. And it hasn't all been lies, not really. I do have experience with children, in and out of the classroom, some medical expertise.

No, I'm not a nurse, but I am well-versed in first aid, something required at the preschool. I've dealt with plenty of injured kids, kids with sprained wrists and ankles, kids with bloody knees from a fall, kids with fevers, kids with stomachaches, earaches, headaches, pea-nut allergies, half the class with EpiPens in their backpacks. Several of my students dealt with medical conditions, too. Riley, a four-year-old in my first year of teaching, had epilepsy; Cleo, in my third year, had diabetes. I'd had conferences with their parents, kept medical files in the top drawer of my desk, knew what to do if Riley began to seize, if Cleo's monitoring device went off. This wasn't much dif-ferent, really. I'll read up on Harper's condition, too. I'll be prepared. And Violet had said it herself, Harper hadn't had an episode in a long time.

"Really?" Violet says, her voice rising a pitch. She claps happily. "Seriously, you'd be a lifesaver."

"Yeah." I nod, grinning. "I'd be glad to."

She beams. "Great! Is Friday too soon to start? Maybe you could come over for a few hours in the morning while Harper's still at school. We can talk logistics."

My stomach flutters. This isn't just a hypothetical; it's really happening. "Sure. Is ten a good time?"

"Perfect," Violet says enthusiastically.

I smile back at her until I notice the time on her Apple Watch. *Shit.* It's almost two thirty. I have to get back to work. If I don't, Natasha will kill me. And then feed me to her Jersey cousins.

"I should go," I say reluctantly. "I have to swing by the pharmacy for a prescription refill."

Violet nods. "We should get going, too," she says. "If I can ever pry Harper from this playground. And seriously, thank you again."

"I'm happy to do it," I say, trying to sound nonchalant. But inside, I am elated. I'm going to be working for the Lockharts. I bite down on the inside of my cheek to keep from grinning. I stand. "See you Friday?"

"Friday at ten!" she says.

I leave on cloud nine.

I'm floating when I get home. Natasha glowered at me when I returned to the chair beside hers, but I didn't care. She'll get over it; she always does. I'll get her two Danishes instead of the one I'd planned on. Another day her attitude might have bothered me, but not today. Nothing could burst my bubble.

My mother notices. How could she not? The happiness is spilling out of me like an overflowing tub, the faucet left cranked too high. It bubbles up and over the porcelain edge, sloshing onto the floor.

"You're humming," she says from her armchair. I pretend not to hear her. She's right, though: I am. I'm in our small kitchen, next to the living room, cooking our dinner. I'm attempting to re-create Violet's pappardelle Bolognese from the other night.

I tip the boiled pasta into a colander in the sink, steam rising from the basin. I take my time mixing in the sauce, weighing what I'm going to tell my mom.

I walk into the living room with two servings, a shaker of Parmesan tucked under one arm, hand my mom a plate, then the cheese. She adds more than she should, but I don't comment.

"What'd you say?" I ask.

"You were humming," she says again. "Good day at work?"

I sit down on the couch, in the seat closest to her, and set my plate on the coffee table. "I met up with Violet again today. And Harper. At the park," I admit. I don't look at her. I keep my eyes on the muted television. A rerun of *Seinfeld* is playing, the one with the babka, I think. "She asked me to nanny for her. A few times a week."

I hadn't planned on telling her—she'll worry; she always does—but I can't help it. I'm so excited about spending so much time with Violet and Harper—and Jay—I want to shout it from the rooftop.

"Nanny for her?" my mom repeats.

I nod. "Yeah, I told her I used to nanny. It's just a couple hours a week." I try to sound offhand, but it's futile. I sound giddy. I glance over at my mom. Her lips are pressed together in a tight line.

"Does she know?"

I stare at her, then shake my head. "No," I say quietly. "I didn't tell her." I'm never going to tell her. Violet can never find out why I don't work at Mockingbird Montessori anymore.

My mom stares back at me. She blinks a few times, then nods.

"It'll be fine," I say. "This will be good for me. I miss being with kids. Plus, the pay is great. Which means one step closer to my own apartment," I add. She knows how much I want this.

Her mouth relaxes. She reaches over and squeezes my thigh. "I'm glad for you," she says. Then she looks back at the TV, picks up the remote. She aims it at the screen but hesitates before pressing the button. "But be careful. You hear me?" She doesn't look at me when she says this.

I nod. She's right. We both know how I am. Then she unmutes it. Kramer bursts into Jerry's apartment, and we both laugh along with the studio audience.

That night, when I go to bed, I realize I'm still humming, my favorite Taylor Swift song, the one about the players and the haters, the heartbreakers and the fakers, the one where she tells you it's going to be all right.

9

The next morning, I'm filling up my basin when Laura walks into the spa. I look up when I hear the jangle of the bell and wave. She waves back, her big hair bouncing, and sashays toward my station.

I don't need to ask her what we're doing today; she comes in every week, alternating between a manicure and pedicure. She gets acrylic on her fingers, gel on her toes, the same deep crimson color for both. When she's finished, she gets her eyebrows waxed with Kristen, our lead esthetician.

"You look like the cat who ate the canary," Laura says, settling into the oversized leather pedicure chair, her feet plunging into the water.

"Me?" I say. I duck my head and bite down on my lower lip; I've been grinning like an idiot since Violet offered me the job.

"She met someone," Natasha says to Laura, leaning toward my station. Her client is on the phone, headphones in. "Some hotshot businessman." She snaps her gum and winks at me.

"A businessman?" Laura says. Her drawl deepens, sounding more like Dolly with every syllable. "How fancy!"

"He's an entrepreneur," I say, blushing. "It's a new thing." For a moment, I consider showing them both a picture of Jay, pulling up his LinkedIn profile, but I know that's crossing the line.

I tell Laura that he's a single dad, detail the afternoon we first met, recounting the bee sting, Harper's cries, how I helped scrape out the stinger. The only things I leave out are my lies. She's happy for me, nodding along throughout my story, beaming.

When I finish her nails, Laura hands me a hundred-dollar bill, giving me a conspiratorial smile. "In case you need something for your next date."

"Thanks, Laura." I smile back and tuck it into the pocket of my scrubs. I loved the cardigan Violet was wearing the other day; maybe I'll buy one, too.

When my chair is empty, I decide to sneak out for a bit, head to the bakery around the corner to buy a pastry for Natasha. Just as I grab my purse from the break room, Lena walks in. I give her a polite smile, try to sidestep around her, but she stands in the doorway, not moving.

"Can we talk? It'll be quick," she says. She pronounces "it" like "eet." "In my office." She motions to the door on my left. It's a tiny square room with a desk shoved up against the wall, a computer, and two chairs. The desk is always piled high with stacks of paperwork, scattered invoices, ledgers.

Fuck. "Sure." I sigh and walk into her office. *Here it comes.*

Lena moves past me and squeezes into the chair closest to the desk. Her office has a distinct smell, a thick, cloying mix of acetone and incense. She crosses one leg over the other, looks me in the eye. One of the things I like about Lena is she's not a bullshitter. Whatever she has to say, she shoots it straight. I brace myself.

"You've been late recently," she says. "Taking long breaks. You missed half your shift on Monday."

"I'm sorry," I say. "It won't happen again. I'll be better."

She shakes her head regretfully. "I can't take that chance. I'm sorry. I told you when I hired you, I need reliability."

I stare at her as the words sink in. The incense smell is making me woozy. "You're firing me?"

Lena nods. "I wish you the best," she says, standing. The legs of her chair sputter across the floor as she pushes out of it. The conversation is over.

I stand, too. Awkwardly, we face each other. Then Lena takes a step closer and gives me a brief hug. "Take care of yourself, Sloane."

I leave her tight office, slightly stunned. Even though it wasn't exactly a surprise, it stings, how abruptly Lena was willing to dismiss me, over a few long breaks and a missed shift, after a year of hard work. It feels like I've been slapped, my cheek hot where she struck me.

I slink through the spa, gathering my nail kit and a few small personal items, and head toward the front door. The other nail techs stare as I walk by. No one speaks to me. Natasha looks like she might get up when I pass her station, but doesn't, turning back to her client. She's probably the one who ratted me out, who told Lena about Allison. I've done a million favors for her in the time we've worked together; she's as ungrateful as Lena is.

I step out onto the sidewalk, out of the air-conditioning and into the heat of the afternoon. The spa door bangs shut behind me. For a moment, I just stand there. Then I smile.

No more neck-hunched days over women's calloused feet, my face stretched by a counterfeit smile so wide I worried my lips might split. No more acetone-blistered hands, knuckles dried and cracking from the too-hot water. No more looking up at women as they looked down on me, literally, figuratively, debasing myself for tips. I'm free, finally free, my servitude ended. At the end of the block, I toss my nail kit into a trash can, hear it clunk against the metal bottom.

Fuck Lena. Fuck Natasha. And fuck that job. I don't need it. I don't need them. I'm Harper's nanny now.

10

The next morning, Friday, I wake up feeling lighter than I've felt in years. I never have to go back to the spa. Never, ever again. And what's better, I'm meeting Violet for a walk. She'd texted me last night, asking if I'd meet her at the playground instead of her house, so she could get some steps in before picking Harper up from school. *Of course!* I answered. I'd have agreed to meet her anywhere. I practically float out of bed, cartoon birds chirping merrily as I dress.

Most of my workout clothes are old and musty-smelling, but I find a pair of barely worn black joggers in the back of my closet that I pair with a loose T-shirt, knotted up on one side. I put on my New Balances, wishing they were a little less worn-out, less scuffed. Then I tuck my hair into a baseball cap, tie a hoodie around my waist. I consider putting in my contacts, but when I glance at my phone, I realize—*shit*—I don't have the time, so I grab my purse and head toward the door.

Fifteen minutes later, I spot Violet at the entrance to the park. She waves when she sees me. I wave back and pick up my pace.

Her dark hair is pulled into a high, bouncy ponytail, a few loose strands on the back of her neck, bangs brushed to one side. Like me, she's in a pair of running shoes—though hers are newer—but she's better dressed, wearing ribbed high-waisted leggings and a matching stomach-baring sports bra, horseshoe logo winking.

"Hi!" she says when I get close. "Thanks again for meeting me here. I feel like I never exercise anymore, so I've been trying to fit it in where I can. Jay bought me a Peloton last Christmas, but I use it more as a clothes rack."

"What's ex-er-cise?" I joke, drawing out the syllables like I'm saying it for the first time. Violet laughs and I feel a little rush.

Frankly, a little exercise would do me well, too. I'm not overweight—or particularly thin—just an average build, a little pudgy around the waist, a bit of a jiggle in my thighs, unlike Violet, who's lithe and long-legged. I could probably stand to lose a few pounds, but I loathe the gym. I hate the sweat-masked Lysol smell, the stuffy air, the women with their pristine Nikes and tanned, flat midriffs. I don't need to feel more schlubby than I already do, thank you very much. Actually, I considered buying a Peloton, too, but when I saw the exorbitant price tag, that bubble burst. The thought of using a three-thousand-dollar gift as a glorified hanger is so ridiculous I almost laugh.

"I've actually been meaning to get back into it myself," I say. "I used to run track in college." It's a nice addition to my list of lies: one, my name is Caitlin; two, I am a nurse; three, my mother has lupus; four, I am a runner. I like the way it sounds.

"I ran in high school, too!" Violet says. "Cross-country."

I smile back, pretending to be delighted at the coincidence. *Shit.* "I loved it, but I tore a ligament in my knee just before graduation. I haven't been able to do it since. So walking's perfect for me, actually." The last thing I want is for her to suggest we jog together instead. The thought alone is horrifying.

"Great!" she says. "I thought we could head to the water then up toward Brooklyn Bridge Park. How does that sound?"

I shrug. "Sounds good to me."

We start to walk, faster than I'd anticipated. To keep up, I do a little half jog every few steps or so. Soon, I start to feel beads of sweat prick at my hairline, my breathing becoming heavier.

"I'm more out of shape than I thought," I say sheepishly, doing my best to keep from panting. Violet smiles at me encouragingly, but doesn't slow down.

After a few minutes, we settle into a comfortable pace, making small talk as we walk, mostly chatting about Harper, about her schedule, her likes and dislikes, eating habits Violet thinks I should know about—like how the only fruit she'll eat is strawberries and how she loves yogurt but only vanilla-flavored.

I manage to slip in a casual question about Jay here and there, learn that he has one older sister, three nieces, that he's always wanted to live in New York. "I wasn't so sure about raising Harper here," Violet says, "but he talked me into it. Jay can talk anyone into anything." She smiles, rolling her eyes affectionately.

By the time we reach the park, the sun is high in the sky, a blazing, bright ball. The temperature is already in the low eighties, the day sticky, hot, even for April. I'm sweaty, my T-shirt damp under my arms, against my back.

Violet looks as fresh as she did when we started the walk. Her face has the slightest tinge of pink, but she's otherwise untouched by the heat.

We slow, strolling toward a bench at the edge of the water. We don't sit, instead standing behind the bench, using its back for balance as we do a few light stretches, heels drawn up behind us, then bending over into a tabletop position. I'm not quite out of breath anymore, but close.

"How do you make this look so easy?" I ask. "I look like I just ran a marathon. I'm a mess!" I pull my wet shirt away from my body, billowing it to get some air, hoping to cool down.

"It's an illusion," Violet says, laughing. "I'm barely holding it together. Underneath it all I'm a disaster."

"You? Sure." I wrinkle my face in disbelief.

She shakes her head. "This"—she motions to herself—"takes a lot of work."

"You're kidding." I raise an eyebrow, a skill I proudly mastered in the long hours I spent alone as a kid, bored in front of the bathroom mirror.

"I'm not. This took me an hour this morning with the flat iron." She points up at her glossy ponytail. "Left alone it's like a rat's nest. The cat-sized kind that live in the sewer."

"I doubt *that* very much," I say, rolling my eyes.

"My bangs alone take fifteen minutes. And without concealer, you could pack a whole wardrobe in the bags under my eyes. More suitcases than bags. And not the carry-on kind. Really, it's that bad." She groans. "And don't forget the eyebrows."

"Eyebrows?" I ask, genuinely curious. "What do you do to your *eyebrows*?" I study them. They're thick and well shaped, but look natural. I've thought little about mine, save for plucking them every once in a blue moon when I notice a too-long hair. They're fairly sparse, not particularly noticeable, though it didn't occur to me to *do* anything about it.

"Trimming, penciling, brushing," she says. When she sees my face, she laughs. "I'll show you. I'll do yours. It actually makes a big difference."

I roll my eyes again, smiling. It's something beautiful women say to ingratiate themselves to average-looking people. She's exaggerating, I'm sure. She probably looks red-carpet-ready when she wakes up— skin dewy, dark eyes bright, eyebrows or no eyebrows. Venus de Milo doesn't need makeup, and neither does Violet.

"Really!" Violet says. "I look like a gremlin without brows. Which is why I set my alarm for five thirty every morning."

I shudder. Any hour before seven feels inhumane. "Oh god, why bother?" Then, quickly I add, "Because I don't, obviously." I give a little self-deprecating snort, motioning to my glasses, my baseball cap. "I mean to—I *want* to—but that snooze button . . . it calls to me. But if you don't want to, why do it?"

Violet laughs. "I don't know," she says finally, slowly, considering. "Jay . . ." She starts, then pauses, stops, starts again. "Not just Jay, but everyone—well, take the other moms, at Harper's school. They make me feel . . . oh, I don't know, they're just so . . . *much,*" she finishes, grasping.

She sees my face and laughs. "I'm not making any sense. You probably have no idea what I'm talking about."

But my expression isn't because I don't know what she's talking about. It's because I do. All too well. Mockingbird, the school I taught at, was the same way—a private Montessori whose tuition ran close to fifty thousand a year. It's why I recognize all the brand names, the designer bags and the jewelry. The parents—the mothers, specifically—looked like they'd stepped off a runway, polished and crisp, Chanel bags and four-inch Louboutin stilettos, Cartier bracelets and three-carat diamond rings, fresh blowouts, unwrinkled, Botoxed foreheads, syringe-filled lips, breezing in and out of the classroom on their way to the office.

They air-kissed their children, also dressed in Balenciaga, Dolce & Gabbana, each other, barely grazing the cheek as they waved goodbye over their shoulders, phones already pressed to their ears. They didn't all work, of course. There were some, like Violet, whose husbands' salaries were more than enough, or who had family money, generations of wealth filling their pockets, who didn't work, at least not outside the home. Instead, they hosted charity events and late lunches at Clover Hill, managed social calendars and household staff, dressed their nannies in last season's Burberry coats, in intentionally scuffed Golden Goose sneakers that looked like they cost sixty dollars instead of six hundred, handed down after only a handful of wears.

"It's stupid, I know," Violet says, "but they make me feel completely inadequate. This"—she motions to herself again—"is my attempt to fit in."

I study her, glancing at her profile out of the corner of my eye. It's funny that someone who looks like Violet, high-cheekboned and full-lipped, feels the same way as I do when I look in the mirror. It makes me wonder, *How do people see me?*

"I think you look great," I say, because she does. Better than great.

"Thanks. I think I look *old*. I'm turning thirty-two soon. In June," Violet says, studying her fingernails. Her face is placid. I can't tell how she feels about what she's just said, excited or disappointed, or something in between.

"June? My birthday's in June, too!" I say.

She turns to me, animated again. "Really? When?"

"June sixteenth."

"Another Gemini!" she says. "I'm the eighteenth. Twins."

A smile lights up my face. I don't know if she means as in the zodiac symbol, or if she's referring to us, because of how close our birthdays are, but I don't care. It's another thing that links us. Born only two days apart. And it's not even a lie.

Maybe she'll want to celebrate together. *It was just going to be the three of us,* I imagine her saying, *just a small celebration, but now, now that I know it's your birthday, too, we should do something special.* A party at their house, a picnic in the park, or dinner at a fancy restaurant where, when we're almost finished, they'll bring two desserts, one for each of us, both topped with candles, flames dancing. Jay and Harper will sing, even though we tell them not to, as we smile at each other across the table.

I'll go to the little shop where I found my necklace and buy another. I'll say I had it made for her, because she liked mine so much. *You shouldn't have,* she'll say, as she opens the box excitedly, her cheeks flushed, but I'll be able to tell that she's happy I did. Then her face will light up when she sees what's inside. She'll grin and put it on, right there, proudly hooking it around her neck. *How do I look?* she'll ask, turning to Jay and Harper. They'll both tell her she looks beautiful, because, of course, she does.

I break from my reverie to find her looking at me expectantly. Did she ask me something? "Sorry, what?" I say.

"I just asked how old you were turning."

"I'm turning thirty-two, too!" I'm not. Lie number five.

"Really?" She cocks her head, her eyes widening. "We should do something together!"

I nod enthusiastically. "I'd love that!"

She beams. Then, "Ready to turn around?"

I nod and we resume the walk, heading back the way we came. She tells me how, growing up, she hated having a birthday in the summer because she never got to celebrate it at school. She was jealous of all the other kids whose parents brought in cupcakes or goody bags, who sat in the middle of the class as the other students sang "Happy Birthday."

"Anyway," Violet says, waving a hand. "I've talked enough about myself. Tell me more about you. Where'd you go to college?"

That's what she doesn't get. I'm not bored of hearing her talk about herself. I don't think I ever will be. But I indulge her, skipping over the two years I spent at community college before I transferred to Brooklyn College, a state university, mixing the truth with some lies. I tell her how my mother raised me on her own, about how we moved from town to town in the South, before settling in New York when my aunt got sick.

"And you said your dad is from Philly?" she asks when I finish.

I nod. "That's what he told my mom."

"I was born there," Violet says. "It's where both my parents were born and raised. They moved to Piedmont, just outside San Francisco, when I was six."

I feel a jolt. A current of electricity lighting up every cell. "That's funny," I manage.

"Small world." She smiles. "Like I said, Gemini twins."

Maybe not twins, but sisters. I've always wished I had a sister, more than anything. What makes it even harder is that there's a chance I do have one, somewhere. I think about it all the time. My dad probably went on to get married and have more kids. And those kids would be my siblings. If Violet's dad is from Philly, then maybe—No. I stop myself.

I smile back. "I visited once, on a school field trip."

"You're probably more familiar with the city than I am, then. I barely remember it." She tells me about what it was like growing up near San Francisco, how she and her friends would take the BART across the bay, how one day, she hopes to move back to California.

Before I know it, we're back in the neighborhood, on the corner of Fifth and Smith. It's almost eleven thirty. We've walked for just over an hour, two and a half miles, according to Violet's Apple Watch. I'm hot and sweaty. Without even seeing myself, I know my cheeks are splotched red, my hair frizzy under my hat.

"Want to grab a coffee?" Violet asks.

I bite my lip. I do, I really do, but I don't want to seem overeager. I know how strong I can come on. I need to bide my time, take it slow. No sudden movements, nothing that might scare her away.

"I would, but I have to get my mom to an appointment," I say ruefully.

"No worries! I'll see you on Tuesday afternoon, then? Harper gets home at one, so do you want to come over a little before?"

"Sure!" I say. "Sounds good."

"Okay, great. Have a good weekend!" She starts to turn, then stops. "Oh!" she says. "I want to show you what I mean. Before I go." She begins rifling through her bag.

"Mean about what?"

Triumphantly, Violet holds up what looks like a pencil. "What a difference brows can make! Come here."

"Right now?"

She nods. "Right now."

Hesitantly, I take a step toward her. She uncaps the pencil and leans in, then gently lowers my glasses. We're almost the exact same height. Her breath tickles my face, warm and minty, and I close my eyes, feeling the light touch of the pencil tip against my skin. "Start at the thickest part," she murmurs. "Then up to the tip. Down, then blend."

Violet moves to the other brow, repeats herself. Then, "Okay, done," she pronounces, stepping back. She takes a compact from her purse and opens it, angling it toward me. "So, do you like it?"

I study myself in the small mirror. My new brows shoot up in surprise. They look fuller, like Violet's, darker, more arched. Even behind my glasses, my eyes seem brighter, somehow, the angle of my cheekbones more pronounced. She's right. I do look different.

"How'd you *do* that?" I ask, still staring at my reflection, turning my head left and then right.

"I told you." She smiles, smug. "With this. Here, take it," Violet says, handing me the pencil. "I have like three others at home."

"Really?"

"Really."

I take it from her, holding it like a treasure. "Thank you."

She smiles. "See you Tuesday!" She turns, waves, and heads down the block.

My smile stretches into a grin. I can't wait. I turn toward home, too. As I do, I catch myself in a reflective storefront window. For the first time in a long, long time, I like what I see.

11

My back and feet are aching by the time I get back to my apartment. I spent the rest of the day shopping for ingredients to make a celebratory meal for my mom and me, in and out of specialty markets: a butcher in Prospect Heights, an artisanal cheese shop in Park Slope, a French bakery Allison once mentioned. My arms are full of groceries when I let myself into the building and cross the small foyer to our apartment door, past the wall of aluminum mailboxes. The light above our door is on the fritz; it flickers on and off intermittently, like a prop in a cheap horror movie.

I set the shopping bags on the floor to open our front door. My key is in the lock when I hear my name behind me. It echoes through the linoleum hall.

"Sloane Caraway?" It's a terse, unfamiliar voice. I stiffen.

Slowly, I slide my key from the doorknob, then turn.

There's a woman in a police uniform, complete with shiny-brimmed hat, brass badge, black lace-up boots. The small metal name tag on her breast pocket reads *Martinez*, C. My stomach drops. I know why she's here. I feel sick.

She must have followed me in, catching the door before it had had a chance to close, quiet as a mouse. "Ms. Caraway?" she says again.

I start to shake my head but think better of it. I don't want to make things worse than they already are. "Yes," I say cautiously. "Can I help you?"

She nods. She removes her cap and takes a step closer, tucking the hat under her arm. Her dark hair is parted down the middle and slicked back into a low bun at the nape of her neck. She doesn't wear any makeup, but not because she doesn't need it. Her nose and forehead are oily, olive skin peppered with faded acne marks, some pocked. Despite this, she's not unattractive. Her eyes are a dark brown, deep-set and almond-shaped with long lashes, lips full. She's younger than I am, maybe late twenties, curvy in the right places.

She clears her throat. "I'd like to ask you a few questions about the other day."

The other day. *The other day.* I'd known that's what this was about, but hearing her say it out loud makes me queasy, a metallic taste rising at the back of my throat. I start to sweat.

"At Rose & Honey," she continues. "You had an encounter with Ms. McIntyre?" She asks as if it's a question, but we both know it isn't.

I imagine Allison leaving the spa, going right to the police station, still shaking. She would have wanted to speak with a supervisor, her arms folded across her chest, foot tapping.

The foyer is quiet. I think I can hear the sound of TV in our apartment behind the closed door, but I might be imagining it. The officer stares at me, waiting. I wonder if she was the one who talked to Allison when she went to the station. Finally, I say, "I didn't do anything wrong."

"No one is saying you did," she says calmly. "Like I said, I'm just here to ask a few questions. Were you aware Ms. McIntyre had booked an appointment?"

I shake my head. "No. I didn't know she was coming in. I didn't know until I saw her."

"And what did you do when you realized it was her?"

"Nothing! She left in a rush. I didn't have a chance to do—or say—anything."

The officer studies me carefully, then nods. "You do understand that the terms of the order say that there is to be no contact with Ms. McIntyre? No communication whatsoever."

I press my lips together. The order. The restraining order. There's a dull, throbbing pain in my chest. "I know," I say quietly. "I didn't plan this."

"Which is why it won't be reported as a violation." I can't tell if she thinks it should be. Has she read the report? I know how it looks. Me, sloppy with a too-big hoodie, smudged glasses, and Allison, neat as a pin, chiseled features, hair like a sunset. I'm not the sympathetic character in this story.

I bite down hard on my lower lip. "Then why are you here?" I ask. But I know the answer. Because Allison had made a scene; because someone had promised, *We'll talk to her.*

"Just as a reminder. The order requires a distance of one hundred yards. It's important that you adhere to these parameters."

"I *have* been." My voice rises an octave. I know what the order says. I have a copy, shoved into the back of a drawer in my bedroom. "*She* came into the spa! *She's* the one who violated the order. Not me."

"I understand," she says. She looks at me, her eyes full of pity, and I want to scream.

"It's not what you think." I can feel my vocal cords straining. I know I sound defensive, pathetic, even, but I can't help it. I want her to know she's wrong, that it isn't what it looks like. "It was all just a big misunderstanding."

She nods slowly. "It always is. Have a good evening, ma'am." She puts her cap back on and starts toward the door. She's stiff, no sway in her step, as if on a tightrope. One misstep and she'll plummet. I wonder if she practices walking that way, carefully placing one foot in front of the other, her spine rigid.

I stand there, watching her leave. When she's gone, I turn and put my key back in the lock. My hand is shaking. I wipe a tear from my eye with the sleeve of my hoodie. I don't want my mom to see me cry.

After a moment, I exhale, then walk into the living room. My mother is in her recliner, legs outstretched and crossed at the ankles. There's an iced tea on the side table next to her, the glass sweating with condensation.

"Who was that? I heard voices," she says, turning her attention from the television. She shifts in her chair, then resettles.

"Gabby, from upstairs," I say. "She was telling me how she broke up with her boyfriend again. She caught him with someone else."

My mom rolls her eyes and looks back toward the TV. She can't stand Gabby.

I know I said I don't lie to my mother. That wasn't exactly the truth, either.

On Monday morning, the day before I'm supposed to start at the Lockharts, I text Violet, telling her I'm looking forward to the next day. When she doesn't respond right away, I text again, just with a smiley emoji, but there's still no answer. Not five minutes later, not ten, not an hour.

Without my job at the spa, I have nothing to keep me busy. No distractions other than the drone of the TV in the living room. By midafternoon, I've picked up my phone a thousand times to see if I missed a text, but the screen is blank. I can't stop fidgeting. Should I text her again, in case she missed the first two? I erase every message I type. With every passing hour, I grow more anxious. I turn off my phone, shove it in my nightstand, leave, then return to my bedroom only minutes later to power it back on. No new messages.

Was it something I said? I replay our conversations over and over again. She seemed fine when we parted after our walk, smiling and waving as she retreated down the sidewalk. Maybe she just hadn't enjoyed our time together. Maybe she was upset I hadn't accepted her coffee invitation. Maybe she didn't think I was a good fit for Harper.

But my real fear—even though I know it's impossible—is that she found out what happened at Rose & Honey the other afternoon. Or worse, about what happened before I got the job, about the restraining order.

At four thirty, I can no longer stand it. It feels like I might lose my mind. I tell my mom I'm going for a walk, shoving my feet into shoes, grabbing my bag. When I push out onto the sidewalk, I have to shield my eyes. The sun is still high in the sky, the days already getting longer and warmer as summer approaches. I'm not sure where I'm going, but I feel better outside. Violet's probably just busy, I tell myself. I almost believe it.

I decide to walk to the park, do a few laps and head home, but I don't stop when the playground comes into view. I keep walking. I already know where I'm going before I get there.

The brownstones get bigger as I turn down the Lockharts' street, the elm trees taller, leaves fuller, the sidewalk wider. I walk on the side opposite their house. When it comes into view, I slow, ducking my head, then stop, half-hidden behind a parked car and tree trunk. I shouldn't be here, of course, but I have to see if Violet is home. I won't be long, just a quick look.

Their front curtains are pushed wide open. It gives me a direct view into their living room. The sun is still bright, the interior of their house well lit.

At first, I don't see anyone. I can see the bookshelves, the couch, the painting above it, their coffee table. Is anyone home?

And then, as if to answer my question, Violet walks into the room. I breathe in sharply, ducking back behind the tree. When I lean forward, just slightly, peering out, she's still there, standing at the bay window. She has a phone to her ear, talking animatedly. She looks upset. Even from here, I can see her brows knit together, forehead creased. She begins to pace, her free hand rubbing her temple.

Then Harper appears through the glass, running up and throwing her arms around Violet's waist. Violet looks down and strokes the top of her head absent-mindedly. Harper looks up, smiling, and Violet holds up a finger. *Give me a minute.* Harper nods and wanders off, toward the stairs.

Now she's listening, the phone pressed to her ear, lips pressed tightly together. Did they quiver? It's hard to tell from here. Then she swipes at her cheek with her palm. She's crying, I think, wiping tears from her face. She nods once, sharply, her eyes fluttering closed. She stands like that, still as marble, until finally, she nods again, her eyes reopening.

She takes the phone from her ear, closing it, two halves snapping shut. For a moment, she just stares at it, her shoulders sagging, face impassive.

Suddenly, without warning, she winds her arm back and hurls the phone at the couch like a pitcher, aiming at a catcher's mitt. Her mouth is open in a soundless scream. The phone hits the back cushion, then bounces off, out of my view. From behind the tree, I flinch.

Violet's shoulders rise and fall as if she's breathing heavily. I know I should leave, but I'm rooted to the ground. Who had she been talking to? What had it been about? A fight with a friend? A family member?

Then she turns her head toward the stairs as if spoken to. She re-arranges her face, anger disappearing. She goes to pick up the phone, slips it into her pocket. She starts toward the stairs, disappears from view.

I wait to see if anyone reappears, but they don't. The living room stays empty. No Violet, no Harper, no Jay. I tell myself I should get going, but one minute turns into five, five into ten, until it's been al-most an hour. The whole time I keep my phone in my hand, hoping Violet will call, but it never rings.

It's getting dark by the time I leave, the sky shifting from a gray to a deep blue as I walk the twelve blocks home, unnerved by what I've seen.

My mom and I don't say much over dinner. I know she notices my mood but doesn't ask. Instead, she reaches over as we watch TV, and squeezes my arm every so often, never taking her eyes off the screen. She's there if I need her, she's saying.

After we eat, I trade my flannel and jeans for pajamas and get into bed without washing my face or brushing my teeth. I know I should do both, but I can't muster the energy.

I reach out and flip off my bedside lamp and lie, staring at the ceiling. What had made Violet so upset? And why hasn't she called me? Are the two related? Dejectedly, I turn onto my side. Maybe my worst fear is true: she knows what I did. She's angry, doesn't know how to confront me.

The darkness of my bedroom is heavy and suffocating, shadows looming large on the walls. I listen to the traffic outside, the distant honking of horns, low hum of sirens, faint voices. Eventually, my eyelids grow heavy and I begin to drift off, gratefully succumbing to sleep.

Then my phone vibrates. My eyes fly open. I jolt upright and grab it off the nightstand, my heart beating. I squint at the screen, aglow in my darkened room. It's Violet. I hold my breath as I open the message. *Hi, sorry for the late text! The day totally got away from me. Are we still on for tomorrow?*

The anxiety I felt all day lifts instantly. I am lighter, brighter. All that worry for nothing. Fingers flying, I type back, *No worries! Yes, I'll be there! One?*

Instantly, I see her typing, then, *Let's say twelve thirty?*

I smile at the screen. *See you then!*

I move to put the phone down, but I hesitate. An image flashes in my mind. The way she looked through her window today, face drawn, angrily wiping tears from her cheek. I want to ask her if everything is okay, but how, unless I tell her what I saw? And I can't admit to having been at their house this afternoon. I know how that would look. Eventually, I set my phone on my nightstand. I'll ask her tomorrow, I decide, if she still seems upset.

I pull the covers up to my chin and close my eyes. This time, I have no trouble falling asleep.

12

At 12:25 the next day, I climb the stairs to the Lockharts' front door. My heart is beating quickly. Starting today, I'm the Lockharts' nanny. No longer a nail tech, but a nanny. It feels right, like I am exactly where I'm meant to be.

The front door to their brownstone is cracked open, resting against the frame. There's muffled music coming from inside. I knock lightly, but when no one answers, I push it open and step into the entryway.

The music is coming from the kitchen. It's blaring loudly, the sound filling the whole house. I recognize the song. I walk toward the source. "Violet?" I call out.

I enter the kitchen to see Violet on the other side of the island, dancing wildly. She's holding a tall pepper mill as if it were a microphone, singing into it with her eyes closed. If it was anyone else—if it was me—they'd (I'd) look ridiculous. Limbs flailing like one of those inflatable tube men, bending and flopping, Elaine in *Seinfeld*. But Violet isn't anyone else. She's magnetic. I could watch her dance all day.

A moment later she opens her eyes. She sees me, standing there in the doorframe, and grins, her performance momentarily paused. She spreads her arms out wide and calls out, "Welcome to New York!" Then the chorus begins and she resumes singing, her eyes on mine, about how the city has been waiting for me. And right now, in their kitchen, it feels like it has. This New York, the one with Violet in it, is different than the one I've lived in for the last fifteen years. It's new and special, and finally, I belong here.

As Violet sings, she picks up a matching saltshaker and dances toward me, the shaker outstretched. I'd planned on asking her if everything was okay, worried about her after what I'd seen yesterday afternoon, but here, now, she's radiant. She seems more than okay.

I drop my bag on the floor and take the shaker from her. I hesitate, only for a second, then start singing, too. We both know all the words. We dance around, shimmying and swaying to the beat, singing into our microphones, the music so loud you can't hear either of us.

When the song ends, Violet yells to Alexa to lower the volume, then drops into a kitchen chair and lifts the hair off the back of her neck, fanning herself with her other hand.

"Sit," she says, and I do, my heart thumping from the dancing, in a seat across from hers. We're both breathing heavily, grinning at each other, delighted with ourselves.

"Some days just call for a dance party," she says.

"I agree wholeheartedly." Actually, it was something I did when I worked at the preschool. Every so often when the mood seemed off, I'd turn the music up and all the kids would dance crazily around the room until they collapsed on the rug in giggles. It would reset our whole day. I want to tell Violet about it, but don't. I can't.

"Harper should be home any minute. One of the other moms offered to walk her home today. Coffee?" she asks, and I nod.

She gets up, returning with two cups, setting one in front of each of us on the table. "I played that song every day when we moved here," she says. "Embarrassing, right?"

"I don't think so," I say. "But I'm a huge Taylor Swift fan."

"Right." She smiles. "You said that the first day we met at the park. That's how I knew we'd be friends."

I beam, tickled that she remembers our first conversation.

She looks me right in the eye. "I know I've said this before, but I really haven't made many friends since we moved. It's nice to finally have one. I'm so glad we met."

I feel a blossom of warmth in my chest. She said I'm her friend. Not her nanny. Her friend.

"Me too," I say. She has no idea how glad. I study her, tucking my hair behind one ear like she's done, sitting up a little straighter.

"You've lived here for a long time; you must know a lot of people." Violet blows on her coffee, then takes a sip.

I press my lips together, nodding slowly. "Sure, I guess." I used to know more. I was friends with a lot of the other teachers at the preschool. We'd go to brunch on the weekends or someone would host everyone for a Sunday dinner, but after I got fired, that doesn't happen anymore. "But since my mom got sick, I've sort of been keeping to myself."

Violet nods. "What about dating? Are you single? Seeing anyone?"

I consider making up a boyfriend, but decide it's too risky. If we become close, like I hope we will, she'll want to meet him, go out to dinner on a double date. I'll have to make up excuses about why he can never join us or how he's away—again—on a business trip.

"Single," I say.

"Single in New York, the dream," she says longingly. "At least, it was for me. Well, high school me, thanks to *Sex and the City*."

"Oh god," I groan. "You have no idea what it's like out there now." I give her a pained expression. "Tinder has ruined everything. It's the bane of my existence."

It's an exaggeration. Actually, it keeps things interesting. I have a dating profile—a few of them, truthfully, all with various pictures of other women I've found online, women that I'm sure will catch the eye of the kind of man I'd be interested in—on several of the apps, Tinder included. It's one of my favorite things to do on a Friday night, sweatpants-clad on the couch with a bowl of ice cream, flicking through the available men, reading their (occasionally successful) attempts to be witty. I'll send a like or a heart to the ones that I find especially clever and wait for the ding of a new message alert. It's fun, having guys tell me how beautiful I am, exchanging charged texts into the early morning hours.

Occasionally, I'll use a profile with my real picture, meet up with someone for dinner or coffee, but the dates are usually awkward, filled with stilted conversation. Every once in a while, they'll end with a make-out session on the sidewalk or mediocre sex on his futon, but there's almost never a second date. They don't ask, and if they did, I'd probably turn them down.

I tell myself it'll be different when I have a better job, or when I finally get my own place. Maybe I'll have a shot at the kind of guys who want to date me when I'm pretending to be someone else.

"Is it weird that I'm a little jealous?" Violet says, laughing. "Jay and I started dating right before Tinder launched. I've always wished that I could try it, at least once."

"Yes," I answer, nodding emphatically. "Very, very weird. Considering. You've seen your husband, right? Do you need your eyes checked?"

Violet buries her head in her hands in mock embarrassment, her dark hair shaking. "You're right," she says, muffled. She sits back up and sighs. "We just got married so young, you know, that sometimes I feel like I missed out on all the fun." Absent-mindedly, she brushes at her bangs, coiling a strand around her finger. "And now I'm a mom with stretch marks."

I smile. I highly doubt she has stretch marks. "You didn't miss out on anything," I say. "I promise you. Unless you like the idea of pervy come-ons and unsolicited pictures of male genitalia flooding your phone."

"That's not a myth?"

"What, dick pics?" I shake my head. "No. Very much not a myth. I can show you if you want . . ." I start to reach for my purse.

"No!" Violet squeals, giggling. "No, I believe you. Please don't!"

I laugh. "Okay, I won't. But what about before Jay? You must have had a million boyfriends in high school."

Violet is a prom queen. A cheer captain. I can see her now, younger, in low-slung jeans and a crop top, surrounded by the other popular kids, the boys elbowing each other to get closer to her, to be the one to carry her backpack home. I was, by contrast—as Taylor Swift puts it—on the bleachers, watching girls just like Violet, wishing someone would look at me like they looked at them.

Violet's smile dims, but doesn't go out, not entirely. "Not really." She shrugs. "I pretty much spent my whole life—before Jay, I mean—in love with this one boy. I went on a few dates with other guys, thinking I might get over him, but it never worked." She lets out a little laugh, like how silly she'd been to believe that could happen.

"What was his name?" I take a sip of my coffee, settle back into my chair. There's nothing I don't want to know about Violet, but I especially love hearing about her childhood, what she was like as a teenager.

She hesitates, then says, "Danny. We were best friends growing up. We were inseparable, did everything together. Everyone thought we'd get married. So did I." She smiles, amused at her younger self. "He had the biggest heart. And he was beautiful. A beautiful boy who grew up into a beautiful man. Messy golden curls. Gorgeous brown eyes." She stares into the distance as if she's remembering. "And he has this little scar, right at the tip of his eyebrow." Violet touches the spot on her own face.

"We were sixteen when he kissed me for the first time. And when he did . . ." Violet trails off. I lean in, my breath hitching. She sees me, laughs. Then she sighs, her eyes softening again. "It was like I'd been waiting my entire life for that one moment."

I can see it, feel it, like it was my heart pounding as his lips brushed against mine. The whole world splitting wide open.

"What happened?" I ask, when she doesn't continue. I'm on the edge of my seat.

"We lost touch, after I went away to college. And then I met Jay." She shrugs, as if that was the end of her love story. Or the beginning. I can't quite tell. "Anyway," she says, smiling. "My point is, no, I didn't have a million boyfriends in high school."

Then she glances at the clock on the wall, frowns. "Harper should be home by now. I wonder what's taking them so long," she says. "The school's like ten blocks away, but it usually doesn't take more than twenty minutes. Mockingbird Montessori. Maybe you know it."

The smile drops from my lips. Suddenly, the kitchen walls seem to close in, the room shrinking. I feel the color drain from my face as a wave of nausea rolls through me, my limbs losing feeling. *Did she say—*

"Mockingbird?" I repeat weakly. My voice sounds watery, warbled, like there's something in my mouth.

Violet turns. "You know it?"

I swallow the acid at the back of my throat. I wonder if I might throw up. How had I not known that Harper goes to Mockingbird? Of course she does; it's the best preschool in Brooklyn, where everyone who's anyone sends their child.

I nod, my head bobbing dumbly. "I used to nanny for one of the families who went there." It's the truth, but not the whole truth. Even still, I regret the words as soon as they leave my mouth. It's more than I want her to know.

"Oh, that's funny. What family?" She cocks her head.

I force my lips into a smile, trying to look nonchalant. "Oh, they moved. To Connecticut, I think." I purposefully don't answer her question. "It was ages ago."

This is, of course, a lie. I'd nannied for them as recently as eighteen months ago. Before I became her nanny, Ellie McIntyre was in my morning class at Mockingbird. It wasn't uncommon for the teachers to babysit the kids on the weekends for extra money. We all did it. The families were well-off, and they paid decently, at least twenty-five an hour, thirty or more for two kids, which was as much as we made in our teaching positions.

Ellie's mom is Allison. Allison McIntyre. She's the reason why I don't nanny anymore, why I'm not a preschool teacher, why I had to work in a place where no one bothered to check my references. She's the one who filed the restraining order. The one who walked into the spa and acted like she feared for her life. Even though it was my life that had crumbled.

She had two kids, both with red hair, just like hers. Ellie, who was four when we met, and Benji, who was seven. Her husband traveled during the week, and she needed help in the afternoons, when school got out and she wasn't done with work. At first, it was just once in a while, on days when she had off-site meetings, a Friday or Saturday night here and there, but soon it became more regular—Monday afternoons when Allison had to go into Manhattan and couldn't get home until after seven, then Wednesdays and Thursdays. Then weekends, too, until I was there more often than not, until it was like I was part of their family. Until I wasn't.

Ellie is probably still enrolled at Mockingbird. She's older than Harper, so they wouldn't be in the same class, but they might play together on the blacktop, on the playground. Violet and Allison likely have seen each other during drop-off or pickup; maybe they even say hello to each other or chat as they're waiting for the kids to come out. The thought of this turns my stomach.

I can't tell Violet her name because if she happened to tell Allison about me, this would all be ruined. Allison's eyes would harden; her face would grow stony. She'd tell Violet things about me that aren't true—at least, not wholly. Don't think I don't see the irony in that.

Then I remember that Violet thinks my name is Caitlin, and for once, I'm thankful I'm a liar, and not ashamed like I usually am.

"Are you okay?" Violet asks.

I make myself nod; I can't get any words out.

Just then, the doorbell chimes. "Oh! That must be Harp," Violet says.

As soon as Violet leaves the kitchen, I drop my head into my hands. I'm sure I was talked about after I left, by the teachers, the students, the parents. It's a close-knit community, which is one of the reasons I loved working there so much: if a child or teacher got sick, even just with a cold, everyone would sign a handmade get-well card; if there was a family emergency, a group of moms would send their au pairs over with ready-made meals. There were flowers on Teacher Appreciation Day and delicately iced cupcakes on birthdays. But there were whispers, too, when a student's parents were getting divorced or when one of the dads was charged with insider trading, so I know there were whispers about me. How loud, I don't know. I don't know if the gossip lingered in the air, in the corners of the classrooms, in the mouths of the parents as they walked their children in and out of the school.

If I'd kept in touch with anyone, I could have asked, but I haven't. I haven't spoken to any of the other teachers since I left. It was a small staff, twelve of us, but only one of them reached out to me after I'd been let go. Her name was Rachel, one of the teachers in the five-year-old class who I often ate lunch with. She called, but I didn't answer. I was too embarrassed. A few weeks later, when the loneliness seeped in, I tried to call her back, but this time, she was the one who didn't pick up. I left a voicemail asking if she wanted to get lunch, then sent a text, but there was never any response. I tried another few teachers over the following months, but no one returned my calls. Not one parent reached out to me, either, not even the ones who had sent gift baskets at the end of the school year or the ones who hugged me tearfully when their child graduated from my class to the next. I'd become infected; no one wanted to catch it.

In the next room, there's the rise of voices. Panic grips me, coiling around my throat like a constrictor. What if Violet invites whoever brought Harper home inside? What if they recognize me? I look around wildly for a place to hide, a broom closet maybe, behind the island.

Just as I'm about to bolt from my chair, I hear Violet say goodbye, the front door closing, Harper chatting excitedly. I exhale, one big whoosh, and shake my head. *Get it together, Sloane.* It was well over a year ago now. I'm sure my name had faded from everyone's lips by the time Harper started at Mockingbird. And if it hadn't, it doesn't matter. To Violet, I'm Caitlin, not Sloane. But even so, from now on, I'll be sure to arrive after Harper gets home from school, never before.

A moment later, when Harper bounds into the kitchen, Violet behind her, I have a smile on my face.

"Caitlin!" Harper yells. "Look what I made at school today!" She waves a round piece of colored construction paper over her head, edges jagged with scissor cuts. "It's Jupiter!"

"Wow," I say, taking it from her. "You must have worked really hard on this!" Praise the effort, not the child! An oft-repeated refrain of the principal at Mockingbird. Old habits, I guess.

Harper and Violet both beam at me.

"Should we go to a new park today?" I ask. "I know of a good one just off Hoyt."

"Yeah!" Harper says. "Can we, Mom?"

Violet nods. "Absolutely! Do you want a snack first?"

"A muffin!" Harper says, doing an excited little wiggle.

"Sure, go wash your hands and I'll get you one."

A pout forms on Harper's face. "I want it now!"

"Okay," says Violet patiently. "As soon as you wash your hands."

Harper's face crumples. "I hate washing my hands!" Harper belts. She drops to the floor and begins to kick her feet against the couch.

"Harper," Violet says. Her voice is stern, but I can see the worry on her face. I feel my hands grow clammy, my heart rate quicken. I'd seen a million tantrums at preschool, but this was different. What if her heart gives out?

Half-panicked, I crouch down next to Violet. "Hey, Harper," I say. "Can you show me how to wash my hands? I forgot how! Do I put water on my feet? Or on my head?"

Harper stops crying, sniffles, and looks up at me. "No," she says, shaking her head.

"Do I put water on my nose?"

She wipes snot from her face with her sleeve, giggling a little bit. "No."

"Will you show me?"

She nods, gets up. Violet shoots me a grateful smile. I smile back, but I'm rattled. What if I hadn't been able to get her to stop crying? What if she'd fainted? Violet would have expected me to know what to do. She trusts me.

Guilt gnaws at me, its tiny teeth sharp. Of course she trusts me. Because I told her I was a nurse. Does that make me a bad person? I don't want to know the answer to that.

Harper is waiting expectantly for me, so I get up and follow her into the kitchen. Something could have happened, but it didn't. It didn't.

"Come on," I say to Harper, taking her hand. "Do I put soap in my ears?"

She laughs and pulls me toward the sink.

13

Over the next few weeks, as the days get longer and hotter, pants replaced by shorts, sweaters by T-shirts, Violet, Harper, and I slip into a familiar routine. Just like I'd hoped, my three shifts a week quickly turn into four, then five, Monday through Friday.

Every day I arrive at the Lockharts' house just after Harper comes home from school. Around one, the three of us head over to the park. On the walk there, she holds both our hands, begging us to swing her until we worry her shoulders might pop from their sockets. We trade off who pushes her on the swings or chases her around the playground. When we're done, I'll take Harper to a ballet class, or gymnastics, while Violet goes home to study.

When Violet and I are together, our conversations are easy. We chat about our days and our lives and the latest celebrity gossip, who got sent home on the latest episode of *The Bachelor*. She mentioned she watched it a few weeks ago, so I started watching it, too, on my laptop, after my mom falls asleep on the couch. I also started buying *Vogue* after she told me about an article she read, so I can be up on the same things she is.

She talks a lot about Harper, funny things she's said or done, her latest tricks to get out of bedtime. Lately, it's asking for her back to be scratched for at least ten minutes. I laugh when Violet tells me how Harper's coerced her into professing her love to each of her stuffed animals, kissing their cheeks and tucking them in before Violet is allowed to leave the room. Sometimes, Harper requires her to give each stuffed animal a back scratch, too. You can tell how much Violet loves being a mom, how much motherhood suits her.

She also talks about Jay. About his likes and pet peeves, the places they've gone together. They traveled a lot before Harper was born, to interesting places like Shanghai and Bali, Patagonia, the Australian outback. I tell her I traveled, too, how I backpacked through Italy after I graduated from college. I didn't, but it feels like I did when I describe the trip from movies I've seen, share details from books I've read. *Eat, Pray, Lie*, if you will.

Actually, I've never left the East Coast. When I was growing up, my mom would take me on weeklong vacations to Daytona Beach, where she used to waitress, where she met my dad. We'd load up the car with beach towels and sand toys and coolers full of lunch meat and jars of peanut butter and we'd get a room in a seaside motel, spend our days baking in the sun, me splashing in the waves, her with a book on a lounge chair. It was always special, but it wasn't Europe.

Violet's favorite vacation was the trip she and Jay took to Scotland right before she got pregnant with Harper. She talks about it with a hint of nostalgia, and I wonder if she ever misses how things were before they became parents. She laughs as she recounts a story of walking into a bar in the outskirts of Edinburgh and how they thought everyone was speaking another language because the local accents were so thick. Jay pulled out his Google Translate app only to realize his mistake when the bartender typed in, "I *am* speaking English, ya dobber!"

I hoard these details about Jay like precious stones, carefully wrapping them up and stowing them away in my memory. It feels like I know him, really know him. Where he was born, where he grew up, what he studied in college. I know how he proposed and what his favorite foods are. I wonder if she tells Jay about me, if he feels like he knows me, too.

Twice, Danny has come up again in conversation. Only briefly, in passing, but both times Violet has looked like a schoolgirl, her cheeks coloring, lips fighting a smile. It's impossible not to wonder if she thinks about him late at night, if she imagines what it would be like if they'd never broken up.

When Violet runs errands, I'll stay at the house with Harper. I'll read to her on the couch or we'll play kitchen, making pancakes and sandwiches and hot dogs out of Play-Doh. She loves listening to Taylor Swift, too, calls her Twaylor, singing along to the choruses of her favorite songs. Three of Harper's classmates have seen her in concert, she tells me wistfully, so the next time I come over, I bring colorful string and plastic beads, and we make Swiftie friendship bracelets, slip them on, and pretend we have front-row seats at her Eras Tour. At first, I was terrified to be alone with Harper, worried what might happen if I was the only one around, but I've gotten more comfortable. I remind myself that I'd call 911 and that I know CPR; if something were to happen, I'd keep her safe.

But my favorite times are when Violet texts me to meet up with her for coffee and take a walk to the marina or up to the Brooklyn Bridge while Harper is still in school. We count our steps on her gold-linked watch, toast with our cappuccinos if we make it to five thousand. Some mornings we take a yoga class, or, if it's particularly hot, we stretch out on blankets in the park, pulling up our shirts to tan our backs and bellies, holding cold cans of La Croix to our necks to cool ourselves down. On these days, I'm not just Harper's nanny, but Violet's friend. And maybe not just her friend, but best friend. I feel like she's mine, at least.

When Violet and I are together, I want to pinch myself that I've been welcomed into her life, that someone like her wants to be friends with someone like me. Sometimes I wonder what she's getting out of it, if maybe I make her feel better about herself, or if she's just grateful to have found child care, but then she'll laugh at one of my jokes, give me a squeeze on my arm, and I know that our friendship is real. Even after all these weeks, I still get a thrill seeing her name on my phone when she texts, a surge of anticipation before I knock on their front door. Some people, when you get to know them, lose their shine. Their newness fades; the mystery evaporates. You start to see the cracks in the surface, their tiny imperfections. But not Violet. She's just as interesting, just as shiny.

I know I have to tread lightly. Even though I'm myself around her, my list of lies continues to grow. I'm Caitlin, a thirty-two-year-old nursing student with a sick mom, former runner, well traveled. I don't have a criminal record. Now that we're friends, I wish I could come clean—really, I do. But I can't. Not ever. If she ever finds out that I lied about having medical experience, that I've compromised her daughter's safety—even though I'd never let anything happen to Harper—it would be over, all of it. And I can't let that happen.

Because here's the real truth. Sometimes, I pretend that we're not just friends, but that we're sisters, ever since she told me her dad was born and raised in Philly. Just like my dad. We have the same dimple in our chin, I've noticed, a similar heart-shaped face, round in the cheeks, slightly pointed chin. Our noses aren't that different, either—both strong, a bit angular. She's prettier than me, of course, her eyes brighter, skin smoother, hair glossier, but the similarities are there.

We could be. Sisters, I mean. It was a game I often played when I was younger. Imagining my dad and his family, make-believe brothers and sisters. They'd be a few years younger than me; my dad was in his early twenties when he met my mom, so it would have taken him another few years to get married and start a family. I'd invent names for my siblings, draw pictures of what I thought they might look like. Violet is only thirty-one; two years younger than I am. Plenty of time for my dad to meet someone and have a baby.

I've never really pressed my mom about him. I only know what she's told me about the night they met: that he was from Philly, that his first name was Joe. Even if the internet had been around when I was a kid, it wasn't much to go on.

I thought I'd grown out of it. I thought I'd accepted that I would never know if I had any brothers or sisters, but it's clear I haven't. And why would I? Doesn't everyone want to know where they've come from? Who else belongs to them? Every so often, I consider taking a DNA test, spitting in one of those little tubes and dropping the envelope in the mail, but I'm not ready to face that the answer might be no one—there's no one else out there, no one else I belong to.

One night, after dinner, after I've spent the day at the Lockharts', comparing Violet's face to my own, I can't help myself. I clear my throat, wet my lips.

"What's my dad's last name?" I ask, a little too loudly. I don't look away from the TV. Out of the corner of my eye, I can see my mom turn to look at me, shifting in her chair.

She doesn't say anything, just stares. Then she looks back toward the TV. "I don't know. It was so long ago, I can hardly remember."

I don't respond. This isn't true; I can tell by the way her body has stiffened. She doesn't want to talk about my dad. And why would she?

"Why?" she asks.

"No reason," I say quickly. "I was just curious."

"It's better not to be," she says. "We've done okay on our own, haven't we?"

"Yeah," I say. I feel a flicker of guilt. "Of course." To admit anything else would be a slap in her face. She gave up everything for me. Even still, I want more than "okay." I want a sister.

14

It's an overcast Friday morning, and Violet's invited me over for a coffee after she drops Harper off at school. Harper has a playdate this afternoon, so my day is wide open. When I leave my apartment, the sky is a deep gray. It's chilly—chillier than it's been in weeks, the final remnants of spring before summer cracks open, heat and humidity infiltrating every nook and cranny of the city. I pull my sweatshirt hood over my head and tighten the strings under my chin. I pick up the pace, hoping I'll warm up.

On the way, I decide to detour by a coffee shop that I know Violet loves. I order us both brown sugar lattes with oat milk, her favorite drink. Now it's mine, too.

I feel myself starting to get nervous as I climb their steps, coffees in hand, wondering if today, Jay will be here. It's something I think about every time I'm in their home, whether he'll stop by for lunch or take the afternoon off, come home early. But he never does. He's always working, always at the office.

Occasionally, Violet will tell me that he says hello or sends his best and I'll feel a rush. An electrical current coursing through me.

Do they talk about me? I wonder. *Does she tell him about our conversations?*

I don't know why I care. Actually, that's not true. Not even partly. I care because I like him. Even though I haven't seen him since that first dinner, I haven't stopped thinking about him. But it's just a crush. A stupid, silly crush. He's my best friend's husband. It's not like it would go anywhere.

Rolling my eyes at myself, I press the doorbell with my elbow. I hop from foot to foot to stay warm. I press the doorbell again, twice. *Come on, Violet.*

But when the door swings open, it's not Violet that appears. This time, it *is* Jay. He looks as surprised to see me as I am to see him. He's half-dressed, in a pair of pressed khakis, no shirt. He has a small towel in his hand, his hair damp, freshly washed. I can smell his shampoo.

"Caitlin?" he says, his eyebrows knitting together, head cocked to the side.

I stare back, momentarily struck dumb. Even though I've been hoping to run into him, I hadn't imagined that I actually would. I blink a few times, wondering if I'm hallucinating. When he doesn't disappear, I decide that I'm not.

"Hi," I say finally. "Good morning."

"Good morning," he answers. He smiles, giving me a once-over, his surprise turning to amusement.

I glance down at my outfit. Jeans ripped at the knee, my oversized hoodie pulled tightly around my face like the little kid from ET. High fashion. Haute couture. I wish I could loosen the strings, but, you know, the fucking coffee. I feel my face flush. At least I did my eyebrows, thank god.

"What can I do for you?" Jay asks.

"Nothing," I say. "I mean, I'm here for Violet. Is she home? We had plans to have coffee." I hold up the two cups in my hands as evidence. "She didn't mention I was stopping by?"

He shakes his head again. "She's still dropping Harper off at school. I was in the shower when she left. She should be back any minute, though." He glances at his watch. "It usually doesn't take her this long."

I shift again from one foot to the other. "It's okay. I can wait outside—"

"No, no," he says. "Come in. I was just finishing breakfast," Jay says, flashing a grin at me. He opens the door wide and motions me inside.

I step through the threshold, into their entryway, then follow him into the kitchen. "Want anything?" he asks over his shoulder. "Toast? Eggs?"

"I'm fine." I shake my head. "I'm not usually a breakfast person." Although, I might be, if I got up early enough to make myself anything. "The coffee is plenty."

On the counter, there's a plate with a half-eaten piece of rye toast and a mug of coffee, still steaming. I perch on a bar stool, setting both cardboard cups down in front of me.

The heat is on in the house, so I shrug out of my hoodie, although the boxy T-shirt I have underneath isn't much better in terms of flattering. I desperately wish I'd spent an extra five minutes getting ready this morning.

I set my purse on the bar stool next to me, and when I hear it clunk, I remember what's inside. "Oh!" I say, reaching into it and pulling out the copy of *And Then There Were None*. "Here." I hand the book to Jay, who takes it from me, looking at it in surprise. "You said you might want to read it," I add. "When we met at the park."

I've been carrying it around for almost two months now. I'd planned on giving it to him the night that Violet invited me over for dinner, but he went upstairs to put Harper to bed before I'd had the chance. I keep telling myself to give it to Violet to give to him, but I haven't. I've wanted to do it myself. It feels like something special between us, just for the two of us.

Jay studies the cover, nodding slowly. For a minute, I think he might not remember our conversation, and I start to feel sick, hands getting clammy. But then he looks at me, a smile spreading across his face, his gold-flecked eyes bright. "Thanks," he says. "Really, thanks. I can't wait to read it."

I smile back. The knot in my stomach unwinds, my limbs loosening with pleasure.

We're still smiling at each other when my phone buzzes. I pick it up off the counter. It's a text from Violet. *Sorry, got stuck at school, heading home now!*

I feel a brief flash of disappointment. I don't want her to come back yet. I've been waiting a long time for this moment to materialize, to see Jay again. When Violet walks in, everything will change. The electricity I feel will dissipate. He'll leave for work, and it'll be just Violet and me again. Then I'm flooded with shame. What's wrong with me? Violet is my friend. And Jay is hers, not mine. He never was, never will be. I shake the disloyal thoughts from my head. *Be better, Sloane*, I think.

Quickly, I type back. *No worries! Jay let me in. See you soon!*

"It's Violet. She says she's on her way home," I say, looking back up at Jay.

He nods and tosses the towel he used to dry his hair on the counter, then picks up his coffee. "So, how's my patron saint?" he asks, smiling at me. "I haven't seen you since dinner. I'm not sure how I've kept myself safe without you."

I blush. "I'm good," I say. "Busy."

"So saving lives one bee sting at a time? No time for needy dads?"

I smirk. "That's right. I race from park to park, ice pack and tweezers in hand. Batgirl's second cousin: Beewoman."

He laughs. "Our own local superhero." Then, smile fading, he says, "You and Violet have been spending a lot of time together." I'm not sure if he's asking a question or stating the obvious, given that I'm on their payroll. Violet pays me each week in cash, crisp bills inside sealed white envelopes. I wonder if he's the one to make the withdrawals, or if she is. "And Harper says you make the best snacks."

I smile. "She's a sweetheart."

"She really likes you," Jay says. "And so does Violet."

It thrills me to hear him say that. "I like them, too. Violet's been a good friend to me." My best friend. I don't say it to Jay, but it's true.

There's a silence as he considers this, then—"Has she said anything to you about us?" he asks. The shift in tone is abrupt. He doesn't look at me. Instead, he opens the dishwasher and begins to unload some silverware. I think maybe I've misheard him.

"You mean you and her?" I ask, frowning.

Jay straightens, shuts the dishwasher, and nods. "Yeah, has she said anything?" he repeats.

I'm still not sure what he's getting at. "Like what?"

He studies me, his eyes searching mine. Then he gives a shrug, a shake of his head, a sheepish smile. "Nothing. Forget it."

"Is everything okay?" I ask.

He nods, but there's something about the way his mouth is set that makes me not so sure. For a moment, the kitchen is silent. I feel uneasy, a little disoriented. What is he talking about? Is there something Violet is keeping from me?

I chew on my lip, staring at him. He doesn't look back at me. Instead, he glances at the clock on the microwave, the blue neon numbers glowing. I'm about to ask if he's *sure* everything is okay, but he speaks before I do.

"I should finish getting ready for work," he says.

But I don't want him to go, not yet. I like talking to him. I wish I didn't, but I do. "How's it going?" I blurt out. It's all I can think of. "Work, I mean."

"Good." Jay shrugs. "But I'm expected to be clothed." He grins at me. "I'm not sure it's appropriate for the founder to show up half-dressed."

"That seems so old-fashioned," I joke back. "What is this, the 1950s?"

"So you don't think anyone would mind if I went in like this?" he asks, looking down at himself, then back up at me.

"I wouldn't," I say, then blush, face reddening. Jesus, did I just say that out loud? "I'm just kidding. I mean, yes, a shirt is probably a good idea." I can't get the words out fast enough. He's going to think I'm deranged. Frankly, I think I'm deranged.

Jay's grin widens, clearly amused.

Then, thank god, I'm saved by the figurative bell. The front door opens and shuts loudly. Violet's home.

"I'm so sorry, Cait!" she calls out. "One of the other moms cornered me. She wouldn't—"

She walks into the kitchen, midsentence, then stops short, seeing Jay. "Oh," she says. "I didn't think you'd still be here."

I feel embarrassed suddenly, sitting here with her shirtless husband, my crush written all over my face in thick, black Sharpie. I can feel the heat rise again in my face.

"I'm just leaving," Jay says. Still holding his coffee mug, he takes his plate from the counter and puts it into the sink.

"Like that?" Violet asks. She raises an eyebrow, then winks at me. Jay makes a face at her, something between a smirk and a grimace, before starting toward the living room.

"Wait, before you go, Jay . . ." Violet calls after him. He turns, pausing beneath the high arch of the doorframe. "I was going to invite Caitlin on the boat on Sunday. You have it on your calendar, right?"

Without waiting for his answer, she turns to me. "We always take a boat out for my birthday," she says. "I wanted to see if you wanted to come, too." Then, to Jay, "Caitlin's birthday is two days before mine. I thought it would be fun to celebrate together." She looks from Jay back to me, smiling. "I meant to ask you earlier, but it snuck up on me this year. Want to join us?"

I feel a rush. I think of the calendar on the wall in my room, both our birthdays circled in marker. I've been waiting for this invitation as the days neared, waiting, wishing, hoping. "Yes!" I say. "I'd love to. That sounds so fun. Just the four of us?"

Violet nods. "Is that okay?"

"Of course," I say. I beam. It's more than okay. It's great, just as I'd imagined.

"Did you make a reservation?" Jay asks. His voice sounds oddly strained.

She nods. "Last week. Why, do you have to work? I already told Harper that—"

"No, it's fine," he interrupts. "That's fine with me."

"Great!" Violet says, grinning at me. "We're booked at ten."

Jay nods. "Okay." Then, "I really have to run. I have a meeting at nine thirty." He picks up *And Then There Were None* from the counter and holds it up. "Thanks again, Caitlin. I appreciate it."

"You're welcome," I say, feeling my cheeks warm again. I don't look at Violet. I hope she doesn't mind that I brought it for him.

"Bye!" she calls after him as he walks out of the room. Then she turns to me, smiling. "I'm so glad you can come on the boat."

I feel warm inside, pleased she remembered my birthday, even more pleased that she wants to celebrate hers with me. "Me too." I smile back. "Really, thanks for the invite."

"Well, thanks for the coffee!" Violet says, motioning to the two lattes on the counter. "My favorite."

We take our cups to the couch. As we settle in, Jay comes back down the stairs—fully clothed now—leather satchel slung over his shoulder, an umbrella in hand. He smiles, waves goodbye, and I blush for the hundredth time. A few minutes later, the rain starts, and Violet and I watch as it comes down in front of the bay window. When the coffees are done, Violet takes some photo books off the bookshelf and shows me pictures from their wedding. I love looking at the shots of her and Jay, dressed like royalty, glowing.

I study her profile as she stares down at the glossy pages of the book, pointing to different images, telling me about the guests at their wedding, about how the best man made a toast that made Jay's mother blush. Something about Jay's grooming habits before dates. I try to focus, but my mind keeps wandering.

What had Jay meant when he asked me if Violet had said anything about the two of them? Was their marriage in trouble? Did it have anything to do with the phone call that I'd seen through the window a few weeks ago? Had she been talking to him? I'd managed to forget about it—

the anger on Violet's face, her expression as she threw her phone against the couch—deciding it must have been nothing; she's seemed fine. If something was going on between her and Jay, she would have told me, right?

Violet's confided in me about any number of things these last few weeks, about how she's worried no one will hire her in New York, especially since she has to take the bar again and doesn't know if she'll pass, about how she feels out of place among the other moms at Harper's school, how she thinks she might be coddling Harper. I can't believe she wouldn't have mentioned something so big as marital problems. She trusts me; I know she does.

Finally, when Violet shuts the book, I clear my throat, take a deep breath. "Is everything okay?" I ask tentatively.

Violet frowns. "What do you mean?"

I shake my head. "I mean, with you. Just, you know, checking in." I don't want to tell her what Jay said. I don't want her to think we were talking about her behind her back. And I don't want him to think he can't trust me.

She smiles. Her face is sunny, eyes bright. "Yeah, I'm great, thanks. Want more coffee? I can make a pot."

I nod. Maybe they'd had a fight recently but had since made up. Maybe he wanted to know just how close we were, if she talked to me about their sex life. Looking at her now, at the open-book expression on her face, I'm sure: if something was wrong, she would tell me. "I'd love another cup," I say.

When it's time for me to leave, Violet walks me out. "See you Sunday? I'll text you the address," she says. She's standing in the doorway, leaning against the frame. Sunday, for our birthday boat ride.

I nod, feeling that rush again, and smile. "See you Sunday," I say. Happy birthday to me.

15

On Saturday night, I set an alarm for seven thirty the next morning. It turns out I don't need it, even though it was past midnight when I went to bed; I wake when the sun rises, just before six.

I tried to go to bed early to make sure I was well rested for the day, but I was too excited to sleep. As much as I tried, I couldn't stop thinking about spending the day with Jay. I know I promised myself I'd be better in the name of friendship, but I can't deny how I feel when I'm around him, the way my heart flip-flops, the flush in my cheeks. It's harmless, I keep reassuring myself, as most crushes are. And who wouldn't have a crush on Jay? I'm a woman with a pulse, last time I checked.

Now, I take my time getting dressed. I find a pair of dark jeans in the back of my closet and a flowy boho top from my teaching days. Then I wash my face and put in my contacts, rummage through the bathroom drawers until I find a bottle of half-dried-out foundation and some cakey blush. I dot the foundation over a smattering of pimples on my chin—something I was sure I wouldn't be dealing with in my thirties, but alas, here we are—and rub some of the blush on my cheekbones. It's subtle, but it helps.

Before I leave my bedroom, I don the hat I bought from the shop and the necklace Violet complimented me on. In my purse is a small box with a similar necklace inside. I found it at the same store. It's not quite identical, since the one I'm wearing is supposed to be a family heirloom, but it's close. They wrapped it for me in gold glitter paper, topped with a bow. I can't wait to give it to her.

In the kitchen, I toast some bread and pour a cup of coffee. I hardly taste either. My whole body is wired with energy. An entire day with the Lockhart family. I feel so lucky I could scream. When I'm finished eating, I step into a clear morning, the sky a brilliant, cloudless blue. The marina is only a little over a mile from my apartment, so instead of the subway, I decide to walk.

I arrive quickly, in fifteen minutes instead of the twenty shown on my phone, and walk up the dock. The air is different here than in the neighborhoods—crisper, cleaner, wet with salt. The yachts and sailboats that line the path are oversized, looming tall, sunlight glinting off their shiny exteriors.

The weather is warm but not hot, a faint breeze skimming across the water, a perfect early summer morning, the kind you wait all year for. The smile on my face feels permanently affixed.

As I near the end of the dock, I hear Violet calling to me. I put my hand to my brow, squinting into the sun.

"Caitlin, hi!" Violet is standing on the bow of a large sailboat, waving. Next to her is Harper, her arm also above her head, swinging it back and forth. They're both in straw sun hats and wear matching red plastic sunglasses.

I wave back, grinning. I want to run down the dock, fling my arms around them, squeeze them tightly.

When I get to the boat, Jay is standing on the side, Violet and Harper behind him. He offers me his hand, and I take it, then take a step off the dock. The boat rocks with the shift in weight, and I almost fall backward. Jay grabs me by the waist, pulling my body to his to steady me. Suddenly, we're face-to-face, so close I can feel his chest against mine, the tickle of his breath on my lips. He smells like spearmint gum.

"Whoa, there," he says, smiling, and everyone laughs. He doesn't let me go right away, holding another few seconds. When he does, I breathe out, my heart pounding.

"Welcome aboard," Violet says, extending her arm, motioning around the boat. "And happy birthday!"

"Thanks! Happy birthday to you, too! It's beautiful out here," I say, looking around. "I've never been boating. Do you guys come out here a lot?"

"We started the tradition in San Francisco," Violet says. "Jay surprised me with a sunset cruise around the marina the first year we moved there, and we've done it ever since. We've upgraded a little over the years, haven't we, babe?" She laughs a little sheepishly.

Jay gives her a strange smile. I'm not sure if he doesn't like her calling attention to their money, or something else. Maybe I was wrong before; maybe something is going on between them that I don't know about. I look to Violet, but she seems unbothered, still smiling.

"Well, I'm going to take us out," Jay says, starting toward the back of the boat. He brushes against me as he walks by, and I can smell the spearmint again. My heart skips a beat.

"Can I pour you a glass?" Violet asks me, holding up a clear plastic cup. There's a cooler at her feet with a bottle of champagne on ice, as well as a bottle of sparkling apple cider. Both are open, half-full.

"Sure," I say, and she reaches for the cider. She tips the bottle too quickly, and the cup overflows, bubbles spilling over the side. Violet shrieks and we all laugh.

"Whoops!" she says, holding the glass out so she doesn't get wet. "I'd be a terrible bartender!" When the bubbles subside, she hands it to me. "For the birthday girl." I take it from her, smiling.

"Cheers!" Violet raises her cup. Harper and I do the same. "Cheers!" we both echo, our plastic cups all knocking together. The cider is crisp and sweet, its bubbles effervescent in my mouth. Everything is as perfect as I imagined it would be.

"Ready?" Jay calls out, and we all nod.

The three of us climb to the front of the boat, Harper in Violet's lap, our faces to the wind. Behind us, the sail unfurls, billowing in the wind. The boat begins to move, slowly at first, then faster, until we're out of the marina, into the harbor on open waters.

"I love it out here," Violet says, inhaling deeply. "Jay's colleague has a boat that we go out on sometimes, too. It's one of my favorite things to do in the summer." She tips her head toward Jay. "If you've never been sailing, you should ask him to show you how."

"To sail?" I look back toward Jay. He's standing at the back of the boat, holding a rope in his gloved hand. He has a pair of tortoiseshell-rimmed Wayfarer sunglasses on, his hair tousled by the wind. He's as handsome as I've ever seen him.

She nods. "It's fun. It's easier than it looks."

I hesitate.

"Go!" She smiles encouragingly.

Cautiously, I stand, the boat rocking over the small waves, and, wobbly, make my way toward Jay. I glance back at Violet, who has already turned back around. She's pointing something out to Harper—another boat, maybe—who is nodding emphatically.

Jay smiles at me as I approach. "Everything okay? Not seasick, I hope."

I shake my head. "Violet said you'd show me the ropes." I look down at the ropes in his hand. "Literally, I guess. I've never been sailing before."

"Yeah, sure, I'd be happy to." His smile broadens into a grin, white teeth appearing. He looks genuinely excited by my interest.

I smile. "Okay. So." I look up at the sails and the ropes and pulleys. "This looks complicated."

He laughs. "It really isn't. We'll start with the basics," he says. "This is the tiller." He points to a wooden stick-like thing behind us. "It's used to steer."

I nod. "Got it."

"Go on, then," he says, like he's daring me.

Hesitantly, I reach out, wrap my fingers around it, then look back toward him.

"Nice grip," he says. His tone is teasing. My whole body flushes, heat radiating through me.

He grins again, bites his lip. God, he's good-looking. I press the back of my hand to my flaming neck. Is he flirting with me?

"And these"—Jay points to the ropes, still smiling—"are called sheets. Each sheet refers to the sail that it controls. This sail"—he points to the sail directly in front of us—"is the mainsail. The front sail, toward the bow, is the jib. So, when you want to move the mainsail you use the mainsheet; if you want to move the jib, then you will pull the jib sheet. Make sense?"

I swallow hard, willing my blush to fade. "Yep, seems easy enough," I manage.

He shows me the boom, which, apparently, I should watch out for, lest it knock me over, and the stays and shrouds, which look like wires, and the halyard, which looks like more wires.

"You with me?" Jay asks.

"Mm-hm." I nod, trying my best to sound convincing. I am not, in fact, with him. I'm having trouble focusing on anything besides the way his arm keeps brushing against mine.

"Great. The sailing part is actually pretty simple. There are a few rules to get us started. First, you can't sail directly into the wind. So if we want to go there"—he points directly in front of us—"we'll have to sail forty-five or fifty degrees to the left or right of the wind, then back the other way. And that's called tacking. We do that by moving the sails we just talked about."

"That doesn't *sound* simple. It sounds like math class."

Jay laughs. "I promise you, it's easy once you get the hang of it. Look how well you handled the tiller." He winks.

I blush again, knees turning to jelly.

"Seriously," he says. "You'll see. Are you ready to give it a shot?" He takes a step back and motions for me to take his place.

"What? No way," I say, shaking my head and holding my hands up, palms to him. "I'll capsize us! It'd be like *Titanic*, round two!"

Jay smiles, amused. "I'm going to show you what to do," he says. "The only real way to learn is by doing. And lucky for us all, there are no icebergs in the East River. Come on, grab the rope," he says, holding it out to me. "Right hand above left."

Reluctantly, I do what he says. Although, truthfully, if he'd asked me to jump off the boat with a brick tied to my ankle, I'd probably do that, too. Aye, aye, Captain!

The rope is thick and braided, taut, under my hands. "Like this?" I look over my shoulder at him.

"A little higher." Jay takes a step closer and reaches around me. He puts his hands over mine on the rope and slides them up. My heart rate quickens at his touch, the closeness of our bodies. "Okay, now we pull. Lean back, just a little."

I ease back, into his chest. It's warm and sturdy. Is it my imagination or does he move even closer? "Good," he says. His breath is in my hair, against my ear, my neck. I want to close my eyes, but I don't. I keep them trained forward, body stiff.

The bow of the boat begins to turn. "Oh!" I say, looking back at Jay, surprised by the movement. He laughs. "Pretty cool, huh?"

I nod. We begin to pick up speed. I tighten my grip on the rope. His arms are still around me.

"Okay, now, let go and pull here." He guides my hands to another set of ropes. "Watch the boom! And, oh, loosen your hold, now pull again. Yep, just like that."

The boat begins to shift in the other direction. He takes a step back. "See, you're doing it!" he says proudly.

I grin at him. "I'm doing it?"

"You're doing it! That's it. Well"—he laughs—"not exactly it, but it's a start. We'll adjust the mainsail as the wind changes, but until it does, you can relax and enjoy the ride."

"Where'd you learn all this?" I ask him.

"Summer camp. When I was ten."

Naturally. The only boats at the summer camp I went to were old, rusty canoes, floating in warm swampy South Carolina lake water. No one minded, though. We splashed through the inky water, feet sinking into the muck, trying not to tip the boats as we hoisted ourselves in. It was just a rinky-dink YMCA day camp; my mom couldn't afford to send me to the sleepaway kind with cabins and bunk beds and bonfires. So sailing? Yeah, right.

Jay sees the look on my face and laughs. "What?"

"I was just thinking about the boats we had at the camp I went to. We were told they were canoes, but they were more like old sardine cans. We used branches we found on the shore as oars."

"I was on scholarship, if that makes you feel any better," he says. "We didn't have a lot of money growing up."

"Really?" I say. I turn toward him, surprised. "You don't seem like . . ." I trail off.

"What, a poor kid?" He smiles wryly. "Thanks, I guess. But I was. Neither of my parents graduated from high school, so they always had pretty shitty jobs. They made ends meet, but we never had much."

We're both quiet. He isn't looking at me anymore, instead staring out ahead. I clear my throat and say, "I grew up without money, too. My mom worked as a housekeeper, but she had health problems. She called out sick all the time, always ended up getting fired for missing too many days. We moved around a lot because we couldn't pay the rent."

It's more honest than I've been with anyone in a long time. Even Violet. Maybe because he was like me, a poor kid who just wanted to fit in.

This time when Jay looks at me, it's like he's seeing me for the first time. Slowly, he nods. "It's a hard way to grow up. I hated it."

"Me too. Which is why I never told anyone. I made excuses about why I could never invite anyone over to our apartment. And since no one visited, I was free to tell them we lived in a mansion. And that my dad was a movie star in Hollywood. I thought that would make people like me." I shrug.

Jay nods. "It's hard to explain it to people. What it's like. I don't think Violet's ever really understood. But I shouldn't be surprised, considering."

"Considering what?" I ask.

He shrugs. "Her family has always had money. Her dad is some hotshot lawyer—Violet worked for his firm in San Francisco—but they have generational wealth. Her grandmother left a trust for her when she died."

I frown, confused. She's never mentioned money. Or a trust. But it makes sense: the big brownstone, the expensive clothes, the ease with which she glides. Still, I'm surprised it never came up.

He sees the look on my face. "She doesn't usually talk about it. She thinks people will look at her differently if they know she comes from money. Even in Brooklyn, where everyone comes from money. I think she likes people thinking that we're self-made, but I'm not sure why. No one here is impressed by new money." There's a hint of resentment in his voice. "It's funny, I grew up wishing I had the kind of money she did, and all she wants to do is hide it."

"Unless you're a member of the Poor Kid Club, you just don't get it, do you?" I give a little laugh. "No dues required, thank god."

Jay laughs, too. "I'm glad you came today. I like you."

I grin at him. "I like you, too." And I mean it. I mean it more than I could ever tell him.

Then, "Oh—!" I say in surprise, "—that moved. The direction thing."

"Good eye! Okay, grab the mainsheet, there. Right, you got it. And pull a little. Exactly, nice! You're a fast learner," he says appreciatively.

I shrug modestly, though inside I am giddy. *He likes me.*

Jay sits down on the bench beside me and clasps his hands behind his head, leaning back, eyes closed, face toward the wind. It ruffles his hair, leaving it standing on end. He's so handsome it almost hurts. I look away, back to the water, before he opens his eyes and catches me staring.

I spend the next hour with him as he shows me how to speed up and slow down, change directions, maneuver the sails. I listen attentively, eager to please. He moves my hands, my body, into the right positions, demonstrating the proper techniques. When he touches me, I feel like I'm on fire. The air is warm and wet, sea spray misting our faces, dampening our skin. Once, just once, I allow myself to imagine him lowering his mouth to mine, the taste of salt on his lips, his tongue.

Finally, Jay glances down at his watch. "Are you hungry?" he asks. "We can take a break."

I don't want to, not really—it's too easy to pretend that it's just me and Jay on this boat—but I nod. "Sure, sounds good."

He cups his hands around his mouth and yells, loudly, so his voice carries, "Here okay for lunch?"

From the front of the boat, Violet gives us a thumbs-up.

He turns to me. "I can take over from here. I'm just going to anchor us. I'll meet you up there in a few minutes."

I start to leave, then turn back toward him. "Thank you," I say.

"For what?" Jay cocks his head.

"For teaching me. For letting me sail the boat with you."

"You're welcome." A mischievous smile plays at his lips. "Maybe next time you can teach me a few things." He's trying to make me blush again. It works.

"Stop!" I say, giving his shoulder a soft shove. There's a familiarity between us now, a closeness that wasn't there before.

"Stop what?" He laughs. It sends a warm feeling through my limbs.

I shake my head, laughing, too. "You're terrible."

"I'm kidding," he says. "Really, I'm glad you enjoyed it."

We stand there, smiling at each other, until finally, I thumb toward Violet and Harper. "Well, I guess I'll head back now. See you in a bit." *Cool, Sloane. Très cool.*

I turn and carefully make my way back up to the bow, the boat rocking over the waves. I hold on to the rail to steady myself.

"How was it?" Violet asks as I take my seat across from her.

"Really fun," I say. "Just like you said."

Violet beams at me. "I knew you'd like it." She drains her glass, as if in a private cheers with herself for a job well done. She seems looser than she normally does, more relaxed. She sees me staring and raises up her red plastic sunglasses, winking at me.

Instantly, I feel guilty. She's such a good friend. And how do I repay her? By flirting with her husband, wishing he was mine, that he would kiss me. I force myself to smile back at her. I'd never *do* anything, I tell myself. It's a silly infatuation, like my high school obsession with Robert Pattinson, lusty, fevered, and forever confined to the darkened recesses of my bedroom, where I spent night after night fantasizing about him sinking his vampire fangs into my tender teenage flesh.

Jay joins us a few minutes later, carrying the cooler and a brown grocery bag. He sets them between us and sits down next to me, across from Harper and Violet. His thigh brushes against mine. Our eyes connect. *Just a crush.* But I know it's not.

"Refills?" Violet asks, reaching for the cooler. Jay and I both nod and pass her our cups. Even though it's just cider, I feel a little drunk, light-headed and euphoric, high from the day, the salt air. Jay. His leg.

"For you," she says, handing me my glass, "and you." She gives the other one to Jay. Then she picks up her own cup and raises it to mine. "To my Gemini twin."

I beam and touch my glass to hers. "Cheers."

Jay reaches into the paper bag. "Who's ready to eat?" he asks.

"I am!" Harper yells, her hand shooting above her head and waving wildly. "I'm so hungry I could eat ten sandwiches!"

"How about you start with one?" Jay says good-naturedly as he unpacks paper-wrapped deli subs, a few bags of chips, and a parcel of grapes, and passes them around. We eat leisurely, the boat bobbing beneath us, the sail rippling in the wind.

"Something about being on a boat makes me so hungry," Violet says, opening a second bag of chips. "Jay, are you going to finish that?" She eyes his sandwich longingly.

"Here, you can have mine," I say quickly. I've only eaten half. I slide it toward her, happy to make Violet happy.

"You better thank Caitlin, Jay," Violet says, winking at me. "Otherwise I would have left you to starve."

"Thank you, Saint Cait. My hero. Again." He gives me that slow smile that makes me tingle, my stomach flip. I blush, smile back.

When we're finished and everything's been cleared away, Violet clasps her hands together. "Should we do presents?" she asks.

"Yes!" Harper shrieks, bouncing up and down in her seat. "Open mine first! Do mine, do mine!"

Violet laughs and cups her hand around Harper's cheek affectionately, kissing it. "Okay, okay, darling girl, I will."

Jay reaches into a big bag and hands Harper two gifts wrapped in silver paper. "Give these to Mom," he instructs.

Harper happily does as she's told, presenting them proudly to Violet. "This is the one from me!" she says, holding up the bigger of the two.

Violet pulls off the ribbon and tears into the wrapping. There's a large white box inside. Violet opens the lid, lifts out its contents. It's a light pink robe, soft-looking, like you want to bury your face in it. "I love it!" she says. She runs her hand over the soft material. "Thank you, Harpie, it's beautiful!"

"I picked it out myself!"

"She did," Jay confirms. "We spent all afternoon looking for the right gift, and she decided this was it."

Violet pulls Harper into her arms, covering her with loud kisses. Harper squeals and wriggles away. "Now open Dad's!"

Violet glances at Jay, then picks up the second package. Carefully, she unwraps it, more carefully than she'd unwrapped Harper's. She turns it over in her hands, studying it. It's a book, a hardcover copy by Bill Bryson.

She flips open the front cover, then to the title page. Both are blank. Quickly, she shuts the book and looks up, smiling at Jay. "Thanks, Jay. Bryson is his favorite," she says, turning to me. "Have you read any of his books?"

I shake my head. I've heard of him—he's a travel writer, I think—but have never picked up anything he's written.

"He's the best," Jay says. "*In a Sunburned Country* is my favorite."

"It's why we went to Australia for our honeymoon," Violet adds.

Jay shifts, clears his throat. "Well, should we—" he starts, but I interrupt.

"Wait, I have a little something for Violet, too," I say, reaching into my bag. "Here."

I take the small, wrapped box, bow on top, and pass it to her. My heartbeat starts to pick up, my stomach feeling like it does on a too-fast roller coaster. What if she doesn't like it? What if she thinks it's stupid? Or ugly? Maybe she complimented me on mine just to be polite. I smile at her. My lips feel tight.

Violet takes it from me, smiling back. She unties the bow and removes the wrapping paper, then lifts the lid of the little box to reveal the necklace. The tiny pearl glints in the sunlight.

"It's like mine," I say tentatively. "Like my grandma's."

"Thank you, Caitlin," she says quietly, looking up at me. The wind has ruffled her hair. It's wild and loose, framing her face. "I love it."

I smile broadly, relieved. She likes it—but I realize she isn't putting it on. I feel a tinge of disappointment, but then see that she has turned around, rooting through a large canvas tote. When she turns back toward me, she's holding a small gift bag stuffed with gold tissue paper. "Great minds," she says, winking as she hands it to me.

"For me?" I say, even though I know it is. I'm beside myself. Violet nods.

Delighted, I reach into the gift, my fingers brushing against a small packet, a folded square of tissue paper. I take it out and unfold the paper. Inside is a gold pendant hanging from a thin gold chain. The pendant is a nickel-sized square, a starburst etched into the metal. It has an antique feel, a vintage relic of the past, but I've seen it before. Around Violet's neck.

"I have one, too." She smiles and reaches into her sweater, pulling the chain out for me to see. "Gemini twins." My heart swells.

"Want me to put it on?" she asks, and I nod, unable to speak. She takes the necklace from me and scoots closer. I can feel her breath on the back of my neck as she hooks the clasp together, light and feathery.

"Let's see," she says and leans back.

Proudly, I lift my chin, put my shoulders back. "Beautiful," Violet pronounces, and both Harper and Jay nod.

"Now time for cake!" Violet announces. She reaches into another bag and pulls out a miniature cake with a plastic lid. She uncovers it and gently places two candles into the icing. She lights the wicks and Jay and Harper begin to sing to us, loudly and off-key.

Looking around at Violet, Jay, and Harper, everyone windblown and rosy-cheeked, I don't think I've ever been happier. I close my eyes and blow out my candle.

16

It's a few weeks after our day on the boat, and I'm sprawled on the couch at Violet's house. Outside, the early July humidity is like a thick and oppressive blanket. The air conditioner is on high, but the heat still lingers in our limbs.

I'm officially full-time as Harper's nanny, at their house five days a week and an occasional Saturday or Sunday, sometimes both. It feels like I'm more than a nanny, though. It feels like I'm part of their family, interwoven into their days, their lives, like I belong here, in this house, laying opposite Violet, my head on one arm of the sofa, hers on the other, fanning ourselves with magazines. As the pages flap, Taylor Swift's lyrics pop into my head. It feels exactly like the title of her song, like karma, honey-sweet.

Harper is asleep upstairs. Instead of going to the park, we made a pillow bed on the floor of her room, took turns reading aloud, her little body wedged between us. When my book was done, Harper begged me to read another, so I did. Storytime had been my favorite at the preschool, with all the kids gathered around me in a circle, their small chins in their hands as they sat cross-legged on the rug. I'd change my voice for each character, facing the book toward them so they could see the pictures. As I read, Harper had tucked under my arm, snuggled in close. By the time the book was over, Harper had her eyes closed.

We tiptoed out, and Violet eased the door shut behind us. We didn't talk as we padded quietly down the stairs. In the living room, Violet sank into one end of the couch, and I plopped onto the other.

Now, she leans her head back, her eyes fluttering closed. "I don't know what I did in a past life to deserve a child that still naps at this age, but it must have been saintly," she says.

"Mother Teresa, for sure," I agree.

"Or Joan of Arc?" She lifts her head, opens her eyes.

"Maybe Eleanor Roosevelt. She was instrumental in the women's rights movement, among other things. Not a looker, poor dear, but that didn't stop her. Huge legacy in her wake."

Violet laughs. "Well, maybe someone a little less honorable, like—"

She's interrupted by her phone. It vibrates loudly on the coffee table. We both turn toward it.

"Sorry," she says, picking it up and frowning at the screen. When she looks up, she sighs. "Jay forgot a flash drive he needs for a client presentation. He wants me to bring it to his office."

She looks at her phone again, then back at me. "Do you mind if I run out? I won't be gone long. Thirty minutes, forty-five at the most. Unless I die of heatstroke on the way back."

"Of course," I say, shrugging. "That's why I'm here!"

Violet beams at me. "You're the best! I'll be back in a heartbeat."

Quickly, she runs up the stairs. A few minutes later, she returns, holding up a small stick. The flash drive. "I'll be back soon," she says. "Call me if you need anything!"

Then she shuts the door behind her. There's a click, a turning of the lock. The house is quiet, refrigerator humming in the next room. I glance around the living room, taking stock. Then I get up.

It's rare that I'm here alone, without Harper coloring in the corner or sitting at the kitchen counter with a snack. It feels different, being here like this, like I have the house to myself.

I wander aimlessly through the living room, first to the little side table by the window, picking up the stacked magazines one by one, then to the bookshelf, running my fingers across the spines of the books. Popular thrillers, pulp mysteries. There are a few classics: *Pride and Prejudice, The Sun Also Rises, East of Eden,* and—*The Great Gatsby*. I smile and pull it from the bookshelf. The spine is stiff when I open it, as if it hasn't been cracked in a long time. It has that old book smell, like dust and mothballs, and I put my face to it and inhale deeply. Then, I flip to the title page.

In black ink, large looping letters: *To my Gatsby. You make my heart sing. To many, many more. xx.*

It was a gift to Jay from Violet.

I imagine her giving it to him, paper-wrapped, tied with twine, for his birthday, an anniversary gift, maybe, in bed one morning, unearthing it from beneath her pillow. I picture them both in their pajamas, her in one of his T-shirts, swimming in it, him in just boxers. He'd have smiled when he opened it, glancing up at her as she watched with eager eyes, hands clasped together as if in prayer.

Then they'd have lain in bed, reading passages aloud, his head on her stomach as she ran her fingers through his hair. Maybe they never got out of bed that day, except to make coffee, open the door for the delivery boy, eating a pizza in bed, ice cream from the carton.

Carefully, I shut the book. The empty slot where it was is gaping, like a missing tooth. It leaves me a little unsettled, ill at ease. But it's not the space on the shelf that's bothering me, not really.

It's the question Jay asked me in the kitchen a few weeks ago. *Has she said anything to you about us?* Is their marriage in trouble? It seems so unlikely, but what else could it be? Have they been fighting? I hate thinking that there's a secret between us, that there might be something Violet's not telling me. I've wanted to ask her, but it felt private, between me and Jay, like it would be a breach if I said something. It leaves me stuck between her and him, both yanking on an arm. I want to cut myself in two, give half my body to each of them.

I put the book back on the shelf and head into the kitchen. I grab a can of seltzer from the fridge and open the tab, the crack of the lid sharp against the silence. I take a sip, glance around. The clock on the microwave reads two fifteen. Violet's only been gone five minutes. I go back into the living room. I should sit back down, I know I should, but I don't.

I resist the temptation for as long as I can. Then I set the seltzer on the coffee table and slowly walk to the staircase. At the bottom, I slip out of my sneakers, arrange them side by side on the first step. I put a hand on the railing, ever so gently, like it's made of glass.

I breathe out, then I pad up the carpeted stairs, my footsteps silent. At the top of the staircase, I pause. To my left is a closed door. Harper's bedroom. I take a step toward it. There's a muffled whirring that gets louder as I near. Her sound machine cranked up. Violet turned it on just before we walked out. Waves, I think, or the sound of a heartbeat, soothing and steady. Halfway down the hall is another door that's closed, and at the other end of the hallway a third door, this one cracked open. I walk toward it. As I approach, I see the foot of a bed: Violet and Jay's bedroom. Carefully, I push the door open.

The floor creaks when I walk in, the caramel-colored floorboards moving under my weight. The bedroom is bright and airy with two large windows overlooking the street. There's a Peloton bike in the corner, a pair of shorts draped over the screen. The midcentury bed frame is wooden, but everything else is white. The billowing curtains, the linen sheets, the duvet cover, the throw pillows. I run my hand across the soft bed cover and inhale deeply. It smells like Violet in here, like a bloom of gardenias, lilacs in the springtime.

The bed is flanked by two nightstands, a gold lamp on each. On one side, a few hardcover books, a box of Kleenex. On the other, a small jewelry dish, hand cream. I go over to Violet's side of the bed, closest to the window, and sit down, the mattress giving beneath me. Gingerly, I lie back, my head sinking into her pillow as I swing my legs onto the bed. The sheets smell like they've been recently laundered, like detergent and fabric softener. I close my eyes briefly, breathing it all in.

I open my eyes and turn onto my side, facing Jay's side of the bed. I stare at his pillow, trying to imagine him next to me, so close that I could touch him. I remember how his chest felt against my back on the boat. Broad, firm. I've only seen him a few times in passing since then, but I haven't forgotten the way he teased me, his hands on mine, our legs brushing.

I sit back up and get off the bed, wander to the windows. I push aside the curtains and look out. A few kids are playing on the sidewalk across the street, two of them tossing a ball back and forth as the others sit on a stoop and watch. Through the glass, I can hear their muffled yells, whooping.

I could stare out this window for hours, watching the neighborhood unfurl beneath me, a tiny, beautiful vignette of the borough. It looks a little like a stage, the way the sun shines through the branches, lighting up the sidewalk like a spotlight.

It's probably the first thing Violet does when she gets out of bed. She stretches, arms above her head, then walks to the window, opens the curtains to let in the morning light. Maybe Jay groans, pulling the comforter over his head.

What does she do next? Get dressed for the day? I scan the room. There are two doors on the wall opposite the bed, both closed. I cross the room and open the door closest to me, the one on the right.

It's a small walk-in closet. On the left are Jay's clothes; on the right, Violet's. His side is organized by type—first pants, jeans and slacks, then shirts, then jackets—hers are by color. There are two sets of small drawers under the hangers. I pull the top drawer out, discover Violet's underwear. Dozens of lacy thongs, matching bras and bralettes. I finger the stitching. Is this what Jay likes? I picture Violet in a black panty set. Of course it's what he likes. I feel the sting of jealousy, then an immediate wave of guilt. I shut the drawer.

On the back of the closet door is a hook where two robes hang, one hers—lavender silk with hand-sewn flower buds on the trim—one his, a white waffle cotton. I take hers off the hook and slip it on over my T-shirt, tie the belt around my waist. The fabric is cool against my skin.

On Violet's side of the closet, there's a shelf above the clothes rack, lined with shoeboxes. I reach up, pulling one of the top boxes down, peek inside. It's a pair of strappy nude stilettos, with TOM FORD written in big block letters on the sole. They likely cost as much as a month's rent. I put the lid back on and slide it back onto the shelf, then reach for the next box. There's a thunk as I tilt it toward me, something sliding from the back of the box to the front. Frowning, I lift the lid. Inside, next to a pair of Manolo Blahnik pumps, is a phone.

It's a small gray plastic flip phone. I stare down at it, puzzled. Then, in a flash, an image pops into my head. Violet in the living room talking on the phone, on the day I'd waited across the street from their brownstone, standing behind one of the tall elms, watching her through the window. Violet ending the call. Violet flipping the phone closed when she was done. *Flipping it closed.* It hadn't been her iPhone. It had been this phone.

Gingerly, I pick it up, open it. The screen is dark. It's off. I hesitate, but only for a second. I hold the power button down. The screen lights up, loading. Then—a lock screen pops up. Password protected. Harper's birthday? Hers? I start to punch in the numbers then shake my head. No. I can't. I shouldn't. Then I do.

I type in Harper's birthday, hold my breath. But no, that's not it. I try Violet's. Also, wrong. Jay's? January fourth, right after the holidays. Violet had once mentioned how hard it was to think of something to get him so soon after Christmas. When she said it, I spent the rest of the day imagining what I would buy him if I were her: a watch, our initials engraved on the back, a fisherman's sweater, one with wool to match his eyes, then imagined him opening the gift, wrapping his arms around me as he told me how much he loved it. Oh-one-oh-four, I type. My stomach is tight.

No, it's not his birthday, either. I let out a breath. I'm going to put it away, I decide. I'm going to put it back in the box, back on the shelf. But as I move my finger to the power button on the side, the phone vibrates. My whole body tenses. It's a new text alert. I flip open the phone.

I can only see a preview, just the first line of the message. It's from a saved contact. Not a name, but initials: DS. It reads: *I need to know which day you—*

I frown at the phone, stare at it until the letters blur. Who is DS? Which day Violet *what*? I try to click into the message, but it takes me back to the password screen. *Shit.*

Is the text from the same person I'd seen her talking to the other day? *DS. DS.* I mouth the letters, whisper them into the closet. *DS. D* for . . . Danny? Isn't that the name of Violet's childhood crush? The boy she said she'd been in love with her whole life? She'd said she'd lost touch with him, but maybe, recently, they'd reconnected and were planning to meet up. Were they having an affair?

Sloane, stop it! I tell myself. I shake my head. *This is what you do: you make up stories, let your imagination run wild.* There's probably a per- fectly reasonable explanation for all of this—even though, right now, I can't think of one. There are plenty of people with the first initial D, a million reasons someone is texting her that don't have anything to do with a secret lover. Right?

I wait, hoping for another text. One minute goes by, then another. The phone stays silent. Finally, I power it off and put it back where I found it.

It doesn't make sense. If she's not having an affair, why does Violet have a burner phone hidden in a shoebox? I can't exactly ask her. *Oh, Vi, what's with the phone I found while I was snooping through your things?* I know I have secrets from her, but I hate that she has secrets from me. I leave the closet feeling uneasy.

Back in the bedroom, I listen for Harper. The house is still quiet. I'll go downstairs in a minute, I tell myself. In just a minute. I shut the closet door and open the other one, thinking maybe, just maybe, I'll find the answers I'm looking for. It leads to a large, en suite bathroom that looks like it's been recently remodeled, with black-and-white geometric tiled floors, and white marbled countertops.

There are his-and-hers sinks, both with their own mirror, a single globular light above each one. To the left of the sinks, a toilet, and next to it, a walk-in shower, no tub.

The countertop is messier than I would have expected, more cluttered. The first thing my eyes land on is a box of hair dye, a deep brown color, the same shade as Violet's hair. I pick it up. It's unopened, unused. I'm surprised to discover that she dyes her hair herself. The woman on the box smiles brightly, her hair lustrous, gleaming. I hold the box up to my head, look in the mirror. Next to the model, my hair looks especially drab and straw-like—not quite blonde, not quite brown. It hasn't always been this color, but it's been a long time since I last dyed it.

Before setting the box down, I make note of the color—Dark Chestnut Brown—and the brand—a generic drugstore name—then move on with my search.

I know I shouldn't be here, I know it deep in my bones, but it's like I'm five years old with a marshmallow on the table in front of me, and just before leaving the room, someone said, *Don't eat it.* How can I not? I know how sweet it'll be when I do.

I scan the countertop and see a tube of acne cream next to the sink, several bottles of lotion. I can't picture Violet with pimples. Her skin is creamy and unblemished, like a polished stone. Maybe because she takes better care of it than I do mine. I study my reflection, the soft glow from the lighting fixtures more forgiving than in my own bathroom with its fluorescent bulbs, their yellow tint. Still, my complexion is uneven, dry in some patches, oily in others. I lean in closer to the mirror. A trail of red zits lines my chin, small but noticeable. I unscrew the tube of acne cream and squeeze, dabbing some onto my finger. I rub it into my skin, then recap the tube, set it back down on the counter.

Next to the lotion, to the right of her sink, is an unzipped makeup bag. I rifle through it, pulling out a tube of mascara, a blush brush, a powder compact. I think about using them, but decide against it, quickly loading them back into the bag before I change my mind.

The floor creaks again when I step back into the bedroom. There's a small ray of sun lighting up a spot next to the window, and I move toward it, into the warm beam. I lean against the window frame, looking out for the kids I'd seen, the ones playing ball.

Then I suck in sharply. Instead of the kids, I see Violet, walking up the street, back toward the house. *Shit.* I glance around the room, looking to see if anything is out of place. There's an indentation on her pillow from where I rested my head, creases on the duvet cover. I fluff the pillow, then run a hand over the covers.

When I'm sure everything is in its place, I exit their bedroom, jog down the hallway to the stairs, trying to keep my steps light. As my hand grabs the banister, I realize I'm still in Violet's robe. My throat constricts. I turn, run back down the hall into their bedroom as I wriggle out of it. I throw the closet door open and try to hook the robe back where I found it, but it won't catch.

I don't have time to waste, so I drop it and dash out, sprint down the hallway and down the stairs, two at a time.

I'm on the bottom step when the front door swings open, Violet appearing. I take a deep breath, try to control my breathing. "Hi," I say, forcing a smile on my face.

"Oh, hi," she says, looking up at me. "Everything okay?"

I step down, nodding, then bending over to put my shoes back on.

"I thought I heard Harper, so I went upstairs to listen. But she's quiet. It must have been a noise from the street."

"Thanks for checking," Violet says, smiling. "And for staying. I appreciate it."

"No problem." I shrug nonchalantly.

"I'm going to grab a seltzer. I'm parched. Want one?" she asks. "We could put on a movie. Harper should be asleep until three, at least."

I shake my head. "Actually, I forgot my mom has a doctor's appointment this afternoon. Do you mind if I head out early today?" My heart is still pounding.

"Of course not," she says.

Violet walks me to the door and waves goodbye from the stoop. I force myself to wave and smile back, fighting the urge to sprint down the sidewalk.

I keep my pace neutral, in case Violet is still watching, and by the end of the block, my breathing has returned to normal. *It's not a big deal*, I tell myself. *So I had a little look upstairs, a peek into her closet—what does it matter? We're friends.* I breathe out some of the tension I've been carrying, let my shoulders relax. *No big deal*, I repeat.

But I can't help thinking about the phone in her closet, what she might be hiding. *Who* she might be hiding.

And the box of hair dye on the counter.

On my way home, I make a brief stop into Duane Reade, the one on the corner with the flashing twenty-four-hour sign out front.

At the checkout counter, the bored, glazed-eyed teenager barely looks up as I set the box of hair dye—Dark Chestnut Brown—in front of him, along with a tube of acne cream, concealer, a palette of blush. My purchases mean nothing to him, but everything to me. It's a risk, but it's different this time, I know it is.

On the way home, I wonder how I'll look as a brunette. I tell myself that I haven't decided whether or not I'll go through with it, but it's not true. I know that I will.

The sincerest form of flattery is imitation, right?

17

That night, after dinner, my mom falls asleep with her plate in her lap, snoring quietly. Her chest rises and falls in slow, steady exhales. Careful not to wake her, I take the dish from her and set it quietly in the sink.

I don't want her to know what I'm going to do. She'd look at me with disappointment, shake her head. She wouldn't believe me that it's different this time. It doesn't seem different, but it is. It's not like the last time, with the box of red dye, dye so red it stained our towels. My relationship with Violet is different. Different, different, different. Even with the discovery of the burner phone, I feel like I know her better than I've known anyone for a long time. She'd tell me to do it; I know she would.

In the bathroom, I hold the box to my head, like I'd done at Violet's. It looks darker now than it did this afternoon, at least three or four shades darker than my current color. I hesitate, but only for a moment. Then I open it.

Thirty minutes later, I step into the shower to rinse the dye from my hair. It runs down my face, into the drain, black as ink. My heart beats excitedly. I did it. Steam rises around me as I imagine what I'll look like when I get out. When the water at my feet turns clear, I shut off the faucet and wrap a towel around my head like a turban.

Quickly, I put on my pajamas and return to the bathroom to unveil the color. The reveal is markedly underwhelming. My hair hangs in wet, stringy clumps. It's so dark it's almost black, especially stark against my pale complexion, nothing like Violet's soft, chocolatey color, warm and rich. It reads a little Wednesday Addams, which, of course, is not the look I was going for.

It's too long, I decide. It would look better if it was shorter, like Violet's. And it needs bangs.

Heartened, I reach into the drawer and take out a pair of scissors, then comb my hair until the front pieces cover my eyes. My hand is steady as I cut. The scissors close easily with a quiet snipping. Hair falls into the sink.

Then I gather it into two pigtails. Holding my breath, I cut about three inches off the first one. And the second. My hair lies in two big piles in the basin. I take out the rubber bands and wince. The right side is about a half inch shorter than the left. I cut a bit, then a bit more.

Finally, I put down the scissors. I stare at myself in the mirror. I want to cry. The length, as you might have guessed, was *not* the problem. Now, the color is wrong *and* the length is a mess. The bangs are jagged, too long, but I'm afraid to cut them any more and make it worse.

I should blow-dry it, but I don't. Dyeing it took longer than I expected and it's late, so instead, I run a brush through it and tie it in a loose low ponytail. Suddenly, I'm exhausted. Maybe it'll look better in the morning, when it's dry. Or it won't.

Defeated, I climb into bed and flip off the light.

As soon as I wake up, I go to the mirror. I cringe when I see myself.

My hair is frizzy and matted from sleep. Now that it's dry, it's even more obvious that I did a terrible job applying the color; my roots are much lighter than the ends, some patches more saturated than others. It's a shade or two too dark for my skin tone. I look pale as a ghost, my eyes rimmed purple from the late night like a tired raccoon. Like the girl from *The Ring*.

Sighing, I brush it into a high bun on top of my head. The bangs hang limply into my eyes. Truly fetching. I find a wide headband in the back of a drawer and put it on, pushing the strands out of my face. With the bangs out of the way, I put on a little makeup, use the brow liner Violet gave me, the concealer and blush from Duane Reade. When I'm done, I look marginally better, but not *good*. *Ugh*.

I walk out into the living room, then stop. My mom is in the kitchen, filling the coffee filter with grounds. I feel my stomach sink. I'm not ready for her to see my hair, to see what I've done. I consider darting back into the bathroom, waiting until she's retreated to her room, but before I can, she looks up.

Her eyes flick to my hair, then meet mine. She walks out of the kitchen, crossing the living room to where I'm standing. She sighs, her mouth set in a thin line. "Sloanie," she says, shaking her head. She's seen pictures of Violet; she knows what this is.

I bite my lip, working the soft tissue between my teeth. The room suddenly feels stuffy, the air thick. "It's different," I say, looking down at the ground.

And it is. The last time I dyed my hair, it ruined everything.

I wouldn't have made the same mistake again. I couldn't bear it if

Violet looked at me the way Allison did, slack-jawed, eyes rounded, horrified by the sight in front of her. Horrified by me.

I'll never forget the expression on Allison's face. I can see it so clearly, even now, as if it happened yesterday. I was in her apartment, cross-legged on the floor of their oversized master closet, my back to the door. It smelled like laundry detergent, a fresh, comforting smell that made you feel at home. In fact, I'd felt so at home, so caught up in the moment, that I hadn't heard Allison come in. But when I turned, she was in the doorway, hands on the frame as if bracing herself.

"What the fuck are you doing?" she asked, almost in wonder. Her voice sounded funny, warbled with confusion.

I didn't have a good answer. I just sat there wearing her dress, her shoes, her earrings, my freshly dyed hair gleaming.

"Your hair . . ." For a moment, she didn't say anything else. Then, "Those are my clothes."

"I just . . ." I began, but what could I say? I just *what*? "You're home early," I said finally. My voice was weak, pleading. I could see that she was angry, even though I hadn't meant any harm.

I adored her. I looked up to her. And I wanted to be just like her. Why couldn't she see it was flattery, nothing more?

Her eyes moved from me to the rest of the closet. All the drawers were ajar. I'd gone in to find a scarf, something to complete the outfit, but once I started looking, I couldn't stop, sinking to my knees as I combed through the contents, searching for I don't know what. One drawer, I discovered, had a cache of old photographs. They spanned years, some from college, Allison's face young and bright, her arms around friends, laughing, some of her and her husband when they'd first started dating, from their honeymoon, of him and her both naked, photos of her in lingerie. Now, the pictures lay around me, scattered like confetti. Her eyes landed on one of her in bed, dressed only in a pair of black panties. I felt my stomach turn.

She wasn't supposed to be home until Monday. No one was. They were spending a long weekend with her parents in Boston. The whole family was going to a Red Sox game that evening. I was there when she bought the tickets. *Should we sit here or here?* she asked me, pointing to the seats on her computer screen.

Her eyes returned to me. The color had drained from her cheeks.

I thought I might faint. I'd been so caught up, I hadn't even heard the front door open. Did I say that part already?

I'd come by to check on their cat, Nibbles. I was only there to refill her food, to make sure the water bowl was full. Allison offered me an extra hundred bucks on top of the coming week's pay if I stopped by, but I waved her off. I didn't have any plans; I was happy to help a friend out. Don't forget that—I thought we were *friends*.

I planned to leave as soon as I fed Nibbles. I just had to use the bathroom first. Normally, I'd use the one in the hall, but that day, I found myself walking into Allison's bedroom.

I stood in front of her sink when I was done, washing my hands, staring at myself in the large oval mirror. I looked almost like a different person, my hair shining, fiery red under the bathroom lights.

I'd dyed it only the day before. It wasn't something I planned, either. None of it had been planned. I know that sounds like I'm trying to buck responsibility, but it's the truth. We'd had an early release from school; it was the Friday before a holiday weekend—Labor Day, I think, which is why Allison and her family were traveling—so I decided to stop at the drugstore for a few things: shampoo, cotton balls, a replacement pair of tweezers for ones I'd misplaced.

On the way to the register, a box of hair dye caught my eye, a red-maned woman on the front. It wasn't the first time I'd wondered how I'd look as a redhead; looking at Allison, it was hard not to imagine what it would be like if you were the one with hair like hers, who you might be if you looked like that.

Casually, almost without thinking, I put the box into my basket. It wasn't the exact same shade as Allison's, but it was close. An hour later, I was toweling off my damp, newly dyed hair.

Seeing myself, I was pleased. Of course, the color wasn't as flattering on me as it was on her, but it looked good. And here's how stupid I was: I thought Allison would be tickled by it. *People will think we're sisters!* I imagined her saying, smiling at me. I repeat, how stupid I was.

Then, standing in Allison's bathroom, I saw a tube of mascara on the counter and thought, *I wonder how I'd look with a little makeup.* So I opened it. One thing led to another. I dabbed her perfume on my wrists, brushed my hair with her brush, slipped a pair of hoop earrings into my lobes. Before I knew it, I was stepping out of my jeans and into one of her dresses.

It was fun, pretending, for a moment, to be her, to feel what it was like to wear her clothes, her shoes, her jewelry. I'd meant nothing by it, really.

I wanted to tell her that, as she stood in the doorway staring, but I couldn't open my mouth. Not with the way she was looking at me. Then she spoke. "Get out. Get the fuck out." Her voice was strangled.

I rose clumsily from the floor, trembling, my movements jerky. As I started toward the door, still in her dress, her stilettos, I stepped on the swath of fabric swirling at my feet. I lurched forward. My arms shot out as I stumbled, reaching for something, anything, to steady myself. It was only by chance that I grabbed the marble jewelry stand atop her dresser. I took another step before regaining my balance, teetering in the pencil-thin heels, my arm outstretched, pointed at her.

Both Allison and I stared at the heavy weight in my hand. When she looked back up at me, there was fear in her eyes. My jaw dropped open. I shook my head. No, I would never. But then, for the briefest millisecond: if I did, she wouldn't be able to tell anyone about this, about what she thought I was doing in her closet.

No, I would never. I released my grip and the stand thudded to the floor, a heavy thunk against the soft carpet. Then I bolted, our shoulders brushing as I left the closet. I wondered if she could smell her perfume on me and thought I might be sick.

I went straight to my room when I got home. I locked the door—something I almost never did—and didn't answer my mom's knocking. When I finally opened it later that night, my mom wrapped her arms around me, holding me tightly. I told her everything.

The next morning felt brighter, more promising. It was a misunderstanding, my mother and I repeated to each other over breakfast. She reached across the small table in our kitchen and patted my hand. A simple misunderstanding. Although it wasn't, not exactly.

When I returned to work, the long weekend over, the school director was waiting for me outside my classroom. Her normally cheery face was grim. She glanced up at my dyed hair, then away as if she'd seen something she wished she hadn't. Nervously, I made a stupid joke, something dumb about the odds of running into each other like this, but she didn't smile. She'd gotten a substitute for me, she said, and could I please follow her? We walked down the hall, side by side. Neither of us said a word.

When we sat down, I tried to explain, but she held up a hand, shaking her head. She talked, but I barely heard her. She droned on and I tuned in every so often. She had no other choice, she said at one point, then, something about unacceptable behavior. Then, *effective immediately*. I looked up from the spot I'd been staring at on her desk. Her eyes wouldn't meet mine. I'd have the chance to say goodbye to my class, then I'd be escorted out.

This time, when we walked down the hall, I walked behind her, instead of next to her, shamefaced, trying not to cry. I'd worked there for six years. Six years and with one misunderstanding, it was over.

When I left the school, pushing through the heavy double doors, I thought that was the end, that that was the worst of it. I'd get a new job, I told myself. At a different school, in another borough. I was wrong, of course. The next day, two police officers knocked on our apartment door and charged me with stalking and menacing in the third degree.

At the station, they told me I could call a lawyer of my choosing or the court would appoint one to me. I ended up with the latter, as I couldn't afford anyone else, especially now that I no longer had a job. The first time I met with my attorney, it was in a shitty office building in midtown. He was young and his suit was ill-fitting—too big in the shoulders, pant cuffs that dragged on the floor—an overstuffed messenger bag slung over one shoulder. I thought he could help me. I thought he wanted to.

"I didn't break in," I insisted, before he had a chance to open his mouth, "she gave me a key. I was there to feed her cat. We were friends. I would never hurt her." And I wasn't lying to him. We were friends. Sometimes, if the kids were asleep when she got home, she'd uncork a bottle of wine and pour herself a glass at the kitchen counter, a tea for me, and we'd talk, about her day, about mine, our families, stories about growing up, some true, some not. Then, when it was late, she'd walk me to the door and give me a quick hug, tell me she'd see me the next day. We were *friends*.

My attorney listened wearily, nodding as I explained, but I don't think he heard me. His eyes were vacant, a half-lit neon motel sign, flickering every so often. He was overworked, I'm sure, buried by cases just like mine, overtired and underpaid. When I was done, he took a breath and told me he'd worked out a deal with Allison's lawyer, that I should take the plea. They agreed to drop the menacing charge if I pled guilty to stalking in the fourth degree, a misdemeanor. No jail time, but there would be an order of protection in place, of course, he said. Of course. Of course, tacked onto the sentence like it was the only thing that made sense. "An order of protection?" I repeated, voice hoarse, watery. He nodded. "It would prohibit all contact between you and Ms. McIntyre."

I asked to be excused to the bathroom and walked down the speckled linoleum hallway, my shoes squeaking, and threw up in the toilet. The retching echoed off the walls.

As soon as I sat back down, he repeated himself: I should take the plea. Employers can't ask about a criminal record during the hiring process, he said. It was a best-case scenario. If this went to court, I could face felony charges. "Take the plea," he said for the third time.

I looked at him, gaping like a stupid fucking fish. Had he already forgotten what I did for a living? I was a teacher. Any reputable school would run a background check. A misdemeanor would show up. Everything shows up. And no one would hire a teacher with a stalking charge, against a parent, no less. If I accepted the plea, it would be like tying a noose around my own neck, or at least, letting him tie it for me.

But in the end, that's what I did. What else could I have done?

Which was why I'd spent so long out of work, how I'd ended up as a nail tech instead of at the front of a classroom. Because of a box of hair dye. More or less.

So I know why my mom is looking at me the way she is. I'd be looking at me that way, too, if I didn't know any better. But my friendship with Violet is different.

"This is different," I repeat. There's a pleading note in my voice.

My mom doesn't say anything else. Gently, she puts her hand to my cheek, then nods and goes back to the kitchen.

My shoulders slump. I wish I could make her understand. I wish I could put into words how lonely I'd been before I met Violet. Allison and her kids were like my family. Mockingbird was my home. Without either, it felt like I was drowning.

I was finally coming up for air when I met Violet. There she was, like a life buoy, bobbing on the surface. I grabbed on and breathed in, my lungs full for the first time in months.

But the best part about Violet is that she needs me like I need her. She's told me so. Over and over again. Maybe I misread things with Allison, maybe I mistook courtesy for friendship, but I'm not wrong this time. I know I'm not.

I straighten and smile to myself. This time is different.

18

At a quarter to one, I'm standing on the Lockharts' stoop. The certainty I felt this morning that Violet would be flattered by my new hair color is quickly dissipating. What if she hates it? I put my hand on the doorknob—Violet told me to stop knocking weeks ago—then pull it back quickly.

I rock nervously from foot to foot. The fabric under my armpits is damp. The small of my back slick. The summer heat is making it hard to breathe.

Even though Violet isn't Allison—I reminded myself of this again and again on the walk over—now that I'm here, in front of her door, the thought of her seeing me like this churns my stomach. But what can I do? Leave? Call her and tell her I'm sick? Even if I did, there's no way I can get it back to my normal color without bleaching it, and that seems like an even stupider decision than the one I made last night. I believe this is called making your bed and having to lie in it. I just wish I'd known that the mattress would be so goddamn lumpy.

Fuck it, I think. *Rip the Band-Aid off.* I open the door and step inside, the air deliciously cool.

Violet is coming down the stairs as I walk in. "Oh!" she says when she sees me. She stops on the bottom step, staring. Her left hand grips the banister. There's a flicker of—something—across her face that I can't quite place. Not surprise, exactly, but her eyebrows rise, mouth slightly agape. Then she smiles, a wide grin.

"I needed a change," I say, smiling back tentatively, repeating what I'd told myself last night as I'd slipped on the gloves, mixed the dye into the accelerant.

"It looks good!" She steps into the foyer and ushers me into the living room. "Who'd have known you'd make such a dashing brunette!"

A rushing tidal wave of relief washes over me. She's not mad. I could cry.

I sink onto their couch, pull my knees up under me. "It's sort of patchy. I'm terrible at dyeing my own hair," I admit. "It never comes out well. But your color is just so nice, and I thought . . ." I trail off awkwardly. "It doesn't look as good on me as it does on you," I say finally.

"No, I think it looks nice," Violet says. "It suits you, it really does. Take your bun down, let me see."

I hesitate. Dyeing my hair the same color as hers is one thing; cutting it is another. "Come on," she urges.

Here goes nothing. I unclip my hair, letting it fall from the bun, then take off the headband, bangs flopping into my eyes.

She studies me carefully, her hand to her mouth, brow furrowed. She reaches out. Her fingers brush against my forehead as she straightens the bangs.

"It's a little uneven," I say, holding up one choppy strand.

"It looks . . . good," she says, unconvincingly. She presses her lips together. I raise an eyebrow skeptically.

Then, Violet starts to laugh. Not meanly, but in a good-natured sort of way. I start to laugh, too. Then we're both wheezing hysterically, tears streaming down our faces.

"Oh my god, I can't breathe," she says, holding her stomach.

"It's a disaster," I say, finally, when we've stopped laughing, wiping my cheeks with my shirt. "Like code red. Or code black. Whatever the bomb one is."

"It is," Violet agrees, still giggling. "Let me call my hairdresser," she says. "He's the best. I'll see if he can squeeze you in and fix it for you."

"Now? Where's Harper?" I look around, just realizing she isn't here.

She nods. "I meant to text you, she's at a playdate this afternoon. She won't be home for a few hours. It'll be fun! I could use a break." She motions to the kitchen. Textbooks and note cards are strewn across the island counter, her laptop open. "What do you think? Should I call him?"

I smile, nodding happily. I was right. She's not mad.

An hour later, I'm sitting in a salon chair, nylon barber's cape draped around my shoulders as Nolan, Violet's hairdresser, runs his fingers through my hair.

"So," he says, addressing me in the mirror. He's tall and lanky with a beautiful face, his brown skin bright and clear, sculpted cheekbones. His fingers snag in a tangle. "What are we doing today?"

"Do it like mine," Violet interjects. "Shoulder length, bangs. I think it would look good on her. We have a similar-shaped face, don't you think? And a little color correction. Like this." She puts her head close to my face and holds up a strand of her hair against mine. "Do you remember what shade you mixed for me last week?"

Nolan nods. "With the warm undertones. It'll be perfect for her."

Violet beams, silently clapping. I like how they're talking about me as if I'm not here, how Nolan's hands are absently tousling my hair as he listens to Violet.

I follow Nolan to a sink, where he leans my chair back and instructs me to close my eyes. A light mist of water tickles my face as he wets my hair with the spray nozzle. His fingers knead my scalp as he works the shampoo into a lather, rinses, then conditions. When he's done, he wraps my hair in a towel and points me to his chair.

Violet brings me magazines and we chat as he works, using a brush to paint the dye into my hair, section by section. I sit as it saturates, then follow him back to the sinks, where he rinses it out. When we get back to his chair, he turns me around, away from the mirror. "No peeking," he tells me, "not until I'm finished." He's serious as he works, brows knit as the scissors open and close, pieces of my hair floating to the floor.

Next to me, Violet grins. "It already looks so good," she crows, and I grin back.

When, finally, Nolan swivels the chair and I see myself in the mirror, I put my hand to my mouth, lean toward my reflection. I'm gone. At least, the me that walked in here two hours ago. Goodbye, Sloanie, Sloanie, full of baloney. He's fixed the color so it's a deep, rich brown, almost golden under the salon lights. It's as shiny as Violet's, glossy and smooth. I turn my head to the left, then the right. It's shorter, another inch gone, just brushing my shoulders, with bangs like hers, framing my face.

"Do you like it?" Nolan asks. He takes a hand and runs his fingers through my hair, shaking out the waves. "You look gorgeous."

I nod, speechless. Gingerly, I reach up and touch it. The strands are soft to the touch, silk-spun.

Violet bends down next to me, so her face is next to mine. "We look like twins!" she says excitedly.

She's right, we do look similar, now that our hair is the same color, the same length, with the same bangs falling into our eyes. Pleasure bubbles up in my stomach. I had no idea I could look like this. Like her.

With my shorter hair, my eyes seem bigger, cheekbones higher. Somehow, my skin looks better, too. I used the acne cream last night, spreading a thin film of it over my face before bed; the smattering of pimples on my chin has already gotten smaller. I can't stop staring. Or smiling. I wonder what Jay will think when he sees me.

Nolan walks us to the front of the salon. He gives both of us a hug goodbye. "Thank you," I keep saying to him, and he squeezes my hands before he leaves, smiling.

The receptionist, young and dewy-faced, smiles and asks how everything was. "Great," I say. "Really great." I reach into my purse, looking for my wallet. I brace myself for the bill.

"No, no," Violet says, pushing my hand away. "It's my treat."

I look at her in surprise. "What, no, you don't have to do that!"

"I know. I want to. It was my suggestion, so I'm paying."

As she takes her credit card out, handing it to the person behind the counter, something else comes out with it, flutters to the floor. It's a business card. Violet doesn't seem to notice, so I reach down to pick it up. When I see what it's for, my breath catches. Suddenly, I have trouble swallowing.

Is it—? Yes, it is. I lose feeling in my fingers. It's a card for Rose &
Honey. Why was it in Violet's wallet? Has she been in? The thought
gives me heart palpitations, makes me want to throw up. She hadn't
seen me there—*had she?*

When I look up, still crouching, both Violet and the receptionist
are staring down at me. "Are you okay?" Violet asks. Her forehead is
creased with worry.

My head bobbles up and down weakly. "Yeah, sorry. Here." I
stand, offering her the card. "This fell out of your purse." The words
stick in my throat like flies to a flytrap, their legs bonded to the gluey
paper. I sound froggish, voice thick.

"Oh, thanks," Violet says, taking it from me. She glances at it, then
tucks it back into her wallet.

"Have you been?" I hear myself ask in that same congealed voice.

"Where?" Her brow wrinkles.

"To that spa. On the card . . ." I can't bring myself to say the name.

"Oh, no," she says, shaking her head. "Not yet. Have you? One of
the moms at Harper's school recommended it to me." Her face is open,
innocent.

She hasn't been in. I breathe out. She hasn't been in. But—someone
else from Mockingbird has. Maybe the same person who recommended
it to Allison. Maybe that's why she made an appointment. But who? I
would have recognized any of the mothers had they been in, especially
if they came in often enough to recommend it.

"Are you sure you're okay?" Violet asks. "You're looking a little
green."

"Oh yeah, I'm fine." I shake my head. "Maybe it's just the fumes
from the hair dye. I do feel a little high," I say, trying to sound like
I'm not on the verge of a meltdown. "And it's been a long time since I

was stoned at three in the afternoon. Not since college." I force a little laugh.

Violet laughs, too, then she links her arm through mine. "Then let's get out of here. Maybe we should go shopping! A new outfit to go with your new hair." She starts to steer me toward the door.

I smile back. I want to, I really do, but seeing that card has left me uneasy, the floor quaking beneath my feet. I want to reach out, steady myself. It's stupid what I'm doing. I forgot how small this neighborhood is, how routine to cross paths with people you know. I often ran into the parents of my students on the weekend, at the market, restaurant patios, on the sidewalk. Someone could see us together, someone from Mockingbird. It hadn't occurred to me until now. If they did, my cover would be blown. This life I've built would crumble. I have to be more careful. I should go home.

"Violet, I—" I start to say, but stop, catching sight of the two of us in a mirror on the salon wall.

The resemblance is uncanny. We look so much alike. Like twins, just like Violet said. Our matching sunburst necklaces catch the light, glint. Maybe, I think, the idea of us being sisters really isn't that far-fetched. Stranger things have happened. Just last week I read an article about triplet brothers, separated at birth, who ended up at the same college.

"You know what," Violet says. "I have an even better idea. Come back to my house instead. I have a few things that I think will fit you perfectly. I won't take no for an answer."

I look from the mirror to Violet, her face open and eager, as familiar to me as my own. I smile back. If anyone from Mockingbird sees me, they'll have no idea who I am. "Okay," I say. "Let's go."

Sloanie, Sloanie, full of baloney is gone.

VIOLET

19

The look on Sloane's face when she sees the Rose & Honey business card is priceless. I think she may keel over. I bite the inside of my lip to keep from smirking. I thought it was a nice touch, pretending to drop it like that, letting it flutter to the ground, seemingly unnoticed. I purposefully ignored it, waiting for her to stoop down and pick it up.

She is pale, queasy-looking, as she hands it back to me. Her face is a chartreuse color, a sickly green.

"Are you okay?" I ask, hoping to sound concerned. I am, actually; it looks like she might vomit on the floor.

Sloane nods unconvincingly, head wobbling. Her face isn't hard to read. She's wondering if I've ever been to the place she used to work—and the answer is yes, I have.

"I'm fine," she says. "Maybe it's just the fumes from the hair dye. I do feel a little high." She gives a little laugh, more high-pitched than normal. "It's been a while since I was stoned at three in the afternoon. Not since college."

I laugh like she's made an incredibly clever joke. "Well then, let's get out of here," I say brightly. "Maybe we should go shopping! A new outfit to go with your new hair?" I link my arm through hers, begin pulling her toward the front door.

She smiles back at me weakly. She's unnerved. Good. But I can't let her go home. Not yet. Her makeover isn't done. When I'm finished with her, she'll look more like me than I do.

"Violet, I—" She starts to protest, but she stops, seeing our side-by-side reflection in a mirror on the wall. Gemini twins, our faces almost interchangeable. We both smile, pleased. For different reasons, obviously.

"You know what," I say. "I have an even better idea. Come back to my house instead. I have a few things that I think will fit you perfectly. I won't take no for an answer."

And I don't. Thirty minutes later, we're standing in my bedroom, Sloane in a crocheted Carolina Herrera tank, admiring herself in the full-length closet mirror as I lean against the doorframe. With her new haircut, it's almost as if I'm looking at myself. It makes me want to dance, leap up and click my heels together. Look what I did, Ma!

"I can't accept this," Sloane says, her eyes not leaving the mirror.

"Well, how about if I trade you," I offer. "The top for your flannel." I motion to the shirt tied around her waist, even though it's pushing ninety today. It should have been tossed in the garbage years ago, worn and faded, frayed at the cuffs, but she wears it everywhere—and I want it.

Sloane raises her eyebrows. "You want *this*?" she asks incredulously, holding up an arm of the shirt. "In exchange for Carolina Herrera?"

I laugh. It *is* an absurd trade, if you didn't know why I wanted it. "I have two others just like it. But no flannel. What can I say, I like your style. So is that a yes?"

"*Obviously.*" She unties it and hands it to me.

I take it from her, surprised at how easy this is, then motion around my closet. "Is there anything else you like? I have too many clothes. Way too many. I've actually been meaning to do a purge." Sloane looks at me skeptically. "Come on, a new pair of jeans, maybe?" I say teasingly, pointing to the gaping holes in the knees of hers.

"What's wrong with these?" Sloane jokes. "Jeans from two thousand five must be considered vintage, right? I thought holes were in!"

"Eh," I wheedle. "Holes are in, caverns are not. Plus, they're a little big on you." I cock my head. "Have you lost weight? You look great. Despite the pants."

Sloane blushes, oblivious that she has me to thank for it. When we met, she was a little heavier than I was; not by much, ten or fifteen pounds, maybe. To close the gap, I started increasing my portions, but I also invited her on as many walks as I could, briskly setting the pace, asked her to piggyback Harper around the park, introduced her to yoga. It's worked. I've noticed most of her pants have been a little looser, sagging around the waist, in the thighs. Her already-too-big T-shirts have become baggier, so I haven't quite been able to tell how much weight she's lost—until now.

"Here." I reach into my closet and hand her a pair of dark denim. "Try these on. And this . . ." I turn around, grab a high-necked Trina Turk blouse off the rack, shove it into her hands.

Sloane spends the next hour wriggling in and out of my clothing. I clap excitedly when something fits as she poses for me in the mirror. There's a growing stack of shirts, dresses, and pants that I've insisted are now hers. I'm glad to see them go; they're beautiful and expensive, what I should want to wear, what I look good in, but none of it is me. I hate all of it. I'd like to put a match to the whole closet, but if I can't, giving it to Sloane is the second-best thing.

When she finally leaves, it's in an entirely new outfit—fitted, high-waisted jeans and the Carolina Hererra she first tried on. She's also carrying a full shopping bag of clothes, stuffed to the brim. At my insistence, the clothes she arrived in are folded in a pile on top of my dresser. I offered to donate them along with a bag of things Harper has outgrown later this week. It wasn't anything special, just a thread-bare T-shirt and old jeans, worn-out from too many wears, but she'd hesitated when she'd handed them over. Then she let go. We both had smiled at her reluctance, then at her concession. What she doesn't know is that instead of donating them, I'll put the pile in my dresser.

I watch as she disappears down the sidewalk. From behind, you wouldn't know that she wasn't me. When she's out of sight, I ease the door shut and check the time. Four thirty. Harper won't be home until six. And Jay is on a work trip; he isn't coming home until tomorrow. Although never would be too soon.

I cross the living room into the kitchen and grab a step stool to reach the cupboard above the fridge, carefully taking out a bottle of Grey Goose from behind some extra paper towel rolls. I pour it over ice, the cubes cracking as the glass fills, then top it off with a squeeze of lemon.

I take the drink back into the living room and settle onto the couch. The vodka is cold and smooth. I smile. This whole thing is almost funny, Sloane and I lying to each other. She doesn't drink? Oh my god, neither do I! Her dad is from Philly? What a coincidence, mine, too! Big Taylor Swift fan? Well, come on, who isn't?

This whole time she thought she lied her way into our lives, but the truth is, I lied my way into hers.

Here's what happened. A year ago, when I was walking Harper into Mockingbird one morning, I overheard a group of moms gossiping in the schoolyard. We were still new to the preschool, Harper and I, both of us hesitant at drop-off, me smiling awkwardly at the other parents, her tightly holding my hand as we approached the play yard. We looked like we belonged—me in a Marni midi, Harper in a Pepa London pinafore, both gifts from Jay—but we didn't, not yet.

"I still can't believe it," one of the moms was saying vehemently—and loudly—"she was in my apartment. In my clothes." A redheaded woman stood in a small circle of wide-eyed mothers, her voice carrying across the blacktop. She had sharp, fine features, porcelain skin. Her arms were wrapped around herself, hugging tightly.

She looked up as she said this last bit, about someone being in her clothes, and our eyes connected. The other women turned, too, saw me staring.

"A former teacher," she said, raising her voice slightly as an invitation for me to join the conversation. I took a step closer to the circle. Then to Harper, I motioned, *go play, darling*. The women parted, opening themselves to me. "I'm Allison," the redhead said, touching her hand to her chest lightly. One by one, the other mothers introduced themselves as well, offering their hands in delicate handshakes. "Violet," I said, over and over again, smiling politely at each woman.

They were desperate to share the story with someone new, all of them, about how, a few months ago, one of the preschool teachers had become obsessed with Allison. She had found her one evening in her closet, dressed in one of her formal dresses—a Jason Wu, if you can believe—her hair dyed the same shade of auburn as Allison's. Allison shuddered at the retelling. "I let her watch my *children*," she said, shaking her head. All of the other moms tsked, murmuring unintelligible noises of dismay.

"It was so unsettling. I think she wanted to *be* me," Allison said in a low, hushed voice.

I stifled a laugh at the melodramatic delivery. It sounded like an overreaction. It made me think of when I babysat for my next-door neighbors when I was in high school. When the kids were asleep, I'd sneak into the parents' room and experiment with the mom's makeup, try on her expensive jewelry, diamond earrings, emerald rings. I'd thought it was something everyone did when they were alone in some-one else's house. But I'd been fourteen, not a teacher at a preschool. So I arranged my face in an expression of distaste and mimicked the con-cerned sounds of the other mothers.

I didn't think of the teacher until a few months later, after the night my world exploded, shrapnel flying, leaving me pulverized and desperate, when I was lying in bed at three in the morning, moonlight streaming through our bedroom window. Jay was down the hall in his office. I could hear his snores through the walls. I wasn't sleeping at all. How could I, rage in my heart and in my bones?

Allison's words rang in my head. *I think she wanted to be me.* I imagined the teacher as a younger version of Allison, clear, pale skin, waify, her long hair dyed a shocking red. Maybe she'd gotten bored one night, decided to play dress-up; the hair could have been a co-incidence. Or maybe Allison was right. Maybe she'd crossed a line, admiration turning into something else. Something darker. It gave me an idea. A late-night, pitch-black idea.

I picked up my phone and started sifting through archived news-letters on Mockingbird's website. I found what I was looking for quickly: an article announcing a new preschool teacher, starting mid-year. The last line read: *Former teacher Sloane Caraway will not be return-ing.* I googled Sloane Caraway and found her picture easily. She looked nothing like Allison: light brown hair, a heart-shaped face, a strong nose, not unlike my own. Not particularly pretty, but not unpretty, either.

I stared at her face on my phone, the tint of the screen lighting up the room. She looked so *ordinary*. I wanted to know more. It didn't take me long to discover she was working in a day spa in the next borough over, her picture on the *About Us* section of the spa's website. From there, I found her Instagram, her TikTok. When I finally fell asleep, I was still scrolling through her pictures, my phone lying on my chest when I woke the next morning.

After I dropped Harper off at school, I found myself heading in the direction of the spa. I slowed as I neared. Instead of continuing past, I stopped, peering through the large front glass window. Past the reception desk I could see a row of pedicure chairs against the left-hand wall. And there she was, in the flesh, bent over someone's feet, carefully applying polish to each nail.

Finally, she looked up, over at the manicurist next to her, her whole face visible. I almost snorted thinking about Allison's claim. They couldn't look less alike. But—I realized with pleasure—even though she didn't look like Allison, she *did* look a little like me. A similar profile, the same color complexion, though hers flecked with acne. My hair was darker than hers, and she was a little heavier than me, wore glasses, but the resemblance was there. My fury-fueled idea might work.

Then I shook my head, turned, and started back toward our brownstone. *No, it's crazy*, I thought as I walked away, *it would never work*, but then, in the next moment—*Maybe it could.*

I returned to the spa the next day, and the next. The day after that I followed her home. I followed her everywhere until I knew her schedule, when she took her breaks, the little corner park where she took them, the patch of grass where she lay down and opened her books.

And then, on a whim, I sent Jay to the same park with Harper, telling him it was her new favorite, hoping Sloane would be there, hoping she'd notice him. It wasn't a stretch; everyone notices Jay. If I was lucky, she'd find a way to talk to him. Women often do, especially since he no longer wears his wedding ring. And Jay always welcomes the attention; he isn't particularly discerning. If Sloane approached him, he'd engage, his ego pulsing, ready for stroking.

If a chance run-in with Jay didn't happen, I planned on taking Harper to the park the next week and finding a reason to introduce myself, accidentally bumping into her while playing tag with Harper or tripping over one of her shoes, which she always left kicked off beside her in the grass, but I thought Jay was clever bait. At the least, he'd catch her eye. Then I could say, *You might have seen my husband here? He's tall, dark hair?* Her eyes would light up, and suddenly, I'd be interesting to her. And that's all I needed.

I'd followed Jay and Harper to the park, settled onto a corner bench, my hair tied under a scarf with big *Breakfast at Tiffany's* glasses on in case anyone looked my way. Sloane was where she always was: on the grass, reading a book. When I saw her glancing around, her eyes landing on Jay, I grinned to myself. When she didn't speak to him, I gave Harper a handful of M&M'S to ask Jay to take her back the following day, and the next. Instead of reading her book, Sloane watched them while I watched her.

I was there, too, when Harper stepped on the bee. I didn't know exactly what happened, only that she started screaming. It took everything in me not to rush over and scoop her up. I might have, too, if

Sloane hadn't reached her first. As soon as Harper stopped crying, I went home. I wanted to be there when they got back, eager to hear about the interaction.

"I got stung!" Harper announced as soon as she'd walked through the front door. She raised her foot in the air to show me. I pulled her into my lap, carefully examined the welt, then kissed it until Harper dissolved into giggles. "Want a Band-Aid, baby?" I asked. "I got new Minnie ones."

"A nurse helped us," Jay said to me as I stood up, Harper still in my arms.

"A nurse?" I'd looked at him, puzzled. Had Sloane told him she was a nurse? I must have sounded funny because Jay gave me a strange look. "I mean, how did you find a nurse?" I said quickly. "That was lucky."

He shrugged. "She said her name was Caitlin. She was nice."

What a liar, I thought. And that's when I decided my plan might actually work.

"I'll look for her the next time we go," I said. "So I can thank her for helping out." And the rest is history, as they say.

I drain my glass, feeling the alcohol spread through me. I smile. I've been waiting a long time for this day, Sloane in my clothes, my makeup, my haircut and color. Sloane as me. I debate pouring another drink to celebrate, but I decide against it. It's not worth the risk. Instead, I take my glass into the kitchen, wash and dry it, put it back into the cabinet where I found it. Me, drink? Never!

20

The next afternoon, when I open the front door and see Sloane on the stoop, I smile broadly. It's like I'm looking into a mirror. She looks so different from how she looked just a few days ago.

She's wearing some of the new clothes I gave her yesterday, a pair of dark jeans and cream-colored tank, and makeup again, too. But it's not only the new haircut, the clothes, the mascara and blush. She's standing up taller, shoulders back. Tits out, the minx, a newfound confidence about her.

Sloane pauses before stepping inside, her head cocked slightly, studying me. I'm dressed more casually than she's used to seeing me, in joggers and a workout tank, my hair unwashed, tied up in a high bun, my bangs clipped up. It's not a complete transformation—I still have some makeup on, my clothes still name-brand, well fitting—but it's a start.

Because here's the other piece of the puzzle: I don't just want Sloane to look like me. I want to look like her, too.

"Look at you!" I say. "I almost didn't recognize you! You look gorgeous in that shirt. Jay's going to be mad—it's his favorite!" It's a silk camisole, a gift he gave me soon after Harper was born. His favorite, but never mine—uncomfortable, impractical. I was more than happy to offload it.

Sloane blushes. "Thanks to you. I was precariously close to shaving my head when I looked in the mirror yesterday morning. And I'm certain that would have been an even bigger mistake. Huge."

I wave my hands dismissively like it had been no trouble at all. In truth, I promised Nolan five hundred dollars on top of the price of a cut and color if he made himself available when I called. I left the store-bought box of dye on my counter, hoping it would get her gears turning, which, to my pleasure, it did.

"Come in, come in." I usher Sloane inside, motioning for her to follow me into the kitchen. "I just made a fresh pot of coffee—want a cup? An afternoon pick-me-up? I know Thursdays are long."

On Thursdays, Sloane picks Harper up from gymnastics, shuttles her to swim, then takes her to the park so I have a few extra hours of "studying." Usually I go home, spread out the law books I ordered, then turn on a podcast. *Crime Junkie* or *My Favorite Murder*, you know, for inspiration. Today, I asked her to come to the house under the guise of having forgotten to pack Harper's swimsuit. In truth, there's something I need to ask her. Something important.

Sloane nods and takes a seat at the counter, setting her bag on the bar stool beside her. "Hey," she says. "Has Harper ever been to Coney Island? I loved it there when I was younger. I'd love to take her!" Then her brow furrows. "Can she go on roller coasters, with her heart?"

I nod. "Actually, we took her last year and she had a blast. No problems on the roller coasters at all!"

That's because her heart is, in fact, completely fine. It always has been. We had a scare when she was a baby—the doctor thought he heard an irregular heartbeat—but the echocardiogram was clear. But when Sloane told Jay that she was a nurse, well, I just couldn't help myself. It was the perfect excuse to offer her the nanny position.

"Great!" Sloane says. "Maybe we can go again? Harper has all of August off from school, right? Isn't her last day a week from Friday? We can go next weekend!"

I feel my heartbeat accelerate. Here it is. The opening I was hoping for.

"That sounds so fun!" I say, setting a mug of coffee down in front of her. "But . . ." *Gently, Violet, take your time. Play it right, go slow.* ". . . we're not going to be here that weekend. Or the weekend after that, actually."

"Oh?" Sloane's face falls, the corners of her mouth turning down. She looks like she's been punched in the gut. Just the reaction I was hoping for. "Where are you going?" she asks bleakly.

"Up north, off the coast of Rhode Island. A little town called Block Island—tiny, only like a thousand people, but beautiful. We spent a weekend there last summer when we first moved and I've been dying to go back. It'll be our last vacation before Harper starts kindergarten." I sigh dramatically. "I can't believe I'm going to have a *five-year-old*."

Sloane forces a smile on her face. "It sounds fun," she manages. "Maybe we can do Coney Island when you guys get back."

"Well, I'm glad you think so," I say, smiling. "Because I've been meaning to ask you . . ." I pause for dramatic effect. *Get ready.* ". . . if you wanted to come with us."

"Come with you?" Sloane echoes. Her eyes widen, round as saucers.

I nod enthusiastically. "It's a big house, three bedrooms, so you wouldn't have to shack up with Harper." When she doesn't reply, I add, "Ocean views! And only a two-minute walk to the beach. What do you think? We could all use a vacation!"

I hold my breath, waiting, hoping I don't sound too eager.

Sloane swallows hard. "I'd love that, but . . ." She shifts uncomfortably in her chair. My breath catches. Is she going to say no? "I'm not sure I can afford it."

Oh, that's all? I relax. I upped her hours when I found out she'd been fired, wanting to weave her into our family as best I could. That had been my intention when I'd given Allison the Rose & Honey card, telling her I'd found the *best* manicurist. "The cutest little place, too—you *have* to go," I'd said. "On Mondays, that's when she's there." I'd hoped there would be a scene—shrieking, maybe. Allison seemed like the shrieking type. When I called the spa later that week, pretending I wanted to schedule an appointment with Sloane, I was pleased to hear: "I'm so sorry, she's no longer with us." I hung up thrilled; it left her free to become our full-time nanny, available to join us on the trip to Block Island.

I dropped the card at the hair salon yesterday as another provocation. *Look how easily you could be found out,* I wanted to remind her. *Here, people know you. They know you're Sloane, not Caitlin. As long as you are in Brooklyn, there is a chance I'll discover that, too.* But I didn't think it would take much convincing. The summer heat alone was enough to drive anyone out, steam practically rising from the sidewalks, the city and everyone in it baking.

I shake my head. "Oh, I'd pay you!" I say, smiling apologetically. "Sorry I didn't make that clear. I mean, you'd be our guest, of course, but I'd still need your help with Harper. Same rate! Jay is going to have to work while we're there, so it would be great to have an extra set of hands. And—"

Sloane lights up. "Then yes!" she says, not waiting for me to finish. "I'd love to!" She's grinning broadly.

"Really? Oh, I'm so glad!" She has no idea how glad. My body is vibrating with an electric energy. It's happening.

"Jay will be glad, too," I say, knowing how happy this will make her. "He's the one who suggested it, actually. He knows how much help you've been lately, and when I told him how much I'd miss you when we were gone, he said I should invite you. That it would be silly not to."

Sloane's cheeks redden at his name. She's smitten. She thinks she's discreet, I'm sure, but it's written all over her face. It doesn't bother me, though. It makes it easier. I want her to want him. In fact, I need her to. It's also why I've told her about Danny, ease her guilt by pulling back the curtain to show her the cracks in our deteriorating marriage. If you can even call it that anymore. The word in my mouth makes me want to retch.

Of course, Jay *hadn't* suggested inviting Sloane. He was apprehensive about the whole trip. In fact, convincing him to go was one of the hardest parts of my plan.

I brought it up last week as he was eating breakfast with Harper, both of them distractedly spooning cereal into their mouths, Jay on his phone, Harper staring at the comic strip on the back of the box. "Let's take a trip," I said casually. He looked up at me, confused. "Back to Block Island." I offered him a smile.

He had cocked his head, eyed me suspiciously. "Together?" he asked. A few months earlier, shortly after Sloane came into our lives, I told him I wanted to work on things. He agreed, but he was wary. He was right to be. In fact, if he knew how hard it was for me to even look at him, how the mere thought of him made me seethe, he would have been terrified.

I nodded. Then I bit my lip, softened my face, and smiled, hoping to look a little nostalgic. "I think Harper would love it," I said. "We had so much fun last time." *Well, you did, prick.* Jay always has fun. He can't seem to help himself. At least, that's the excuse he gives.

Then I said, louder, "Harpie, do you want to go to the beach with me and Daddy?"

It was a cheap trick, and I knew it. So did Jay, his mouth set in a thin line as Harper swiveled to look at me, her spoon suspended in midair, an expression of pure excitement on her face.

"Come on, Jay, what do you say? You loved Block Island."

We spent a long weekend there shortly after we moved to New York. Harper was almost four at the time, Jay and I optimistic about our future, hopeful that we'd left the hardest days, the fighting, the arguing, behind us in San Francisco. We spent every day on a beach blanket, Harper digging in the sand at our feet, strolling through the little town when we got hungry in search of lobster rolls and hand-churned ice cream, sunburnt and happy.

It was Jay's first time to the island, but it wasn't mine. Far from it. I'd spent every summer growing up there, from the week after school let out in June to the last weekend in August, in my grandmother's vacation home. She'd spent her summers as a girl there, too, then after she retired and my grandfather died, she moved there permanently.

At first, we went as a family, but as I got older, my parents would fly me out, stay a week or so, then fly back to San Francisco, which was fine by me. *Don't let the door hit you on the way out,* I wanted to call after them as they rolled their suitcases down the pathway to their town car. I was happy to see them go, happy to stay. I loved it there. I loved it so much that in my senior year of high school, I moved in, unpacking my things into the dresser in my grandmother's spare room. It felt like more of a home than I'd ever had before.

I adored my grandmother. She wasn't one of those older women with a stiff perm and even stiffer upper lip. Unlike my parents, she didn't care if my T-shirts were Popsicle-stained or if I never used a brush, if my skin was sticky from sunscreen. Her shirts were stained, too, hair also wild. She wore cutoff jean shorts and went barefoot. She sailed, shucked oysters, laughed with her mouth wide open. We were equals from the start, partners in our island adventures. With her, I could be myself, and she loved me for it.

We'd start our mornings on the front porch with a coffee, mine mostly milk and sugar, flipping through the paper, then bike into town to pick up groceries for that night's dinner. During the day we swam in the ocean, searched for shells in the sand, read on beach towels. I told her everything, about my life at home, about what I wanted to be when I grew up, how I really felt when Caroline, who I thought was my best friend, didn't invite me to her birthday party, even though I pretended not to care.

She was the first person I told when Danny kissed me. I'd had a crush on him since the first day I set foot on Block Island. We'd met when we were six, on the beach in front of my grandmother's house.

"Want to help me build a castle?" he had asked. He had these bright amber eyes, a mop of curly hair to match, a dusting of freckles on his nose, and, even then, this deep, melodic voice that made anything he said sound like a serenade. I'd waited ten long years for him to kiss me. Ten years that we'd chased each other around the island, fished in his boat, snuck out to swim in the dark, that we'd jumped on my bed singing Prince songs at the top of our lungs, *I would / die for / you / yeah / darlin' if you want me to!* He knew me better than I knew myself. The real me, not the me I had to pretend to be for my parents, always prim and smiling, never a hair out of place.

Danny was one of a handful of true locals whose family lived on the island year-round. His dad was a doctor, his mom a waitress in his aunt's restaurant. They weren't wealthy, and even though they did well, it wasn't enough to keep my parents from looking down their noses at Danny, telling me I could—and should—do better. But no one was better than Danny; no one had a heart like he did.

Then, a few weeks after our first kiss, just after my sixteenth birthday, he told me we couldn't be together anymore. He'd met someone else. My grandmother wiped my tears. "It'll all make sense one day," she whispered into my ear, and she was right. She'd seen the bigger picture, she always did. She was everyone's lifeline, her hand always outstretched to lift you up, pull you out of the depths of whatever murky water you were flailing in.

I was a freshman in college when she died, suddenly, of a heart attack, only a few weeks before I was supposed to fly to the island for Christmas. My mom called me at six in the morning on a Sunday with the news. It was the first time I'd heard from my mother in months. I was bleary-eyed, confused, last night's mascara still gluey on my lashes, then, when it sunk in, devastated. I wrote a speech for the funeral, but I never read it; I was crying too hard to speak. Jay and I had just started dating, and he sat beside me on a pew, his arm around my shoulder.

When Jay and I took Harper to Block Island last May, it was the first time I'd been back since I was eighteen. My heart ached when we disembarked from the ferry. It felt like coming home. The island was more crowded than it had been when I'd left—more tourists, new hotels and houses dotting the coastline—but it smelled the same, like hand-pulled saltwater taffy, had the same dreamlike quality to it that it always had, its edges soft and hazy.

On the way to our rental, I asked Jay to drive by where my grandmother's bungalow had been. I frowned, confused when I didn't see it, only to realize that the lot had been bulldozed, a modern three-story monstrosity built in its place. I was surprised, but more than surprised, I was angry. What kind of person would tear down a historic landmark? I wanted to take a bat to the floor-to-ceiling glass windows, drag its occupants out by their hair. *This land doesn't belong to you*, I'd yell. But I sat in the passenger seat quietly, my nails digging into my palms. Jay didn't notice a thing.

I'd thought that I would recognize everyone, that everyone would recognize me, but for the most part, I was anonymous, another tourist, another New Yorker passing through. I turned heads in my Missoni cover-up, high-cut bikini bottoms, but it wasn't because anyone knew who I was. It had been too many years, the ties that I'd had long faded.

On our last afternoon, I snuck out to browse in the little boutiques while Harper napped, stopping for a glass of wine at a sidewalk café before I went home. The waitress was in her fifties or sixties, with graying hair and an open, pleasant face. "Violet?" she'd asked, studying me. "Rebecca's granddaughter?"

I'd nodded and then realized it was Danny's aunt, his mom's youngest sister. We hugged and she told me how sorry she was about my grandmother's passing. "Wait until Danny hears I saw you," she said. "He's always had a soft spot for you." I hadn't spoken to him since my grandmother's funeral over ten years ago; I'd closed that part of my life, of myself. I'd packed her away, hidden her under clothes that weren't my style, a life I barely recognized. I'd thought I had to. I'd thought that's how I made people love me. In fact, Harper was the only glimmer of who I'd been on the island: her giddiness, giggles, wild curls a vestige of the old me.

But now, I needed to go back again. It was the only place that made sense. So I put on an amiable face, smiled at Jay. "Come on," I had said. "Remember the lobster rolls?"

"I'll think about it," Jay answered. But he agreed, finally, after I asked again, this time in the dark, under the covers, his hand between my legs. I bit down on the inside of my cheek so hard it bled, but I needed him to remember how things used to be, how things could be again, maybe, if he said yes. I squeezed my eyes shut as he touched me, pretending I was somewhere—anywhere—else.

Now, to Sloane, I say, "Harper is going to be so excited when I tell her. She loves you, you know."

Sloane smiles broadly, flattered. "I happen to adore her, too."

I believe her. I was hesitant, at first, to leave Harper alone with Sloane, busying myself with the laundry while they played in the next room, making excuses to join them at the park, but the more I watched them together, the clearer it became how much Sloane enjoyed spending time with Harper, how good she was with her. Little things like squatting down to Harper's level when they talked, making up silly songs when Harper's on the verge of throwing a fit, assembling snacks to look like animals—pretzel butterflies and peanut butter toast in the shape of a cat, sliced strawberries for the ears. It's one of the things that endears her to me. Funnily, I don't hate her. You'd think I would, given what I'm planning to do, but I don't. In some ways, I'm grateful. She's a means to an end. The answer to a problem. And she makes me laugh.

"Then it's settled!" I say. "You're coming. The only thing I need from you is your driver's license. For the ticket."

Sloane's face changes, paling. "My driver's license?" she squeaks. For a minute, I'm confused, but then I remember. It has her real name on it. She doesn't want me to see it.

I nod. "Yeah, it's some new security requirement for the ferry. And I'll add you to the rental car reservation, in case you want to take Harper anywhere."

Sloane's throat moves as she swallows hard. "Sure," she says slowly. "No problem." She opens her purse and begins to rifle through it. She looks back up, furrowing her brow, in faux surprise. "It's not in here. I must have left it at home. Can I swing it by tomorrow?"

"Of course," I say. I can't wait to hear the lie she comes up with when she hands it to me.

After Sloane leaves to get Harper, I take my laptop to the kitchen counter, then pour a full glass of wine. As I sit down on a bar stool, my inbox dings. It's the travel agent I've been working with. I click into the email excitedly.

Good news, it reads. *Call me.*

I grin, picking up my phone.

I'd spent hours in the weeks before on the phone with various travel agents making sure we were in a house next to another young family with kids. Many of the rental companies wouldn't give me any information about other occupants, but eventually I found Gina, who was more than willing to help, once she learned about the commission she'd earn on the booking, given that I was happy to pay a premium for whatever rental she found for me. Money, I've known for a long time, will motivate people to do almost anything.

"I found the perfect house," Gina says when she answers. "There will be a family next door the whole time you're there, two kids, four and six. Three bedrooms, just like you asked. Across the street from the beach. It just popped up, thanks to a last minute cancellation. It's a little more expensive than—"

"Let's book it," I say. I don't care about the price.

There's the sound of a keyboard clicking on the other end of the line. "Done!" Gina announces.

I hang up, take a long, celebratory sip of my wine. It's happening.

21

The next morning, when I get back from dropping Harper off at school, I get a text from Sloane: *When should I drop the license by?*

Now? I write back. *If you're free.* The sooner I get it, the better.

Thirty minutes later, I open the door for her. She doesn't look good. Her hair is still glossy, skin clear, but her eyes are bloodshot, purple-rimmed, and bagged as if she hasn't slept. She probably hasn't, worried about how she was going to explain that the name on the license wasn't the one she'd told me, worried I might recognize it.

"Come on in," I say. "Want a coffee?" It's clear she needs one.

But she shakes her head no. She reaches into her back pocket and hands me her license. "Here," she says, almost shoving it into my hand.

"Thanks." I glance down at it. When I see the photo, I forget about the name discrepancy. Her picture is hysterically bad. Her mouth is half-open as if she's about to speak, lips sort of pursed, teeth showing. She's combed her hair into a bun on top of her head, but it's flopped to one side and she's missed a piece near the front. She looks pale,

COUNT MY LIES

really pale, likely an effect of the harsh DMV lighting, but startling nonetheless, and one eye appears much smaller than the other. On the whole, it's one of the worst driver's licenses I've seen.

I choke back a laugh. "Wow!" I say. "Just wow!"

"What?" Sloane says. She sounds on the verge of panic.

I angle the license toward her, tapping my finger on the photo. She cringes. "Oh god. I forgot how bad it is. I've trained myself never to look at it lest I drop dead of embarrassment. I look like an extra from *The Walking Dead*. More brains, please." She rolls her eyes into the back of her head, sticks her tongue out.

I snort. Like I said, she makes me laugh. Then I look back down. "Oh," I say, pretending to have just noticed something. "Your name, it says . . ." I look up at her quizzically.

"Oh, right." Sloane makes a noise that I think is supposed to be a chuckle. "I was a weird kid."

I cock my head, not sure where she's going with this.

She rolls her eyes. "For some reason, I told everyone to call me Caitlin when I was little. I thought it was pretty, I guess. And it stuck. Obviously." She lets out a high-pitched giggle, rubs at the back of her neck. "Like I said, I was weird." The corner of her mouth twitches as she gnaws on the inside of her lip. These are her tells: a hand to her neck, a twitch of her lip. Sometimes she shifts in her chair, crossing and uncrossing her ankles.

She watches nervously for my reaction, whether I'll care, whether her real name rings a bell.

I wait a beat before answering, afraid I might start laughing if I speak. That's the best she could come up with? How fucking lame. Frankly, I'm disappointed; I expected more from her. Finally, I'm able to say, "Well, I pretended to be a cat for most of first grade, which made me just as popular as you'd imagine, so you weren't the only weird one." I didn't. My mother would have had me institutionalized.

I see Sloane's shoulders drop in relief. She grins back at me.

Then I cast my eyes down toward the countertop. I begin to move my hands back and forth over the smooth marble, hoping I look uneasy. "Can I talk to you about something?" I ask.

There's one more thing I need from her. Something big.

"Sure," Sloane says slowly, searching my face, puzzled, unsure of what is coming.

I give her a smile. "Will you sit?" I motion to the couch.

We move into the living room, taking a seat facing each other. Around us, the house is quiet. I wait to speak, letting the tension build between us.

"What's going on?" Sloane finally asks, her voice an octave higher than usual. She wipes her palms nervously on her pant legs.

"Well." I clear my throat, take a deep breath. "I wanted to ask you—if anything happens to me, to *us*, I mean, Jay and me, we were wondering if you'd take guardianship of Harper." I keep my eyes on hers, don't blink.

For a minute, she stares at me blankly. "Guardianship?" Sloane shakes her head. "You want me to take guardianship of Harper?"

"I know," I say, giving a small, apologetic laugh. "It's a big ask. Monumental. But Jay's parents are in their late seventies. In a few years, they won't have the capacity to take care of her." Also, they barely had the capacity to take care of their own kids. Look how Jay turned out.

"But . . ." Sloane is still gaping at me. "What about your family?"

"We're not particularly close." I say it lightly, shrugging. It's a gross understatement; we haven't spoken since I left San Francisco. I plan never to speak to them again.

Growing up, my relationship with my parents had always been strained. When I was little, I was pawned off to nannies and tutors, shuttled from piano to ballet, horseback riding on the weekends. I ate dinner with the housekeeper, wishing I had a sibling to eat with instead, while my parents worked long hours, my dad a partner at his law firm, my mother a well-regarded art dealer. They never bothered to kiss me good night when they got home, never tucked me in. If I was ever pulled into a hug, it was with stiff arms, left me cold. I was merely an accessory to their busy lives, a collectible from Christie's, a Porta Volta chair, admired but never sat in. We were publicly cordial because I was required to be—any perceived disrespect would be met with a sharp slap—but privately distant. The expectation was clear: I played the part of the perfect daughter, my private school uniforms hand-pressed and wrinkle-free, my hair neatly combed, while they played theirs, well-dressed, well-coiffed, smiles bright. My father was handsome, my mother beautiful, both gregarious.

Everything was about appearances, our lives just for show. It was stifling, at best. I felt like a plastic doll they occasionally took out of its packaging, then stored back on the shelf, the closet door shut tightly behind them. They never knew me, never wanted to.

I stood it as long as I could, resentment eating me from the inside out, until I had to surface for air, my lungs on fire. I'd just turned seventeen, at the tail end of my junior year in high school, when it finally became too much to bear.

I'd come home early from school—I had a headache, I think—had pulled into the driveway, was sitting in my car, checking a text that had just come through. When I looked up, about to get out, I saw our front door open. A woman stepped out, her blonde hair swept up into a twist. I'd never seen her before.

My father appeared behind her. He hooked her by the waist and she turned, smiling flirtatiously up at him. Then, he kissed her, hard, his hand sliding over the curve of her hip. My heart dropped into my stomach, a brick. I felt sick.

That evening, I stood nervously in the doorway of my parents' bathroom, picking at my nails. My mother was removing her makeup; my dad was at a late dinner with clients. "Stop that," she said without turning around. She hated it when I picked. I put my hands by my sides, cleared my throat. "I saw Dad," I started, haltingly. "This afternoon. With—"

"I know," she said, not letting me finish. She didn't look at me, staring into the mirror instead as she applied eye cream, dabbing gently. Then she met my eyes. "I know," she said again, more firmly this time, and I understood. This was something she tolerated. But then her mouth quivered, just slightly. She looked back into the mirror. She tolerated it, but she wished she didn't have to. The conversation was over.

I hated her as much as I hated him. I hated him for his infidelity, her for accepting it. I hated them both for the lies. Their marriage, like everything else, was a sham. I couldn't stomach it for another second. I wanted no part of their fake fucking lives. When I asked to move out, to stay with my grandmother at the end of the summer instead of flying home, they shrugged, *sure*. It was like salt in an open wound. Even though I was the one who wanted to leave, it stung that it bothered them so little, that they said yes without a second thought. They rarely called that year. On Thanksgiving, Christmas, my birthday, but otherwise, silence.

After they dropped me off at college, I didn't hear from them until my mother called to tell me my grandmother had died. I think it might have been one of the reasons I fell in love with Jay. I'd been living in a loveless desert; his desire felt real after a lifetime of insincerity. What a fool I'd been. Sure, his desire had been real, but almost nothing else was.

Then, four months after the funeral, when I was home for spring break, they asked me to join them in my dad's office. They had a lawyer on the phone. Through the tiny speaker, he informed me that my grandmother had left an eight-figure trust in my name; I'd receive it when I turned twenty-five. You could see the anger on my parents' faces, the resentment in the way their jaws twitched. The only thing I cared about, though—the Block Island house—was in my mother's name.

By the time I found this out, they'd already sold it, the money used to upgrade their country club membership. I was livid. They knew how much the house meant to me. It was punishment for my grandmother's love. That was the last straw, the final nail. I told them I hated them, screamed it again and again until I was hoarse, slamming the door on the way out so hard I thought it might crack in two.

But they were the only family I had left. So when my father called me after three years of no contact, my anger wavered. He'd found out I was applying to law school and offered to write a letter of recommendation from his firm, where I'd interned all throughout high school. I accepted.

We spoke sporadically after that, brief texts or calls, then more frequently, resuming holidays together as a family. I agreed to an externship with his firm as a 3L, then a full-time position when I graduated. Their efforts increased in the months leading up to my twenty-fifth birthday, my dad including me on high-profile cases, invitations from my mother to dinner. He offered to make me partner; she asked me to be on the board of a foundation she belonged to.

It wasn't hard to see what they were doing. I was interesting to them now that the money was in sight. But I played along because they were finally offering me what I'd always wanted: their attention, their love. It might have come with strings, but it was something.

I thought, maybe—stupidly—our time together was a start, an opportunity for a real relationship. So I let them in, basked in the closeness. Then, after Harper was born, when I brought up moving to New York, Jay's business opportunity, the illusion fractured, splintered into itty-bitty pieces. Jay and I had been married for five years by then, college sweethearts, like I'd told Sloane, but they'd never warmed to him. They begged me not to go, tried everything to change my mind, heartfelt cajoling at first, then bitter, empty threats.

I saw their desperation for what it was. They were worried their well would dry up, that Jay would take what they felt was theirs. Not *me*, but my money. I was gutted.

When we moved, I changed my number, deleted my social media. I didn't give them our new address. There's been no communication since.

But this is more than Sloane needs to know, of course.

I smile shyly at her. "The truth is, over the last few months, you've become like my family." I look away, then back at her. Then I add, "It feels like you *are* my family." It's a line I've been waiting to use for weeks now, for just the right moment.

Sloane stares back at me, her eyes wide. "I feel the same way," she says hoarsely.

I thought she might. So I put down another card. "This might sound crazy," I say, leaning forward, "but have you ever thought we might be?"

"Related?" Sloane leans in, too. She sounds almost breathless.

I nod. "Sisters, I mean. I don't know, it's just that the only thing you know about your dad is that he's from Philly. And my dad is from Philly. And we look so similar, now that our hair is the same." Then I give a little laugh, shake my head. "I mean, it's probably one in a million, but I guess that's why you taking guardianship makes sense to me." I lick my lips. "But if you feel like it's too much of a responsibility, I completely understand."

Sloane looks at me, her eyes bright. I know I've said the right thing, about us being sisters. Another brick in the house of lies I'm building; I don't think my dad's ever set foot in Philly, let alone Daytona, where she was conceived. Then Sloane nods. "Of course I will."

"Are you sure?"

"Completely," she says.

I reach across the couch and put my hand on top of hers. "Thank you," I say. "Really, thank you."

Then I get up and take a sheaf of paper-clipped papers and a pen from my purse. I set the stack on the coffee table and uncap the pen.

"Here." I tap my finger on a blank line. "This is where you sign."

I hold my breath as Sloane picks up the pen. She presses it against the page. The dark blue ink bleeds through the page, leaving the paper wet. I'm pleased to notice that instinctively, she signed her real name. Her real name is also listed throughout the document, but I correctly assumed that she wouldn't ask to see it, too swept up in the fantasy I've just sold her.

I downloaded the form—an addendum to our will—off of a legal site last night and forged Jay's signature earlier this morning, laying the paper over an old signed check and tracing the curvature of his name. It's critical to my plan, as is the other legal document I'm bringing with me to the island. The other, however, I didn't need to download—or forge Jay's signature. My lawyer prepared it and couriered it to me yesterday. I've already hidden it in my suitcase, tucked the manila folder between the pages of a magazine in a zippered pocket.

Later, when Sloane leaves, I'll log into Jay's email and send the newly signed documents to our lawyer from his account, copying myself. Then I'll block our lawyer's email address so when he writes back a confirmation of receipt, Jay won't get it, Jay none the wiser. Who's the fucking fool now, Jay?

Sloane finishes signing, then re-caps the pen.

"Seriously, thank you," I say again, with as much earnestness as I can muster. I shuffle the papers back into a neat stack. Then, "Oh, before I forget!" I get up and go to the hall closet. I return with a big Bloomingdale's gift bag, a crumple of pink tissue paper peeking up from the top. "Here." I hand it to Sloane, grinning.

"What is it?" she asks.

I shrug coyly. "Open it."

Carefully, Sloane reaches inside and pulls out a soft bundle, unwrapping it gently. It's a white, gauzy, robe-like shirt, soft and expensive-looking, delicate stitching around the seams and a braided tie around the waist. She looks up at me in wonder. "It's a swimsuit cover-up," I say. "Keep opening!"

She reaches in again and removes another wrapped item, this time a sleek black bathing suit. It's a one-piece, but sexy, with a plunging neckline. "There's more!" I wink.

When she's done, she's opened three swimsuits in total, another cover-up, a pair of brightly patterned, wide-legged linen pants, shorts, a button-up cotton shirt, and two pairs of sunglasses. I spent the afternoon at Bloomingdale's with Harper last Sunday, picking out a new summer wardrobe for Sloane. I wanted to make sure she was dressed the part of Mrs. Lockhart. I have a look, remember? Carefully cultivated, aimed to please—please my husband, to be specific. Speaking of Jay, he'll love Sloane in these clothes.

Like my parents, Jay has always been clear about what he thinks a woman should wear, what she should weigh, the clothes he prefers. Of course, his preferences were different from theirs, though, again, like my parents, the more zeros on the price tag, the better. I loved it, at first, when he came shopping with me, grinning wolfishly as I twirled around in an outfit he'd picked out. "Now try that one," he'd say, and I would, gladly. Once, he went down on me in a dressing room, following me in and locking the door behind him. I came hard and fast, my left hand gripping his hair, my right clasped over my mouth as I moaned. He always knew how to touch me, what I liked. I was happy to fill my closet with things that made him happy, to keep my stomach flat, my body tight, happy knowing he couldn't wait to take off what I put on. This was before I knew he'd be happy to take off anything, off anyone.

"Violet, this is—" Sloane starts.

"For the trip!" I say, shrugging. "As a thank-you for coming with us."

"I should be the one thanking you!" she says. No, she shouldn't. Really.

I tell her to take the rest of the day off to pack, then walk her to the door, giving her a quick hug before she steps onto the porch. "Be here at nine on Sunday," I say. "Our car leaves at nine thirty!"

When Sloane's gone, I check my watch. It's only ten, which means I have almost three hours until I have to go get Harper. Plenty of time to take Sloane's driver's license to the DMV.

Before I leave, I change out of my clothes into the ones Sloane left for me to donate, then scrub the makeup from my face. I rake my hair into a messy bun and take a pair of plastic-framed glasses out of a shopping bag I've hidden in the back of my closet, put them on.

In the dingy, poorly lit DMV waiting room, I sit for almost an hour and a half before my number is called. "I was hoping to take a new picture," I say, sliding Sloane's license across the counter, underneath the plastic partition. The woman on the other side of the desk barely glances at me or the license before directing me to another line, where another monotone employee instructs me to look straight into the camera. We look alike, yes, but I want the picture on her license to be of me. It'll make things easier, more believable.

I update Sloane's mailing address to a PO Box I set up on Block Island, so when it's mailed out, I'll be the one to receive it, and pay an extra thirty-five dollars for expedited processing. I should receive it by the end of next week. Then I leave, smiling, with just enough time to change back into my own jeans and reapply the makeup I removed before leaving to pick up Harper.

Now, the only thing left for me to do is pack.

22

Normally, I'm up before Harper, but this morning, the day of our trip, I purposefully didn't set an alarm. Today is my first official day as Sloane, not Violet. I'm giving Violet to Sloane, stepping out of my life, letting her step in. If I know her, and I think by now I do, she'll accept happily, slipping into it—into me—with pleasure. We'll both get off the ferry as someone else, as each other. Only Sloane doesn't know it yet.

I wake to the sound of Harper's footsteps thudding down the hall from her room to ours. I pull myself into a sitting position as she leaps onto the bed, the mattress bouncing beneath her. I didn't fall asleep until early this morning, going over the plan again and again until I drifted off as the sun rose. Now, I'm groggy, eyes burning.

"Daddy says it's time to get up!" Harper says, pulling the covers off of me. "We're going to the beach today, remember?"

"I remember, baby." I smile at her, my eyes still closed, reaching out to ruffle her hair. I'd felt the same excitement when I was a kid, suitcases packed, headed for the airport. It was the best feeling in the world. "Are you all packed up? What about books? Do you want to bring your CD player?"

"Oh yeah!" Harper says. My parents bought her an old-school Discman before we moved, along with a dozen CDs of Disney music and kids' audiobooks. Harper loves it, lies on her floor listening for hours, changing out the discs, carefully replacing them into their cases. It was one of the most thoughtful things they'd done as grandparents. She leaps off the bed, starts running back down the hallway to her room. "I'll put it in my backpack!" she yells.

I pull myself out of bed and head into the bathroom. I skip my usual morning shower and instead tie my hair back into a messy bun. I brush my teeth but forgo makeup, then dress quickly in a pair of black yoga pants and a loose-fitting T-shirt, a pair of beat-up Converse that I found in a thrift store last week. Finally, I tie Sloane's flannel around my waist, the one she traded me for my Carolina Herrera shirt.

When I'm done, I stand in front of the full-length mirror leaning against the wall. I smile. I look younger than I usually do, more nanny than mom, like Sloane did when we first met that day in the park. It's not a drastic change—I'm still me—but it's the beginning.

"Mom!" Harper is yelling from her room. "Mom, I can't find my shoes!"

I glance back at my closet. I finished packing last night—almost. I have a few more things to zip into my suitcase, but I want to wait until right before we leave.

"Coming!" I call.

I'm still in Harper's room, helping her comb through her closet, when the doorbell rings. Sloane's here. I check my watch. *Right on time.*

"Can you get that?" I yell down to Jay. A moment later I hear the door open and shut, Sloane's voice in the foyer.

"I'm going to go say hi to Caitlin," I say to Harper. "Keep looking for your shoes, baby, okay?"

I clomp loudly down the stairs, but Sloane barely notices me. She's leaning against the closed front door, gazing at Jay, her cheeks flushed as he makes a joke, something about how many suitcases are piled at the foot of the staircase. Sloane's in a pair of my jeans, a light, high-waisted pair that makes her hips look tiny, and the ivory camisole I told her was Jay's favorite, her hair glossy, eyes bright.

This is the first time Jay's seen her since her haircut and new clothes. By the way he's looking at her, his eyes lingering, it's clear he appreciates the transformation. He's probably imagining her ass up, bent over the edge of a bed—his favorite position.

"Morning, Caitlin!" I say loudly, stopping a few steps from the bottom. Both Jay and Sloane turn toward me abruptly.

Sloane blinks at me for a minute as if she doesn't recognize me. Then she smiles. "Morning," she says brightly. "Can I help with anything?"

I gesture around wildly. "All of it!" I say, giving a little laugh. "But mainly, can you help me find Harper's shoes? I've looked *everywhere*."

"I just saw them . . ." Jay looks around, then points to a pair of Harper's shoes near the couch. "There they are."

I peer over the banister, shaking my head when I spot her white lace-up sneakers. "No, not those, her *red* shoes. The jellies. She refuses to come out of her room until she has them."

"I'm on it," Sloane says, dropping her bags by the rest of the luggage.

I put my hands together, pantomiming a prayer. "Thank you. I just have a few more things to pack up. And could you make sure Harper pees before we go?"

She nods and I run back up the stairs.

"Fifteen minutes," Jay calls after me. "The car will be here in fifteen minutes. We'll miss the ferry if we don't leave by nine thirty."

"Mm-hm." I make a noise to signal I've heard him. As if there would be anything that would keep me from getting on that boat.

I go back into my bedroom, locking the door behind me. There are a few things I need in the closet. First, the burner phone I've stashed in a shoebox, a cheap Nokia that I bought a few months ago from a dusty electronics store in midtown, paid for in cash, preloaded with minutes. And second, the gun. My mother, before we stopped speaking, insisted on giving it to me as I packed for New York. Despite her outwardly liberal art-loving persona, her closeted conservative values often peeked through the cracks, their rays shining brightly. She spouted crime statistics, citing surges in burglaries and home robberies throughout the city. I'd rolled my eyes—San Francisco had some of the fastest-rising crime rates in the country—but agreed to take it. We store it in a lockbox on a high shelf in our closet, the key hidden separately, on another shelf, out of reach of Harper. The gun is registered in both Jay's and my name.

When I've packed the gun, I take the phone into the bathroom and lock the door. I turn on both faucets, sit down on the closed toilet seat lid, then click on the only number I have saved.

He picks up after the first ring. His voice is deep, cooling, like a balm. It always has been.

"Hi," I say softly. I tell him that we're packed, almost ready to go, that I can't wait to see him again. "Soon," I say, then ask if he's ready. He says that he is and I smile, even though he can't see me.

Ten minutes later, I open my bedroom door at the same time that Sloane and Harper are coming out of the bathroom, Harper in the red jellies I buried under a pile of stuffed animals so I'd have something for Sloane to do while I packed.

"You guys ready?" I ask.

They both nod. "You?" Sloane says, her voice slightly higher than its normal pitch. She doesn't want to ask outright, but she can't imagine I'm planning to leave the house like this, like I just rolled out of bed. So unlike the Violet she thinks she knows.

I hadn't been lying when, on one of our first walks together, I told her how much time I spend on my appearance. It's been a habit for as long as I can remember. I was a gawky kid, big-eared, big-toothed, big-nosed. Eventually, I grew into my features, but during those long, painfully awkward years, my mother would stand behind me in the mirror, a curling iron in one hand, a brow brush in the other. "It's important," she would say as she smoothed and styled, tugging at my hair until tears pricked my eyes, "the effort you put in." The implication—if you don't care how you look, no one will care about you—has been reinforced a million times over in the course of my life. Now, I hope that it's true. Already, I feel lighter.

"Yup, ready!" I say. "Let's go!"

Sloane does a good job of hiding her surprise, smiling pleasantly. The three of us traipse down the stairs, Sloane, then Harper, then me. The front door is open, everyone's suitcases but mine already down on the sidewalk. I keep my hand tightly gripped around my bag's handle.

Jay is standing next to a black town car, staring at his phone. "Come on," he calls, opening the back door. "Everyone in!" Harper and Sloane start toward the car.

"Wait!" I call and everyone turns. "Let's take a picture! Do you mind, sir?" I ask the driver.

"Now?" asks Jay. He looks at his watch, then back at me. "We really should get going."

I nod. "It'll be quick. Just in front of the stoop is fine. Go on, get together." I motion for them to stand next to me.

Jay sighs but picks up Harper and carries her back to the stoop. Sloane doesn't move, waiting by the car.

"What are you doing?" I say. "I meant you, too, silly! Get up here! Can we use your phone?"

Sloane hands her phone to the driver and hurries back up the stoop to stand next to me. "Cheese!" I say as the driver holds the phone up.

When the photo's been taken, we all load into the car, packing in like sardines. Harper sits between me and Sloane, headphones plugged into an iPad. Her neck is bent, eyes focused on the cartoon show on the screen. Sloane and I grin at each other over her head. We're both excited, but only one of us should be.

Four hours later, the car drops us at a sunny dock, swarming with other travelers. We unload the suitcases from the back of the trunk and begin lugging them toward the boat.

"Smile, you two!" I say to Sloane and Harper. I hold up my phone. Sloane squats to Harper's level and puts her arm around her small shoulders. I want there to be as many pictures as possible of Harper with Sloane, Harper with Jay and Sloane. I want there to be evidence of them as a family.

The ferry ride is just under an hour. While Jay is inside the cabin, pretending to work, Sloane, Harper, and I spend the trip on the top deck, counting seagulls and looking for whales. It's hot and cool at the same time, the sun pounding down on us, the wind blowing, skimming across the cold salty ocean surface. When a cloud passes overhead, we all shiver, huddling together for warmth.

I keep snapping pictures, mostly of Harper and Sloane, a few selfies of the three of us, waving Sloane off when she offers to take shots of just Harper and me. "I'm a mess," I say, "I overslept," covering my face with my hands, "seriously, don't aim that camera at me!"

A short while later, the ferry docks and everyone pours off the ship, down the ramp. I stop at the bottom, breathing in the taffy-sweet, sea-spray air. My grandmother used to wait here for us, her arms open wide. I close my eyes, picturing her big smile, her hand on top of her big floppy hat so it wouldn't fly away in the wind. It's hot here, just as hot as in the city, but it feels different. There, the heat makes you want to crawl out of your skin, but on the island, it makes you want to take off your clothes, slowly unbuttoning your shirt, sliding your shorts down over your hips, panties on the floor. It's a sultry heat, unwinding everyone, loosening everything.

We wait with the luggage while Jay goes for the rental car. When he pulls up, I insist Sloane rides next to him, up front. "So you have the best view of the island!" I tell her, climbing into the back seat of the car. Harper looks exhausted, her eyes glassy, drooping at the corners. I pull her close to me, letting her head rest against my body.

The car moves slowly down the gravel driveway, from the boat-yard out onto a paved road, our windows down, the salty air warm and pungent. I'm home.

Soon, we reach the town's main street, a bustling block of ice cream parlors, souvenir shops, restaurants with signs offering lobster rolls and fried clams. People are strolling on the sidewalks in sun-glasses and sundresses, wide-brimmed hats, licking their melting cones, slurping cups of lemonade and crushed ice. It feels half real, half like you've walked onto a movie set. At the end of the block, I direct Jay to turn onto a one-lane road that runs next to the ocean. To our left is the water; to the right, beach cottages, all in a row, with wooden porches, wet swimsuits and towels slung over the railings to dry.

As we drive, the houses become farther apart, separated by stretches of bushy seagrass, tall stalks of feathered plants swaying in the wind. I glance down to see that Harper has fallen asleep, her head lolling forward, mouth slightly open, her body heavy. Sloane catches my eye in the rearview mirror and we smile at each other.

A few minutes later, we slow toward the end of a long block. I look down at the map on my phone. "It's the next house," I tell Jay. "The one with the shutters."

Jay turns slowly into the gravel driveway then kills the engine. Carefully, I unbuckle Harper and lift her onto my hip, her head resting on my shoulder. She shifts, then snuggles her face into my neck.

Jay, Sloane, and I pause in the driveway, staring up at the house. It's a two-story cottage with blue thatched siding, a bleached roof, and white shutters around the windows, not unlike my grandmother's. There's a covered porch with two Adirondack chairs facing toward each other. Across from it, a trail leading to a stretch of white sandy beach, the ocean.

We walk up the cobbled path to the porch in a single, quiet line. There's a lockbox attached to the front door, just like Gina told me there would be. I tell Jay the code, and he lets us in.

Gina hasn't disappointed. The inside of the house is as picturesque as the outside. It's large and airy with whitewashed wood floors and shiplap siding, rattan furniture, cushions upholstered in pastel blues, nautical stripes. The décor is classic beach cottage: framed pictures of wooden lifeguard towers and old VW vans parked on sandy shores; a rusted anchor hanging on the wall next to the front door; conch shells and starfish in a glass bowl on the coffee table. On the bookshelves are classic vacation reads: summer romances, and detective novels, their covers sun-faded and worn. The kitchen, at the back of the house, is charmingly vintage with retro black-and-white-tiled floors, an old-school stove and matching refrigerator, teal-blue cabinets. It has a round table with four chairs and a back door that looks like it might lead out onto a deck. I almost expect my grandmother to walk in, a pitcher of iced tea in hand.

I tilt my head toward the stairs to let Jay and Sloane know that I'm going to take Harper up to her bedroom. I take each step carefully. Upstairs, there's a beachfront bedroom to my left, a small bedroom across from it, and, to my right, at the end of the hall, another big bedroom. I take Harper into the small bedroom with a twin bed and lay her gently down on top of the covers. She rolls onto her stomach, sighs, and settles back to sleep.

I shut the door behind me and head back downstairs. I step back into the living room just as Jay and Sloane come through the front door, their hands full of suitcases.

"Upstairs?" Jay asks.

"Here is fine." I motion to a corner of the living room. "We can take them up when Harper is awake. Poor thing is *wiped*." I plop down on the living room couch. "So am I, actually. I was thinking about making a run to the store to stock up on a few things, but"—I look to Jay—"would you mind going instead?" I give him a hopeful smile.

Jay shrugs. "Sure."

"Thanks." I smile at him. "Maybe some hot dogs for dinner? Milk, eggs. Bread for toast tomorrow."

"Anything else?"

I shake my head. "No, but hey! Why don't you take Caitlin?" I say. "You could give her the full tour of the island! There should be cruisers in the garage. Take her by that little ice cream store! Oh, or that café next to the kayak rental!"

"Oh, it's okay . . ." Sloane starts to protest. She looks nervously from me to Jay. "He doesn't have to—"

"Jay doesn't mind, do you, Jay?" I interject. And before he has a chance to respond, I continue, "The whole island is less than a two-hour bike loop. Then you can stop by the market on the way back. You can ride a bike, right, Cait?"

Sloane nods. "Then it's settled!" I pronounce. "I'll take Harper down to the beach when she wakes, and we can make dinner when you get back."

"Are you sure?" Sloane asks. "Because I can stay with Harper if you want."

"Completely," I say. "Really, I'm exhausted. And it'll give me some time to unpack. You guys have fun, enjoy the island!"

I pretend not to notice the look Jay gives me. He's confused at my enthusiasm, doesn't quite know what to make of it. But I keep my face blank and after a beat, he turns and smiles at Sloane. "All right, let's do it," he says, holding the front door open for her. She smiles back, blushing slightly. She's besotted, poor thing.

When the door closes behind them, I smile. It's important that they're seen together from day one. Mr. and Mrs. Jay Lockhart.

23

When I'm alone, I take my suitcase and lug it up the stairs, down the hall to the master bedroom. The room is beautiful, beachy and light-filled, with two big windows looking out over the ocean, the sand stretching out to meet the frothy surf. On the wall to my right, there's a king-sized bed flanked by two doors, one to a large walk-in closet, one to a bathroom. On the left wall, a modern dresser, armchairs on either side.

I toss my suitcase onto the bed. First things first. Gina, the agent, assured me that there would be a safe available somewhere in the house. I find it in a linen closet in the master bathroom; I use my grandmother's birthday as the code, the same password to my burner phone. In it, I put three things: the gun, the phone, and the manila folder my lawyer sent me last week, divorce papers inside.

Once I relock the safe, I unpack only one thing, a red Hervé Léger dress that I purchased last week, hanging it up in the walk-in closet. The rest—two modest one-piece swimsuits, shorts, a few T-shirts— I leave in my suitcase. I want to be able to easily move everything into Sloane's room later this week.

I go back downstairs and take the remaining luggage up: Jay's into our room, Sloane's into hers, Harper's outside her door. As I set it down, I hear a rustle inside.

"Mama?" Harper calls out. Her voice is small and froggy with sleep.

I ease the door open gently. "Did you have a good nap, lovey?" I ask. "You fell asleep on the way to the house."

Harper sits in the middle of the bed, bleary-eyed, her hair sticking up in fuzzy tufts. "Are we at the beach?" she asks.

I nod. "Want to go play in the sand?"

Thirty minutes later we're on a beach blanket, our skin glistening with sunscreen. Harper is using a little plastic shovel to dig a hole next to the blanket, searching for sand crabs. I lie back, arms behind my head. *Maybe,* I think hopefully, *Jay will get hit by a car on the way back.*

We've been on the beach about an hour when I see Jay and Sloane approaching on their bikes. "Look!" I say to Harper. "There's Daddy and Caitlin!" I raise a hand above my head and wave. Harper waves, too.

Both Jay and Sloane wave back. I see Jay say something to Sloane, then they both dismount from their bikes. He takes a paper bag from the basket of his bike and heads toward the house while Sloane starts down the path leading to the beach.

Sloane approaches us with a wide smile. She looks giddy, her eyes sparkling, cheeks flushed. They had a good time, I can tell. I knew they would. Jay, with his easy smile, the way he looks at you, makes you feel like you're at the top of a roller coaster, just about to tip. Exhilaration and anticipation, stomach flipping, heart pounding. It's like a drug. If you're not careful, you'll turn into an addict, track marks on your arms, veins shot.

It's the way I felt when I first met him. He sat in the desk next to mine my freshman year in college, smiling at me as he lowered himself into the chair. It was only the second week I'd been on campus. "Is this seat taken?" he'd asked.

"It is now," I said.

He walked me back to my dorm but didn't leave. We sat on my bed, talking, our thighs touching. I could barely breathe around him. He was the kind of good-looking that makes you ache. And he was funny, made me laugh until my sides hurt. But really, it was how his eyes never left mine, how everything else disappeared around us. He asked me to be his girlfriend two weeks later, and then, when we graduated, to be his wife. Both times, I said yes before he'd even finished the question. I knew I'd never get tired of the way he looked at me; it never occurred to me that he'd ever get tired of looking. I worked so hard to make sure he wouldn't, my body sweaty and sore from the effort.

"Jay's going to start the grill," Sloane says as she nears. "He said to come up in an hour."

"Did you have fun?" I ask. I motion for her to join me on the beach blanket.

She nods as she sits, stretching her legs out into the sand. "It's gorgeous here." She tilts her head back and breathes in deeply. "Like nothing bad could ever happen, right?" she says, looking over at me, smiling.

I nod. I know what she means. Except bad things do happen here. Drownings, overdoses, drunk-driving deaths. More than you might think, dozens each summer, careless tourists with too much money and not enough regard for themselves or anyone else.

Bad things happen, but they're cleaned up quickly, wiped away, made neat by money and power. Nothing examined too closely. Accidental deaths or natural causes, always, the coroner's signature loose and sloppy, just like him. Rumor had it he was happy to look the other way, sign the paperwork, no questions asked—as long as it was worth his while.

Like the time an intern disappeared from a senator's vacation home, poof, just like that. Everyone had seen them together that summer, noticed how beautiful she was, how young she seemed—especially compared to his wife. Her sudden absence was explained away, never mind the shouting we all heard the night before we never saw her again, the cleaning crew at his house the following morning. It was something only the locals knew about, our secret to keep, one of our many own Chappaquiddicks. No one wanted the beauty of the island untarnished more than we did, not even the ones writing the checks.

Nothing—no one—is perfect, not even the things you love the most. Growing up, I couldn't quite make sense of it, how a place so bright could also be so dark, but now, it suits me. In fact, it's one of the reasons we're here.

I reach out and squeeze Sloane's hand. "Thanks for coming, Cait."

She squeezes back. "Thanks for inviting me."

When we get back to the house, sun-flushed and salt-caked, Jay is on the back patio off the kitchen, standing over a smoking grill. "Who wants a hot dog?" he calls when he sees us. "Harper?"

"Yes!" Harper yells. "Ketchup only, though. I don't like it with mustard," she tells Sloane, who nods intently, like she's just received incredibly important information. I feel a surge of affection, both for Harper and for Sloane. Then, a flash of anger at Jay. He never remembers that Harper hates mustard, always offers it to her no matter how many times she reminds him.

We eat at the little table in the kitchen nook, still in our bathing suits, towels wrapped around our waists. Jay has a beer while the rest of us drink cold lemonade from plastic wineglasses.

Sloane barely takes her eyes off Jay. She laughs loudly whenever he speaks, hangs on to every word. He seems to enjoy the attention— of course he does; he always has—glancing at me every so often to see my reaction. I pretend not to notice, laughing along, keeping a happy smile stretched across my face.

At seven, our hot dogs eaten—I had three—and our glasses empty, I look to Harper. "Okay," I say. "Time for a bath, little bean. Jay, you ready?"

Harper juts out her lip. "I want you to give me a bath, not Dad!" *Good girl, Harp.* I'd told her earlier that I had a plan to make her bath extra fun tonight.

I give Jay a helpless look, like, *Well, what do you want to do here?* He holds up his hands in surrender. "I'll do the dishes; that's fine with me."

"I'll help," Sloane says quickly. She glances toward Jay, then looks away. Silently, I congratulate myself. Hook, line, sinker. Nothing but net.

"Great!" I say. "Thanks." The more alone time they have together, the better. "Come on, then, let's go." Then, to Jay and Sloane, "I'm probably going to head to bed after I've tucked Harper in. I'm still beat from today. See you in the morning?"

They both nod.

While I'm in the upstairs bathroom with Harper, Harper splashing in the tub, I hear the clink of dishes being washed, the refrigerator opening and closing. If I had to guess, Jay is scrubbing the plates while Sloane dries, tidies up the kitchen. There's the rise and fall of their voices, laughter, a happy yelp every so often. He's probably flicking soap bubbles at her as she leaps away, swatting at him with a dish towel, grinning. They're both high from their afternoon together, light-headed. I imagine the electricity when he passes something to her, their hands brushing. With Jay, there's always electricity, the snap and crackle of heat, the promise of something more.

I'm reading to Harper in bed when the door slowly creaks open, Jay's head appearing. "Night, Harp," he says softly when he sees she's still awake.

He crosses the room and gives her a kiss on the top of the head. She reaches up and wraps her little arms around his neck. "Night, Dad," she says. "I love you." I feel a pang. She'll miss him when he's gone. But I'll make it up to her. I'll love her enough for the both of us.

When he leaves the room, I hear his footsteps descending on the stairs. I haven't heard Sloane come up yet. Maybe they'll end up on the couch together, watching a movie, sharing a blanket; I wonder whose pants would unzip first. But when I step back out into the hallway, closing Harper's door behind me, Sloane is coming up the stairs.

She smiles at me. "Is she asleep?" she whispers, motioning to Harper's room.

"Out like a light." I nod. "And no need to keep it down. Once she's out for the night, she's out. She'll sleep through anything."

Anything. Even yelling, the sound of glass breaking, sirens. How she slept through that night, about a year ago now, I'll never know. But I'm so grateful I could bend down, kiss the ground.

"Well, I'll see you in the morning," Sloane says. "I'm exhausted." She gives a little wave when she enters her room, then closes the door behind her.

Thirty minutes later, Jay comes into our bedroom. I slow my breathing, pretend I'm asleep. He undresses and climbs into bed next to me, the mattress sinking under his weight.

"Violet," he whispers into the darkness. "Violet?" He moves against me, and I feel him press into my back, body warm, wanting. I stay still. He presses harder, breath in my ear, in my hair, then, when I don't respond, he gives up, rolling over.

Even if I'd wanted to, which I don't—I'd rather fuck a cactus—I'd have turned him down. The sting of rejection has always been too much for Jay to bear; he'll need something to soothe it. Someone, rather.

Lucky for him, he won't have to look far.

24

The next morning, I wake to sunlight streaming through the window, the whole room awash in it, so bright I have to cover my eyes, blinking to adjust. Jay is still asleep, his mouth slightly open.

Slowly, as not to wake him, I grab my phone from the nightstand, squint at the time. It's just before seven. I ease out of bed, grab a few things from my suitcase—a thick-strapped striped swimsuit, faded tank, cutoff shorts, baseball cap—and dress quietly in the bathroom. I don't wash my face, don't apply any makeup.

As I leave the bathroom, I catch sight of my reflection in the mirror. It surprises me how I feel, seeing myself like this, undone and bare-faced. It's like a deep sigh of relief, like I've finally exhaled after holding my breath for too long, my whole body unclenching. I feel, now—again—like the girl I used to be on the island. It's not because of what I'm wearing, the too-big shirt and comfortable swimsuit, but because for the first time in I can't remember how long, I'm not dressing for someone else. I don't care what anyone thinks when they look at me. I've stepped out of Jay's box. I'm free.

It's how I thought I would feel in college, finally on my own, my parents' expectations and private school uniforms left crumpled in my closet. But before I found myself, I found Jay. I thought he was the antidote to the straitlaced dear daughter I was expected to be at home, the liberation I was chasing, an authentic love-me-for-me kind of love. I was wrong. Instead of becoming the person I wanted to be, I became who *he* wanted me to be. The girl from the island was buried again, just like she had been in my parents' house. But now, she's resurfaced, she's here. I smile at myself. *Welcome back, Violet. It's good to see you.*

Downstairs, I pack a beach bag: a stack of towels and a blanket, waters and a few cans of soda, snacks, sunscreen. I find a couple of beach chairs and an umbrella in the garage that I set on the porch.

Just before eight, I hear Harper's door open. I pop two pieces of toast in the toaster, then meet her coming down the stairs. She's still blinking sleep from her eyes, yawning.

"Hi, lovey," I say softly. "Everyone's still sleeping. Let's get your swimsuit on and we'll go to the beach!"

She nods as I direct her back up the stairs. I manage to get her dressed without much resistance, her limbs still heavy and sleep-laden.

When we get back downstairs, the toast is finished, edging on burnt. I butter it quickly, hoping Harper doesn't notice. But she does. "This is too black," she says, wrinkling up her nose.

I roll my eyes. "Okay, I'll eat it. How about this one?" I hold up the other slice, slightly less done.

"No! It's burnt, too!" She glares at me, her bedhead pointing in every direction. She's not a morning person.

Normally, I'd fight her on it, press the importance of not wasting food, but I want to get to the beach early, and unless I give in, I'm in for a raucous brawl. I put two fresh pieces in the toaster.

As Harper eats her perfectly browned bread, I rifle through the kitchen drawers until I find a piece of scrap paper and a pen. I quickly jot down a note for Sloane, clip it to the fridge: *On the beach, join us when you're ready!*

"Come on, let's go," I say to Harper. It's important we get to the beach before Sloane wakes up.

We've been on the beach for an hour or so when I spot a woman and two children making their way from the house next to ours down the grassy path to the beach. I already know her name and the names of her two children, courtesy of a generous tip to Gina, travel agent extraordinaire. They arrived two days ago. They're the reason I shelled out the big bucks for the house we're in.

I watch as the woman lays out a big blanket, unfolds a beach chair, dumps a pile of sand toys out of a bag. "Come on," I say to Harper, "let's go make friends."

I slip my hand into hers and we make our way across the beach toward their setup.

"Hi!" I call out as we near.

The woman looks up from a weathered paperback, her face shaded under a woven straw hat.

"We're your neighbors," I say. I point up toward our house. "We just got in yesterday. I saw your kids and thought it would be nice for Harper to have some playmates. Harper, can you say hi?"

"Hi," Harper says shyly.

The woman smiles and gets to her feet. She's a young-looking mom, light blonde hair, freckled and pale skin, tall and thin with a slightly boyish figure, birdish in her face, but cute. She has on a too-large faded blue chambray shirt, open over a string bikini, sleeves rolled and pushed to the elbow. Her hip bones jut out angularly beneath the bikini ties.

"Hi," she says. "I'm Anne-Marie. And that's Rooney and Claire." She points to the two kids down by the edge of the water, first to the boy, then to the girl.

I kneel next to Harper. "Harper, do you want to go play with them?"

She nods, then skips off happily. I watch her, smiling, heart expanding in my chest. That's my girl, my social butterfly, my golden retriever child.

"How old is she?" Anne-Marie asks.

"Five at the end of the month," I say. "I'm Caitlin, by the way. Harper's nanny." I offer her my hand, and she takes it, her palm cool, fingers slender.

"Nice to meet you," she says. "You said you got in yesterday? Where from?"

"New York. What about you?"

"North Carolina. Charlotte. We've been here since Friday. You're lucky; you just missed the storm. It was torrential, poured the first two days we got here. The kids almost lost their flippin' minds! But then, just like that"—she snaps her fingers—"it cleared. I was worried we'd be stuck inside the whole trip, thought we might have to fly home! And the idea of getting back on a flight with those two . . ." She shakes her head emphatically. "Well, let's just say I need a stiff drink just thinking about it!"

Anne-Marie is, I discover, a mile-a-minute talker, as she launches into another story about their trip down, how Rooney got airsick, which made Claire sick, and her husband was no help whatsoever, since he had downed two Valiums and a glass of wine for his flying anxiety before takeoff and was passed out against the window. "I could barely get him off the plane," she says. "Meanwhile, both kids and I are covered in puke." Anne-Marie rolls her eyes when she says this, like, *You know, husbands.* I do, of course. Mine happens to be even worse than hers, although Fitz—I quickly learn his name—seems like he's a real piece of work himself.

After finally pausing to take a breath, Anne-Marie points behind me. "Oh," she says, shielding her eyes from the sun. "Is that Harper's mom?" I turn to see Sloane making her way down the path toward our umbrella. I'm pleased to see she's in the cover-up I bought her, the oversized Dior shades, looking chic, poised. A New York mom on vacation.

I nod. "Violet Lockhart. You'll love her. I should get Harper back, but bring your kids over this afternoon, I'll introduce you two!"

"We'd love that!" Anne-Marie says enthusiastically.

"Come on, Harp!" I call. "Let's go get a snack!" Then, to Anne-Marie, "Great meeting you!"

Harper comes predictably running at the promise of something to eat, and we both wave as we leave, heading back to our own setup.

"Morning!" I call to Sloane as we near. She's situated herself under the umbrella on the blanket, legs outstretched in front of her.

"Morning!" Sloane says. She smiles brightly up at us.

I take a seat next to her, begin to rifle through my bag for a granola bar for Harper. "Sorry," I say apologetically. "We were just meeting the neighbors. They're staying in the house next to ours." I point up the bluff to a pale pink house with the same gray-thatched roof as ours. "They have two kids around Harper's age."

"One's named Rooney and one's named Claire!" Harper pipes in. "Claire is older than me. And Rooney is a boy. But there's a Rooney in my class that's a girl."

Sloane stiffens at the mention of Mockingbird, her jawbone clenching slightly. She probably knows her; Rooney's mom told me she's been at the school since she was eighteen months. Then Sloane relaxes her face, smiles widely at Harper. "How lucky!"

"Isn't it?" I say. "I invited them over later so the kids could play some more. And you can meet the mom. She's a trip. A real talker. Like, I could barely get a word in."

Sloane laughs. "Well, I'm glad Harper will have playmates."

I nod. "But here's something funny," I say. "She thought I was the nanny."

Sloane cocks her head, gives a little snort. "That *is* funny," she says. "Why would she think *that*?"

"I think she saw you and Jay at the grocery store yesterday and assumed the two of you were together."

Immediately, Sloane's face flushes. "What'd she say when you told her he was *your* husband?" she asks.

"I didn't correct her! I told you, I could barely get a word in edge-wise!" I bury my face in my hands in mock embarrassment. "And I didn't want to make her feel bad, so I just went along with it. I told her my name was Caitlin when she asked!"

"*What?*" Sloane laughs. "So she thinks you're the nanny and I'm Harper's mom?"

I laugh, too, like it's a delightful mix-up. Oh, tee-hee, *hilarious*, right?! "Yes! I figured we probably won't see much of them, what harm would it do?"

"You just said they might come by later!" Sloane says.

"I know, I know! My mistake! Just go along with it, okay? Promise? I'd look like a nutcase if I came clean now."

Sloane shrugs. "Okay, fine, but it *is* loony, you know that right?" she asks pointedly, raising an eyebrow.

I laugh again. "I know! Can we talk about something else, please? How'd you sleep last night?" I ask.

She nods. "Like a rock. You should have woken me this morning!"

I wave my hand dismissively. "We're on vacation," I say. "And if you were able to sleep through Harper's meltdown about her toast this morning, then I probably wouldn't have been able to wake you anyway."

"It was burnt!" Harper says indignantly. "It would have scratched the roof of my mouth!"

Sloane smiles good-naturedly. "Well, I'm not usually such a heavy sleeper. It was glorious. Although, I did wake up with a nasty sunburn this morning." She pulls the neck of her shirt to one side to expose a reddened shoulder.

"Ouch!" I say. "We'll get some aloe at the store later. Here, let's not make the same mistake today." I hand her a can of aerosol sunscreen. "Do my back and I'll do yours. Harper, let me spray you again, too."

When we're all sufficiently oiled, we rest our heads back against our chairs, chins tilted toward the sun, our hats shading our faces.

After a few minutes, Sloane asks—casually, of course—"Is Jay—"

"Working." I finish her sentence without opening my eyes. "He said he'd try and join us later for a bit."

Obviously, I didn't talk to Jay before I left, but I assume he'll come out at some point, happy for an excuse to take his shirt off. And it will give Sloane something to look forward to. It's impossible to miss the hopefulness in her voice.

And just before noon, he does. I'm in the surf with Harper, running up and back as the waves ebb and flow. She squeals when the water catches her, lapping at her ankles. I see him as he walks over the dune, starting down the sandy slope toward our umbrella. He's carrying a big brown bag in one hand, and he waves with the other.

Harper starts shrieking when she sees him. She runs to him and leaps into his arms. He swings her around, Harper giggling happily. I force a broad smile onto my face.

"I brought sandwiches," Jay says, holding up the bag. "I hope everyone's hungry." He loves this: looking like the stand-up guy, the good dad. Jay saves the day! What a fucking hypocrite. I smile widely at him as I select the largest one.

When we're done eating, Harper hops up excitedly. "Can you swim with me, Dad?"

He gives her a rueful smile. "I have to get back to work, Harp," he says. "Sorry, baby."

Harper's lower lip juts out, trembles. "You just got here!"

My stomach hardens. *Yeah, Jay, you just got here. And we both know what you're doing up there in that office, that there's no reason you can't spare ten minutes for your daughter.* It kills me, his dismissal of her, the hurt on her sweet face. He deserves to be quartered, all four limbs tied, splayed, pulled apart, *pop pop pop pop.*

Jay sighs. "I'll try and get off a little early today, okay?"

She glares at him. "I want to go in *now!*"

"I'll go in with you, Harper," Sloane offers.

"I want to go with Dad!"

"Are you sure you don't want me to take you? I can teach you how to catch a mermaid." Sloane shrugs nonchalantly. "I mean, if you're interested." I hide a smile. I have to hand it to her: she is great with kids.

Harper doesn't look at Sloane, instead kicking at the sand in front of her. "Mermaids aren't real," she says, but she doesn't sound completely convinced.

"How do you know?" Sloane asks.

The corners of Harper's mouth twitch. Sloane stands up, offers her hand to Harper. She takes it. "You've really seen one?" Harper asks.

Sloane looks to me, then Jay. He mouths *thank you* to her, and it's clear how pleased she is. "Just once," she says to Harper. "Come on, let's go!" They run hand in hand down to the water. Harper shrieks as she leaps into the waves.

"Thanks for the sandwiches," I say to Jay. "Where'd you get them?"

"From the deli with the market attached, right before the main drag. I picked up some groceries, too. Just a few things for the next couple of days. Burgers for dinner tonight. And Popsicles."

"Great," I say. I asked for ice cream, but it's just like Jay to think he knows better. I'll go back to the market later. I know it well; I went in every day during my summers here with a gaggle of friends, barefoot and sandy, lingering with the refrigerator doors open until Mr. Menna yelled at us to move it along. We'd grab bottles of cold Snapple and bags of sweet-and-sour candies to bring back to the beach, eat on our towels. There was no exchange of money, no wet dollar bills tucked into our swimsuits. If you were a local, you had a tab everywhere on the island, settled somehow, some way. Mr. Menna must have been in his seventies by the time I was a teenager; I wonder if he's still there, white-haired, wrinkled.

"Was there an old guy working there?" I ask Jay.

He shrugs. "I don't know."

I nod curtly. Of course he doesn't. It takes a specific type to catch Jay's eye. And an aging male shopkeeper isn't it.

"Well, thanks again for lunch," I say. I force myself to smile. "We'll be up in a few hours."

Jay leaves, and I settle back into my chair, watching Sloane and Harper splash around in the waves.

The afternoon stretches on, bright white and hot. Music plays from a Bluetooth speaker, Sloane's Taylor Swift mix that we all sing along to. Harper's favorite song, "Bad Blood," plays over and over and every time it does, I smile to myself. How fitting. I take a million pictures of Harper, her belly still baby-fat pudgy in her little two-piece suit, hair curling in the humidity like a wild halo, sand freckling her sticky skin. She crouches at the edge of the water, looking for seashells, running back up to our umbrella when she finds a good one. She poses for me when she sees me holding up my phone, grinning, hand on her hip like she's fifteen instead of almost five. Not everything about being a mother is easy, but this, this right here, right now, is magic.

Around five, when the heat of the sun begins to subside, I call down to Harper. "Ready to go back home?"

"No, not yet!" Harper says, looking up from the hole she's digging.

"Dad bought Popsicles," I singsong. "You could have one while I get dinner started."

Harper scrambles to her feet. "I love Popsicles!"

I laugh. "I know you do. What about you, Cait, you want a Popsicle?" I turn to Sloane. "And Jay said he got burgers for dinner."

"Sounds good," she says, standing and stretching her arms above her head. The sunburn on her shoulders has already started to turn from pink to brown, her skin slick from all the sunscreen.

We fold up the chairs, unwind the umbrella, then start our trek back to the house, up the sand and through the tall, reedy grasses.

The three of us have just settled in the kitchen, Harper at the little table waiting for her Popsicle, legs dangling off the chair, when there's a rap on the front screen door.

"Hello?" A woman's voice carries into the house.

I take a step into the living room and see Anne-Marie and her two kids on the porch.

"It's our neighbors!" I say, leaning back into the kitchen. "Come on, I'll introduce you." I motion for Sloane and Harper to follow me.

"Remember," I say on the way to the door, winking. "You're me."

Sloane rolls her eyes good-naturedly. "Right," she says. "I remember."

I open the screen door. "Hi! Come in, come in!"

"Is it a good time?" Anne-Marie asks.

"Yes, totally," I say. "We were hoping you'd stop by. Violet," I turn to Sloane, "This is Anne-Marie. Anne-Marie, Violet. They're staying in the house next door."

"Hi," Anne-Marie says, extending her hand to Sloane. "So nice to meet you!"

"Do you want to show Rooney and Claire your room?" I ask Harper.

"What about the Popsicles?" Harper says, frowning.

I smile apologetically at Anne-Marie. "We were just about to have Popsicles. There's enough for everyone if it's okay with you."

She waves me off. "Of course. They'd love that, wouldn't you, guys?"

Both of her kids nod shyly.

I usher everyone into the kitchen and take out the box, doling the Popsicles out one by one. "Go eat them on the back porch," I say, opening the door. The three kids happily parade outside.

"Would you like anything? Iced tea, water, beer? A Popsicle?" I say to Anne-Marie.

"A Popsicle sounds great," she says. I hand one to her and Sloane, then take one for myself.

"Where'd you find her?" Anne-Marie says to Sloane, tilting her head toward me as she unwraps her Popsicle. "I'm lucky if my nanny puts her phone away long enough to pick up the kids from school! I'm not kidding, she forgets one of them like twice a month."

Sloane smirks at me. I smile prettily back. "Just lucky, I guess," Sloane says. "Where are you guys vacationing from?" *Smart, Sloane, change the subject.*

"Charlotte," Anne-Marie says. "Have you been?" She doesn't wait for either of us to answer. "I'm originally from Vermont, but my husband was born and raised there. We met at a sales conference and one thing led to another! He was adamant about raising kids close to his parents, and since mine are thoroughly enjoying retirement in Boca, I thought, *what the hell*, and we've been there for almost ten years now! It's a cute city, growing like crazy."

I give Sloane a look like, *See what I mean?* and she suppresses a smile.

Anne-Marie continues. "It's not as big as New York, of course. Caitlin said you're from the city?" she says to Sloane.

Before Sloane has the chance to answer, there's the sound of footsteps on the stairs. We all turn to see Jay descending into the living room.

My smile freezes on my face. I'd assumed he wouldn't come down. That was stupid of me. I should have suggested we all take our Popsicles on the porch with the kids. *Shit.*

"Anne-Marie," I say quickly, "this is Jay. Harper's dad. Jay, this is

Anne-Marie, and that's Claire and Rooney on the deck with Harper. They're staying in the house next door."

"Hi," Jay says, crossing the living room, coming into the kitchen to shake Anne-Marie's hand. "I was just coming down to grab something to drink." He gives her his wide, movie-star smile. "Nice to meet you."

Anne-Marie runs a hand over her hair to smooth it, tucking a strand behind her ear. "Nice to meet you, too," she says, smiling back.

Then Jay cocks his head. "Didn't I see you this morning? Out for a run?"

"Oh, probably," Anne-Marie says. "I try to do five miles before breakfast."

"Every day?" Jay asks. He sounds impressed.

Anne-Marie nods, blushing slightly. "I try. Some days it's less. Some mornings I can hit ten, if I get started early enough. I ran the Boston Marathon a few years ago. I went to college there. At BU. I'm training for another next spring."

"Wow!" Sloane says as Jay nods appreciatively.

"It's a good excuse to get out of the house," she says. "Fitz—my husband"—she clarifies to us all—"lets the kids watch cartoons when they wake up—it's *vacation*, he says—and they're demons when it's time to turn it off. So I let him deal with the aftermath. It's his mess, really. Are any of you runners?"

Both Sloane and I shake our heads, but Jay makes an affirmative noise. "When I have the time," he says. "I love running. In fact, I was hoping to squeeze in a few jogs while we're here." I try not to roll my eyes. I haven't seen him lace up a pair of running shoes since we moved to New York. But Jay, predictable Jay, won't miss the chance to make someone feel seen. And Anne-Marie offered one in an outstretched hand.

"You should join me!" Anne-Marie says.

Jay nods thoughtfully. "Maybe I will. When do you go?"

"Seven-ish," she says. "Before it gets too hot. And before these monkeys are hungry for breakfast. Fitz couldn't scramble an egg to save his life." She rolls her eyes. "But speaking of hungry—and Fitz—we should be getting back. He'll be home from golf soon and wondering where dinner is."

"And I should head back upstairs," Jay says, smiling. "I have a little bit more work to do." He takes a can of seltzer from the fridge. "Nice to meet you, Anne-Marie. Maybe I'll see you in the morning."

He smiles, gives a wave, and the three of us watch as he makes his way back to the stairs. I let out a sigh of relief, glad Jay hadn't said anything that would have given me away.

"My husband has never *once* joined me for a run." Anne-Marie gives a little laugh. "Can you tell him to talk to Fitz?" She directs the question to Sloane. Then she pushes open the screen door to the back patio. "Kids! Let's go!"

We all walk them to the front door. Harper and Claire are giggling among themselves, already fast friends.

"Thanks for the Popsicles! Can you guys say thank you?" Anne-Marie says to her kids as they step out of the house. Then to us, "Beach again tomorrow?"

"We'll see you there!" I say.

"Nice to meet you!" Sloane calls as they reach the end of the walkway.

I ease the door shut behind them. "That Fitz really sounds like a catch," Sloane says when it's closed.

I snort. "Husband of the year." Well, runner-up to Jay, of course.

When I get into bed that night, I have a smile on my face. The meeting with Anne-Marie couldn't have gone any better. She's going to be a witness for me, even though she doesn't know it yet. It's another checked box on the list, another step closer.

Soon, this will all be over.

25

The next few days blur together, the bright blue skies bleeding from one afternoon into the next. We spend most waking hours on the white sand beach, every morning setting up an umbrella for shade, unfolding beach chairs, spreading a blanket out, and doling out shovels and buckets for Harper to play with.

We apply and reapply sunscreen to ourselves and Harper, offering each other our backs, slathering on coat after coat until our skin shines. We take turns wading in the water with Harper, splashing in the surf. Taylor Swift plays on repeat as we trade magazines, reading articles out loud to each other, talk about nothing, everything. When Harper yells, "Mom!" we both look up and wave.

Anne-Marie and her kids pop by every so often to dig in the sand, share juice boxes, snacks. Anne-Marie gossips about the families on the island, complains about her husband, and, along with Sloane, ogles Jay when he comes down to swim with Harper.

Jay is mostly holed up in his makeshift office upstairs in the oversized laundry room, but he joins us for lunches and dinners and will occasionally appear on the beach under the pretense of saying hi to Harper, instead flirting with Sloane, predictable as always. He's taken Anne-Marie up on her offer to run together; every morning he disappears for an hour, comes back brow beaded with sweat, his T-shirt soaked through, clinging to his chest and back. Already his skin has darkened, deepening into a golden hue. If it's possible, he's becoming even more handsome, ripening in the sun. Soon, he'll be ready to pick. Then I'll squeeze, letting the juice run down my arms, stain my clothes.

At night, he puts Harper to bed while Sloane and I do the dishes. When the kitchen is clean, we change into our pajamas and binge-watch *Bridgerton*. Jay usually comes back down to grab a beer, then disappears again, back up the stairs to his office.

I stock our fridge with ice cream and Popsicles, help myself to extra scoops and oversized portions at dinner. It doesn't take long for me to gain weight, my cheeks becoming a little rounder, stomach a little softer. I don't wash my face at night, either, pleased in the mornings when there's a new smattering of pimples on my chin, along my jawline. I don't pluck my brows, never blow-dry my hair. I look less and less like my old self each day. I catch Jay staring at me one morning while I'm changing into a swimsuit, but he doesn't say anything. He doesn't have to.

Things have changed between Sloane and me here, too. A subtle, almost imperceptible shift. In New York, we were close; it wasn't real, not all of it, but I really had begun to enjoy her company. She's funny, self-deprecating, thoughtful. A liar, yes, but desperate, mostly, for people to like her. And she wanted me to like her, thought I was special. It made me feel special, something I haven't felt for a long time. I'd been lonely in New York. I told her the truth that first night; I hadn't made many friends since the move, spent most of my time with

Harper, or by myself. By the time we left for Block Island, I looked forward to seeing her every day, glad when she walked through the door.

But now she looks at Jay the way she used to look at me. She lights up when he walks into a room, her eyes bright and shining. It's his desire she wants, not my friendship. I don't fault her, especially since I've been gently nudging her to him. Even though it's necessary, it leaves a bitter taste at the back of my throat, a hardened pit at the base of my stomach.

It's Thursday night, our sixth night here. Sloane and I have just finished cleaning the kitchen when Jay comes back down from putting Harper to bed. Normally, he stays upstairs, claiming he has to work for another hour or two. But tonight, he had three beers with dinner. I can tell he's restless, will likely open a fourth, maybe a fifth, tired of being alone. I want to be asleep when he's ready for bed, or at least pretending to be.

I let out a loud yawn, stretching my arms above my head. "I'm going to head upstairs. Can we rain-check *Bridgerton* tonight?" I say to Sloane, pretending to suppress a second yawn. "I'm beat. I think I'm going to take a bath and get into bed."

"Of course," she says. She flicks her eyes to Jay. I can tell she's excited by his presence, by the possibilities.

"Okay, good night!" I give a general wave and make my way upstairs. A moment later, they begin to banter, Sloane giggling.

I'm just changing out of my clothes and into a pair of sweatpants when I hear the squeak of the front door opening and closing. I lean my head out into the hall to see if I hear anything downstairs, but the house is quiet. Did they leave together?

I cross the bedroom and slowly slide the window open. The ocean is loud, rushing, but their voices carry. They're both on the porch. I strain to hear, but only catch a word here and there. I need to be closer.

Quietly, I ease the bedroom door open and tiptoe down the hallway. The downstairs is dark, the lights shut off. Holding my breath, I make my way down the stairs. From the last stair, I have a clear view of the window that looks out onto the porch. I creep toward it. It's open; I can hear them perfectly. I'm hidden in the shadows of the darkened room, but even if I wasn't, they're distracted, their backs to me, each in an Adirondack chair.

"Over there," Jay's saying. "See, low, in the grasses?" He leans toward Sloane, his arm outstretched so she can see where he's looking.

Then, after a pause, "Oh!" Sloane cries. "I think I saw one! And—another! There are a ton!"

Even though I can't see, I know they're talking about the fireflies that light up the dusky shoreline, blinking on and off like neon dots, glow-in-the-dark confetti. He's showing her like I'd shown him when we last visited. When I was little, my grandmother and I would come down to the beach after dinner, running through the sand to chase them, shrieking if we caught one, their wispy wings tickling our palms.

Jay laughs. "Is this the first time you've seen them?"

"No," Sloane says. "But it's been ages. Not since I was a kid. My mom and I used to live in Florida; there were millions of them there."

They sit quietly for a moment, but I can feel the charge from here. I remember that feeling, alone with someone, the air thick, heavy with anticipation. Her heart is pounding, I'm sure of it.

"I'm glad you came on the trip," says Jay. He's lowered his voice, and Sloane shifts to look at him.

"Me too," she says.

Then, slowly, so slowly, his head begins to tilt toward hers. As if by magnetic force, she leans in, too, millimeter by millimeter. I hold my breath.

Then, as their lips are about to touch, Sloane pulls back, shakes her head. "I can't . . ." she says, but I can hear in her voice how much she wants to. "I can't do that to Violet." I bite down on the inside of my cheek, internally screaming, *Do it!*, the voice in my brain sharp and shrill.

Jay pulls back. He studies her, then shakes his head. "You don't know," he says. "Do you?"

"Know what?" Sloane asks.

"We're separating. Violet and me. I'm moving out when we get back to the city." I breathe in sharply. We've discussed divorce, of course, but he agreed to work on things. It's why he thinks he's welcome in my bed on this trip. But it should be no surprise that he's chosen to leave that part out.

Sloane's quiet at first. Finally, she asks, "Why?"

That's a great question, Sloane. Why, Jay? Are you going to tell her why we've discussed—well, shouted, screamed, about—divorce? Tell her, I dare you, I want to hiss through the open window, my breath hot in his ear.

Jay sighs. He leans his head back against his chair. "A million reasons. But mostly, she's changed. We both have. And we've been fighting a lot. It feels like we don't want the same things anymore. She hasn't been happy here. In New York, I mean. I think she resents leaving San Francisco for me."

I dig my fingernails into my palms to keep from screaming. It's not that he's wrong, but he's not right, either. He's so far from right. It's true, we'd been arguing, like we had been for years, but that night—

the night that we said everything, when divorce was said out loud—was different than our previous fights. The limit had been reached.

"You're not the woman I married," he'd said, shrugging, by way of explanation. Like I was an old rag, once new and bright white, now disappointingly faded, stained, tossed into a bucket of dirty water and used to mop the floor one last time before being thrown into the trash.

At that, I threw my glass of wine at him, overcome with fury, incensed by his nonchalance, how blasé he seemed about it all. Cabernet and glass shards exploded against the wall to the right of his head.

No, I wasn't the woman he married. The woman he married was a meticulously curated version of myself, a boxed-in twenty-four-year-old with a round ass and a tight dress, in lacy bras and thongs, who gave him head in the bathrooms of bars, drunk and uninhibited. Now I was the mother of his child. But it shouldn't have been a denigration, should it?

I wasn't naïve; I knew that things would be different once I had Harper. I knew I'd be different. I thought Jay knew that, too. I thought he'd understand that our lives would change, our relationship would change. I thought he wanted it to. I did.

But he wasn't happy. "You never want to do anything anymore," he'd say. "You never want *me* anymore. You're always tired."

Of course I was tired. I had a baby who woke up three times a night and every morning at five thirty, sometimes earlier. Who I carried everywhere, who wanted something from me every second of every day. I was swollen, puffy, both before I gave birth and after, my face sallow from the lack of sleep, nerves frayed from the crying—hers and mine. It's not that I didn't want to go out, that I didn't want him, it was that I couldn't. I was consumed by Harper, by her milk-sweet smell, her velvet-soft skin, by the warmth and weight of her, by how much she needed me.

And, I wanted to know, if we did go out—who was going to get up with her in the middle of the night? Who was going to make her a bottle in the morning if we drank too much, were hungover, too sick to get out of bed? Not him. Never him. Where was his sacrifice? I was the one who'd given up my body, yes, willingly, of course, willingly, but what had he given up? Nothing. Not a thing.

But I tried. When Harper began sleeping for four-hour stretches instead of three, when I weaned her from my breasts, I put myself back in the box. In his box. I dressed up and smiled. I sucked his dick again. And I agreed to move, to uproot our lives. I left my job and my friends and my support system. For him. For us. Because he promised things would be different. That they'd be better. But instead, he removed my heart from my chest and crushed it with a sledgehammer.

So when he told me I wasn't the woman he married anymore, like it was something he could no longer abide, I threw a glass and started screaming. The night dragged on for hours, slogged on, yelling and shouting, then a blur of red-and-blue lights. When it was over, the sun rising, I knew nothing would ever be the same. How could it be?

"I had no idea," Sloane says to Jay. Her voice is hushed.

Jay goes on. "We agreed to live together through the divorce proceedings, but we've been sleeping in separate bedrooms, living two separate lives. The only time we talk is around Harper, or about her. Up until recently—right around the time she met you, now that I think about it—she wouldn't even look at me. Lately, it's been better, though; she's been pleasant, friendlier than she's been in a long time."

This is what he thinks Sloane wants to hear, what it will take to convince her to sleep with him. If he could only hear how it sounds, if he was just a little bit smarter, he might put two and two together. But it just wouldn't be fair if he had looks *and* brains, right?

"Do you think she wants to get back together?" Sloane asks. I almost laugh out loud. Even though it's what I'm pretending to want, I'd rather choke on my tongue.

Jay nods slowly. "Maybe? But it's over. For me, at least. I think she knows that. I've made it clear." *See?* he's trying to say, *I'm a stand-up guy. A good guy. Are you wet yet?*

Sloane doesn't say anything for a few minutes, then finally, she asks, "Why did you come on this trip?"

Jay sighs. "For Harper. Violet said she wanted to keep as much normalcy as we could. I said no, but she begged me. She wanted Harper to have one last happy memory of her family together."

"I can't believe she didn't tell me," Sloane says softly. I have to lean closer to the window to hear. "I wish I'd have known."

Is she upset that I didn't tell her the truth about me and Jay? That I lied? I hold back a snort. Come on, Sloane, really?

"You're a good friend," Jay says. He reaches out and tucks a strand of Sloane's hair behind her ear. My stomach turns. I can't believe this shit used to work on me.

They both fall silent. A minute passes, then two.

Finally, Sloane shifts. "I should go to bed," she says.

I can see Jay's head nodding. "Me too."

Carefully, I sneak back up the stairs. My blood burns hotly in my veins, anger boiling, simmering. Jay's lies burrow under my skin like a tick, latching and feeding, making me sick. He'd told Sloane a sliver of the truth, a tiny, microscopic piece; the rest was bullshit.

Shortly after I close my door, I hear the door to Sloane's room shut, too. Briefly, I wonder if Jay followed her upstairs, into her bedroom, but a minute later the doorknob to our bedroom turns. I squeeze my eyes shut. I feel the mattress shift as he climbs into bed next to me.

It's time. I was going to give it a few more days, but I can't wait any longer.

Strike while the iron is hot, isn't that the saying?

26

The next morning, we're all in the kitchen, bustling around. Sloane came down shortly after I did, giving me a small, hesitant smile. I waited for her to ask me about the divorce, about what Jay told her last night on the porch, but she didn't.

If she had, I planned on confirming what he said—that we've been fighting a lot and have decided to end things—and tell her that I've been embarrassed to say anything, that I'm still coming to terms with it myself. It doesn't really matter if she knows or not at this point; in fact, it might be just what she needed to hear, the permission she would never ask for.

Jay has just come back from his morning run with Anne-Marie, sweaty in workout shorts and an old, faded T-shirt from our alma mater, hair damp. The smell of his sweat is salty, ripe. I'm at the stove scrambling eggs; Sloane's at the toaster. Harper is already seated at the table, pretending to feed two of her Barbies. She lifts an empty fork to one of their mouths, then the other.

Sloane and Jay are trying to avoid eye contact, but I notice when they accidentally brush against each other, Sloane's face reddens. She turns, busying herself with buttering toast, pretending to concentrate deeply on the task. It's clear that their conversation last night has changed things between them.

When the eggs are done, I join Harper at the table, dishing some onto a plate for her, then setting the bowl in the middle of the table. "Want some?" I say to Sloane.

"Huh?" she says after a beat, looking at me in surprise.

"I asked if you wanted some eggs."

"Oh, sure," she says. She pulls out a chair and sits down across from me. "Thanks."

Jay finishes at the coffee machine, then grabs a bagel from a brown paper bag and starts toward the stairs. He smooths Harper's bangs as he passes her. "Have a good day, baby," he says.

"Oh, before you go . . ." I say. Jay pauses, turns. "I made dinner reservations for tonight at five thirty. For all four of us." I look at Harper and Sloane. "At the lobster house. Murph's. And"—I turn back to Jay—"don't say you have to work late. You can take one day off early."

Jay holds up his hands in surrender, the ever-so-gallant knight. "Okay," he says. "Dinner at five thirty."

I want people to see them together. With Harper, as a family. It's not entirely necessary, but it'll make things more believable, give credibility to my story. Murph's is the perfect place.

When Jay's out of the room, I turn to Sloane and Harper, a big smile on my face. "So, what do you say we go shopping? Should we buy you a new dress for tonight, Harp?"

Harper lights up. "Can it be green? Tiana's dress is green. From *The Princess and the Frog*," she says matter-of-factly, as if it's something we all should already know, which of course, I do, given how often she watches the movie. It's recently replaced *Moana* as her favorite.

"We can look for a green one," I say, and she claps happily.

"And I have a dress for you, Cait," I say, looking to Sloane. "It's a little too short for me, but I think it'll fit you perfectly."

The red Hervé Léger. I bought it before we left, the same day I bought all of the other outfits for her. "I need a dress," I told the saleswoman. "Something head-turning." She'd nodded, returned shortly, clearly understanding what I was looking for. At home, I took off the tags, wore it around for a few hours to break it in a bit.

"Thanks," Sloane says. Her eyes don't meet mine. Does she feel guilty about their almost kiss? She shouldn't. I practically shoved her into Jay's lap. Turned her into someone I knew he'd want to put his hands all over.

"Great," I say. "I'm just going to get dressed, meet you downstairs in ten? Do you mind getting Harper ready?"

She nods. I bend to kiss Harper. "Don't forget to brush your teeth, lovey, okay?"

Upstairs, I dress in a college T-shirt and cutoff shorts, the Converse sneakers. It'll be the first time the three of us go into town together, and I want to look our parts. Me, the young nanny; Sloane, the Brooklynite mother, polished, put together. After I sweep my hair back into a ponytail, I take the pair of plastic-rimmed glasses that I bought for the DMV picture out of my toiletry bag, put them on. It's one more thing that separates the Violet I was before, from the one I am now.

As the three of us walk down the driveway to the car, I toss Sloane the car keys. "Will you drive?" I ask. "My contacts have been bothering me, and this prescription is a little out of date."

"Of course." She nods, catching the keys, turning to look at me. "I didn't know you wore glasses."

I nod. "I mostly wear contacts, but they've been uncomfortable recently. I thought I'd give my eyes a break."

"Oh," Sloane says, cocking her head. I can tell she's not sure whether to believe me. She's suspicious of me now, now that she thinks I lied to her about Jay. *Hysterical.*

From the passenger's seat, I direct Sloane to the small main street of the island. It's a cloudless, still day, the sky impossibly blue, air thick and warm. It's busier than it was when we first arrived, which is good. More people to see us together, Sloane as me, me as Sloane.

The street is lined with a number of upscale clothing boutiques, their glass storefronts filled with well-dressed mannequins adorned with oversized leather handbags, long necklaces, bangle bracelets; home furnishing stores with island décor; sidewalk cafés and hand-churned ice cream parlors. We stroll up the street, one of Harper's hands in each of ours, wandering in and out of shops without buying anything until we reach a children's store, the mannequins small instead of adult-sized.

"Let's look in here!" I suggest, opening the door for Harper and Sloane to go in.

Harper's eyes light up when she sees the racks of brightly colored clothes. She sprints to a row of sequined T-shirts. "Look at this one! And this one! Oh, and this!" she says, flipping through the hangers.

In the end, Harper decides on a green dress with a rainbow-colored tulle skirt that flares when she twirls. She begs to wear it out of the store, but I convince her to re-dress in her shorts and T-shirt by promising her ice cream later.

As we start toward the register with the dress in hand, Harper sees a display of headbands. She dashes over to it, then turns back to us, her face lit with delight.

"Can I get one of these, too?" Harper asks, looking from me to Sloane. "Please, please, please?"

It's my biggest weakness as a parent: saying yes, never no. I love the way Harper squeals when she's happy, how her cheeks scrunch up, the little gap between her two front teeth peeking out when she smiles. I love making her that happy. Jay thinks I should be stricter, but I can't, not when she clasps her hands together like that, her eyes shining.

"Sure, baby," I say. Then, to Sloane, "It might take a while for her to pick one out. Why don't I grab us a table at the restaurant across the way while you finish up with Harper?" I reach into my purse and take a credit card from my wallet, pass it to Sloane. "Just meet me there when you're done. Do you mind?"

"No." Sloane shakes her head. "Sounds good." I like the idea of Sloane and Harper being seen together alone, a mother and her daughter on a shopping excursion.

I cross the street to a little café with a sidewalk patio. The waitress seats me in the back corner, away from the sidewalk, but with a clear view of the store across the street.

Ten minutes later, Sloane and Harper emerge from the store, and I lift my hand above my head, wave them over. They hold hands as they cross the street, shopping bag on the crook of Sloane's elbow. They really do look like they could be mother and daughter, if you didn't know any better, with their dark hair and heart-shaped faces.

"How'd it go?" I ask when they sit down, both Harper and Sloane across from me, next to each other. "Did you pick a headband?"

Harper nods. "It's green to go with my dress," she says. "The lady wrapped it up for me like a present."

"I can't wait to see it." I smile at her. "Let's order. I'm starving!"

I tell Sloane about Murph's, the lobster joint I made reservations at for tonight, how it has the best reviews of all the restaurants on the island. It's the place to be seen, a favorite of locals and tourists alike, where I'd go with my grandmother for any special occasion. In the red dress I bought for her, Sloane is sure to turn heads; she and Jay will be noticed by everyone.

At the end of lunch, when the server drops the bill at the table, I smile at Sloane. "You have my card, I think."

"Oh, right, here," she says, reaching into her purse, then extends my credit card across the table.

I don't take it from her. "Actually, why don't you keep it," I say. "In case you need to buy anything else for Harper while you're here."

"Are you sure?" she asks.

I nod. "It's easier that way. You never know when you'll need to treat this monkey to ice cream." I reach over and pinch Harper's cheeks. She swats me away.

Sloane smiles, shrugs. "Okay."

"Lunch is on you, then, I guess." I wink at her.

"Well, my pleasure." She puts the card in the leather check presenter and holds it up, signaling the server. She hands him the book, then, as she turns back to us, she freezes, staring at something across the street. Her eyes widen, breathing slows.

I follow her gaze. Sloane is watching a woman on the opposite sidewalk coming out of the children's store we were just in, her arms full of shopping bags. The woman is in an expensive-looking dress that shows off her heavy chest, and strappy gold sandals, with big, coiffed blonde hair. She looks to be in her midfifties or early sixties, draped in jewelry. She hardly looks out of place—the island is filled with rich women on weekend shopping excursions—but Sloane doesn't take her eyes off her.

Sloane visibly tenses as the woman steps off the curb and begins to cross the street in our direction. When the woman reaches our side of the street, she scans the restaurant patio, then smiles broadly when she sees Sloane. I think she might come to our table, but she just lifts a hand in a wave and continues down the street.

"Who was that?" I ask, looking to Sloane. What are the odds Sloane knows someone who vacations here? It's not exactly the social circle she runs in. But it would be a problem if she did. The whole plan hinges on her anonymity, on mine.

"No one," Sloane says quickly. "Just a woman we chatted with while shopping. She was looking for a gift for her granddaughter and asked Harper's opinion."

I study her. It sounds like another lie. I look for her tells, the twitch of her mouth, if she's touching her neck, but her hands are in her lap, a tight smile on her face. Is she telling the truth? If she didn't know that woman, why had she looked so alarmed?

I decide to let it go. She probably lied to the woman in the store about something, was worried I'd find out about it. I smile back at her, then look to Harper.

"Should we get that ice cream I promised you?" I ask.

While we wander around the downtown with our cones, I keep an eye out for the woman, but I don't see her. Sloane seems to have forgotten about it, happily trading licks of ice cream with Harper, a relaxed expression on her face. I feel a twinge, sorry that for Sloane, this vacation is almost over.

27

When we get back to the house, I ask Sloane to take Harper upstairs for a nap, then get her ready for dinner.

"I'm wiped," I say, plopping down onto the couch. "I'm going to lie down for a bit, too, if that's okay." I close my eyes, hoping to appear exhausted. "The dress for you is in my closet, Cait. Shoes, too, if you need some."

"Of course," Sloane says, taking Harper by the hand. "Let's go, Harp."

I hear their footsteps on the stairs, then above me in the hall, Harper's bedroom door closing. An hour later, it opens again. They scuttle around upstairs, in and out of the bathroom, my room, Sloane's room. There's the sound of the shower running, a blow-dryer.

Finally, I hear giggling at the top of the stairs. "We're ready!" Sloane calls out.

They descend, hand in hand, Harper in her new tulle-skirted dress, a perfect French braid down her back, Sloane in the dress I bought last week, red, hip-hugging, neckline low. Her hair is blow-dried and shiny, skin golden from the sun, cheeks flushed. They both look beautiful.

Harper lets go of Sloane's hand and leaps onto the couch, flinging her arms around my neck. I squeeze her, then pull back to touch her braid, her hair like silk. "I love your hair, baby. And your dress!" Then I look up at Sloane. "That dress is amazing on you!" More importantly, Jay will think so, too. The dog might try to finger her under the dinner table.

Sloane smiles, then frowns, seeing that I'm not dressed. "Oh, are you—?"

"I'm actually not feeling great," I say, drawing my knees closer to my chest, my arm encircling my stomach.

"What's wrong?" Sloane looks concerned. "Do you need a doctor?"

"No, no." I roll my eyes, muster a smile. "I'm fine. It's that time of month," I say. "I get pretty bad cramps that come on out of nowhere. I just need some ibuprofen and a heating pad. No lobster for me." I arrange my face into a disappointed expression.

Sloane's face falls, too. "Well, we'll go to dinner when you're feeling better."

"No, no, you guys go," I say, moving into a sitting position on the couch. "They're hard reservations to get. You should still go."

"It's okay, we can—" Sloane starts, but I cut her off.

"No, really." I smile. "Harper would be so disappointed if we canceled. Is it okay if Caitlin and Daddy take you to dinner, Harpie?"

Harper nods.

I look back to Sloane. She has a funny look on her face, a sort of half smile, and I realize that she's happy I'm not coming. She's excited to have Jay to herself, especially now that she knows we're no longer together. *Good for you, Sloane. Enjoy it.*

Just then, Jay comes down the stairs in slacks and a collared shirt rolled at the sleeves, carrying a beer. He's freshly showered, hair damp, face shaved clean. Sloane is blushing already, just at the sight of him. I remember looking at him like that once. Now, I want to gouge him in the throat with a butcher knife.

Harper jumps off the couch. "Look at my new dress, Dad!" She twirls around so the skirt lifts in the air.

"Wow!" he says. "You're gorgeous!" Then he picks her up, hoists her onto his hip. "Ready?" Harper nods. He looks to me, then Sloane, holding a beat longer on Sloane, on her body in the tight dress, then back to me. "Should we go?"

He doesn't even notice I'm not dressed. "You guys go," I say. "I'm not feeling well. I'm going to stay home and rest."

Jay turns back to look at me, then nods slowly.

"We can bring you something back," Sloane offers. "Dessert or something?"

I shake my head. "I'm going to get in bed early, so hopefully I'll be asleep when you're home. I'll be fine by tomorrow, I promise. Give Mama a kiss goodbye, baby."

Harper does, then runs back to Jay, and the three of them walk out together, down the path to the driveway. I get up, watch them from the doorway. They look like a perfect family. Before Sloane gets in the car she pauses, then turns back to look at the house. I lift a hand, wave. "Have fun," I call. She waves back, a small, tentative smile on her face.

I go back inside and ease the door closed behind them. The house is uncharacteristically quiet. I can hear the rush of the ocean, a clock ticking in the kitchen.

From the front window, I watch the car back out of the driveway, drive down the road toward town. When I can no longer see it, I go upstairs, into the master bedroom, then to the bathroom, where I punch in the four-digit code to the safe. It beeps twice. The lock releases.

I reach in and take out the burner phone. I power it on, the little screen lighting up. Then I call him.

He answers on the second ring. "Hi, Danny," I say.

Danny Shepherd, my first crush, my first kiss, my first boyfriend. The boy who broke my heart when he told me that he didn't feel the same way about me, didn't feel that way about any girl. My grandmother wasn't surprised. Looking back, maybe I shouldn't have been, either; after all, he loved Prince more than I did. When he came out to his parents, shortly after we broke up, they ordered him out of their house. Not knowing where else to go, he showed up on my grandmother's doorstep, and she welcomed him in.

"He needs us," she told me, and one look at him told me she was right. I sat beside him on the couch as he told us how his dad watched him pack a bag, his arms folded, didn't say a word to Danny as he left.

He slept in my bed that first night. I woke to the noise of him crying at two in the morning, his side of the bed empty, and found him in the bathroom on the tile floor with a cheap razor in hand, his wrist upturned. I took it from him gently, led him back to the bedroom, held his hand until he fell asleep. My grandmother said he could stay as long as he wanted, as long as he needed. When he left a month later to move in with his cousin, he'd become like blood, like a brother. We whispered to each other when we hugged goodbye: *I would / die for / you*, the song we sang as kids, our fists imaginary microphones.

After Jay and I visited the island, when I realized our marriage was over, I called him. His aunt had given me his number, but it hadn't changed. I wanted to hear a familiar voice, someone who wouldn't say *I told you so*. Someone who knew me before I became Jay's wife. When he answered, I almost wept.

We talked for over two hours. I told him about Jay and leaving

San Francisco. He told me how he'd stayed on the island, how he'd reconciled with his parents, decided to follow his father's footsteps in medicine, begun working as an EMT when I left for college. He'd loved it so much he never looked back; he oversaw the department now, made captain a few years ago. He'd thought about leaving, but by then his parents were aging, his mom's health declining, and it didn't feel like the right time. He'd never married, had just ended things with his long-term partner.

I hadn't known it, but he'd seen us that May, when I'd come back with Jay and Harper, at dinner one night, the three of us sharing a pizza in a corner booth of a popular restaurant. He'd almost said hi, but we'd looked so engaged, with the food, with each other, that he didn't want to interrupt. I was thinner than he remembered, my cheekbones and collarbone sharp and angular, my clothes expensive, a bracelet on my wrist that cost as much as his car. A distorted version of the girl he knew growing up.

So he'd sat at the bar, with his back to us, pint glass in hand. Which is where he was when he saw Jay and the waitress, not thirty minutes later. They were in the dim corridor leading to the bathrooms. Jay was stooped, his mouth to her ear, their bodies close. She was giggling, a pretty young thing, slender and in a short skirt, and Danny understood what he was seeing, the kind of man I was married to, why I'd lost so much weight. It broke his heart. He set his half-drunk beer on the bar and walked out.

He'd been waiting for my call ever since, waiting for me to wake up to the truth. When I did, the morning after that night, that night with the cops and the blood, that fucking night, he said he knew I would.

We've talked almost every day since. He's the only one who knows everything. When I first saw Sloane, it was his number I dialed, he who I told about my idea.

In the beginning, he indulged the fantasy, but when he realized I was serious, he tried to talk me out of it. A few days after I'd invited Sloane into our lives, he called me on the burner phone, said he couldn't go through with it. He couldn't help, couldn't be a part of it. "Please," I begged, voice cracking, "I can't live like this. I need you." But he hung up.

I'd thrown the phone across the room in anger. I was alone again. And I was drowning. But then he called back a few hours later, his voice quiet. "Okay," he whispered. "I'll do it. You and your grandmother saved me that summer. Now I'm going to save you." *Darlin', if you want me to.*

I smiled through my tears. "Thank you," I whispered. "Thank you."

Now, on the phone, I tell him, "Tomorrow. I'm going to do it tomorrow afternoon. Are you ready?"

When he says that he is, I tell him that I love him and I hang up. I put the phone back in the safe and relock it.

Around eight, I turn out all the lights, close my bedroom door. I want the house to be dark when they pull up, for them to think I'm in bed, asleep.

At 8:50, I see the flash of headlights, hear the crunch of wheels on the gravel driveway. I creep to the window, crouching low, and slowly lift up the bottom slat of the blinds. The headlights turn off, but no one gets out of the car.

I wait, still no movement. It's dark in the car, and I can't see into it. A minute goes by, then two, then five. What are they doing in there?

Finally, both the driver's-side and passenger's-side doors swing open; Jay gets out from behind the wheel, Sloane from the other side. Jay opens the door to the back seat and bends down. When he stands back up, Harper is in his arms, cradled, how he held her as a baby. My throat tightens. I remember those early days so clearly, Harper teeny tiny, wrapped tightly in muslin, snug against Jay's chest as he gazed down, his eyes soft, his finger gently stroking her downy cheek. I felt so lucky. I thought I had everything.

Sloane follows Jay up the walkway to the house. Faintly, I hear the front door opening, then footsteps on the stairs. I listen for Sloane's bedroom door to open and close, but it doesn't.

I get out of bed, quietly crossing the room, my footsteps light, and crack the door open, just a sliver. It opens soundlessly. I hold my breath and peer through the slit.

Pale yellow moonlight streams into the hall from a small window. Sloane is outside Harper's bedroom, her back to me, waiting. Waiting for Jay. I hold my breath as I watch.

A moment later, Jay emerges from Harper's room, easing the door slowly closed behind him. He turns to Sloane, takes a step toward her. At first, they just stand there, unmoving. Then she tilts her face upward. Jay lowers his lips to hers, his hand slipping around the back of her neck, pulling her to him. They kiss tentatively at first, then harder, more urgently, pressing into each other, Jay moving her against the wall. He's a good kisser, good with his tongue, good with his hands.

"Do you think she wants to get back together?" Sloane had asked Jay. *Never*, I'd wanted to yell. He disgusts me. And yet. And yet, seeing him with her makes stomach acid rise in the back of my throat, turns my mouth sour, my intestines twisting.

I step back from the door. That's enough. I was starting to feel bad about what I'm planning to do, about the gun in the safe, but not anymore.

Back in bed, I lie on my side, staring at the wall, facing away from the door. A few minutes later, the bedroom door opens, hinges creaking as it swings wide. Then I hear the buckle of Jay's belt being undone, his pants fall to the floor.

He wants me; he's pressing himself against my back, his hips grinding rhythmically. He's already hard from Sloane, from their foreplay in the hall. His body against mine sickens me. I move away from him. When he reaches for me again, I throw the covers off and grab my pillow, go to the bathroom and lock the door.

He deserves everything that's coming to him. And Sloane, well, she's not so innocent now, either, is she?

28

I get up early the next morning. I hardly slept. Jay is still snoring when I leave the room. It takes all of my willpower not to hold a pillow over his face.

Downstairs, I make a cup of coffee, wait for Harper to get up. Our beach things are packed, ready. We have a big day ahead of us.

I take my mug onto the porch, walk down the driveway toward the water. It's a warm morning, hotter than it's been, the air heavy with humidity. There's only the faintest of breezes, the tall grasses swaying gently. I squint at the beach. Anne-Marie and her kids have already set up camp down near the water.

At eight thirty, I go back upstairs and wake Harper. Sloane's door is still shut. Poor thing must be tired from her big night on the town, the heavy petting in the hallway. It's exhausting sneaking around.

It's just as well. I need to talk to Anne-Marie. And I'd like to do it alone.

When Harper is dressed and fed, the two of us make our way down to the water. I set up our umbrella and chairs, then motion for Harper to follow me. "Want to go play with Rooney and Claire?"

We walk along the surf until we reach their beach chairs, the towels spread out in the sand, all covered in beach toys. Anne-Marie waves from her spot under the umbrella.

"Morning!" I call out.

"Where's Fitz today?" I ask, dropping down into the beach chair next to her. Fitz is both Anne-Marie's favorite and least-favorite thing to talk about. It's clear she thinks he's a semi-functioning baboon who doesn't know his ass from his elbow. She enjoys his paychecks, but not much else. She's like a wind-up doll on the subject. If you turn her key, she'll yak for hours, pausing only for the occasional inhalation.

Anne-Marie groans. "Golfing. Again. We're here for almost ten days, and I think he'll have spent nine of them with a golf club in his hand. I don't get it," she says. "Really. Golf? It's so *boring*. I know it's his vacation, too, but honestly. Last year, we went to Barbados and . . ." And she's off.

I half listen, my eye on Harper kneeling in the wet sand with Rooney and Claire. I could watch her for hours. Study the freckles on her nose, kiss her eyelids, listen to her long-winded stories, her breathy pauses, her laugh. She's the greatest thing that's ever happened to me. The meaning of my life, every good part of me distilled into her tiny, perfect body.

When I tune back into Anne-Marie, she's staring at me expectantly. "I'm sorry, what was that?" I ask.

"I said, Jay doesn't seem like that kind of guy, though," she says finally, glancing back up at our house. "The kind that plays golf all day. He seems great. A really involved dad."

"Oh." I smile politely. "Yeah, he's great. Friendly, too. Really friendly." I let out a little nervous laugh. "Sometimes a little too friendly, you know?" I laugh again, uncomfortably, like I don't want to make a big deal about it, even though it's clear what I'm insinuating.

Anne-Marie's eyes widen. "Jay? Do you mean—?"

"Oh, I don't know," I say hurriedly. "It's totally possible I misread the situation. He probably didn't mean for his hand to . . ." I shake my head, dismissing the whole thing. "It was nothing, really. I shouldn't have said anything. Don't mention it to anyone, okay?"

She nods, of course she'll keep it to herself—as if Anne-Marie has ever kept anything to herself—but I can see the gears turning. When she learns of the murder, her blood will run cold, remembering our conversation. It won't surprise her. Men who are capable of infidelity are capable of anything.

"Oh!" I say. "I almost forgot. Violet wanted me to ask you—would it be okay if Harper spends the night at your house tonight? She's been begging for a sleepover. Then we could return the favor, have your kids sleep over at ours?"

"Absolutely!" Anne-Marie says. "The more the merrier! Claire and Rooney are ten times easier to manage when Harper's around."

"Great!" I say. "I'll feed her lunch at home, then maybe Violet can bring her over after?"

"She's welcome to eat with us. It's supposed to be in the nineties today, so I was planning to head in early anyway to get out of the heat. I can make an extra grilled cheese for her."

"Perfect." I smile.

When Harper and I start back to our umbrella, I see Sloane, already sitting in a beach chair. She lifts a hand up and waves tentatively as we approach.

"Hey," she calls out. She keeps her eyes on me as we reach the edge of the blanket, searching my face. Do I know?

I stare back for a moment, enjoying watching her sweat, then relax my face. *Know what, Sloane?* I smile broadly. "Hi! How was dinner last night?"

Sloane returns the smile uneasily. "Really nice," she says carefully. "I think Harper had a good time, didn't you, Harp?" She looks to Harper, who nods in agreement. "And the lobster was delicious. I'd never had one before."

"Really?" I ask, surprised. "So good, huh? It's my favorite lobster house. And did you get the molten chocolate cake?" I sigh wistfully. "The best I've ever had."

Sloane nods. "We shared one. Jay was worried Harper would be up all night if she had her own."

Oh, wow, what a good dad! Should I give him a standing ovation? The bar for men is unspeakably low. I smile tightly. Except that isn't why they shared one. It's funny, how well Sloane thinks she knows Jay, when in truth, she knows nothing about him except the lies we've both been feeding her.

"Are you feeling better?" Sloane asks, quickly changing the subject. She probably finds it uncomfortable talking about the date she had with my husband. A date that ended in a kiss. Well, more than one.

"Much," I say. "Thanks. I took an ibuprofen eight hundred and it knocked me out. I slept like the dead. I didn't even hear you guys come in."

The relief on Sloane's face is clear as day. I wonder if it kept her up, worrying if I'd heard them together in the hallway, if I lay in my bed, ears straining. Then her face tightens again. She chews on her lower lip, brow slightly furrowed.

Here it is. Here's where she confronts me about Jay, about our divorce. I glance at Harper, digging a hole in the sand a few feet away.

Sloane clears her throat. "You told me you don't drink." She says it lightly, carefully, like she's on tiptoe, stepping softly across a creaking floor, hoping not to make a sound.

I stare at her, surprised. What did Jay tell her? Did he tell her about the night things ended? About the shattered wineglass? The police officers on our doorstep?

I force my mouth into a placid smile. *Play it cool.* "I don't."

Sloane pauses, then, haltingly, "But Jay said . . ." she starts. She's not sure how to finish that sentence without it sounding like an accusation.

"He said what exactly?" I raise an eyebrow wryly. *Don't be defensive, Violet.*

Sloane shrugs. "Just that you drink sometimes. And I was confused because you told me you don't."

I lick my lips, exhale through my nose. Blink a few times, stalling, thinking. "Well," I say. "I used to. It's why I don't anymore. It's been a few months now, since I stopped. When we first moved, I was lonely, the days were long. I started drinking at five, having a glass of wine before dinner instead of with. Then five o'clock became four. Then three thirty. Then, before I knew it, I was pouring myself a drink at noon, drinking steadily until I put Harper to bed."

This part isn't a complete lie. It's true that I was drinking more than I should have been. Anyone would have, if their husband did what mine had.

I sigh. "Anyway, eventually I realized something needed to change." I don't tell her why I've cut back, why I hide the bottle of vodka, why I only allow myself a glass or two every once in a while. It's none of her business what happened that night.

"So I quit," I say, shrugging. "One night I dumped all the bottles down the drain, like they do in the movies." I smile at Sloane. "I didn't say anything to Jay because then I would have had to admit I'd had a problem. And who wants to do that? But"—I shrug—"I'm not surprised he hasn't noticed. He's been a little . . . preoccupied."

I don't look away when I say this, holding Sloane's gaze. You, *calling me a liar, Sloane? That's fucking funny.*

Sloane blinks, reddens, then shifts her gaze to the sand at her feet.

Then, abruptly, she says, "You know, I'm a little hungry. I didn't eat anything before I came down. I'm going to head back up to the house and grab something. Want anything?"

I smile, shake my head. "No, thanks."

I watch Sloane leave. She's walking a bit more stiffly than usual, her shoulders held higher, back straighter.

I know for certain now. Our friendship, or whatever Sloane and I had, is gone, dissipating like a trail of smoke from a blown-out candle, a thin gray trace in the air, then nothing. She's chosen Jay. Good. It's a relief. It will make what I have to do easier.

Thirty minutes later, when I see Anne-Marie and her kids head toward their house, I pack up and tell Harper we're going in. I'm thrumming with adrenaline, my whole body vibrating. The day seems hotter, crisper, clearer, than it normally does, the blades of beach grass sharper, pale against the bright blue sky. It feels like we're in an oven, the temperature creeping up with every passing minute.

When we get to the house, I open the front door, then pause. I hold my hand out behind me to keep Harper from walking in.

From the doorway, I have a clear view into the kitchen. Sloane and Jay are standing together near the sink. Her back is to me as she faces Jay, her face tilted toward his. I can't see if they're kissing, but they're close enough that they could be. They haven't heard us, too caught up in whatever they're doing, saying.

Then I let the door slam. Sloane and Jay jump apart. Sloane looks toward us guiltily, like she's been caught red-handed, elbow-deep in the cookie jar.

"Hi!" Sloane calls out, a bit too loudly. "I didn't think you guys would be back so soon!" Her cheeks are aflame. Jay, unsurprisingly, doesn't say anything.

I wait a beat before giving a tight smile. Then I take Harper's hand. "We're going to go get rinsed off," I say. "Let's go, Harp."

Upstairs, Harper and I pack a bag. Even though it's supposed to be for one night, it'll likely be many, many more, so I stuff a few extra T-shirts, undies, and shorts into her backpack. "In case you want options," I tell her, ruffling her hair.

Harper is bouncing around the room, thrilled at the prospect of her first sleepover with a friend.

"What kind of pajamas do you think Claire will have?" I ask as I put her *Frozen* ones at the top of the bag.

"Maybe she'll have Elsa, like me," says Harper. "Maybe we'll be matching. Or maybe she'll have Ana. Or maybe she won't have *Frozen*. Maybe she'll have *Encanto*. Do you think she's seen *Encanto*?"

I nod, laughing. I'd bet my life that every warm-blooded five-year-old on the planet has.

Then, before I open her bedroom door, I bend down, circle my arm around her tiny waist. "When I pick you up from Claire's house, let's play a game, okay?"

Harper nods. "Okay. What game?"

"We're going to pretend I'm Caitlin. And every time you call me Caitlin, you'll get an M&M. Deal?"

She nods again. I bring her to me, hugging her tightly. "That's my girl. I bet you'll be so good at it, you'll get a whole bag!"

Then, together, we walk down the stairs, back into the living room. Sloane is still in the kitchen, sitting at the table. She's gnawing on a fingernail, brows knit together. She looks up sharply when she hears us, then stands, the chair almost toppling over.

"Hi," she says. She's nervous. She thinks I saw her and Jay kissing, or at least, is worried I did. There's guilt on her face, too, smeared all over it.

"Will you take Harper next door?" I ask. "She's going to spend the night at Anne-Marie's house, with her kids."

"I'm having a sleepover!" Harper announces. She's wearing her backpack over her shoulders. It's almost as big as she is, stuffed to the brim.

Sloane looks surprised. "Sure. Is everything okay?" she asks cautiously.

For me it is. For you, Sloane, not so much. "Fine," I say. I try to keep my voice even. My heart is starting to pound. *This is it.* "So, you can take her?"

She nods. "Now?"

"Yeah, you're ready, right, Harp?"

Harper nods happily. I stoop to kiss her, but she's already out the door, starting down the stone walkway. My heart lurches. I want to run after her, scoop her up and hold her one last time, squeeze her until she squirms out of my arms, giggling. *Mo-om, stop!* But I don't. Soon, it'll just be her and me, together.

"See you soon," I call after them. I lift a hand, wave.

Sloane turns back. "See you soon," she echoes.

29

I shut the door and go up the stairs, taking them two at a time. From our bedroom window, I watch Sloane and Harper begin their walk from our house to Anne-Marie's. It's a five-minute walk there, ten minutes round-trip, longer, of course, if she goes in to chat.

Either way, I don't have much time.

I take my suitcase across the hall into Sloane's room. Sloane's barely unpacked either, clothes spilling out from her oversized suitcase in the corner. I stuff them all back inside and wheel it into the master.

Then I go into the closet and find Jay's empty duffel bag, start grabbing his things from the dresser drawers, tossing them inside, trying to fit in as much as I can in the short time I have. I keep an eye on the window, checking for Sloane.

In the bathroom, I grab his toothbrush, his electric razor. When I come out, I glance again out the window. My heart skips a beat. Sloane is starting down Anne-Marie's walkway, back to the road leading to our house.

Here it goes.

"Jay!" I yell. "Jay!" When I don't hear him, I yell a third time. "Jay!"

Finally, "What?" he answers, his voice faint from the laundry room office. I don't respond.

Then, I hear a door opening down the hall, and a moment later he appears in the doorframe. "What—?" he asks, then stops short. He looks around the room, sees his half-packed bag, the open drawers, the piles of his clothes. "What are you doing?" he asks, looking up at me in confusion.

"I changed my mind," I say. I shove a pair of his board shorts into the bag, not bothering to keep them folded, then a stack of his shirts. "I want you gone."

"Are you kidding?" he asks. His face darkens. "You begged me to come here."

"Well, now I don't want you here anymore." I stop for a moment, folding my arms across my chest. "Take your things and go."

"Why? What the fuck did I do?"

"I saw you with Caitlin," I say.

Jay shakes his head, raises his hands defensively. "Violet," he says, lowering his voice, "she was coming on to me, and I—"

I almost laugh. He's used this line before.

The first time I heard it was after his company Christmas party, back when we lived in San Francisco. I was a month or two into my pregnancy with Harper, not showing, but naueous all the time, puking most mornings. But Jay had just gotten the job, and I wanted to support him, so I put on a dress and a smile and accompanied him to the restaurant.

Halfway through the evening, I realized a woman was staring at him, a young sales associate he worked with, caramel-colored curls, pretty. Jay pretended not to notice, but I watched as his eyes kept darting toward her, as he bit his lip to keep himself from smiling at her.

When he excused himself, my eyes followed as he went to the bar, where she was standing with a glass of wine. Then they were both gone. Not for long, five minutes at the most, but it was something. Maybe a blow job, maybe just his hand up her skirt, the other on her breast. Something quick. I knew it in my gut. He was twitchy when he came back, his arm slipping back around my waist, fidgeting by my side.

When I confronted him at home, he told me I was being paranoid. That it was the pregnancy hormones. "I saw how she was looking at you," I insisted. "Look," he said, holding his hands up. "You're right, she was flirting with me, but I—"

But I—always *but I*—never at fault, never to blame. I believed him then. Because I loved him, because I wanted it to be true. Because I was hormonal. Because I was stupid. I'm not anymore.

Now, I hold up a hand to quiet him. "I don't give a shit. In fact, I'm happy for you two. It's exactly what I hoped for."

Jay glares at me, eyes flashing. "You're fucking crazy," he says. "You know that?"

I stare back at him. He's so handsome. I loved that face once. Now I hate it.

"Maybe I am," I say. He's probably right. But aren't all mothers when it comes to their children? There's nothing we won't do. "Now get the fuck out." I zip up his bag and shove it at him.

For a minute he doesn't move, then takes it from me roughly. "You're such a bitch." He gives me a long once-over, his lip curled with disdain. "Who could blame me?" he says.

There it is: his other favorite excuse. If I looked different, *better*, put out more, he wouldn't have done what he did. It's pathetic.

"Get *out*."

His jaw twitches. "Where's Harper?"

"A sleepover next door. She won't forgive you if you make her leave early. Just go back to the city. I'll bring her home on Sunday."

"I'll see you in court," he says. He slams the door on the way out. It rattles in its frame.

No, you won't, I think.

His footsteps are heavy on the stairs. I hear the front door open and the bang of the screen, then the car starting, the squeal of tires as he peels out.

Then there is quiet again. He's gone. There's only the sound of my breathing and the ticking of the clock on the wall, the steady rhythm like a metronome. I walk back into the bathroom, punch in the code to the safe for the last time.

I take out two things, the gun and the divorce papers, the ones my lawyer drafted before we left.

My trust, since it was set up before we were married, is not considered marital property; if we divorce, Jay is not entitled to it. I'd likely owe him alimony from the income I earn from it, but the trust itself would remain in my name. The only way the money would be his is if something happens to me; he's the primary beneficiary on our life insurance policy—as long as we are married at the time of my death. If we divorce, however, it all goes to Harper. It's very much in Jay's best interest that we remain together. It will be clear to anyone: these divorce papers would make him very, very mad.

I imagine the surprise that will register when he learns about them; perhaps it will mirror my own when I learned that our marriage, like my mother and father's, had been a sham from the start.

I was heartbroken when we moved to New York, grieving the loss of my parents. I had been the one to sever ties, yes, but it hurt, a deep, throbbing ache in my bones. I felt like an orphan.

I told myself that it didn't matter because I had Jay. He'd fallen in love with me before he'd known about the money. He cared about me for me. And when I finally told him the amount, after he proposed, three years after we'd started dating, he kissed me and said it didn't change anything. That he wanted to be self-made, earn his own money. He might need an initial investment, but after that, he'd be on his way.

He'd sounded so earnest. I believed him. Even as he flitted from job to job, always quitting after a few months, hopping from one new venture to the next. I was happy to support him, happy to seed his start-ups, to write checks with strings of zeros; I thought he was brilliant.

And then I found out he'd known about the money all along. He'd been on the phone with his sister one night, shortly after we'd moved into the brownstone, a few whiskeys in. Their dad had had a health scare; they weren't sure if he was going to make it through the night. I was upstairs with Harper, he in the living room, but his voice carried and I heard his side of the conversation clearly. His sister must have said something about their father's will because Jay snorted. "Don't be too sure," he said, "Violet's mom only got a vacation shack when her grandmother died. And that was after they petitioned a judge."

I'd stiffened. *What?* How did he know they'd petitioned a judge? I hadn't known that, so how did he?

Sheepishly, later, he admitted that he'd heard my parents discussing the division of my grandmother's assets at the funeral, in hushed, angry tones. "All of it?" my dad had said. "To Violet?" Then, "The house isn't worth a tenth of that." And, "Yes, we'll contest it, see if it holds up in court." It had, of course.

I sat down on our bed, my legs buckling. Jay had known about the money since the beginning. He swore it made no difference, knelt down and looked me in the eyes. But it made a difference to me. How could it not? How could I not question everything?

New York was supposed to be our fresh start. Jay's big break. I wanted it so desperately to be. For us, for him. And we were already here, my family already lost. So I decided to give him the benefit of the doubt. The chance for him to prove himself, finally. "This is it," he said, "you'll see." With him still kneeling in front of me, I nodded. "Okay, I believe you," I said, for the ten thousandth time, about the ten thousandth thing.

This won't be a surprise to anyone: it wasn't the business opportunity he promised it was. It quickly became clear that "online gaming start-up" was a euphemism for a slapdash gambling site; he'd joined a group of midlevel investors who thought they'd cash in on the recent online frenzy, though none of them had any expertise in the field whatsoever. The hours Jay was holed up in his office were hours spent in virtual poker rooms—for market research, as he put it. The truth: like always, he was giving into whatever impulse struck his fancy. Today, gambling; yesterday, a line of coke in the bathroom, sex with a stranger at a party. Jay only thought about himself, did what felt good, looked good. After three months in New York, he came to me for another check; nothing had changed.

He, like my parents, would never be able to separate his love for me from his love for my money. It was a crushing realization, to say the least. I hope, when this is all over, he is similarly crushed, his heart smashed to smithereens under the weight.

I place the divorce papers on the dresser and take the gun back into the bathroom. Then I wait.

A minute or two passes, then the front door opens and closes again. I hold my breath.

"Violet?" I hear Sloane call out.

I cock the gun, let out the air in my lungs.

Sloane's footsteps are on the stairs, then in the hall. I clear my throat. "In here," I call out. My voice echoes off the bathroom's tiled walls. It's reedy, thin. The jugular vein in my neck throbs.

I hear her open the bedroom door, then the knob to the bathroom door turns. My back is to her. I'm facing the vanity counter, my head hung.

"Violet?" Sloane says again, almost a whisper this time. "Are you okay?"

I open my eyes and look up. I see Sloane's face in the mirror behind me. The face that now looks so much like my own. Our eyes meet. For a moment, neither of us moves, both staring at the other's reflection. I breathe out steadily. Then I turn to face her.

"No, I'm not," I say. "Okay, I mean." My heart is a drum in my chest. "I haven't been okay for a long time."

Sloane's brow crinkles with concern, her face softening. "I'm sorry," she says tenderly. "Is there anything I can—"

Then she stops, her eyes landing on my right hand, dangling by my side. She sees the gun. Her jaw goes slack, color draining from her face.

When she looks from the gun to me, her eyes are wide, pupils so big and black they look like inkwells. I stare back at her. It's like looking into a carnival fun-house mirror. A warped, almost-true version of myself.

I see her swallow. "Is this about Jay?" she asks, her voice wobbly, tiny.

I nod.

Sloane's eyes flutter closed. "I'm sorry," she says. "It just happened. I never meant to hurt you!"

I can't help but laugh, a short bark. "You think this is because I'm jealous?" I shake my head. "No, I'm not jealous. That's not why."

She sighs. Then, gently, "He told me everything, Violet. He told me he was leaving you and that you weren't taking it well—"

"He's lying," I interrupt sharply. "You think you know him, but you don't. He's a liar. Just like you, *Sloane*."

When I say her name—her real name—her face changes. She swallows hard, opens her mouth to speak, but nothing comes out.

I give her a small, rueful smile. "We've all been lying to each other, haven't we?"

Finally, her voice strained, she asks, "How long have you known?"

"Since the beginning."

She presses her lips together tightly. Her eyes fill with tears. She looks like a wounded puppy. I feel nauseous. I swallow the sour spit at the back of my throat. *Think of Harper*, I tell myself. *This is for her.*

"But—" Her voice shakes. "Why are you going to kill me? If you're not jealous?"

"I'm not killing you," I say. "Look in the mirror, *Violet*. I'm killing *me*."

Sloane stares at me, not understanding, her face contorted in confusion. Then her eyes widen with the dawning realization. Slowly, she raises her hand to her mouth, covering it in horror.

"Well, technically, Jay is going to kill you," I continue. "At least, that's what I'll tell the police."

I feel a sharp pang in my gut. The truth is, I wish I didn't have to kill her. I wish I could have aimed the pistol at Jay's chest, blown a hole right where his heart should have been. I thought about it. And thought about it and thought about it. I wanted to kill him, wanted to with every fiber of my being, but it would be too risky. If I was caught—I'd be the prime suspect, probably the only suspect—I'd lose everything. Everything Jay was already threatening to take.

Then I met Allison. And she told me about Sloane. It gave me an idea. What if, instead of me killing Jay, Jay killed me? What if people thought I was dead and he'd done it? Then when I took Harper, no one could question it; she'd be in the loving, legal care of our trusted nanny. And Jay would be in jail, where he belonged.

But for it to work, I needed a body. I needed Sloane. If I could get her to dress like me, look like me, act like me, then, well, when police arrived on the scene and I told them it *was* me, there'd be no reason for them to believe it wasn't. Violet Lockhart would be dead, and Jay Lockhart would be the one who had done it. At least that's who I'd point my finger at.

It would be my picture on Sloane's driver's license. And then there are all the pictures I've taken of Harper and Sloane together, pictures I'll show the police. If they take the photos to Anne-Marie, she'll point to Sloane and say, *Yes, that's Violet Lockhart.* It sounds simple, and it is. Because it's always the husband, even when it's not. What would there be to refute? There would be a body and a motive. They'd find out about the life insurance policy and how it is null and void in the event of a divorce, then find the divorce papers I set out on the dresser. Case open and shut.

Jay would go to jail, and I'd leave with Harper. Thanks to the updated will, Sloane Caraway is the named guardian. From Sloane's phone, I'd text her mother, let her know what had happened to Violet Lockhart, that Sloane would be taking Harper back to the West Coast. Maybe I'd FaceTime her a few times—her mom's vision and hearing are starting to go—just long enough for her to think Sloane is all right. She's unlikely to pose any real threat, even if she suspects something.

Sloane said she's housebound; there's not much she can do from an armchair. Then we'd go away, maybe back to California, maybe to the Pacific Northwest, a little town in Oregon.

"Please," Sloane whimpers, voice muffled from behind her hand, breaking. She's scared, so scared. "Please don't do this."

"I'm sorry," I say. And really, I am. I don't want to, but I have to. The pain in my stomach is throbbing. "There isn't any other way."

My finger hooks around the trigger. I raise the gun.

Sloane begins to back up, legs quaking beneath her, arms outstretched as if to shield herself. There's terror in her eyes.

I feel like I'm floating above myself. Blood rushes in my ears. I see her mouth moving, but I can't hear anything but static.

She turns to run. *Now. Now, Violet, now. For Harper.*

I close my eyes and squeeze. The gunshot is deafening, sharp, like the crack of a whip, but louder, my ears ringing, aching.

When I open my eyes, Sloane's body is on the floor.

The gun clatters to the tile. I fall to my knees.

JAY

30

She said *what*?" I ask. I raise an eyebrow in surprise. In the distance, the faint wail of sirens.

Anne-Marie grins cheekily, then shrugs, brushing a strand of her blonde hair from her eyes. "She said you were coming on to her."

"I came on to *her*? Caitlin said that? When?" I try not to sound as irritated as I feel. Why had Caitlin been talking to Anne-Marie about us?

"Look, don't shoot the messenger," Anne-Marie says, crossing the kitchen and taking another beer out of the fridge. "But don't worry, I didn't put much stock in it. All nannies think the dad is interested in them, ever since Ben Affleck ran away with his. It goes with the territory."

She winks and takes my empty bottle from me, hands me the full, cold one. I take a long drink, then another. The beer's relaxed me; when I first got here, forty-five minutes ago, right after my fight with Violet, I could have put my fist through a wall. Thank god for Anne-Marie. She was on her porch when I drove by, waved at me to stop. "The kids are upstairs," she said, motioning to follow her inside, "zonked out in front of the TV." I can hear it now, volume at full blast.

Now, even over the sound of the TV, the sirens are louder, getting closer. I realize it's the first time I've heard them since we left the city. In New York, they are a constant part of the background noise, an ever-present whine, swelling and fading throughout the day, quieter sometimes than others, but always there. Here, where the only noise is the rushing of the waves, the sound is grating, out of place.

I cock my head toward the street. "Think Caitlin called the cops?" I joke.

Anne-Marie looks at me, amused. She opens her mouth, but doesn't have a chance to speak, because suddenly, the sirens are right out front. We turn to see two police cars, their lights strobing, parked outside of the house. The doors of each car open, sirens still blaring.

"I'll go check on the kids," I say to her. I set my beer on the counter. "Maybe one of them got ahold of a phone?"

But before I can move, there's pounding on the door. Heavy thudding, a closed fist banging against it. We look at each other, frowning.

Then it bursts open. We both recoil, backing away from the door until we're pressed up against the living room wall. Three police officers stand in the doorway. Their guns are drawn.

"Jay Lockhart?" one of the officers booms.

Instinctively, I raise my hands above my head. "Yes, that's me. I—"

"Sir, you are under arrest for the attempted murder of Violet Lockhart." He approaches me with handcuffs, roughly turns me around. I feel metal against my wrists, cold, hard.

Attempted murder? What the fuck? My head is spinning, body unmoving. I stare at him, shell-shocked.

The cop continues, "You have the right to remain silent. Anything you say can be used against you in a court of law."

"There's been a mistake," I finally manage, trying to turn to look at him, but I'm jerked back around, my body propelled forward toward the door. "Please!" I'm yelling now, panic rising.

I glance back at Anne-Marie. She's pale-faced, staring at me with her mouth hanging open, arms clutching at herself.

"It's a mistake," I yell again. "Anne-Marie, call a lawyer. You have to help me!" But she doesn't move, her eyes wide, round and unblinking.

Outside, I'm shoved into the back of a police car, its lights flashing. My head knocks against the side of the car on the way in.

No one speaks to me on the ride to the station. I sit, reeling, a numb, heavy feeling making it hard to breathe, hard to think. Attempted murder? Of Violet? No, there has to be some mistake.

At the station, I'm dumped in a dingy holding cell, drab, gray, humid. There are no windows, no air-conditioning. My shirt sticks to my back, sweaty and grimy. I sit on the hard bench, then stand, then sit again. I shouldn't be here. I don't know what the fuck is happening, but I know I shouldn't be here.

Twice, I get up, yell for water, desperate for someone to talk to me, to look at me, but no one comes. Finally, after what feels like hours, a guard opens the door, calls my name.

He leads me down a cement corridor to an interview room. Like the holding cell, it's hot and run-down. In the middle, there's an aluminum table and two chairs, one on each side. The chair is uncomfortable, too small.

The guard leaves, and I'm alone again, but this time, not for long. There's a loud buzz and the click of the door unlocking.

A man walks in. He's wearing a pair of slacks, a dress shirt with rolled cuffs, unbuttoned at the collar to reveal a faded white under-shirt. He pulls out the chair opposite me, lowers himself into it. He's a thin, sharp-featured man, forties, early fifties, maybe.

"I'm Detective Edgerton," he says. He's brusque, but not rude. "You're on camera, okay?" He shifts to point to a small video recorder behind him, in the top, right-hand corner of the room. Then he turns back toward me. "Do you want to tell me what happened?"

I shake my head. "*Nothing* happened! This has to be a misunder-standing!" I'm on the verge of hysteria. "You have the wrong guy! I never hurt Violet. I would never. I—"

"Jay." He holds up a hand. "Let's take a step back. When was the last time you spoke to your wife?"

I breathe out shakily. "Earlier this afternoon."

"And what happened during that conversation?"

"We . . ." I swallow. I know how this will sound. "We had a fight. She asked me to leave."

"What was the fight about?" he asks.

"She thought . . ." I stop again. I rub my temple. My brow is slick with sweat. *Fuck.* "She thought she saw me with the nanny." My head is pounding, pain wrapping from the back of my skull to my forehead. "Can I get a water or something?"

The detective ignores me. "Did she?" He's straight-faced, doesn't blink.

I shift in my chair. "Look, my wife and I, we've been having some problems. We've discussed separating." I know this doesn't answer his question, but I want him to know that it's not what it looks like.

"Who suggested the separation?"

I shrug. "I don't know, we both agreed that things haven't been working." This, too, isn't exactly the truth. But the truth won't help me.

"But initially, Mrs. Lockhart was the one who wanted to end things?"

I'm not sure what he's getting at. Or who told him that.

"She was angry, and yes, she might have been the one to first say it, but we were working on things—"

He interrupts me. "So, she wanted out and you didn't. Is that why you shot her?"

I stare at him incredulously. "What? Shot her? No! I didn't shoot her. Did she say I did? She's lying! *Jesus.*"

I drop my head into my hands. I know Violet's been upset with me; of course I know. Things have been rocky between us for a long time. It's true I haven't always been the best husband, but it hasn't always been easy to be who she wants me to be. It's been lonely, and I'll admit, I've been weak. The last year in New York has been especially hard. We've both done things, said things, to hurt each other, but *this*? To say I shot her? *What the fuck, Violet?*

"Look." I raise my head. I'm exhausted, every part of my body like deadweight. "Can I talk to her? If I could just have five minutes, I'm sure I can clear this all up. *Please.* Just a quick call." I'm begging now. "She'll tell you, this is all a mistake!"

Detective Edgerton sighs. Then he leans back in his chair. He looks tired, too. "I'm afraid that's not possible."

"I haven't had my phone call yet!" I say, realizing. "Don't I get a phone call? Please. Let me talk to her!"

The detective clears his throat. There's a long, heavy pause before he says, "Unfortunately, Mrs. Lockhart died two hours ago, on the way to the hospital."

I stare at him in disbelief. *What? No. No. She can't be—*

"Which"—he clears his throat again—"means you're looking at a first-degree murder charge. Are you ready to tell me what really happened the last time you saw Mrs. Lockhart? If I know the truth, I can help you."

The room seems to expand then shrink, my vision getting darker. Suddenly, it feels like I'm underwater, everything distorted. I'm waterlogged, sounds muffled, my eyes bleary.

"Mr. Lockhart?" Detective Edgerton's voice booms loudly. "Someone get me some water!" he calls. "Mr. Lockhart, are you okay?"

"I need a lawyer," I hear myself say.

No one comes for me until the following afternoon. My body is stiff and aching, head still pounding. My eyes burn from the lack of sleep. After my interview with the detective, I was booked—fingerprinted, photographed, clothes exchanged for oversized sweatpants and a stained T-shirt—and led to a cell with a thin mat in one corner and metal toilet in the other. The small room was hot and reeked of piss.

Exhausted, I lay down on the mat. I drifted in and out of sleep, jolting awake whenever I dozed too deeply, chest seizing, remembering. *Violet's dead. Dead. Dead. Dead.*

A guard banged on my door early this morning, signaling breakfast. Four hours later, lunch. Both were served on plastic trays, both inedible.

Finally, the guard unlocks my cell, swings the door wide. "Your lawyer's here," he says apathetically. "Get up."

Before he left the interview room yesterday, after I steadied myself, lifting my head from between my knees, Detective Edgerton slid a list of names across the metal table. "Attorneys on the island," he said. "If you don't have one."

I pointed to the first name I saw. Javier Delgado. I could have called Kathleen, the divorce lawyer I met with a few times, but what good would a divorce lawyer do me now? And I wanted someone local, on the island. Someone who could get me out of here as soon as possible.

The guard leads me to the same interrogation room I was in yesterday. Javier is in the same chair as the detective was, a file folder open in front of him on the table. He stands when we walk in, smiling politely at me as he reaches to shake my hand.

Javier is well-dressed in a nicely tailored gray suit, expensive tie, leather loafers. He's late thirties, early forties, maybe, with thick salt-and-pepper hair, a pair of wire-rimmed glasses on his clean-shaven face.

I know how I look in contrast, steeped in grime and sweat, eyes bloodshot, rimmed with deep bags. I smell, too, a sharp acrid smell, like sweat and urine, the stench of the cell clogging my pores. I need a shower. I need to go home, get the fuck off this island.

"Mr. Lockhart—" Javier starts, a pleasant, almost vacant expression on his face.

"I didn't do it," I interrupt. He has to know this. It's the only thing he has to know. "We had a fight, but when I left, Violet was fine! I swear, I had nothing to do with this!"

He smiles kindly at me, nodding. He believes me. I slump back in my chair. For the first time since I got here, I feel relieved. He's going to help me.

"I talked to the prosecutor this morning, before I came here," Javier says. "They've offered us a plea deal." He looks at me as if this is good news. When I don't react, he continues. "If you plead guilty, they'll reduce the sentence to man one. Fifteen years in prison."

I stare at him blankly. *What?* "But I told you, I didn't do it," I say, shaking my head. "Why would I plead guilty?"

Javier sighs. He takes off his wire-rimmed glasses and drags his hand down his face, forehead to chin, as if he's already exhausted by this case.

"Mr. Lockhart, I'm going to level with you. This doesn't look good for you. If we take this to trial, there's a very good chance you're looking at life in prison."

"But I didn't do it," I repeat dumbly.

"That may be the case, but it could be hard to prove."

I slam a fist down on the table. "Isn't that your fucking job?"

The placid expression on his face doesn't change. He looks down at the file in front of him. "Your wife told police before she died that you shot her. Ms. Caraway corroborates this story. That makes two witnesses. Then there's the life insurance policy."

I don't know who the fuck Ms. Caraway is, but I'm too tripped up by the mention of our life insurance policy to give a shit right now.

"What are you talking about?" I ask, leaning forward, my hands on the table.

"The one that names you as the sole beneficiary of her trust. Unless, of course, you were to get divorced."

Javier pushes a stack of papers across the table.

"What is this?" I flip through the pages.

"Those are the divorce papers. They render the insurance policy defunct. Mrs. Lockhart had them drawn up before you left New York. Prosecution will argue that you were angry when she served you. You tried to talk her out of it, but when you couldn't, things escalated."

I shake my head. "No, that's not what happened! This is the first time I'm even seeing these! But"—I look down at the pages, trying to make sense of them—"even if that were true, I would never have shot Violet! I'd never hurt her!"

"There's been a history of physical altercations, correct? The police came to your house on a domestic disturbance call last year?"

"Because she threw a glass at me!" I run my hands through my hair, pulling at it. I feel like I'm losing my mind. "The neighbors heard us arguing and called the cops. I never touched her!"

"Listen, I'm not saying you did. But it could be seen as a pattern of behavior. At least, that's how the prosecution will present it. And the fact that you were found next door, that you were planning to take your daughter without the consent of her mother—"

My mouth drops open. "Take her? I wasn't there to take Harper. I . . ." I stop abruptly. The real reason I was there won't make things any better for me.

Javier shrugs. "It's a compelling case against you, Mr. Lockhart."

I stare at him incredulously. He doesn't care whether or not I did it. Not even a little.

"Think about it," Javier says. "Fifteen years if we plead out. You'll probably only do twelve with good behavior. You'll be able to see your daughter graduate high school. If this goes to trial, you may not even get to walk her down the aisle." He shuffles the papers sprawled across the table into a stack and puts them back into a folder. "Sleep on it. I'll be back in a few days."

Javier gets up, starts toward the door.

"Wait!" The thought of him leaving, of me being alone in that cell again, lurches me into a panic. "Don't go!"

He stops, raises his eyebrow. *Yes?*

"When can I get out of here?" I ask. I want to run to him, clutch at his suit jacket, beg him, *Take me with you.*

He stares at me for a moment before answering. "I'm sorry, Mr. Lockhart," he says, shaking his head. "There's no bail. Not for capital cases."

31

It's two days before Javier comes back. Two more sleepless nights in the dank cell. It feels like my mind is unraveling. I can't make sense of how or why I'm here.

The hours tick by. To pass the time, I replay my fight with Violet over and over again as sweat beads along my brow, gathers under my arms, the cell humid and hot.

When I first walked into the bedroom, she'd been packing. Quickly, by the look of things—clothes strewn about, dresser drawers open. She didn't seem mad, at least, not at first. She bustled around, stuffing things into a bag. It took me a minute to realize they were my things, my bag.

Then she saw me in the doorway. There was a twitch at the corners of her mouth. "I want you out," she said. "I saw you with Caitlin." Her voice was as emotionless as if she were telling me we were out of milk.

It was so different from last time, from that night she'd thrown her wineglass at me, her eyes wild, face contorted into a furious snarl. No, this time, it was almost as if she was enjoying it.

What else did she say? Right. *It's exactly what I hoped for.* Then the twitch at the corners of her mouth blinked into the briefest of smiles that, when it was gone, I thought I might have imagined it.

It's exactly what I hoped for.

Why? Why?

I don't know. The only thing I do know is that when I walked out of the house, Violet was alive. What had happened after I'd left? How had she ended up dead? The question pounds inside my skull like a drum.

Finally, when I'm on the brink of losing it altogether, a guard unlocks my cell door and takes me back to the interrogation room. Javier is waiting inside, his hands folded on the table.

I sit down in the chair across from him. He smiles at me expectantly. "Have you—?" he starts.

"I need you to tell me what happened," I interrupt. "After I left. I swear, when I walked out, Violet was alive! Did someone come into the beach house? Is that where she was shot?"

Javier stares at me as if trying to determine whether he should answer me, as if he thinks I might be fucking with him. Then he says, "Your nanny said she heard you and Mrs. Lockhart arguing. A few minutes later, a gunshot. When she felt safe enough to come out of her room, she found Mrs. Lockhart bleeding in the master bathroom. When the police arrived, Mrs. Lockhart confirmed she had been shot by you."

I shake my head. "There was a gunshot after we argued?"

Javier looks down at his papers. "According to Ms. Caraway. It says she told the police that—"

"Wait." I hold up my hand. That's the second time he's said that name. "Who is Ms. Caraway?"

"Sloane Caraway. Your nanny."

What the fuck? "No," I say. "Our nanny is named Caitlin. I don't know anyone named Sloane."

Javier takes a photograph from his folder, slides it to me. It's a picture of Violet and Harper on the beach with Caitlin.

"Yeah, that's Caitlin," I say, looking back up at him.

"She told the police her name is Sloane Caraway," Javier says, shrugging. "I'm sure they asked for identification."

I stare back at the photo. Sloane Caraway? Why had she told us her name was Caitlin?

"Look," Javier says. "It's a pretty airtight case against you. The prosecutor emailed me this morning. They found the gun that was used to shoot Mrs. Lockhart. There were no prints, but they ran the tags. It was registered in your name. I understand you don't want to plead guilty, but that, along with Ms. Caraway's testimony—"

"Violet's mom gave her that gun! I've never touched it!" My voice is strained. "I won't plead guilty. I can't. I didn't do it."

Javier's face tightens, his mouth puckering. He sighs. "I think that's a mistake. Like I said in our last meeting, this might be your best chance at a reduced sentence. I know it's not ideal, but you have to consider the alternative. If this goes to trial and you're convicted, it could be decades before you're released. And what about your daughter, Jay?"

My shoulders sag. Harper. My beautiful brown-eyed girl.

"Where is she?" I ask. I drop my head into my hands. "Is she okay? I need to call my sister. She'll come out. She can stay with her."

I haven't spoken to Denise in months, despite the fact that she calls me every few weeks. I ignore her calls, don't call back. I plan to, but I don't get around to it, never quite in the mood to rebuff her requests for money. She lives in Ohio with her three kids, two stepkids, and her second husband, and is always short on funds, for rent, for groceries, for clothes for the kids. "I wish I could enroll Penny in ballet," she'd said irritably, last time we spoke, like somehow it was my fault she couldn't afford it.

Javier opens his manila folder, flips through it, and pulls out a typed sheet. "She's in the custody of Ms. Caraway."

I jerk back up to look at him, frowning in confusion. "Caitlin? Why is Harper with her? She should be with family."

"Well, it looks like Ms. Caraway"—Javier says her name slowly, emphatically, to correct me—"is listed as Harper's guardian. In your will. Should you and Mrs. Lockhart become incapacitated."

"What?" This doesn't make sense. "No, no, there's been a mistake. My sister is the designated guardian."

It was a point of contention when Harper was born, a hard sell to both Denise and Violet. Unsurprisingly, the two didn't like each other. Denise thought Violet was a snob; Violet thought Denise was a freeloader. Neither was wrong, exactly. But I couldn't stomach the idea of Harper going to live with Violet's parents, or my own, for that matter. "She should be with her cousins," I argued to Violet, "other kids, family. And anyway, what is the likelihood of something happening to both of us?" Violet relented eventually, as did Denise, when she realized custody would come with a check. Had Violet updated our will without telling me? Why?

"Your signature is on the paperwork. Right next to Mrs. Lockhart's." He takes another document from his file, hands it to me, taps a finger near the bottom of the page. "It was forwarded to us by your lawyer in New York. He said you sent it to him."

I stare at it, speechless, my name—next to Violet's—in blue ink.

Finally, I look up, shaking my head. "I didn't sign this! And I definitely didn't send it to him. I don't want her with Caitlin—or Sloane—whatever her name is! Please, let me call Denise."

"Look," Javier sighs. "Apparently, Ms. Caraway has a lawyer. A good one. If you want to dispute the will, we'll have to send it through the proper channels. It could take months." He closes the folder. "I'm happy to start that paperwork if you want."

My head is spinning. *What is happening?* "Yes! Harper doesn't belong with her!"

Javier nods. "Okay, I'll work on that. But the plea—you're sure?"

"How many times can I say it? I'm not going to spend fifteen years in prison for a crime I didn't commit!" Spittle flies from my mouth, lands on the table.

Javier nods. "I understand. Let me talk to the prosecutor again. I'll see if there's room for negotiation." Then he stands up. The chair legs squeal against the concrete floor. "In the meantime, try and get some rest, okay?" His voice is gentler now.

I nod dumbly, still breathing heavily. Rest, sure. I wonder if I'll ever feel rested again.

"And Jay?" Javier puts a hand on my shoulder. When I look up at him, I can see the pity in his eyes. He thinks I'm a sad sack of shit. "I saw Harper with Ms. Caraway, leaving the station. She looked like she was in good hands. She was smiling, going to town on a big bag of M&M'S."

In my cell, I sit with my back against the wall. It feels like I'm on the brink of a black pit, about to be swallowed whole.

I run my fingers through my hair, yanking, pulling. Why would Violet have signed over parental rights to Caitlin? Why has Caitlin been lying about her real name?

For the hundredth time, my last fight with Violet snags in my head, a broken record. Her voice echoes loudly, reverberates throughout the cell, off its concrete walls.

It's exactly what I hoped for.

What had she meant? That she *wanted* me to have an affair with Caitlin? Why would she have signed custody over to a woman she'd wanted me to have an affair with?

But what had happened between Caitlin—*Sloane?*—and I had hardly been an affair. It was innocent, mostly—a handful of flirtatious looks, a few kisses. It was a distraction, nothing more. We both knew it. It was just that Violet had been so hot and cold the last few months, then frigid since we'd arrived at the beach, with her tight smiles, pretending to be asleep every night when I came to bed, that I'd been restless, wound tight. And Caitlin was there, waiting.

Who could blame me? I barely recognized Violet anymore. And not because she looked different, although she did. I think of the picture Javier showed me today of her and Caitlin on the beach, Harper between them. She's gained weight in the last few weeks—heavier than I've ever seen her, outside of pregnancy—and her skin has worsened—zits around her chin, on her forehead. The Violet I knew, the one I've gone to bed with, the one I've brushed my teeth next to for more than ten years, was fastidious about her weight, went to painstaking lengths to keep her skin clear—nighttime serums and creams, scrubs and facials. But other things were different, too: the way she'd dressed, for one, in clothes that didn't fit, that were ugly and worn-out. And, maybe, the biggest change of all: the way she carried herself, like she was untouchable, like if you reached out, your fingers would pass right through her.

On the island, Violet retreated, and when she did, Caitlin took a step forward. Caitlin, with her bedroom eyes and throaty laugh. She looked at me the way Violet used to.

In some ways, actually, Caitlin reminded me of Violet. The old Violet, at least. It's funny, now that I think of it: on the morning we left for the island, when Caitlin showed up on our doorstep, for the briefest of instances, I thought it *was* Violet on the stoop. Caitlin's hair was darker than it was the last time I saw her, and shorter, the same cut and color as Violet's, in clothes that looked so much like what Violet would wear. She blushed when I complimented her, told me Violet had given her the shirt—the whole outfit, actually. I didn't think much of it at the time; isn't that what women do, share clothes, swap style tips?

But now it needles at me. Had Caitlin been jealous of Violet? Had she been dressing in Violet's clothes, acting like her, because she wanted to *be* her? I feel a thick wave of nausea roll through me. Could she have been jealous enough to murder her?

I rub my temples. *No.* If it was Caitlin who shot Violet, why would Violet have told the police it was me? It doesn't make sense. I'm missing something. But what? I lie on my back, my bones jutting into the cement floor beneath me, staring at the cracks in the ceiling. I feel like the answer is just out of reach.

Eventually, I fall asleep, my eyes burning, head pounding. I toss and turn, body aching. I sleep dreamlessly.

Then, in the middle of the night, I sit up. My eyes fly open, a cold sweat drenching my shirt.

Javier said that Caitlin had overheard us arguing. But she hadn't been home. I brushed by her on my way out; she was coming in.

So how would Caitlin have known we'd been fighting? Unless the person who told the cops about the argument wasn't Caitlin. The truth slams into me like a freight train.

Caitlin didn't shoot Violet. Violet shot Caitlin. She shot Caitlin and told everyone that Caitlin was her, that it was Violet Lockhart lying on that floor. And that I was the one who killed her.

Caitlin wasn't trying to look like Violet; Violet was trying to look like Caitlin. She wanted Caitlin to look like her. And she wanted Caitlin and me together so people would think Caitlin was Violet Lockhart, my wife. *It's exactly what I hoped for.*

I scramble to my feet and begin banging on my cell door. "Someone, help! I need help!"

I bang and bang until finally, there's a loud buzzing and my door opens. A guard eyes me with irritation. "I need you to call my lawyer!" I say.

"It's four in the morning," the guard says. "You can call tomorrow." The door slams shut again.

"No!" I yell. "No, wait!"

But no one comes back. I slump to the floor. Eventually, I lie back down on the mat, but I don't sleep, wired. Violet is not dead. Not dead. Not dead. Not dead.

I'm pacing when a guard finally buzzes me out of my cell, tight figure eights around the small room. My whole body is pulsating, like how I feel after snorting a line, lightheaded and everything crystal clear.

As soon as I'm inside the interview room, uncuffed, I rush to Javier, grabbing his shoulders. "Violet isn't dead!" I say. "Caitlin is! I mean, Sloane. Violet killed her!"

Javier takes a step back from me, straightens his suit jacket, then gestures to a chair. "Why don't you sit down?" he says calmly. "Have you slept?" He touches me on the elbow, an attempt to steer me toward the table.

"No!" I jerk away. I know he thinks I'm crazy—I would, too; I know how I look, how I sound—but I'm sure I'm right. I'd bet my life.

"Listen," I say, lowering my voice. "Violet is framing me. She shot Caitlin and said it was me. Now she's pretending she's Caitlin. That's why she was dressing like she did. I thought maybe Caitlin was trying to be Violet, but it was the other way around! Can you bring her here?"

I'm breathing heavily now, panting almost, staring at him. He doesn't have to believe me, he just has to hear me out, give me a chance to prove it.

Slowly, Javier shakes his head. "I can't bring a witness to see you. Even if she agreed, which . . ."

Then something else hits me. The other thing nagging at me. "The M&M'S! You said you saw Caitlin giving Harper M&M'S. Violet gives those to Harper! As a reward! It was her—you probably didn't realize it because she was dressed differently, but you have to believe me!"

"Jay, I'm not going to accuse Ms. Caraway of stealing your wife's identity because she gave your daughter M&M'S. It's—"

"She's not Ms. Caraway!" I practically yell. "Didn't you hear me? It's Violet! Please, you have to find a way to meet with her! Or, no—I have a better idea! The body! Can you order a DNA test on the body? It'll be Caitlin's—Sloane's, whatever her name is!"

"Jay, please sit down," Javier says.

I do, even though I don't want to. Underneath the table, my knee jiggles wildly. Javier takes a seat across from me. For a moment, he says nothing. Then, "The body was cremated yesterday."

I stare at him. "*What?*"

"I'm sorry."

It feels like I've been socked in the stomach. How did Violet orchestrate all of this? I begin to laugh in disbelief, a hysterical giggle that overtakes me. That *bitch*. She thinks she's smarter than me; she always has. This was her chance to prove it. But I won't let her. I sober, stop laughing as quickly as I started.

I set my jaw. "I want to go to trial," I say.

"Jay—" Javier starts, reticent.

"No!" I interrupt. "If Caitlin is the only witness, then that means they'll have to call her to the stand. Violet will have to show up."

Javier takes a seat at the table. He sighs. "The prosecutor said they could offer twelve years if you take the plea," he says. He doesn't believe me. Not even a little bit.

I shake my head. "No. Do I need to hire another lawyer? I'm taking it to trial. With or without you."

There's a long silence. "If you want to go to trial, we'll go to trial," Javier says finally. "But it could take months, up to a year even, if not longer."

"I don't care." I don't care how long it takes. I will not let Violet get away with this. I will not let her take everything from me.

"Okay," Javier says, nodding slowly. "I'll let the prosecutor know. And if you change your mind—"

"I won't," I say.

Three months go by. At my request, Javier successfully petitioned for the case to be tried in Brooklyn, so I was transferred to a holding prison in Queens. It means I'm closer to Harper, but no one will bring her to see me. It means I'm closer to Violet, too. I know she's out there, can feel her, hear her laughing at me.

Then, one afternoon, news. In another concrete room, just as bleak as the others, Javier tells me that Sloane Caraway has agreed to meet with me. She'll be accompanied by the prosecutor. Javier will be there, too.

"Will you take the plea," Javier wants to know, "if it is, in fact, Sloane Caraway and not your wife?" I nod. It will be Violet. I know it will be. She can't help herself; she wants to rub it in, wants me to know she's punishing me for what I've done.

"Good." Javier nods, and I know he and the prosecutor have come together, both with the same goal: to stay out of the courtroom, to close the book on this case, on me.

I don't care about their motivation. The only thing that matters to me is that she's coming. I didn't kill her, but when I see her, I might.

Two days later, Javier and I sit side by side in a windowless room in the cellblock, two empty chairs across from us. My ankles are shackled to each other, to the legs of the chair. A guard stands in the corner.

The room is stiflingly quiet.

I can't take my eyes off the door. Any minute, she'll walk in.

My heart is pounding violently in my chest. It's like sitting at the top of an amusement park ride, legs dangling, waiting for the drop. It's coming, you know it is, but you don't know when. Now? Now? *Now?*

Finally, a loud buzzing. Now. My stomach plummets.

The door opens. Two women walk in: the prosecutor first, a tall woman in a boxy suit, gray-blonde hair, and behind her, Violet, her head ducked, dark brown hair silky and smooth. My breath hitches, catching in my throat. It's her. A triumphant smile spreads across my face, adrenaline coursing through me.

Then she looks up. Her eyes meet mine, and my smile fades, drips from my mouth onto the floor, a puddle at my feet. Both she and the prosecutor take a seat on the other side of the table.

The woman across from me is not my wife. She looks like her, almost—the same haircut, the bangs, the heart-shaped face. She's wearing Violet's clothes, too, a crisp pin-striped shirtdress I always loved, the top two buttons undone, her gold sunburst necklace.

But it's not Violet.

It's Sloane.

SLOANE

32

I turn my key in the lock, opening the door to the Lockharts' brownstone. The smell of freshly cut peonies fills my nose as I pause in the entryway, surveying the living room, the kitchen.

A dozen half-full moving boxes cover the floor, the kitchen counter, the dining room table. Books have been taken off the shelves, picture frames from the wall, plates and glassware from the cabinets, all bubble-wrapped and carefully packed. Two weeks ago, I put the house on the market; already six offers have come in, two over asking. The real estate agent told me she thinks we can close by the end of the month. By then, Jay will have accepted the plea, will be behind bars for good.

I smile, then start up the stairs. "I'm home!" I call out.

When I reach the top, the bedroom door at the end of the hall opens. Violet emerges. "How'd it go?" she asks.

"You should have seen his face," I say, grinning. "I wish I could have taken a picture."

She grins back, her face mirroring my own. Violet, my Gemini twin.

I'd almost lost her, so soon after I'd found her. We'd both been careless, letting Jay come between us, our feelings for him—infatuation in my case, hate in hers—distract us from what really mattered. But in the end, when it counted, we chose each other.

Three months ago, I stared at Violet in horror as she pointed a gun at me. As her finger slipped around the trigger, I turned, prepared to run, then, when the gun went off—the noise so loud it felt like my eardrums were bleeding—I dropped to the floor, my hands over my head.

When I realized she'd missed, I began to crawl, panicked, then scrambled to my feet.

It was something I learned in active shooter training as a teacher at Mockingbird—the only chance you have against someone with a gun is to run; it's harder to hit a moving target than a still one. So I ran. I ran out of the bedroom, down the stairs, out the front door. I didn't look back.

By the time I reached the road, I was panting and crying and yelling for help. I had no phone, no car keys.

Frantic, I started toward Anne-Marie's house, legs pumping. Twice, I glanced behind me, but both times no one was there. Still, I kept running, my face streaked with sweat and tears.

I slowed only when I reached Anne-Marie's house, gasping for air, lungs burning.

As I started up the walkway, I paused, noticing the car parked in their driveway. It was ours; our rental car. Relief pummeled through me. Jay was here. He was here to get Harper.

I'd heard his fight with Violet as I'd walked up the path to our house after dropping Harper off at Anne-Marie's, the disgruntled shouting as I stepped onto the porch, both of their voices loud, enraged. Before I'd had a chance to go inside, the front door had opened with a bang. Jay had his duffel bag slung over his shoulder, his face twisted into an angry scowl. He'd brushed by me, barely registering my presence, muttering something about going back to the city. I'd been stunned, slightly hurt, but mostly confused. Now it made sense. Of course he'd come here. He would never leave without Harper.

Half sobbing, I climbed the stairs to Anne-Marie's front door. But then, on the top step, when the living room window came into view, I stopped abruptly, my breath catching, a hand squeezing my heart. *No.* No, it couldn't be. I wanted to cry out in pain, but I didn't.

Through the glass, I could see Jay. And Anne-Marie. Together. Kissing. They were leaning against a wall, his body pressed against hers, Anne-Marie's hand groping the front of his pants. I stared, gaping, the image not quite computing.

Jay with Anne-Marie. Jay kissing Anne-Marie. Kissing her like he'd kissed me, just the night before. It felt like a kick to the gut, like someone had reached down my throat and ripped out my insides. Five minutes before, I thought I might die; seeing Jay with Anne-Marie, I wished I had. When had it started? During their morning runs? Or some other time, after we'd all gone to sleep?

Since we'd arrived on Block Island, my feelings for him had intensified until it felt like I was on fire, my body aflame, hot, burning. I thought I had found my soulmate.

That first day, when he took me on the island tour, his hand rested on my lower back as we walked into a restaurant, lingering. In the booth, our thighs brushed. Our chemistry had been palpable. He'd teased me, grinned at me, his eyes on mine. I told myself it was all in my head, but I spent every night in bed, hoping it wasn't, heat between my legs. He was all I thought about, all I wanted to think about.

Then, the night we went to dinner. "I've never felt this way before," he whispered into my ear, Harper asleep in the darkened back seat of the car. "Me either," I breathed. By then, he'd told me about the divorce, and while I knew what it would do to my friendship with Violet, I was in too deep.

I thought Jay and I would be together when we got back to New York. He'd said as much. "I can't wait until we're alone," he said. "Until we don't have to sneak around."

But I'd been a fool. As I watched him through the window, watched his mouth open into Anne-Marie's, I remembered Violet's words.

"You think you know him," she had said plainly, "but you don't. He's a liar. Just like you."

I assumed she was angry at him for leaving her. The bitter, cast-aside wife. But then, when I saw him with Anne-Marie, I realized she meant something else. He'd only told me what I wanted to hear. He told everyone what they wanted to hear. How had I been so blind?

So I went back. To Violet. Without Jay or Anne-Marie seeing me, I walked back down the steps, back to our house.

"Violet?" I called out, easing the front door open. "You're right. I'm a liar. A good one. Let me help you." I wasn't scared anymore. She didn't want to hurt me; she wanted to hurt Jay. And now so did I.

She was still in the upstairs bathroom, on her knees, the gun tossed aside. Her face was pale, eyes red and puffy. She looked so young. When she looked up at me, tears ran down her cheeks.

I sat down in front of her and told her what I saw. Then she told me everything.

Jay had started cheating on her when she was pregnant with Harper. Well, that's when she first found proof. When she accused him, he told her she was jealous, making things up. He almost convinced her, too, but then she found the messages on his phone. Nudes from a coworker, plans to meet at a hotel.

He cried when she confronted him. Told her he'd felt lonely, was scared about becoming a dad, that it wouldn't happen again. Except it did. When Harper was only six months old. And again, a year after that. Those were the times she knew about, at least. Every time, he swore things would change. She wanted to believe him. Needed to.

So when he asked her to start over with him in New York, she agreed. He said it would be his chance to be the breadwinner, to prove to himself that he could provide for their family. They'd relied on her family's money for so long that he'd lost sight of who he was as a man. That he'd looked to other women for validation. In New York, he promised, things would be different. Things would be better.

And they were, even after she found out he'd known about the trust. He'd been devoted, focused on his start-up. That's what she thought. Then came the request for a cash infusion, the admission he'd gambled the company dry. And only a few weeks later, the final kick to her gut.

Violet came home early one afternoon to find the house seemingly empty, a Disney movie playing on the living room TV. Nina, their nanny, hadn't mentioned plans to take Harper anywhere. "Hello?" Violet called out. Then, rustling. She followed the noise into the kitchen, found Harper standing on the counter in front of their snack cabinet. Harper turned at the sound of Violet, wobbled, almost falling, a guilty smile on her face. She knew she wasn't supposed to be up there. "I was hungry," she said. She didn't know where Nina was.

Violet settled Harper back onto the couch with a bowl of Honey Nut Cheerios, then went to look for Nina. The door to Jay's office was closed. Slowly, barely breathing, she opened it. Jay was in his desk chair, head leaned back, eyes closed, Nina on her knees. Violet pulled the door shut and went back downstairs. Quietly, she packed Harper up and took her to the park.

Suddenly, it became clear to her, like a match had been lit in a pitch-black room. She was living her parents' life. The one she'd tried so hard to run from. She'd become her mother, her head buried so deep in the sand she was choking on it, married to the same type of man as her father. At the expense of her daughter. Her darling Harper. She was incensed. At herself, yes, but at Jay, too. Finally at Jay.

She waited until Harper was asleep that night before shutting the door to their bedroom. He was already in bed, head crooked over his phone. Texting Nina, probably—maybe a picture of his dick he'd taken earlier that day.

"What?" he asked when he looked up, saw the look on her face.

"How could you?" she yelled. "You left her alone! And for what? A *blow job*?" Her voice was shrill, tight.

At first, he acted dismayed. Harper was fine; nothing had happened to her. And Violet was confused; it wasn't what it looked like. Eventually, he stopped lying, but this time, he wasn't remorseful.

He just looked at her with a *what do you expect?* expression. "You're not the woman I married anymore," he said. Like it was Violet's fault that he couldn't keep his hands to himself, that he did whatever he wanted, whenever he wanted. *There's nothing wrong with me,* he meant. *Nothing wrong with what I did. There's something wrong with you.*

That's when she saw red. That's when she told him she wanted a divorce. That's when the fighting escalated, when he followed her downstairs, where she smashed every photo of them together, when she screamed so loudly that the neighbors called the cops. That's when she threw the glass at him. When it shattered, a shard nicked the side of Jay's face. The cut wasn't deep, but blood rushed from the gash, ran down his neck. He played it up, holding his hand to it, wincing like a wounded puppy. No one was arrested, but a report was filed. Violet was drunk, and even though so was Jay, it was her broken glass, his dripping blood.

Jay could have pressed charges, but he didn't. He would, though, he told her when the police left, as the sun was rising, if she tried to divorce him; the officer on the scene said he had a year to file if he changed his mind. Then he would apply for sole custody. If there was a hearing, what judge would grant custody to a mother with a domestic violence record? He'd take Harper and as much money as he could. If she left him, he threatened, she'd be leaving alone and broke. He was holding her hostage, her hands tied, dirty rag stuffed into her mouth. Their marriage, like her childhood, was a prison.

She tried to fight it, but her lawyer said there was a chance Jay was right, that a judge might deem her unfit, strip her of custody. And order her to pay alimony and child support. There was that trust fund from her grandma, after all. Yes, it was hers, but there were ways to access the income she made from it. It wasn't worth the risk, in his six-hundred-dollar-an-hour opinion. Could she try and work it out? the lawyer had asked.

But hadn't she already tried? For years, she'd tried because she loved him, because she believed him when he said he would change. Because despite everything—the infidelity, the money, the digs about what she should wear and how she should look—she thought he was a good dad.

At least, she thought that he *could* be, if she showed him how to love unconditionally, how to love without expectation.

But now here was proof, definitive proof, that she was wrong. He would never be a good dad. A good dad would never care more about his hard-on than his daughter. And worse, a good dad would never steal a child from their mother. Harper needed her. He might as well be severing their daughter's limb.

She could finally see the forest through the trees. Who Jay was, why he'd never change. At his core, all he cared about was money and appearances. *Himself.* And Violet, better than anyone, knew what that could—no, *would*—do to a child. Maybe, if she was there, she could lessen the blow, but if he was left alone with Harper, who knows the damage he'd do.

It was the other thing she'd turned a blind eye to, subtle now, but for how long?: comments about how much Harper was eating, her portion sizes. He hated the M&M'S, glared at Violet when she offered any treats. How he made sure Harper's hair was neatly braided, her bangs smoothed, that everything she wore had the right label. If you didn't know any better, you might mistake it for concern. I did. But Violet saw through it. Jay was teaching Harper—like he had taught her, like her parents had taught her—that her worth was inextricably tied to how she presented herself to the world.

So the answer was no, she couldn't work it out. Jay had broken Violet's heart, again and again, and one day, he was going to break Harper's; of this Violet was sure. And that was the one thing, the only thing, she would never allow.

So together, in the bathroom of the beach house, we came up with a plan. There was just one rule: no more lies. At least, not to each other. Never to each other.

When we both had agreed, Violet handed the gun to me. Instead of her shooting me, I would shoot her.

Before I did, Violet called Danny on the burner. When he answered, she began crying again. "I couldn't do it," she told him. Her shoulders shook as she sobbed noisily, snot leaking from her nose, voice breaking. "I couldn't." On the other end of the phone, I heard his voice. "I know, honey." It's why he'd agreed to go along with it. He'd realized that when she picked up the gun, her finger slipping around the trigger, she wouldn't be able to shoot me. It wasn't who she was. He'd known it before she had.

The gun was heavier than I expected it to be. I could feel my heartbeat in my palm, pulsing against it. I breathed out shakily. Violet stood only a few feet away, her back to me as if she were running, like I had from her. I needed to shoot her at close range so I wouldn't miss. Danny had told us to aim for her lower thigh. There would be a lot of blood, but it would be far enough away from any organs, and he could say her femoral artery had been hit. No one would question him; he was at the top of the ladder, his word incontestable.

Violet cried out when the gun went off, a low, guttural wail. I ran to her, but she waved me away. "The gun," she said, teeth gritted, eyes screwed tightly closed. "Take care of the gun."

I wiped it down and tossed it under the bed for the police to find. Then, pressing a washcloth to her thigh, I called 911. I was grateful for my too-large hands, my *mitts*, how they covered the wound, stopped the bleeding. "Help!" I yelled into the phone. "You have to help us! My friend, she was shot. Her husband, he shot her, then left!"

As we waited for the sirens, I couldn't help but imagine what it would be like: me moving into their big house, Violet and I going shopping to redecorate Jay's office, turning it into a bedroom for me. I'd be like an aunt to Harper, a sister to Violet. I saw myself waking up early to pack Harper's lunch, braiding her hair, taking her to the park after school, helping Violet make dinner, her at the stove while I chopped onions at the island. We'd take turns putting Harper to bed, trade off doing the dishes. At the end of the day, we'd collapse on the couch, bicker affectionately about what to watch.

I smiled down tenderly at her as I squeezed her hand with my free one. Violet had gone from being who her parents wanted her to be, to who Jay wanted her to be, stifling herself until she could barely breathe. She'd given everything she had. Still, it wasn't enough. Still, *she* wasn't enough. But she would be enough for me. We would be enough for each other.

Violet opened her eyes, smiling weakly. "I'm sorry I tried to kill you."

I let out a half laugh, half sob. "I'm sorry I tried to sleep with your husband."

Violet was drenched in sweat by the time help arrived on the scene. Danny arrived first, as promised, along with another EMT, a young, zit-speckled kid who looked barely eighteen, then two cops, one around the same age as the EMT, the other pushing sixty, a round paunch above his belt. In the commotion, I studied him. Violet was right; Danny was beautiful. When he went to her, his touch was tender, his eyes soft, voice low and soothing. It was no wonder every girl—and boy—on the island had been in love with him.

As Danny worked on Violet, bandaging her wound, strapping an oxygen mask to her face, loading her onto a stretcher, I sat with the officers. I told them what we'd rehearsed, that I came home from dropping off Harper from Anne-Marie's and heard Violet and Jay arguing, him yelling at her. Something about divorce papers, how he'd never let her go. He sounded so angry, I said, my voice quaking. Then I heard a gunshot. Terrified, I hid in a closet. I heard him drive off, but I wasn't sure if he was planning to come back, so I waited. When I came out and went upstairs, I found Violet like this, on the floor, blood everywhere. "I think he went to find his daughter," I said finally. "She's at a sleepover next door."

At this, the older of the two cops got up abruptly. He made a call on his radio, said the word "backup." Then they both left, their boots thudding down the hall, the bang of the front door, the wail of police sirens. *Sorry, Jay,* I'd thought, though I wasn't sorry at all.

Danny and the other EMT wheeled Violet out of the bedroom, down the stairs, and out of the house. I followed them into the back of the ambulance, Violet lying supine on the stretcher, her face pale. Once the stretcher was secured, the second EMT closed the doors, then, a moment later, appeared in the cab of the ambulance, behind the wheel.

Danny hooked an IV into Violet's arm. Fluids and painkillers, he told me. Violet's eyes fluttered closed. Her breathing grew shallow. I couldn't tell if she was acting or not.

Five minutes into the drive, Danny looked up at me. "She's lost too much blood," he said, shaking his head.

His face was so solemn, so drawn, that for a minute, I almost believed him. Then he pounded on the plastic partition to the driver's cab. "Redirect," he said. "Redirect to the morgue."

Our siren cut out abruptly, the ambulance slowing. While we drove, Danny called the police. It was a short conversation, but when he hung up, he told me that they wanted me down at the station to give an official statement. Someone would meet us at the morgue to pick me up.

When the ambulance finally slowed to a stop, Danny pulled a thin white sheet over Violet's face.

I stood in the parking lot while Danny wheeled her in, feeling like I was in a dream.

A few minutes later, he came out with an empty stretcher. The coroner had been two sheets to the wind, as usual, bottle of gin half-drunk on his desk, barely acknowledged Danny as he signed the intake form, waved him into the back, where Violet got off the stretcher and waited, in a coat closet, for Danny to pick her up after his shift ended. The morphine he had given her in the ambulance would hold her until then.

As the coroner took another swig in his office, his eyes glazed, head lolling, Danny took Violet's file into the body storage facility in the back of the morgue. The occupied refrigeration units had similar files affixed to their doors in plastic sleeves. That day, there were three flagged for cremation; there were always at least that many, especially in August, at the height of the heat, throngs of tourists who'd over-imbibed, overestimated their swimming abilities, careless with their suntanned bodies, their lives.

There, Danny slipped one of the files out and, in its place, slipped Violet's in. When the body was cremated, no one would know it hadn't been Violet. If the cops—or anyone—came looking for her, asking for an autopsy, the coroner would come up empty-handed. It wouldn't be the first time there'd been a mix-up, intentional or otherwise, not the first time someone wanted something to seem different than what actually was. If it were another police department, another city, another town, there might have been an investigation, but here, the cops wouldn't press the issue. The coroner was one of their own; the sooner this was buried, the better for everyone.

None of this would have worked anywhere else, but on this tiny island, things were different. Violet knew that when she brought us here; it was why she brought us here.

Danny waited with me until a police officer pulled into the parking lot. I rode in silence to the station where I repeated the same story I'd told the cops at the house. They thanked me, then brought me to Harper. She flung her arms around my neck and I held her tightly.

"Where's Mom?" she asked finally, pulling back to look at me.

"It's just going to be us for a little bit," I told her. I hugged her again, then, into her ear, whispered, "But don't worry, you'll see her soon." Then I handed her a king-sized pack of M&M'S, her favorite.

An officer gave us a ride to a nearby hotel; the beach house was now a crime scene. There, when Harper was asleep in the double bed next to mine, I called Laura. Laura, my Dolly Parton client from the spa.

I'd run into her while we were shopping for Harper's dress the day before. As Harper and I started toward the register, Violet waiting for us next door, I heard my name. "Sloane? Is that you? Hi, sweetheart!"

When I turned, I did a double take. I hadn't expected to see anyone I knew on the island, especially not a nail client.

I told her I was visiting with a friend and her family, introduced her to Harper. She gave me a hug, her heady perfume thick in my nose, then her number. "Call me," she said, smiling. "If you ever need anything."

When I did, only two days later, she gasped when I told her what had happened. "How *awful*," she'd said in her deep Texan drawl.

She put me in touch with her lawyer, said her retainer would more than cover a few phone calls. Within a week, I'd been granted temporary custody of Harper; I was awarded full guardianship two months after that.

Ten days after the shooting, Danny drove his car onto the ferry, Violet tucked out of sight in the back seat, and brought her home, home to Harper and me, our arms outstretched.

With the help of Laura's lawyer, everything has been transferred into my name: the Lockhart home, money for raising Harper.

Violet almost never leaves the house. We don't want to risk anyone recognizing her. Which is why, as soon as Jay takes the plea, we're packing up a moving van, driving to California. Not to San Francisco, but somewhere sunnier. We're looking at houses in San Diego, bright bungalows within walking distance from the beach.

There, we can be a real family, the three of us. Thanks to Violet's grandmother, we'll have more than enough money; neither of us will have to work. Legally, we'll share my identity, both Sloane Caraway, but tell everyone we're sisters. I go by Caitlin now, to make it easier.

Once we're settled, I plan to convince my mom to join us. The warm weather will be good for her joints. But not just that. She loves Harper as much as I do; she even comes with us to the park on Fridays, pushes Harper on the swings. She dotes on her the way a grandmother would, pinching her cheeks and slipping her Hershey's Kisses when she thinks no one is looking.

My list of lies is shorter now. One, I am the only Sloane Caraway. Two, Violet Lockhart, Harper's mother, is dead. Three, I felt nothing when I saw Jay this morning in the cellblock.

This last lie, about Jay, is what I wish were true. But when our eyes met, my heart skipped a beat, my stomach tightened. This is the only lie Violet can never know. The one I'll bury so deep it can't breathe.

Because I've found my happy ending. It's not the ending I fantasized about when I first met Jay at the park, not the one I thought I wanted, but it's better. Thanks to him, I've found what I've spent my whole life looking for. A sister. And not just a sister: a Gemini twin.

Not by blood, but by choice.

ACKNOWLEDGMENTS

To Elisabeth Weed, for believing in this book—in me—from the first page, for taking my wildest dreams and turning them into reality. Your insight, guidance, and support have been a true gift that I will never take for granted. I am forever grateful. Huge thanks to the entire The Book Group team for their support and to DJ Kim whose name in my inbox always brings a smile to my face.

To James Melia, whose keen editorial vision and brilliance is only matched by the enthusiasm and warmth with which he delivers it. It has been a joy working together; you promised that this would be great fun and you've delivered in spades. I am the luckiest. Vroom vroom!

The entire S&S team who has worked passionately and tirelessly to bring the best version of this novel to readers, especially: Jennifer Bergstrom, Sally Marvin, Jessica Roth, Mackenzie Hickey, Aimee Bell, Wendy Sheanin, Liv Stratman, Caroline Pallotta, Alysha Bullock, Esther Paradelo, John Vairo, and Matt Attanasio. Thank you for every minute of your time.

To Michelle Weiner, film agent extraordinaire, who has championed this book from the very beginning. I am so honored to have you in my corner.

ACKNOWLEDGMENTS

To Jenny Meyer and Heidi Gall, thank you for sharing this manuscript with the world. You've made magic happen.

To Liz Gazin, for the friendship that inspired this whole book. You have a heart of gold; to know you is to love you. You're the best cheerleader anyone could ask for.

To the McGibbon women: my godmother, Josie; and godsisters, Amalia and Chloe, who have wholeheartedly shared in my joy in this journey, in all my journeys. Chloe, my best friend from the beginning, forever and for always, thank you for being there every step of the way.

To Kelsey Cox and Marcie Haydon, who were there when I got the email that kickstarted this adventure, who have cheered me on, celebrated with me, and crowned me. You're the best.

To Shannon McClintock, for the endless supply of enthusiasm and encouragement, who has lifted me up and never not answered the phone when I've called. I couldn't have weathered these last few years without you.

To Jenna Newburn, who has always encouraged my dreams, who has been by my side at every costume party I've attended, and who taught me, long ago, if you've lost something, check your pockets. You are pure sunshine. Carpe diem, gorgeous friend.

To Martha Scurr, my favorite reading partner, who has been cheering me on every step of the way, who has read every Word document I've sent her. I am so grateful for your friendship. Don't forget, if I can do this, so can you!

To Miranda Leggett and Rachel Rose, for their brilliant beta reads. Your seals of approval were the push we needed to send this baby into the world. Thank you for your insightful edits, unmatched wit, and friendship.

To Emma Pattee, Kate Fagan, Clare Leslie Hall, Christina Li, and Sanam Mahloudji, it's an honor to debut alongside your brilliant novels. Your friendship has been an unexpected treasure.

To Liane Moriarty, Katy Hays, Amy Tintera, and Liv Constantine, for the generosity of your time and support; thank you for the road you have paved for aspiring writers and the willingness to lift those up who are following in your footsteps.

To my aunts and uncles and cousins, coast to coast. Family is everything. You are everything. I am so lucky to belong to the funniest, kindest, warmest group of humans. Extra special thanks to my Aunt Dina, who has taken me seriously as a writer since my first book, who invited me to speak at her book club many moons ago, whose generosity is limitless, and Aunt Lori who has requested a copy of every manuscript I've written, who has been a fan long before I deserved it.

To Teresa Morrissey, Laura Rubenstein, and Alexis Donaire, for twenty years of friendship that has buoyed me up, given me love and laughter, and nurtured my spirit. Thank you for being the ones to remind me I have always been a writer because I write; the rest is icing on the cake. We are so very fortunate to have each other, through everything—and all that is to come!

To Jim and Holly Stava, my loving in-laws who welcomed me into their family with open arms from the day we met. Thank you for always believing in me.

To my brother. Someone once asked me if I ever wished I had a sister and I answered honestly: no, not once, I have Noah. Of course, if they'd asked me if I wished I was an only child . . . Just kidding, obviously. I love you. You are an inspiration and the best brother a sister could have. I hope I make you half as proud of me as I am of you.

To my parents, I won the lottery with you. Thank you for the endless love and support, for filling our house with books, for making me believe the world was mine for the taking. Mom, you knew what this story was about long before I did—but of course you did, you've always seen the bigger picture, have always been my guiding light. Dad, it has been the greatest gift to share a love of books with you. Your red pen—and quick wit—has been sharpening my writing, making it better, making me better, for as long as I can remember.

To Beckett and Margot, the lights of my life, for opening my heart to a love I never knew possible.

To Jensen, for your support and encouragement, for never, ever doubting that this would happen, but most importantly, for the beautiful life we have built. Thank you for all of your love.

ABOUT THE AUTHOR

Sophie Stava received her BA in English literature from UC Santa Barbara. She currently resides in Southern California with her family.